The Cylinder

Richard J. N. Copeland

To my wife Ann

The Cylinder

1

The ancient army field telephone rang once, then again, more persistently. Professor John Black lifted the receiver and listened to the faint, crackly voice on the other end of the line. He had insisted on using this museum piece instead of more modern technology since the region in which they were working was remote and mobile phones were at best unreliable if they worked at all. All this system needed to work was a battery and a length of cable.

'John, I think you should take a look at this,' the voice said. 'We've found something unusual.'

'I'll be right over.' He replaced the receiver and abandoned the laptop on which he had been constructing a three dimensional model of the Iron Age site that they were excavating, then left the old shooting cabin in which he had improvised some kind of office. Zipping up his jacket against the wind, he walked over to the dig which was about two hundred yards away from the hut. He could see the team members in a group, looking at something still hidden from his view. One of them looked up as he approached.

'Here John, have a look at this, will you?' The speaker was Dr. Bernard Savage, his team leader.

'What have you found?'

Bernard tipped back his waxed cotton bush hat and scratched his head. 'I don't know. This thing doesn't seem to belong here.'

John stepped down into the pit and looked at the focus of their attention. Part of something protruded from the freshly dug edge of the excavation. It was pale grey and his first thought was that it might be an old gas cylinder that someone had dumped there. Then he had another thought. He decided to err on the side of caution. 'I think we ought to clear the site and call the Army in to take a look at this.' As he spoke, he waved the others away from the area.

The team backed away towards the edge of the pit, leaving the two men alone with the cylinder.

Bernard looked at him. 'You think it might be an old wartime bomb? That's what I thought at first. Now I'm not so sure. What do you think this might be?' He pointed with his trowel to a pattern on the side of the cylinder. 'It looks like some sort of writing. Whatever it is, it's definitely not German; in fact, I don't know what it is.'

The other team members had left the pit and were wandering away in the direction of the cabin as he leaned forward to take a closer look. The characters, if that was what they were, were meaningless to him. 'This doesn't look like anything I've ever seen before,' he muttered. 'It's not a modern European script. What do you think? Has Barbara seen it? She's our linguist.'

'She gave it a cursory look.'

'Nothing?'

Bernard shrugged in reply. 'No, and she doesn't think it's a bomb either. For one thing, there's no sign of corrosion; not even a speck of rust and it'll have been down here for a long time if it dates from the war. Can you think of any metal other than gold or platinum that could be buried all that time in these conditions without corroding?'

'It's definitely not gold. Are you sure it's metal?'

Bernard pulled a face. 'Nope.'

He ran a finger over it, feeling the smoothness of its surface. 'I think we should take a closer look.' His initial caution had waned and his natural curiosity had got the better of him. 'I want photographs and measurements. Who's got the camera?'

'Barbara has already photographed it. She wants to analyse that script, if that's what it is.'

'Call her back, will you? And bring the other team members with her. I want exact measurements as to its depth and location before we go any further. Why did this thing not show up on the magnetometer scan or on the ground penetrating radar?'

Bernard shrugged. 'Not everything does.'

'You would expect something like this to show up though, wouldn't you, especially with GPR?'

He nodded. 'I'll get Barbara.' He turned and climbed out of the pit, leaving John alone with the cylinder.

He squatted in front of it and ran his finger over its surface again. It looked like a gas cylinder and it was as smooth as glass. Even the inscription seemed to have smooth contours as if it had been moulded into its surface. He could make no sense of it. It was like no writing he had ever seen before. He racked his brain for all the ancient scripts he could recall and nothing fitted. Perhaps Barbara might shed some light on it. The edge of another inscription caught his eye. It was just visible as an arc with what appeared to be part of a circle inside it. The rest was hidden in the damp earth. He wiped some of the soil away and then, with the aid of his pocket knife, he carefully picked away some more, exposing the rest of the pattern. It appeared to be a set of overlapping circles within a larger circle as if someone had doodled on it with a pair of compasses. It gave him an odd feeling. He thought of the cabalistic symbols used in ritual magic and dismissed the thought. It did not fit. He tried to estimate the overall size of the object from what was visible and guessed it was about one metre in length and, from its visible radius, twenty to forty centimetres in diameter. Although it appeared to be ancient, it was impossible even to guess its age. Mud still clung to it in places, but where it had been wiped clean it looked new. He was impatient to completely unearth it so that it could be examined in more detail.

'What do you think of it?' Barbara's voice interrupted his reverie. Dr. Barbara Sedgwick was a PhD in archaeological studies and an expert in ancient languages. Her voice was cool, but she was unable to completely conceal her excitement at the sight of the thing. A digital camera hung from a strap around her neck.

John looked up. 'Have you seen this?' He pointed to the circular pattern that he had partly uncovered.

She crouched in front of it while Bernard craned his neck for a closer look. 'Odd,' she muttered. 'It looks like some kind of diagram. It could be decorative, I suppose.'

'It's smooth,' he said. 'Like the inscription, it seems to be moulded into the body of the thing. It's not engraved; there are no sharp corners.'

'I noticed that. It could have weathered, of course.'

'But there's no corrosion.'

'Odd, that,' she said. 'I'm going to take some more pictures of it and then we'll take some measurements before we go any further. I want a complete record of this thing; exactly where it is located and its depth. I particularly want to see if there has been any disturbance of the soil. I suspect this might be a hoax.'

'It's a possibility,' John agreed.

Bernard removed his hat and ran his fingers through his tousled hair. 'I think it's a racing certainty. Remember we had those students up here a couple of weeks ago?'

John grinned.

'Anyway,' Barbara said, 'I'm not leaving anything to chance. We should examine everything to the finest detail.'

'Are you sure it's not a bomb?' John asked uneasily.

'Pretty sure,' said Bernard. 'I am not a weapons expert, you understand, but I don't think either the Germans or the Allies had materials as resistant to corrosion as this and even if they did, what would be the point of using it for a bomb casing? Besides, why would they have engraved those symbols on it?'

'Some sort of code?' John suggested.

'Maybe,' he said, 'but I doubt it.'

Barbara stroked its smooth shell with a kind of tenderness. 'I know this sounds unscientific, but I have a feeling about this and I'm ninety-nine percent certain that it's not a bomb. Also, I'm beginning to have doubts that it may be a hoax. We shall examine the site for recent disturbance of course, but I don't think we'll find any.'

John left them to it and returned to the cabin and his computer. He stared at the screen, taking little in. The cylinder bothered him. No explanation for its presence seemed to fit. He toyed with all the various possibilities that had already been guessed at and felt dissatisfied with all of them. The most likely explanation was that it was a student hoax. If it was, it was a good one. There was no visible sign of soil disturbance.

There was a knock on the door and Barbara entered. A laptop case was slung over her shoulder. 'You might want to see this,' she said, setting up the computer on the table. 'I've enhanced the detail of the photograph of the inscription and frankly I'm baffled.'

She selected the appropriate picture file and a close-up image of the inscription appeared on the screen. 'It looks like an Egyptian cartouche,' she said, 'only the inscription is like nothing I've ever seen before.'

'Beats me,' he said, looking closely at the screen.

'I'm going to email these pictures off to Lars Ericsson at Uppsala University when we get back to town. If he can't identify the script then I think we've found a new form of writing.'

John had heard of Lars Ericsson. He was regarded as one of the world's leading philologists and was highly esteemed in his field.

'Well,' he said at length, 'if you don't know what it is, we have little option.' He sucked a knuckle. 'This thing bothers me.'

'I know what you mean.'

They sat in silence for a while as he studied the script on the screen. It looked otherworldly. It occurred to him that it might possibly be extra-terrestrial in origin, but he dismissed the thought instantly. He was not a believer in such ideas as alien intervention in mankind's development and had frequently poured scorn on the propagators of these theories. Books and papers occasionally appeared on the subject and he had pooh-poohed the lot of them, mostly with good reason. The books were invariably ill-informed works of the worst kind of sophistry or else were just plain fraudulent; a cynical attempt to dupe a gullible, sensation seeking public into believing anything that would boost their author's book sales. The truth, he knew was usually more prosaic than the creators of these wild theories would have their intended readers believe. He was not about to join forces with that particular lunatic fringe unless irrefutable proof was found, and that proof as yet was not here. No, it was possible, even probable that the thing had come from elsewhere, but that elsewhere was more likely to be found on the continent of Europe, Asia or Africa than from some far-fetched remote planet on the outer arm of the galaxy.

'How's it going out there?' he said eventually.

'All's going according to plan.' She paused. 'Bernard noticed something, though.'

'What's that?'

'The thing is not magnetically attractive. He put his compass near it and the needle didn't deviate. Nor did anything register when a metal detector was held near it. Still, that doesn't mean much.'

'It indicates that it's not metallic,' he said. 'I wonder what it's made of.'

'It could be some kind of ceramic.'

'We're talking here of Iron Age people with Iron Age technology. It's possible, I suppose. If so, they were far more advanced than we have ever given them credit for.' He slapped the table. 'This is all getting a bit too sci-fi for me.'

'Dangerously close,' she agreed. 'Want to know something else? Below the level of that thing, there is no evidence of any Iron Age settlement. Given its depth and position, it dates back to the same time as the people that settled here. We seem to be looking at a fully developed culture that appears to have grown out of nothing.'

'Cultures don't spontaneously appear.'

'This one appears to have done so.'

He had noticed this. There was a clear demarcation line between there having been a settlement on the site and there not being one. It had not evolved and developed as communities usually do. It was as if it had suddenly appeared and then, just as mysteriously, disappeared. Lower down, a number of Stone Age tools and weapons had been found and then, almost spontaneously, the Iron Age had arrived. It was like looking at the ancient equivalent of a new town. The Bronze Age seemed to have been passed by. This anomaly had puzzled everyone on the project, but no one had attached much significance to it until now. It had been assumed that these people had arrived as either settlers or conquerors and then, having settled, moved on, perhaps for economic reasons. This remained a possibility. The land was unfit for farming and the hunting would have been meagre. Another possibility was that they had been displaced by other invaders, although as yet little evidence had been found to support this idea. The site appeared to have been simply abandoned.

'I think we should take another look at the artefacts and the bones we've recovered,' she said. 'There may be a few clues there.'

'There may be,' he said thoughtfully. He did not like the way the cylinder seemed to be leading them.

2

It took two days to unearth the cylinder; two days of anxiety and careful excavation during which its exact position and depth were recorded. The soil was examined for any sign of disturbance. None was found, as a result of which the likelihood of it being a hoax diminished. It was improbable, but still not impossible. Meanwhile, in London, Barbara examined the decayed remains of weapons and tools, now little more than rust stains, plus the human and animal remains that had been uncovered. They told her little. The British Museum, who had taken custody of them, decided to conduct their own tests and report their findings. She left them to it and returned to the site. When she got back, the cylinder had been removed from the diggings and was lying on the floor of the cabin. It had been carefully cleaned and now she could see more clearly the designs on its surface. It looked in pristine condition.

'What is it doing down there?' she asked John.

'It's safer on the floor,' he said. 'I doubt that the table would take the weight. It's bloody heavy. It took all four of us to carry it here and we had to stop several times to rest. It nearly gave me a hernia.'

'It must be solid,' she said. 'I emailed the photographs to Lars, but he hasn't come back to me yet.'

'He's probably as flummoxed as we are. You know, the more I look at this thing the less I know what to make of it.'

She crouched in front of it. 'I wish I could identify those signs... writing... it... is...writing... can't think... ooh...' She stood up slowly, staggered a bit and supported herself on the table.

John started. 'What's the matter? You OK?' He dragged a chair over to her. 'Sit down.'

She sat on the chair, staring unfocusedly ahead.

'What is it?'

'I don't know,' she said vacantly. 'It's that cylinder… something odd…'

Panic attack, he thought, or else a fainting fit.

'Be careful with that thing,' she said. 'We don't know what we're dealing with here.'

He tried to make sense of this, but could not. He went over to the cylinder and crouched in front of it as she had. Nothing happened, and then, suddenly something did happen. A loud ringing noise inside his head rocked him back on his heels. He scrambled to his feet and backed away from it, shaking violently as if he had just received an electric shock. 'Bloody hell!'

She stared at him. 'You felt it too?'

'What the hell was that?'

'I don't know.' There was a faint hint of panic in her voice.

'I don't understand.' He said. 'We carried the thing in here and none of us felt anything then. What's happening?' He picked up the telephone receiver and cranked the handle. Someone answered. 'Bernard, come over here, will you? Something's happened.'

'This is Chris,' the voice came back. 'Bernard's busy at the moment.'

'Then call him will you? I want to see him now.'

'OK,' Chris's voice came back and the line went dead.

He replaced the receiver. It felt heavy in his hand. 'How are you feeling now?' He turned back to Barbara.

'A bit better,' she replied. 'That thing gave me something of a surprise.'

'I think you should take the rest of the day off.'

She laughed nervously. 'I'm not that bad. I'm more curious now to know what this thing is and what it's doing. You say nothing happened when you moved it here?'

'No. The only problem we had with it was with the weight.'

The door opened and Bernard entered. 'What's up?'

'Stay away from that cylinder.' John pointed to it. 'Something's happened.'

'What?'

'Barbara got a shock from it, and so did I.'

Bernard stared at it in disbelief. 'What, you mean it's electric?'

'I don't know.'

'But we carried the thing in here and nothing happened.'

'I know, I know. But something has happened now, right? Something we can't explain, and it's getting stronger.'

'What is? Look, what's all this about?'

He considered this. 'I… I don't know. I can't explain, but I think we'd be well advised to get out of here.'

Bernard thought it best to comply with his wishes. He made for the door.

They stood by one of the two Land Rovers and pondered the situation. Bernard could not make any sense of it. From what John had told him, the cylinder possessed some kind of electrical property that was out of place in such an ancient artefact. There had to be some mistake. He was in little doubt that the thing dated from somewhere around the First Century BC. It had not been planted there, of that he was sure, yet now no less than Professor John Black was implying that it boasted a technology that belonged to another age far in advance of anything that they were investigating. It had been inert when they had carried it to the cabin. Now, from what he had just been told, it was becoming active. The more he thought about this, the less he understood. He was every bit as sceptical as John when it came to crazy theories about alien intervention and yet, in this case, the theory would fit. It was the only thing that did.

'Perhaps we should go back to the hotel and discuss this properly,' he suggested.

John grunted an agreement. 'I think we should suspend work here until we know better what we're dealing with.'

'We're not properly equipped to deal with this,' Bernard said. 'I think we should call in a physicist or someone who might shed some light on whatever this thing might be. If what you say is true, none of us should go near it again.' He paused. 'What did you mean when you said it was getting stronger?'

'I don't know,' he said. 'I don't know why I said it. It's just a gut feeling, I suppose.'

Bernard thought for a moment. 'This is getting silly, so I'm going to offer a silly thought. I suggest we black out the windows of the cabin.'

'You're right,' he said. 'It is silly. Why should we do that, do you think?'

'OK,' he said. 'It was inert when we found it, wasn't it? And now something has activated it. What if that something was exposure to light? It would fit.'

John thought about this. 'A photovoltaic element, you mean? Look, this thing is supposed to be ancient. Are you suggesting an Iron Age smith or potter could have known about photovoltaic cells?'

'Let's give it a try,' he persisted.

Before long, the windows of the cabin had been covered with the tarpaulins normally used for covering the dig during the night. John was not keen on this idea, but then he was not keen on anything to do with the way this business was going. Practically everything about it troubled him. He resigned himself to the thought that since the whole project had gone peculiar, unorthodox methods would have to be employed. All his former beliefs were being overturned and he felt helpless in the face of it. He also felt a growing sense of frustration at the way that this new discovery had disrupted all work on the dig. So they wanted to cover all the windows with a tarp, he brooded. Well, why not? Let it rain on all their hard work. He began to wish that this bloody cylinder thing had never been found. At the same time he was aware of a certain fascination with it. It intrigued him. It was a conundrum. It was wrong.

3

'Let's face it. We don't know what we're doing any more, do we?' John said that evening as he sat with Bernard and Barbara around a table in the hotel bar. Without waiting for a reply he continued. 'I'll tell you what we know about that thing so far. Bugger all. That's what we know.'

The others agreed.

'You might not like this,' Barbara said cautiously, sensing his irascible mood, 'but I think we should call on the services of an aerospace engineer. I know a particularly good one...'

John snorted. 'So you think it came from outer space, do you?'

'I think no such thing,' she protested. 'I am trying to keep an open mind on the subject, but you've admitted it yourself; we don't know what we're dealing with here. That thing affected both me and you and neither of us knows exactly what happened back there. We're not equipped to deal with this. Who do you think can?'

He considered this. She had a valid point. The facts spoke for themselves. 'All right,' he agreed. 'Who do you know who might shed some light on this?'

'His name is James Masters. We were at university together. Although still young, he's very bright and he's already become a leading expert in the field of space exploration and rocket science. He's worked with both NASA and the European Space Agency. Now let's get this straight before you start. I am not saying that this object is a spaceship or anything of the kind, but he'll be in a better position to offer some explanation as to what it might be than we are.'

'Good point,' Bernard said. 'Until we get this business sorted, we're stymied. I say we go ahead and call him.'

John gave in. 'You're right, I suppose. OK, call him in. We've got to get to the bottom of this one way or the other.'

'Just how did that thing affect you?' Bernard asked. He wondered about John's uncharacteristically choleric mood and if it was in any way related to the shock or whatever it was he had received from the cylinder. On the other hand, he reasoned, Barbara had had the same experience and yet she was relatively untouched by it.

'It was odd,' John said slowly. 'I can't really describe it. It was something like a loud noise inside my head and this feeling... I don't know, I can't describe it.'

'It was a strange experience,' Barbara added. 'John's right. It's difficult to describe in simple terms. It was a multiplicity of sensations.'

Bernard shook his head. This was not very helpful.

John was perfectly aware of his grumpy mood. He resented the total disruption of his project that this cylinder had produced. All had been normal until its discovery. Now the dig had been halted and was not likely to resume for days, maybe weeks, possibly never. Meanwhile, his delicate diggings had been left exposed to the not too tender mercies of the weather, the tarpaulins having been purloined in an effort to exclude the light from the cylinder. It was utter madness. As if this wasn't enough, the thing had so far defied all efforts to identify it. No suggestion as to what it might possibly be could be taken seriously. Under these circumstances he felt he had a right to be grumpy.

'I just hope it doesn't rain,' he said, changing the subject.

Barbara sensed his unease. 'Have we any spare tarps?'

'If we had, we'd have used them.'

They fell silent and Bernard went over to the bar to refill his empty glass. Normally a man of cheerful disposition, he was beginning to feel as gloomy as John. He had been right to cover the windows. After all, if light had not activated the thing, what had? The thought of Iron Age people devising photovoltaic cells and accumulators was ludicrous, but the whole situation was becoming so bizarre that almost anything had to be considered a possibility. An aerospace engineer was exactly what they needed to analyse the conundrum. Without his expertise they would be going nowhere. He paid for his drink and returned to the table, a curious thought running through his mind.

'I've an urge to examine this thing myself,' he said as he sat down.

Barbara stared at him. 'You don't mean now, surely?'

'You will do no such thing!' John insisted. 'For one thing, it's late at night; for another, you've had too much to drink for driving and in any case there's no knowing what it will do to you if you get too close to it.'

'Of course I don't mean now, but I'm very curious about this business,' he said. 'What exactly *did* happen when you got close?'

John looked up at the ceiling in an effort to recall just what did happen. 'I've already tried to tell you once. I don't know how to describe it. It was strange. I honestly don't know how I felt at the time. It was a kind of shock, but it was probably more the shock of surprise than the electric variety. There was no tingle or convulsion, just a noise inside my head and then this feeling. I jumped back before it went any further.'

'It was an odd, muzzy sensation,' Barbara added, 'as if something was trying to infiltrate my mind or communicate… oh, you may laugh, but that's just what it felt like – a kind of telepathic link.'

Bernard's eyes narrowed. 'I'm not laughing. I'm trying to keep an open mind on the subject, but I'm baffled; we all are. Let's consider what we know about it so far. We know its depth and location when found and there was no sign of recent soil disturbance, so it's almost certainly not a hoax. Most importantly, there appears to have been a great technological advance in the culture under our investigation at about the time it arrived, and that's about it. We don't know what it's made of or what it could possibly have been used for; in fact, we know next to nothing.'

'So?' John cut in. 'Where does this leave us?'

'In complete and utter darkness, that's where. And that's why I want to have a look at this thing myself.'

'You think you might be able to shed some light on it, do you?' John said.

Bernard ignored his sarcastic tone. 'Probably not, but a fresh pair of eyes might see something possibly overlooked in an earlier examination.'

John drained his glass and stood up. 'I'm going to bed. We'll look at it again in the morning.'

The truth was he had had enough. The conversation was going around in circles and further discussion was pointless.

Bernard gave a thumbs-up sign. 'I'll be there.'

Barbara produced her mobile phone. 'I'll call James Masters and ask him if he can find the time to visit us.'

John grunted a grudging approval. It had been a long day and he was tired.

After he had gone up to his room, the others sat in silence for a while. Barbara called James Masters and persuaded him to visit the dig at a time that would suit his usually busy schedule. Eventually, they departed for their separate rooms with muttered goodnights. Bernard typically was the last to retire.

4

John slept badly that night. His sleep was disturbed by dreams of the cylinder. He saw it again as it had originally been found, half exposed in the earth, felt its extraordinary weight and then saw it on the floor of the shooting cabin, glowing in the dark with a bluish white light. Something was bent over it, but he couldn't see exactly what kind of creature it was. It appeared to be human.

He awoke with a start. A chink in the curtains projected a bar of light from the streetlight outside onto the wall. He switched on the bedside lamp and closed the curtains completely, shutting out the light.

Barbara also slept badly. In a vivid dream she saw people dressed in white robes surrounding the cylinder. She knew that they were worshiping it. In their midst was a young woman dressed in an ankle length brown robe. Her face was calm and unemotional. She watched as the girl walked slowly towards the cylinder and, crouching, placed both hands upon it. Her body convulsed once and then became still, the only movement being the even rhythm of her breathing. She held this position for some time. Then, slowly, she arose and turned to face the others. Something in her had changed. Her face seemed to glow with a hidden light. A rhythmic chant came from the others in the assembly, growing in volume as the girl slipped off her robe and stood in their midst, completely naked. Someone stepped forward and draped a new white robe over her shoulders which she then fastened with a cord. The others linked hands and began to dance in a circle around the transfigured girl and the cylinder. The scene bore a passing resemblance to a witches' coven with the girl as a new initiate to their mysteries. Certainly, the ceremony appeared to be more closely related to ritual magic than to any conventional organised religion.

She woke up at this point and had difficulty getting back to sleep again. The dream troubled her. She wondered if the cylinder had once been worshiped by these ancient people. It had been only a dream, she knew, but it had been so graphic that she wondered if she had indeed been given a glimpse of the distant past.

The others slept peacefully.

5

In the morning they drove out to the site and John, Barbara and Bernard assembled in the shooting cabin. In the dim light from the blacked-out windows the cylinder still lay on the earthen floor near the far corner of the cabin's dark interior: an enigma.

Cautiously, John approached and crouched in front of it. He reached out and touched its surface. Nothing happened. 'It's quite inert,' he muttered. It looked as if Bernard had been right after all. He stood up. 'Let's take down the tarpaulins and see what happens. I want to see if this thing really is affected by light.'

Bernard went out and removed the tarpaulins from the windows. The interior of the cabin grew light again as John and Barbara stood silently in front of the cylinder. Neither spoke of their dreams that night, but both were still haunted by them. John recalled his eerie vision of the cylinder as a thing glowing in the dark and Barbara was still disturbed by her dream of the ceremony surrounding the young woman initiate that had disrupted her night's sleep.

John broke the silence. 'I think we should take the opportunity to have a closer look at this thing while we can.'

Barbara agreed. While it was inert, there might not be a better chance.

Together, they took measurements and examined the patterns more closely. It was then that Barbara first noticed something new about the circular pattern. Inside each circle was another pattern, identical to the main one, but lighter and more delicate in its impression. She looked at it more closely through a hand lens. The pattern was repeated again inside the smaller one; and inside that... it was too small to see, even with a magnification of 10X.

'Odd,' she muttered.

John looked up from his notes. 'What is?'

'Look at this.' She handed the glass to him. 'The pattern is repeated. It gets smaller and smaller. I don't know why I didn't notice it before.'

He studied the pattern. 'Is this the most powerful lens we have?'

'Yes,' she said. 'Anything much more powerful is impractical for general use.'

'It would be interesting to know how far down this pattern goes.'

'And so, *ad infinitum*,' she mused.

'I wonder if there's more. Can you take another photograph of this?'

'Sure.'

He rose to his feet. 'Let's take a look at the photograph you took yesterday. This doesn't look right to me.'

'My briefcase is in the wagon.'

They went outside and walked over to the Land Rover where she opened her briefcase and produced the photograph of the pattern. Nothing was visible inside the circles. 'It might have been the light, of course.' She paused. 'But I did enhance the picture on the computer.'

'Hmmm.' John's face was clouded with doubt.

She noticed his unease. 'This business is getting stranger day by day. It's almost as if…' She paused.

'What?'

She took a breath. 'It's almost as if the thing is coming alive.'

He had to agree. Nothing here was understandable. There were too many anomalies for his liking and he was fast reaching a point where he was prepared to believe almost anything.

'I'll photograph it again.' She picked up the camera.

They returned to the cabin where she carefully framed the pattern in the viewfinder and took a photo. She pressed the review button. 'Here.' She showed him the image on the viewing screen. The internal pattern was just visible. It became more visible when she enlarged the image. 'What do you make of it?'

He shook his head slowly. 'I don't know. Let's examine it further. Give me a hand to turn it, will you?'

With some effort, they rolled it slightly, revealing the cartouche-like inscription. It looked much the same as before, but for the sake of comparison she photographed it again. It was then that they noticed another design on the body of the cylinder. It was small and lobed like a trefoil with a complex pattern of squares and triangles inside. It bore a passing resemblance to a Tibetan Mandala.

'I don't remember seeing that before,' John said, as much to himself as to Barbara.

'It wasn't there before, that's why.'

'We must have missed it. It's very small.'

'We examined it minutely,' she insisted. 'It definitely wasn't there.'

'What the hell is going on?'

'I want to photograph this. Help me turn it.'

Again, they turned it over to reveal the pattern more clearly and she took a close-up photograph, holding the camera as near to the object as the macro focus would permit.

John brooded. 'You know what you said a short while ago – about it coming to life?'

'Yes.'

'You might be right. There's something about this business that disturbs me.'

She looked at him. This was not the factual, down-to-earth professor that she knew. His face was haggard as if, like her, he had slept badly. She decided to tell him of the dream she had had that night. When she had finished, he guessed that this would be a suitable time to tell her of his own dream.

'It looks as if we've both been affected by the cylinder,' she said. 'I wonder if anyone else dreamed of it last night. It's a difficult question to ask; sounds a bit screwy.'

'I think we should say nothing about it for now. It may be playing on our minds and consequently it's affecting our dreams.'

His argument, she reasoned, was valid. After all, the thing had disrupted the dig ever since its discovery, as a result of which it dominated their waking thoughts. It should therefore not be surprising if it infiltrated their dreams as well. Indeed, they had all been affected by it in one way or another, particularly John. He was after all in charge of the project and the mere presence of the cylinder was having a disruptive effect upon it. To make matters worse, they were working on a limited budget and therefore were up against a strict time limit.

He bent over it again. 'I wonder what else it has to show us.' He was beginning to talk of it as if it was alive. Barbara noted this but said nothing. It was interesting to see that the arch sceptic was wavering in his previously entrenched views.

'There's been something odd about this whole project,' she said. 'So far, it has thrown up more questions than it has supplied answers.'

'I know what you mean,' he said. 'You think this cylinder may have something to do with the other anomalies?'

'I don't know. But there are too many unanswered questions. Look, the village appears to have suddenly arrived on the site of a long abandoned Stone Age settlement. It didn't evolve as most settlements do. It seems to have just appeared as a pre-formed culture, leapfrogging millennia in the process. There's no evidence of any Bronze Age development apart from a buckle, two clasps and some small pieces of jewellery. Then it appears to have ceased just as suddenly as it appeared. There was no decline, just an abrupt termination. The bones we uncovered are currently being examined for signs of violence, but they're highly decomposed so it'll be hard to spot these signs, even if they are there. It's possible that the settlers were massacred, and that would explain a lot, but so far we have found no evidence to support that theory. It's as if the people suddenly all left at once, abandoning everything. We've found a couple of pieces of high quality jewellery, so I doubt if the place was looted. There's no explanation for any of this.' She paused. 'I know this sounds silly, but I think this cylinder was the focus for some kind of cult that grew up around it.'

'It's your dream, isn't it?'

'That may have some bearing on it,' she admitted, 'but it's a possibility that shouldn't be discounted. After all, it's no more bizarre than anything else around here.'

There was a knock on the door and Chris, one of the younger team members entered. 'I think you should take a look at this!'

'What is it?' John asked.

'I don't know, but it looks like a clock.'

He raised his eyebrows. 'A clock, you say?' His voice was calm and even. He felt that nothing could surprise him now. 'At least it's not a bloody spaceship,' he muttered and made for the door. Barbara followed.

6

The clock, or whatever it was, lay half uncovered in a freshly excavated portion of the dig. It was circular, about fifteen centimetres in diameter and corroded almost beyond recognition, but a number of toothed wheels were still discernable. These were obviously gears. Bernard and Lynda, one of the two younger members of the team, were hunched over it. Lynda was gently brushing earth away from it with a soft paintbrush.

Bernard looked up as they approached. 'This is fantastic!' he said.

John looked at the object. It appeared to be a fine mechanism and was clearly a machine of some description, but its function was anybody's guess.

'What do you think?' Lynda looked up from her work.

John shook his head slowly. 'I think this may be a job for the Science Museum.'

'It's completely out of time, if you'll forgive the pun.' Bernard quipped.

John chose to ignore his little joke. 'Are you sure it's a clock?'

'It could be anything. My immediate guess was that it might be an old brass clock that someone dumped here a century or more ago.'

'It's possible,' John said. 'Still, we'd do well to send it off for verification. If it's not an old clock movement, then we've made a highly significant discovery. It's becoming apparent that we're dealing here with a highly developed culture, possibly more advanced than anything we have yet encountered, so for now, as far as I'm concerned, anything is possible.'

Barbara peered at it closely. 'It doesn't look like an old clock to me. I don't know much about clocks, you understand, but the degree of corrosion and the overall look of it tells me it's a lot older than a mere hundred years.'

'It reminds me of the Antikythera mechanism,' Chris mused. 'It's believed to be the world's first mechanical computer. I think its purpose was astronomical.'

She considered this. It was a possibility, but for now no one could be sure.

Bit by bit, more of it was uncovered; a painstaking process. Finally, it was removed and carefully wrapped in layers of bubble plastic. Before this, however, Barbara photographed it, taking care to record as much detail as possible.

All this time, the cylinder lay on the floor of the cabin, temporarily forgotten.

The mechanism was carried back to the cabin to be packed into an appropriate sized box. As soon as they opened the door they were aware that something was amiss. Barbara was the first to enter and was immediately struck by an odd sensation, as if the air was charged with static electricity, or something akin to it. Bernard and John were conscious of it too. It was John who was the first to realise what was happening.

'The cylinder!' he roared. 'Throw the tarp over it!'

Bernard ran out and grabbed one of the tarpaulins off the pile. He returned with it and attempted to throw it over the cylinder. The first effort failed. His second throw only succeeded in partly covering it. He gathered it in and got ready to throw it a third time.

Barbara stepped forward and took one end of the tarpaulin, then hesitated. 'Wait,' she said and slowly walked towards the cylinder.

'What are you doing?' Bernard asked, his voice rising to falsetto.

'The field is no stronger here than where you're standing,' she said.

'Barbara, don't be a bloody fool!'

Before anyone could react, she knelt in front of it and, reaching out, touched its surface the way the girl in her dream had touched it. Nothing happened. 'It's safe,' she said calmly, 'perfectly safe. You can pass the tarpaulin to me if you like.'

Bernard was clutching the tarpaulin like a lifebelt. He looked at it stupidly, as if uncertain what to do next. His head felt muzzy and thought was difficult. Slowly, he approached the cylinder and froze as a loud note sounded inside his head. The tarpaulin fell to the floor. At the same moment, Barbara convulsed once and then recovered her composure. John was unaffected by it all.

'Are you all right?' he asked unnecessarily.

Bernard staggered back and propped himself against the wall. 'Christ, what was that?' he croaked. His face was pale and he was trembling.

Barbara rose from the cylinder and came over to them. 'You'll be all right in a moment. We had the same experience, remember?' She looked at John. 'I felt an energy surge as it happened. Now I think I'm beginning to understand what's happening here. I believe the thing just probed Bernard's mind.'

John was puzzled. 'Why did it not affect me this time?'

'It already knows you,' she said. Her voice was calm and assured.

John snapped. 'That's it. I'm calling everyone off the project with immediate effect. Until we get someone else in who knows how to handle this situation, I'm declaring this cabin off limits. I'm not going to jeopardise the team's safety for that bloody thing, whatever it is.'

'John, you don't understand. There is no danger. It means us no harm.'

'How can you possibly know that?'

She thought about this, but could find no satisfactory answer. 'It's just... I can't explain... it's just a feeling, I suppose.' As she spoke, she was only too aware of the inadequacy of her words. Something in her had changed, but she did not know what. It was as if the cylinder had communicated with her in some way that transcended language. It had not used words, nor had it projected any kind of image, and yet new thoughts were arising in her head that she could not explain. Indeed, many of them she could not even begin to understand. 'John,' she pleaded. 'Please believe me. It presents no danger to us.'

'No?' Bernard said, still recovering from his recent shock. 'Then what do you suppose happened to me just now?'

'It won't happen to you again,' she assured him. 'It knows you now.'

'What's all this about knowing us?' John demanded. 'It's as if you think the thing's alive.' He paused. 'Do you think it is alive?'

'I don't know. It may be, but not in the sense that we are alive.' She shook her head. 'I can't explain. I haven't thought it through yet.'

'I have,' John said. 'And that is why I'm ordering everyone out of here.'

'If it was going to harm anyone, it would have harmed me,' she insisted. 'I actually touched it, remember?'

But John was implacable. There was to be no further argument. Reluctantly, Barbara covered the cylinder with the tarpaulin to exclude as much light as possible while the remaining tarpaulins were used to cover the dig.

The site was duly abandoned.

7

'Well,' John said to Bernard across the dinner table. 'You got your way.'

'Huh?'

'You said you wanted to get closer to the cylinder and now you have.' He smiled sardonically. 'Scary, isn't it?'

'Scary isn't the word. I thought I was having a stroke. What is that thing? It seems the more we find out about it, the less we know.'

'Barbara seems to know more about it than we do.'

Bernard scratched his head. 'What do you reckon to that? Do you think it really has imparted some knowledge to her, or does she only think it has?'

John considered this. 'I have known and worked with Barbara for five years on and off, and I can assure you that she is the most level-headed and responsible researcher you could ever wish to have for a colleague. She is most definitely not given to wild flights of fancy. You've seen the way she works. She's methodical, she records everything scrupulously and minutely and I have never seen her the way she was today. It's very untypical.'

At that moment, she entered the dining room and joined them, looking from one to the other. 'I've just checked my emails,' she said. 'Lars has responded to my message and he says he cannot make anything of the script I sent him. It's completely outside his experience.'

'Hmmm…' John rubbed his chin.

'There's more,' she continued. 'The British Museum has sent me their findings on the bones and artefacts we uncovered, and it is startling.'

'What is?'

'Well, we thought we were excavating an Iron Age village, didn't we?'

'Of course.'

'According to their test results, and they ran them twice, those remains are over seven and a half thousand years old. Those people belonged to the Stone Age.'

'Impossible! There must be some mistake.'

'They assure me that there is none. We know the radiocarbon test is sometimes less than precise, but it's accurate enough and it could never be that far out. That's why they ran it twice. They didn't believe it either. Oh, and there were definite signs of violence. One of the partial skeletons showed signs of the cervical vertebrae having been severed by a sharp instrument, indicating decapitation. Another had suffered multiple cuts to the limbs and chest area, but it gets worse. Some of the bones had faint but definite scrape and cut marks on them, indicating the possibility of cannibalism.'

Bernard whistled through his teeth. 'What in hell was going on there?'

'We can only guess. Two possibilities come to mind. One is that these people were cannibals themselves, or else they were preyed upon by others, possibly another tribe. It could explain their sudden disappearance.'

'How can we be sure of the evidence of cannibalism?' John asked. 'Some cultures dismember their dead and feed the body parts to scavengers as an alternative to burial.'

'True.' She agreed. 'But these bones show evidence of slight carbonisation, indicating the flesh had been cooked on or over a fire, but I stress that this is only a possibility. We don't really know.'

'Hmmm,' Bernard mused. 'There's food for thought.'

'It's good to see you're none the worse for your ordeal,' John observed dryly.

'I feel fine,' Bernard said. 'It was more of a surprise than anything else. There was no pain or anything like that.'

'Well,' John said. 'All three of us have been affected, or perhaps *in*fected by that thing now. The odd thing about it is that it has not actually affected us outwardly at all. There is no noticeable personality change and we are thinking the same as before, so I'm wondering just how it might have affected us. One thing, though; if any of us start to experience intrusive or unwanted thoughts, we must tell each other about it immediately. We don't know what we're playing with here.'

'Whatever happened to the arch sceptic?' Barbara said, raising her eyebrows.

'I've had cause to reconsider my former views. Oh, one more thing, Bernard; if you have dreams tonight about that thing, tell Barbara or me. I might as well tell you that we both dreamed about it last night.'

'And...?'

'It may be nothing, but it's just possible it may be affecting us on a psychological level. Remember that Barbara and I were the first to be affected by it, and now we are dreaming about it, but that may be coincidence.'

'So you think it might have affected your psychological make-up after all?'

'It's a possibility,' John admitted.

'I think it mind-probed us,' Barbara said.

'What makes you think that?' John asked her.

'It's nothing but a feeling, like everything else concerning the object. I don't know. Perhaps I've watched too many sci-fi films, but it's significant that we only experienced that disorientating shock once. Bernard was the last to be stunned by it while we remained unaffected. I actually touched it, remember? The air was practically crackling with static or something and yet I felt nothing by way of a shock, although I did sense a power surge at that moment. That made me jump.'

'What on earth possessed you to touch the thing?'

'I honestly don't know. It was like a compulsion. I can't explain.'

'You might have been killed. You could feel the energy radiating from it.'

'I somehow knew it would be safe,' she said.

'You see?' said Bernard. 'It *has* affected you psychologically.'

She fell silent, thinking about this. She honestly did not know why she had touched the cylinder when all her natural instincts should have warned her against such a foolhardy idea. It might have been charged to a lethal potential for all she knew to the contrary, and yet she was still haunted by her dream of the girl who had touched it with impunity. The thought occurred to her that it might not have been electricity at all, but some other force as yet unknown to them. She felt an unaccountable desire to touch it again – to get to know it – to find out what it was about. She tried to dismiss this thought but it would not go away.

Here indeed was an intrusive thought. She supposed she should tell John about it but decided not to. She would address this matter on her own.

John drummed his fingers on the table. Here was a pretty pickle. The Museum's findings had, at a stroke, upended everything he had believed to be true about the project. Now the entire history of early mankind would have to be rewritten. He had mixed feelings about this. On one hand, it was exciting to be instrumental in such an earth-shaking discovery; indeed, to call it exciting would be an understatement. On the other hand it was unsettling to have one's former beliefs overthrown. He felt powerless in the face of these events.

'About your decision to cease all work on the dig,' Bernard said to him. 'What do we do now?'

'I need to think about that,' he said. 'I may have been hasty, I agree, but I cannot and will not risk the safety of the team. We are dealing here with an unknown – I shall use the word *intelligence* for want of a better one – and we don't know what it might be capable of doing to us. One thing is undeniable, though: something very strange is going on up there and we are in the thick of it. Barbara might be right; there may be no danger, but I cannot afford to take that chance. I am in charge of this project, remember, and as such I am responsible for the team's safety. If anyone suffers an injury as a result of my negligence or ego, it will be my neck on the block – and yours, as my second in command.'

Bernard nodded. It was impossible to argue with this.

'Something else troubles me,' John continued. 'Concerning the evidence of violence and possible cannibalism, was there something about that cylinder that sent them all a bit doolally? They may have turned on each other.'

'It's a possibility, but then, just about anything else is.'

He decided to confide his feelings on the matter. 'Listen, Bernard, I have to admit I don't know what I'm doing any more. None of us do. We are dealing here with too many unknown factors and now even the things we had previously taken for granted have been overturned. Is it any wonder I sometimes have to act in a way that seems irrational?'

Bernard made a noise of agreement. He could understand it perfectly.

'And now, to cap it all, we find some kind of instrument that is completely out of place: a finely made Stone Age clock, for Christ's sake! Nothing fits. First, we discover the remains of a high culture that's millennia ahead of its time while at the same time we find evidence of murder and cannibalism. How do you equate such barbarism with such a highly developed civilisation?'

He turned to Barbara. 'Have you heard anything from your aerospace engineer?'

'Not yet,' she said. 'He said he would like to see it and would get back to me when he had the time.'

'That's a pity. I could use his services right now. I want to get to the bottom of this cylinder business as soon as possible. It would be interesting to know just what it's made of and who might have made it.'

'I noticed something about it,' Barbara said. 'We have measured it more or less precisely. It is 1.2198 metres in length and 0.4066 metres in diameter; a ratio of exactly three to one.'

'Is that significant?'

'It might be. It indicates that it was made with a degree of precision that is again far ahead of its time, rather like the small inscription we discovered on it this morning. It is so fine it might have been laser etched.'

John considered this for a while. 'Right,' he said at length. 'We shall go up there again in the morning to clear our stuff out of the cabin. There's not much in there anyway. The cylinder should be inert again by that time, for a while at least, and we shall take another look at it, for whatever good that may do us. This time, though, we shall only uncover it for as long as it takes to examine it. It is now becoming obvious that it is activated by light, and it doesn't take long.'

'It hasn't had long, yet,' Bernard said. 'I wonder what would happen if it received a full day-long charge.'

'Difficult to tell,' John said. 'And I, for one, am not prepared to put it to the test.'

Bernard rose from the table. 'I think we've gone about as far as we can go for today. Let's adjourn to the bar.'

'Good idea,' John said. 'I think I need a drink.'

Barbara looked up at them. 'I'll join you later. I want something to eat first.'

The meeting broke up.

8

It was another restless night for John. He lay awake turning over the day's events in his mind. Barbara's news had disturbed him more deeply than he had cared to admit, even to himself. Now paradox was piling up on paradox and he was losing his grasp of the situation. He tried to put it all to the back of his mind, but it would not stay there. Fresh thoughts kept popping up that would not allow sleep to come. Eventually, he switched on the bedside light and tried to read, but he could not concentrate and finally he gave up. He picked up the copy of the email from the British Museum that Barbara had given him and read it again. Then he looked at the detailed photographs they had sent her as an attachment. The cut marks on the bones were plainly visible.

He recalled that few complete skeletons had been found. This was scarcely surprising, given the great age and overall poor condition of the bones, and no one had spared it much of a thought. Now it was significant. He wondered now if these people had all been butchered and their bones simply dumped on a midden or buried without ceremony in a communal grave pit. This thought depressed him. He wondered how such an advanced civilisation could have ended in such a tragic and bloody way.

He put the papers away and looked at his watch. Half past two. He felt he might never get to sleep. Well, he must try. He switched the light off and shut his eyes. Eventually, sleep did come, but it was fitful and again it was haunted by dreams of the cylinder.

He awoke to the sound of a gentle rap on the door. It came again as he got up and pulled on his dressing gown. It was Barbara. She was also in her dressing gown.

'May I come in?' she said. 'I can't sleep and I've been having these dreams again.'

'That makes two of us,' he said. 'Come in.'

She came in and sat on the bed. He sat down beside her.

He looked at her. 'Would it help to talk about it?'

She laughed nervously. 'I don't think we have ever been this intimate before. John, there is something going on in my head that I don't understand.'

'In what way?'

'It's hard to describe. Sometimes there are abstract patterns that relate to nothing in particular, mixed with fragments of thought that are disjointed. Then there are the dreams. Some are good and illuminating, and then there are the bad ones. They're horrible. I'm afraid I might be going mad.'

'I don't think so. You're probably the sanest person I know. I think it's that bloody cylinder. It's affecting all of us except perhaps Chris and Lynda. They've had the least exposure to it, haven't they?'

'Bernard seems all right.'

'So far he is. We shall see how he is in the morning.'

She looked at him. 'Would you mind if I stayed the night with you?'

He blinked at her, surprised by her point blank request.

'It's just that I don't want to spend the rest of this night alone. Please, I'm not trying to seduce you; I really am frightened.'

He put his arm around her shoulders and drew her close. She was shivering. 'Get into bed,' he said gently.

She did as she was told and he got in beside her. She drew up close to him and caught hold of his arm, her head resting on his shoulder. Gradually, her shivers subsided.

'I feel safe here,' she murmured.

'Tell me about your dreams in the morning,' he replied and closed his eyes. The warm company of a woman was comforting to him. He had almost forgotten what it felt like to be in bed with another living body since his divorce from his first and only wife some three years previously and, prior to that there had been little contact between them since his work had taken him away so often. Doing field work and research for his PhD had done much to precipitate the break-up of their relationship. He saw this too late with the benefit of hindsight and, by the time he had realised that there was a problem, the damage had been done. She had eventually found a lover and, blaming him for his devotion to work rather than her, had divorced him. That had been a bleak time in his life. As a result of this, he had immersed himself even more in his work at the expense of all else, including relationships. This ultimately earned him an honorary professorship at Cambridge University, but it had been a costly title.

Barbara's breathing became slow and even. She was asleep. He suddenly felt a great tenderness towards her. They might perhaps have made love, but sex at this time would have been inappropriate and he felt that he would appear to be taking advantage of her present vulnerable state. Theirs was a good relationship on a number of levels. She was a good and capable colleague and a trusted friend, but their friendship had never developed beyond that point. He was content for now to leave it at that. He did not want to spoil a good friendship and run the risk of history repeating itself as he felt would be bound to happen once their relationship developed into anything other than the purely platonic. He was not willing to take that risk.

He wondered what dreams might come to them in whatever remained of the night before he too fell asleep.

Bernard had no difficulty sleeping. He had one dream concerning the cylinder and it was a strange one. In it, he saw in sharp detail the recently discovered small, finely etched pattern with its complex, repeated design and he was drawn into it; that is to say, the tiny image seemed to grow until it was huge, engulfing him. Then he was falling through it and into another one, then through that and into yet another in what appeared to be an infinite progression. It was a dream of very short duration and he awoke with a start, as one awakes from a dream of falling. As soon as he had fully regained consciousness, he sat up, trying to remember as much of it as possible.

He was aware of the volatile nature of dreams and how they could sometimes be forgotten in minutes, so he had had the presence of mind to put a pen and writing pad on the bedside table before going to bed that night. Now he switched on the bedside light and immediately wrote down everything he had seen in his dream, together with a rough sketch. Now he would not forget it. He switched the light off and went back to sleep, determined that if there were any more dreams such as this, they would be captured.

Barbara dreamed again. This time she saw the cylinder glowing with a faint, bluish light in a dimly lit interior. It was hovering a few inches above the ground and slowly rotating about its central axis. From what appeared to be its core, a small, but much more intense light began to pulse erratically, as if sending out some kind of code. At the same time, a sequence of five brittle-sounding notes repeated itself; then the order of the notes changed and changed again. They were a semitone apart and as sharp and brittle as glass.

She shifted slightly in her sleep and John moved too. Their heads came closer together.

People were gathered around the floating cylinder, indistinct in the shadows and, over the five note sequence, they sung a single low note as a kind of drone; something similar to the ohm sound sung in a Buddhist temple.

Again, the dream was of short duration and once more she awoke from it, this time unafraid. It had not been a bad dream this time, quite unlike her earlier nightmare of the indiscriminate slaughter of men and women whose bodies were then stripped and horribly mutilated. It had been graphic in every bloody detail and she had awoken from it in a state of near panic. The terror induced by this vision had driven her to seek the reassurance of John's company.

John awoke briefly from his dream as she moved. He stirred a bit and tried to make a mental note to remember whatever he could of it. What he did not know, and could not possibly have known, was that his dream was exactly the same as Barbara's.

All this time, Chris and Lynda slept peacefully.

9

John finally awoke and looked at the clock on the bedside table. Half past eight. He had missed the alarm and overslept. Barbara was not there. She must have got up and left him to sleep late.

He got out of bed and, after a hurried wash, got dressed and went downstairs to the breakfast room. Barbara and Barnard were sat at their usual table. They looked up as he entered the room.

'Morning,' said Bernard, carefully avoiding any comment on John's tardiness.

'We decided to let you sleep on,' Barbara said. 'If you had a night like I did, you probably needed it.'

'It was a bit restless,' John said, helping himself to a glass of grapefruit juice.

'Dreams?' Bernard looked at him intensely.

'Yes, dreams.' He joined them and sat down. 'Look, I suggest we use what is left of the morning to hold a meeting to discuss this dream thing. I'm in no doubt now that this cylinder, whatever it is, is affecting our minds in some way so, if the conference room is free for an hour or so, I shall book it. We'll give Chris and Lynda the morning off. What is to be discussed is better confined to just the three of us. Anyway, the fewer people who know about this the better.'

The others agreed.

'Where are Chris and Lynda, by the way?'

'They went out to do a bit of shopping,' Bernard said. 'I thought it wouldn't matter much this morning so I said it was OK.'

'That's fine. The whole bloody project's been disrupted anyway.'

After breakfast, they went into the conference room and sat at one end of a long table that looked as if it had been designed for board meetings.

Bernard produced his notepad and described his dream to the other two. Then it was Barbara's turn. First, she described the grisly vision of slaughter that had so disturbed her that night.

'It was mass murder,' she said with a shudder. 'They were shown no mercy, but were indiscriminately cut down or clubbed; men and women alike. Some were stripped and their bodies mutilated; some were disembowelled. It was indiscriminate slaughter. A few were thrown alive into the burning buildings where they died screaming in the flames. It was horrible. I have never dreamed anything like that before.'

She then went on to describe her other dream of the floating cylinder and the strange music. At this, John suddenly leaned forward in his chair, listening intently.

When she had finished, he stared at her in disbelief. 'That was my dream exactly!' he exclaimed. 'To the last detail! There is almost no possibility of this thing being a coincidence.'

'Proof positive of our minds having been affected, I think,' she said. 'Perhaps it has set up some kind of telepathic link between us.'

He fell to thinking about this. As far-fetched as it sounded, this idea could not be discounted.

'It was just the one dream, though,' Bernard said. 'Still, it stretches the possibility of coincidence a bit far.'

'More than just a bit,' John countered. 'Damn it, you know how sceptical I am concerning so-called paranormal phenomena, but lately I've had good cause to reconsider my position regarding this matter. Since just about everything I used to believe has been undermined by this thing, I now find myself forced to consider all possibilities. The mere fact that it exists overturns everything I was ever taught.'

After they had all described their dreams and Bernard had jotted them down, John made an announcement. 'I have decided to contact the university and request an extension to the project. There will be raised eyebrows, I know, but if I stress the uniqueness of our discoveries, I'm reasonably sure I'll be able to convince them – either that or they'll think I've flipped.'

'It would take a lot of pressure off us, that's for sure,' Barbara agreed.

'OK then,' Bernard said, rising and gathering up his notes. 'Meeting adjourned for now. I'm off to do a spot of writing. There are a few things I would like to catch up on. I'll see you in the bar for a snack lunch.' He went out.

'John,' Barbara said when he had gone. 'Thanks for last night. I really did need company. And… and thanks for not taking advantage of the situation.'

Something like tenderness showed in his face. 'Don't hesitate to come again if these dreams persist,' he said in a low voice. 'Who knows? I might need your company as well.'

She smiled and kissed him lightly on the cheek. 'Thank you. You're not the old grouch you sometimes pretend to be.'

'Who says that?'

'Never mind.' She laughed and went out.

He paused and looked at himself in the large mirror over the fireplace. 'Old grouch indeed!' he harrumphed.

10

They met at one o'clock in the bar and chose a table in a quiet corner. Bernard was the first to speak.

'I've noted all the dreams we outlined this morning, and something occurs to me. It's purely a guess at the moment, you understand, but while I was writing, the thought struck me that the cylinder may be implanting its own memories into us: memories of the time when it last saw the light of day.'

'It seems a bit far-fetched,' John said.

'Quite,' Bernard agreed. 'But so is everything else concerning this matter. Now, if this theory is correct – and I emphasise the word *if* – we might be able to assemble them into some kind of history of what really happened to those people and why they disappeared.'

John thought about this for a while. 'It is worth a try,' he said eventually, 'but it's highly unlikely that anyone will ever believe it. It's far too airy-fairy.'

'Then we'll tell them it's a well-considered theory, all carefully worked out and perfectly logical.' He shrugged and became serious again. 'Look, I'm not looking for a lazy way out here, nor is it an alternative to conventional research. We shall be as meticulous as ever – more so if anything. I strongly suspect that any evidence we find will corroborate this idea. Alternatively, these dreams may just serve to fill in some of the missing pieces, that's all. It's worth a try, anyway.'

'It sounds plausible,' Barbara said.

John tapped a one fingered rhythm on the table. 'It is probably the daftest idea I've ever heard in my entire career,' he said. 'Still, it might just work. Go ahead with the project. It would be interesting to see what comes out of it.'

'It might be interesting to see if there are any new patterns on the cylinder,' Barbara said, changing the subject. 'I'm anxious to see it again.'

'We shall look at it this afternoon,' John said, 'but as soon as it starts to show signs of life again, we cover it over. Is that understood?'

She nodded without saying anything. Despite the disturbing psychological effect it seemed to have had on her, she wanted to touch it again, but John was adamant on this matter. She wondered how she could persuade him to let her. She decided she would have to work on this. She had a strong feeling that the answers to a lot of pertinent questions were stored inside that enigmatic hull. These were currently being withheld from her, tantalisingly out of reach.

11

After lunch, they got into John's Land Rover and drove out to the site. Everything appeared to be exactly as they had left it, so the trio went straight to the cabin. John had decided to give Chris and Lynda the rest of the day off. He wanted them to know as little as possible about the cylinder and, since this afternoon's business would be almost entirely to do with that, he had reluctantly decided to exclude them from the proceedings. His chief reason for keeping them in the dark was to avoid any risk of their being contaminated by chance contact with it. Also, the fewer people who knew about the possible implications of its discovery the better and if that involved having to deny this knowledge to fellow members of his team, then so be it.

Their first task was to clear the cabin. They immediately set to work removing the spare boxes and packaging materials that had been stored there along with some other sundry equipment and moving them out to the Land Rovers. The field telephone too was taken away, leaving only the old table and the two chairs. Once this was done, Barbara went over to the cylinder and pulled the tarpaulin away from it. It was inert once more, proof now that light was indeed the agent that energised it. Bernard pointed this out to them, secretly pleased that his initial guess had been correct.

With some effort, they turned it over and examined it for more signs and symbols in case more had appeared overnight. There were no more. They moved it back to its original position.

'Why do you think it's so heavy?' Bernard asked. 'I mean, even assuming it's solid, I still find it hard to envisage any material heavy enough to weigh as much as this thing does.'

'I can't even guess,' John said. He realised that Bernard's question was essentially a rhetorical one, but it nonetheless irritated him to be asked questions for which he had no ready answer.

'We don't know what it's made of,' Barbara said. 'What's more, I have a feeling that no one else will either, not even James Masters.'

John pricked up at the mention of this name. He had temporarily forgotten about Barbara's suggestion. 'Are you sure he can be trusted to keep this secret?' he asked her. 'Only the more I think about this, the more I am anxious to keep as many people out of here as possible.'

'I can always call him off,' she said, 'but you must realise that other people will get to know about it eventually.'

'Yes, I know. But until then I'm not too keen on all and sundry coming around to gawp at it. We don't know what we're dealing with here and I am concerned about the possible dangers attached. We have all experienced some odd effects from it and I am anxious to keep the number of people affected down to the barest minimum.'

'I'll think about it,' she said and began to study the small Mandala-like pattern with her hand lens. 'I wish I could photograph this in more detail, but the camera won't focus close enough. Besides, the definition isn't good enough to capture the finer details of the design... uh, that's odd...' Her voice trailed off and she leaned closer to the design as if to get a closer, more detailed view of it, then she recoiled, as if startled by something.

'What is it?' Bernard asked.

She shook her head as if to clear it. 'A sudden feeling of vertigo, I suppose. That dream you described to us this morning; it was a bit like that. For a moment, I felt as if I was falling into the pattern.'

'Then it's not completely inert,' John said. 'Have you noticed how it gains in strength day by day? Even when we cover it, its recovery time decreases every time we re-expose it to the light.'

Bernard nodded. 'It seems to be acting like an accumulator of a particularly efficient kind. It looks as if every time we expose it we are giving it a top-up charge.' He paused. 'If this is right, the time will come when we'll no longer be able to turn it off.'

John gazed at it, marvelling at the beauty of its symmetry. It was as if he was seeing it for the first time. All the fine details were there, but enhanced to such a high degree that he fancied he could see the very atomic structure of its surface. He remembered the few occasions he had smoked marijuana in his undergraduate days. This feeling was a bit like that; only more lucid, so clear in fact that he could almost reach out and touch some important answer... almost.

It was Bernard who saw what was happening. He grabbed the tarpaulin and threw it over the cylinder. 'Christ!' he shouted. 'Get out of here... now!' He rushed to the door and threw it open. 'Fuck, the thing's taking you, now come on!' He caught hold of Barbara's coat and pulled her away from the proximity of the cylinder, then he went back to John and tried to pull him away, but he resisted.

'What the hell do you think you're doing?' he roared.

'John, get out of here. Do you hear me? That thing is affecting you like never before. Can't you see?'

John got to his feet and walked towards the door. Once outside, he stopped and looked back towards the cabin. Barbara came over and stood by him. 'I didn't realise,' he said. 'I didn't realise.'

Bernard joined them. 'It's getting sneaky,' he said. 'I felt nothing unusual, none of us did, and yet it was going to work on us like Billy O without our knowing it.'

John stared at him. 'You did.'

'I tumbled it, but only just. Another minute and I too would have succumbed.'

'You're new to it,' Barbara said. 'You may still be more sensitive to its effects.'

John swallowed hard and leaned against the nearside wing of the Land Rover. Although shaken, his head felt remarkably clear. The Zen-like experience of the cylinder's apparent psychic power had changed something in him in a way he found hard to define and this troubled him. 'Let's get away from here,' he said.

They climbed into the Land Rover and drove back into town. On the way back, no one spoke. It was as if they were mentally trying to process something too complicated for mere words to express.

Back at the hotel, John purloined the use of the conference room for a special meeting and once more they sat at the end of the large table. Bernard had brought a note pad and pen with him.

'Right,' he began. 'This thing is getting too big for us. We should have realised it a couple of days ago. We are going to have to get someone in to assist us, but who?'

'I don't want anyone else getting involved,' John said. 'We have already been exposed to whatever danger there may be, and I can't risk exposing anyone else to it. Why on earth do you think I'm keeping the other team members away?'

Barbara leaned forward. 'I know I'm likely to get my head bitten off for saying this, but what have we got to lose now if we just carry on and accept the cylinder for what it is?'

'What?' They both looked at her.

'What more can it do to us?' she said. 'I mean: if it's going to harm us at all, then it will have already done so. If we get other people involved, we shall be exposing them to the same risk; then there'll be a big hysterical reaction and the whole project will be on the scrapheap. Do you want that to happen?'

Bernard considered this. She had a valid point. On the other hand, he reasoned, they had all had their minds tampered with in some way and this was without doubt clouding their judgement. He would have to think about it.

'It's possible,' she continued, 'that the Ministry of Defence will get involved; even probable. If that happens, then we really will lose control of everything. The Army will take over the site and all our work will be undone.'

'Then what the hell are we supposed to do?' Bernard said. 'We have already lost control of the situation, so what difference does it make?'

John tapped the table. 'No one else is getting involved at this stage. Now let's move on. I think we should each try to record our experience of what happened back there. It may help us to find out more about what this cylinder is about. The chances are that the news of its discovery will leak out anyway. After all, we are not the only ones involved, are we? There is Lars in Uppsala, James Masters...'

'He knows little or nothing about it,' Barbara corrected him.

'Maybe, but there are those at the University whom I have told about it, and they know that we have made an important discovery, although they don't know what, exactly. I applied for an extension, remember? As time goes on, it is inevitable that more people will get involved anyway, so the best we can do is make the most of what little time we have left before the world gets to hear about it.'

'Something occurs to me,' Barbara said. 'It's now obvious that the thing has affected us all in some way, but it has not altered our personalities at all. I mean, you are still very much John Black and Bernard is still Bernard Savage, and I know I am still me. It has not turned us into zombies, has it, so how do we know it is dangerous?'

'We don't,' John said. 'That is to say, we don't know yet. But then, they didn't know the dangers of radiation until people started falling sick and dying as a result of exposure to it. Do I make my point?'

The others nodded.

'Right, now let's get on. I might as well start.'

Bernard picked up his notepad and pen.

'I was unaware of anything happening at first,' John began and proceeded to recount his experience with the cylinder.

Barbara's experience had been very similar to John's after the initial vertiginous experience that had so coincided with Bernard's dream.

It was Bernard's turn. 'I was beginning to drift when I became aware of what was happening and managed to pull myself out of it, so I can't really tell you what happened to me, if anything.'

This concluded the meeting. They left the room and Bernard went upstairs to log his notes. John and Barbara sat in the bar until it was time for dinner. There was nothing else to do for the rest of the day.

12

Chris and Lynda sat together at a table in a small café. They were both puzzled by the recent behaviour of the senior members of the team. They had been given the day off for no obvious reason and this was not the only unaccountable thing to happen recently. Both wondered why that peculiar cylinder had been kept from their sight since they had released it from the earth and helped to move it to the cabin. Since then the cabin had been declared out of bounds to all but the senior team members. From this it was reasonable to suppose that the cylinder had something to do with this; in fact, it was obvious that they were not being allowed anywhere near it. This was frustrating as it was annoying. Both were young and hungry for knowledge and this was being denied to them, or so it seemed. After all, they wanted to be integral members of the team and not marginalised as they now appeared to be.

'Do you think we should confront Professor Black over this?' Chris said.

Lynda was more cautious in her approach and liked to consider things rather than act instinctively or on impulse. 'If I know John Black, he's not a bad old stick and he must have a good reason for keeping us away. He wouldn't do this normally. He likes to include all his students in his work as much as he can, so if he wants to keep us away from that cylinder, he must have a sound reason for it.'

'I want to know just why he is keeping us away from the cabin,' he said. 'Damn it, I'm supposed to be on this project to learn, not to be used as a labourer and kept in the dark over it.'

'Chris, no one is trying to use you as a labourer and if we're being kept in the dark there must be a good reason for it.'

He supposed she was right but he was bored. If something was going on he wanted to know what it was and be a part of it. It was nice to have the day off, but the town was small and it didn't take long to see all that the place had to offer. He wanted to be back on the site and working. Most of all, he wanted to know what that cylinder was about. There was no doubt that it was an important find; indeed, it was probably unique, but that was no reason to guard it from all but the only three who had been granted the privilege to work with it. The way they regarded it, anyone would think it was the Holy Grail. He decided that he would have it out with John and find out just why all research work on the cylinder was being kept from them, and if he was not satisfied with the result, he would take matters into his own hands and find out for himself. He reckoned the site was about an hour's walk from the town, even allowing for the rough terrain, and both he and Lynda were young and fit. It would be an easy enough walk for them. He didn't impart this idea to her but filed it away for future use.

Lynda also was frustrated by their apparent exclusion from anything to do with the object. It was obvious that it had become the centre of everyone's attention barring theirs. Chris had a valid point, she knew, but she also knew that it was uncharacteristic of John to hide information from any team member. Nonetheless, she thought it would not be unreasonable to politely enquire why they were being denied all access to the cylinder. After all, they had a right to know.

'Leave it to me,' she said eventually. 'I shall ask him.'

13

After dinner, Lynda approached John and asked if she could have a private word with him. He more or less guessed what it was going to be about and agreed to talk, but with some hesitation and grave doubts as to what he might say by way of a plausible reason for withholding so much important information from both her and Chris. It wasn't fair on them, he knew, but the way he saw it, he had no option but to keep them away from that cylinder at all costs. Now he was forced to tell her the truth, but it could not be the whole truth. He thought of something.

He led her into a corridor of the hotel where it was quiet and where they were unlikely to be eavesdropped.

'Now,' he began. 'I shall be as straight with you as I can. You are right, we are keeping information concerning the cylinder from you, but believe me, it is not to keep you in the dark as you believe. We are limiting all access to the cylinder because we believe it might be made from some highly toxic material.'

'But we handled it,' she protested.

'Yes, and that was unwise, but you were subjected to minimal exposure and there should be no harmful effects. You would have to be exposed to it for several hours to suffer any ill effects, but the danger is there.' The thought of having to tell her a half-truth repelled him. It was against all that he stood for, but he had no choice.

She saw through it anyway.

14

That night the dreams came again, and this time they were more vivid than ever. John awoke amid twisted sheets after dreaming of what amounted to a massacre.

What appeared to be an attacking army had breached the settlement's defences and had now gone on a killing spree, lashing out indiscriminately with war clubs and stone axes. Dropped iron weapons were collected and reused to devastating effect and the wounded were simply slaughtered where they lay. He saw the cylinder, blackened with dried blood and in a hut that seemed to be burning around it. On turning, he looked directly into the eyes of a man whose face was a mask of rage and hatred. The man roared, his heavy war club raised and ready to strike. In that moment he knew that this would be the last thing he would ever see, at which point he awoke in a state of panic and terror.

For some time after that he lay awake, afraid to go back to sleep and worrying that he was losing his grip on the situation. He was becoming obsessed with the cylinder and this thought was also disturbing to a mind that was normally so disciplined. He wondered about Barbara and if she too was dreaming. She probably was. It had affected all who had come within close proximity to it and was now dominating their thoughts to the point where not even sleep would come as a release from its influence. As likely as not, Bernard would be dreaming of it too.

He switched on the light and sat on the edge of the bed, wondering what he had done to the team by exposing them to its malign presence, even if it was malignant. He did not even know that much. He picked up a notepad and started to write his dream down, not that he would be likely to forget it. Still, it was important to record what he could of the various details. Of these, he could remember surprisingly little. For instance, he could not quite recall what the people had looked like or how they were dressed. He remembered the shape of one of the iron swords with its simple hilt and leaf shaped blade, broadening slightly towards the point. Such a shape was reminiscent of certain Bronze Age weapons. He sketched it as best he could and tried to remember if such a weapon had been recovered from the site. He could not. The few intact weapons that had been found were so badly corroded as to be almost unrecognisable, being scarcely more than elongated chunks of brittle rust or just iron oxide stains in the soil.

Barbara too was tormented by dreams of the cylinder. One was peaceful enough, depicting what looked like daily life in the village. It was a vision of prosperity, with market traders and men who might have been wealthy farmers, together with their partners and children playing amongst what looked more like houses than simple huts. But there was another, darker side too, for amongst the wealthy she saw what appeared to be a slave class. These people, although well dressed enough, wore around their necks a distinctive cord, reminiscent of a dog collar, made from some kind of plaited rope and spliced so that it could not easily be removed. Then there was the underclass. Beggars sat on corners and keened for alms and signs of the most abject poverty were everywhere beyond what appeared to be a given boundary. Somehow she knew that these were the people who lived outside the settlement's stockade walls; a subject nation, enslaved and dominated by the People of the Cylinder.

She stirred and awoke, and then, following Bernard's example, wrote down what she had seen or at least the bits of it that she could remember.

On going back to sleep, another dream came. This time it was unpleasant and horribly violent. She saw the cylinder in the centre of a round hut, surrounded by people who seemed to be worshiping it. A young girl who might have been either a slave or a captive was led by the lead around her neck into the centre of the circle. She was dressed in a long robe that was tied at the waist by a simple cord and she was weeping. This seemed to have no effect on the watchers as the robe was removed and, now utterly naked, the girl was forced to kneel before the cylinder. The rope lead was released as a man stepped forward and, placing a knee between her shoulder blades, pulled her head back by the hair and, with a long, broad bladed knife, slit her throat from ear to ear. Blood jetted from the deep wound and spattered the far wall and the cylinder as the dying girl's body was released and allowed to slump to the earthen floor of the hut. A cry went up from the surrounding crowd as she awoke again, terrified by this vision of what could only have been a human sacrifice.

She duly recorded this one as well and lay down again, but sleep eluded her this time. She could not forget the image of that wretched girl and her grisly fate. Eventually, she rose and pulled on her dressing gown. It reminded her of the gown the girl had worn. Sitting at the desk, she briefly sketched out a few possibilities as to what the cylinder might be. She was now fairly certain that it was implanting pieces of its history into their minds. It was significant that all who had come into close contact with it had been bedevilled by these dreams ever since it had first become reactivated after so many millennia of dormancy. The possibility that it might be some kind of recording device occurred to her. If so, she wondered who might have put it there and why. She wondered too if it might have recorded the activities of the team as they worked on the dig. It was possible, she reasoned, but only if it was within a given range, for it was constantly at the centre of these visions of the past, if that was what they were. But it possessed no lens that they could see, or any hint of a camera, so how could it see? It was then that an idea occurred to her that was as obvious as it was brilliant. Instead of a camera, it was using the eyes of its acolytes to record what they saw.

She wrote this down and went back to bed, but sleep eluded her. She could not shut out the horrid vision of that throat-slitting ceremony. Had these ancients so venerated the cylinder that they had taken it for a god and even sacrificed virgins to it? It was possible, even probable for a people who could not begin to understand natural phenomena, let alone a thing like this. After all, it was baffling the educated brains of modern academics, so it would be little wonder that a far more simple culture might regard it as divine. She thought of how the Aztecs had sought to placate their bloodthirsty gods by a constant stream of human sacrifice, waging war on neighbouring tribes just to take prisoners for that sole purpose. It was not beyond the bounds of possibility that these people might have been similar.

She arose once more and wrote this idea down as well. Things were beginning to take shape in her mind.

For some time she sat at the desk and tried to think, but no further ideas came. She was tired and yet sleep seemed further away than ever. She thought of her previous night with John. It had been a

58

comfort to have his company in the night. She had not slept with a man since her undergraduate days, since when work had been uppermost in her life. Even John, whom she had known longer than most people in her working life, was first and foremost a colleague and this essentially governed the conduct of their relationship. True, she had always considered him a good friend as well as a colleague and she liked to think that he regarded her in the same light, but up until now that had been the extent of their relationship. Still, their night together had changed something and she felt a small thrill as she remembered lying beside him in the night's stillness. She thought of going to his room again, but hesitated, uncertain this time. It might look as if it was becoming a habit.

In the end, the matter was resolved by a gentle knock on her door. She opened it and saw John standing in the corridor.

'I hope I didn't wake you,' he said. 'I saw your light under the door.'

'No, no. I couldn't sleep anyway. Come in, please.'

He entered and sat on the edge of the bed, looking and feeling awkward at finding himself in this situation. 'Me neither,' he said. 'Christ, I wonder if I'm going mad. I'm having war dreams now.'

'It's the cylinder,' she said. 'It's affecting all of us and I think I'm beginning to understand how.'

'How?' He looked up at her.

'I had a bad dream as well and couldn't get back to sleep, so I made some notes. Here.' She handed him the notepad. 'It may seem off-the-wall, but so does everything else right now.'

He read her notes carefully. She had something, he knew, but it still left too many questions unanswered. Still, he reasoned that she might just be right. He told her this much and then read, with some disquiet, the account of her dream of the throat-slitting.

'It was that which led me to the possibility that they regarded it as a god and even sacrificed to it,' she said. 'Do you think it's likely?'

'It's possible, certainly,' he said.

She decided to change the subject. 'What was your dream, then?'

'Pretty grim,' he replied and outlined it to her. When he had finished he shook his head and banged his fist on his knee. 'What's happening to us?'

She stepped in front of him, pulled his head forward into her belly and held it there. 'Hush, now. Hush. It was just a bad dream,

59

that's all. I think that they'll eventually diminish.' She stroked his back, aware of what she was doing and aware that he needed comforting by whatever means she could muster. In that moment he looked so helpless she might have been comforting a frightened child. She had never seen him like this before. 'There there.' Her words were automatic; instinctive. 'There there.'

He put his arms around her and nestled his head deeper into her belly, feeling the soft material of her dressing gown against his cheek.

'You can sleep with me tonight,' she said. 'It will do us both good.' She opened her dressing gown and allowed his face to press against her bare skin. 'Come to bed,' she whispered.

He released his grip and sat back, looking up at her. 'We have a good relationship. I don't want to spoil it.'

She smiled. 'You won't.'

Despite his misgivings, he found himself powerless to resist. He put his hands under her dressing gown and stroked her smooth skin.

She leaned forward so that her breasts brushed against his face. 'We need each other tonight,' she said, 'and this time you don't have to play the gentleman. I *want* you. I want to feel you inside me. Now, come to bed.'

Bernard was having a bad night. Dreams such as he had never had before tormented his sleep and kept him awake for much of the time. It seemed as if every time he closed his eyes some new vision emerged from the dark recesses of his mind. He duly noted what dreams he could remember and was surprised to notice that the number he had written down seemed to be fewer than the number he had actually had. He sat up and pondered this. It was obvious that he must have gone straight back to sleep after some of these dreams without writing them down. He tried to recall any that might have gone unrecorded, but could not. Of those he had recorded, one was a dream of the ritual slaughter of an adolescent girl, similar to the one that Barbara had had. This had distressed him. Next, he dreamed of the cylinder itself, and saw how a kind of enlightenment arose from physical contact with it. Barbara's dream of the young girl doing that had more or less coincided with this. He wondered why this apparent enlightenment had not affected their enthusiastic attitude towards human sacrifice.

Next he was troubled by a war dream, similar to John's but more brutal. In it, he saw an orgy of slaughter with severed limbs and heads littering a ground that was slippery with blood. Bodies were stripped and mutilated, regardless of age or sex. A terrified youth was held, his arms pinned from behind by one warrior while another, grim-faced, ran him through with his spear.

He awoke from this one in a cold sweat and sat up for a long time, afraid to go back to sleep in case he might dream the same thing again. Eventually, tiredness got the better of him and he slept once more, trying this time to concentrate on the cylinder itself and its enigmatic nature. He was beginning to have an idea.

Sure enough, he dreamed again. This time he saw the cylinder and its mysterious designs. One of these; the smallest, had already occurred in one dream. Now he saw the larger one that resembled a cartouche with its indecipherable writing. Perhaps something lay in this that might help to solve the cylinder's riddle. As he watched, he became aware of a brittle sounding rapid sequence of five notes, repeated at first, and then varying and growing in intensity as the characters within the cartouche began to float, drifting very slowly and arranging themselves into patterns that were meaningless to him. Still the pattern varied until it started to create the illusion of a three dimensional object of great complexity and beauty. Now it merged with the compound circular pattern to form another of even greater complexity. This new pattern grew until it was as big as he was, or else he was diminishing and at the same time it darkened until it became like a photographic negative of its original neutral colour. Then, like the illusion created by an isometric drawing of a cube, the pattern inverted itself and he was passing through it into what looked like another world. Here, nothing was recognisable. Shapes rose in front of him, but they were not shapes that might be seen on earth. They were indescribable. They stretched away for mile after mile to an invisible horizon or far distant vanishing point. It was almost like stepping into a painting by Yves Tanguy, except that here the shapes were three dimensional. They seemed to obey no normal law for, while solid, they were also fluid. Some flowed along the ground like amoebae while others broke free and floated in the air. In the distance, something like a mast rose hundreds of metres into a milky sky. It was slender and its base could not be seen. It seemed to rise out of a ground mist. He could not guess its purpose.

He looked around. The shapes were everywhere. Some were linked together by thin filaments that seemed to grow from the things themselves like strings of protoplasm. Tiny nodes of light pulsed along these and he guessed that they were in some sort of communication with each other. Whatever it was, the shapes seemed to completely ignore his presence there. He was convinced that they were alive. One of the floating ones passed close to him, almost brushing past. It displayed no outward sign of curiosity at all. It was as if he wasn't there as far as they were concerned.

Unaccountably, although this landscape was as alien as anything ever could be to an earth being, he felt at peace there. He somehow knew that these strange biomorphic shapes posed no threat to him and he felt that he had known them for a long time. He wanted to stay with them, and then the conscious side of his brain intruded, telling him that this was only a dream and he awoke; not a violent ejection into wakefulness this time but a gentle drift into consciousness. It was morning. He looked at the clock. It was half past seven and he felt tired. He resisted the strong temptation to turn over and go back to sleep and got up.

Before he dressed, he wrote down this latest dream and tried to remember his last thought before falling into the sleep into which this particular dream had come. If his idea was correct, these dreams could be controlled. He would see.

When John awoke, dawn was breaking. Barbara was asleep beside him. The bedclothes were partly thrown back and she was naked. He wanted to touch her, but he resisted the temptation and let her sleep undisturbed. He stared up at the ceiling with its ornate Victorian plaster rose around the pendant light and considered the complexity of its leaf and flower pattern. This made him think first of an elaborately iced cake, rather like the one with which he had celebrated his seventh birthday. It had been so beautiful that it had seemed a shame to cut it. Then, inevitably, his thoughts drifted to the complex patterns on the cylinder. He tried to put it out of his mind and thought instead of last night when he and Barbara had made love. It had quickly become obvious that they both needed the intimate comfort of sexual union and, more importantly, the security of each other's company. Their lovemaking had been free and uninhibited with fingers and lips exploring every inch of skin with no holds barred and no taboos. Perhaps their heightened emotions had served to

62

intensify their combined sexual appetites, for their lovemaking had been almost savage in its intensity. The bad dreams had ceased and he had slept well after that. Barbara, too, had slept peacefully beside him. Had she had any further nightmares he would have known for he was a light sleeper and any disturbance would have woken him instantly.

He sat up and tried to read the clock, but it was on her side of the bed and he couldn't see it at its present angle. He guessed that it was about five o'clock. He thought about going back to his room, then lay back again. He didn't want to leave her before she woke up naturally. To do so would be churlish. It would look as if he was abandoning her and he did not want to create any false impression at this stage. He looked at her again, vulnerable in her nakedness and he longed to hold her again in his arms – to once more feel her warm body against his, but he let her sleep. She needed it. They both did.

He opened his eyes, unaware at first that he had drifted back to sleep. It was lighter now and she was sitting on the bed beside him in her dressing gown. She stroked his forehead. 'I've made you a coffee,' she said.

He took her hand and held it. 'What time is it?'

'Five past seven. Breakfast is at eight. Did you sleep well?'

'Yes. The dreams stayed away; how about you?'

'Fine.' She gave a naughty little chuckle. 'We really *do* work well together, don't we?'

He sat up. 'I'd better get back to my room.'

She put her arms around him and drew him close. 'Thanks for last night. I'm so glad you came. I really needed your company.' She kissed him.

He looked into her eyes. An almost overwhelming feeling of tenderness welled up inside him. 'We needed each other,' he said softly. 'We really needed each other.'

They made love again.

15

They met for breakfast at eight o'clock and Bernard eventually joined them. He looked rough. 'Christ, what a night,' he said. 'I seem to have had nothing but dreams and, guess what; they were all about the cylinder.'

'Now there's a surprise.' John said.

'I am starting to worry about it,' he continued. 'If they continue like this, we'll all end up in the funny farm. That bloody thing is becoming an obsession. God, I would give anything to have a normal dream again, preferably one with a glamorous page three girl in it; anything but that accursed cylinder. I've never had dreams like these before. Still, there might be a glimmer of hope.'

'Oh?' John looked up.

'It's a new idea and still largely untested, but I think they can be controlled. I'll tell you more about it later. I take it we shall be having a meeting after breakfast?'

'The conference room is booked this morning,' John said. 'Still, I shall have a word with the manager and see if we can have an alternative room. We need to talk. Whatever happens, we shall meet in the lobby at ten o'clock, OK?'

After breakfast, Barbara and Bernard went back to their rooms to do some work, while John negotiated with the manager for the use of a spare room. Successful, he went to his room and got out his laptop. He had neglected his work recently and was anxious to catch up with it. He studied the three dimensional model of the dig and noted the exact position where the cylinder had been found. A grey circle surrounded it, marking where traces of carbon had been discovered, together with tiny fragments of charred wood. He remembered his dream of the burning hut and the mass slaughter. No human remains had been found there, but they may have been incinerated in the intense heat and time would have erased whatever traces remained.

He then checked the exact co-ordinates of where the clock or whatever it was had been found and entered them with the appropriate label. It was important for him to do this in order to at least try and stay on top of a situation that was rapidly moving beyond his control. When he had done that, he closed the laptop and checked the time. Still fifty minutes to go before the meeting. He lay on the still unmade bed and thought about his newly developed relationship with Barbara. The last two nights and last night in particular had seen their friendship grow into something like love. This served if anything to complicate matters still further. He was in no doubt that they needed each other, but how long would it last? Last night had done them both good and she had given herself to him freely with the kind of abandonment that only lovers can do, but had it been just for that particular moment? His main fear, if only he would admit it, was that it might change everything as far as their working relationship was concerned. Tricky indeed... Well, he would worry about that later. They were both professional enough not to let interpersonal relationships interfere with business, or at least he hoped they were. He got up and went over to the window.

Outside, the day was well under way. Shoppers walked the pavements and cars manoeuvred their way along the high street. Out there, it was a normal day while all around him it seemed things were getting progressively more chaotic with each hour that passed. He looked at his watch. Still ten minutes to go. Thoughts of Barbara rose to the surface again. He knew that he was falling in love with her. The way he had seen her this morning was proof, if proof were needed, that this would be more than just a one night stand as far as he was concerned. He had not felt such tenderness for another human being since the early days of his marriage, but that had been different again. He saw with the benefit of hindsight that that episode in his life had been a big mistake, probably the biggest mistake of his life. They had both been too young and inexperienced when they had married and his work had taken him away from her too often. It was small wonder then that she had got fed up and started sleeping with another man. He had to accept his share of the blame. He wondered if it would be the same with Barbara, even assuming that their relationship ever developed that far. He would worry about that later. It was time to go.

Downstairs in the lobby he found a somewhat haggard-looking Bernard.

'I've managed to get us a spare room,' he said. 'Are the others not here yet?'

Bernard looked around. 'No. We're the first.'

John was silent for a moment; then he said: 'I've been thinking about Lynda and Chris. Have you seen them yet?'

'No, I think they may have slept late.'

'Don't you think we should tell them the truth about the cylinder? It seems unfair to keep them in the dark. I had to tell Lynda that the thing is toxic and a health hazard. I wonder now if I did the right thing.'

Bernard thought about this. 'I honestly don't know. I do know how I would feel if I thought someone was hiding the truth from me, and I can tell you that I wouldn't be very happy. No one likes to feel excluded.'

'I'm between the devil and the deep here. On one hand, I am unhappy about concealing the truth from them, and on the other, I want as few people as possible to know about it.'

'They're both trustworthy,' Bernard said. 'I think you could trust them with a secret.'

John smiled at him. 'Thanks. I shall try and find them.'

He left Bernard standing in the lobby and went to the breakfast room. Chris and Lynda were sitting at a table. They looked up as he entered.

'Sorry we're late,' Chris said as he joined them. 'It's my fault, I'm afraid. I overslept.'

'That's all right. Finish your breakfast and then I would like you to join us for a meeting. It's important that you should know one or two things. We shall be in room 109 for the next hour or so. Join us when you can, will you?' He paused. 'Have you been having any strange dreams at all?'

Chris gave him an odd look. 'No.'

'OK, I just wondered, that's all.'

He left them and returned to the lobby. Barbara had joined Bernard and together they made their way to room 109. Here, they sat where they could and John called the meeting to order. He first decided to tell them of his decision to include Chris and Lynda in the proceedings and to brief them on what the situation really was concerning the cylinder.

'Is that wise?' Barbara asked him.

'I don't know,' he said. 'But I think it's only fair that they should know. I'm in a bit of a quandary over this and I'm not happy with either option, but I'm satisfied they can be trusted to keep a secret, so I'm prepared to take the risk.'

Her face still expressed some doubt, but she said nothing.

'Before they get here, I think we should get our dreams out of the way,' he went on. 'I suppose I might as well start.'

They each described their dreams and Bernard duly noted them. 'I am beginning to see a pattern emerging,' he said when they had finished, 'and there are a number of parallels or near ones at least. Here, we have the war dreams, then what appears to be a human sacrifice, and then there is the cylinder itself. That has appeared on two separate occasions. Of these, mine is the oddest.'

'You said they might be controllable,' John said.

'It's too early to say, but if you think in a certain way before going to sleep, it may help to steer the course of these dreams. I think it worked for me once, but it's still too early to tell if it really works.'

'It would be nice if it did,' John said, 'because I don't know how much longer we can take it. Now that you know how violent they can be, you will understand. We are fighting to preserve our sanity here.'

'I was curious to find out more about the cylinder and now I'm reaping the benefit,' Bernard said. 'That'll learn me.'

'Curiosity killed the cat,' Barbara said.

'It won't kill me!' he huffed.

There was a knock on the door and Chris and Lynda entered.

'Find a place to sit and join us,' John said. 'First, I have a confession to make, and an apology. I have not been entirely straight with you concerning the cylinder.'

'I thought not,' Lynda said. 'That story about it being poisonous didn't really fool me, you know. We both of us guessed there was something wrong with it ever since it was first discovered.'

'I suppose it didn't, and I apologise if I insulted your intelligence, but I had my reasons for hiding the truth from you. Look, this may sound a bit cloak and dagger, but before I go on, I want you both to promise me that not a word of this will be repeated outside this room. Do you understand?'

'Yeah, sure,' she said and Chris nodded.

'Right; when I told you that it was toxic, it was not that far from the truth. It isn't exactly poisonous, but it has adversely affected all who have come close to it, and that effect is psychological. When you handled it, it was dormant and therefore safe. Now something has activated it and it is highly dangerous for you to go anywhere near it. That is why I want you to stay away. I don't want you to have to go through some of the things we have experienced.'

'How has it affected you?' Lynda asked, 'and do you know what that thing might be?'

'To answer the second part of your question first, we don't know. The thing is a conundrum. It is like nothing we've ever seen before. As for its effect, it appears to have implanted us with unwanted thoughts and vivid dreams, almost as if it's transferring its memories to us. We think we have all had visions of its past history.'

Chris gaped in disbelief.

'Look,' Bernard said, picking up his notes. 'This is a record of all the dreams that we can remember. You might as well read them, then you'll see how it has affected us, but I'll warn you; some of those dreams are pretty horrible.'

Chris took the notes and read them carefully, looking up from time to time as if uncertain whether or not to proceed. When he had finished he passed them to Lynda and took a deep breath. 'Phew! Pretty violent stuff, some of it.'

'You had to be there,' Bernard said.

John waited until Lynda had finished reading, then he said: 'Now perhaps you will understand why we have kept you away from that cylinder and why I gave you a buckshee day off yesterday. We were going up there to examine it again and I didn't want to take the risk of your being accidentally contaminated by it. As it was, Bernard got hit by it and now all three of us have been affected. We are now trying to understand what's happened to us and find a way of dealing with its effects. That's why we kept it from you. I have now decided to let you in on the secret, but I must insist you don't breathe a word of it outside these four walls. It's potential dynamite.'

'Trust us,' Chris said.

'I am.'

'You said it hit Bernard,' Lynda said. 'What exactly happened?'

'It's hard to describe exactly,' Bernard said. 'I had a kind of muzzy feeling in my head and then something hit me like an atom bomb. Barbara said it had mind-probed me.'

'How did you know that?' She turned to Barbara.

Barbara shook her head. 'I honestly don't know. The thought came from nowhere, like one or two others I've had recently. That seems to be another effect of contact with the cylinder. You begin to feel as if you know it better than you possibly could.'

Chris chuckled. 'Sounds like a mind-altering experience.'

'That's one way of putting it,' she said, but there was no humour in her voice. 'Look, this is not some magic hippy-trip. It's very serious.'

'Sorry,' he said, surprised by her unexpected outburst.

She softened. 'No, I'm sorry. I didn't mean to snap at you. It's just that we don't know what's happening to us and it's... well... frightening.'

Lynda put a comforting arm around her shoulders.

'Well,' John said. 'We've briefed you on the situation as much as we can. I'm sorry we can't tell you more, but we don't know any more at this stage.'

Chris whistled through his teeth. 'Very strange; but what do we do now?'

'We carry on as before, but I don't want you to go anywhere near that cylinder or the cabin. We are currently trying to deactivate it, but it seems to be getting stronger, despite our efforts.'

'Deactivate it?'

'We think it may be light activated. If it is and we exclude the light, then we think it might run down; at least that's the idea.'

'It may only need a small amount of light,' Chris suggested. 'How have you excluded the light?'

'We put a tarpaulin over it.'

'I'll bet some light is still getting in.'

Bernard snapped his fingers. 'I bet you are right. Just one or two lumens may be enough to energise it, and if that is right, it'll be getting stronger day by day. We have already noticed that for ourselves.'

John pondered this idea. 'In that case, it could be reaching peak power right now.'

'Oh my God,' Bernard mused.

Barbara had by now recovered her composure and she said: 'Does anyone here know anything about superconductors?'

They all looked blank.

'I don't know much about them either, but I understand they're a very good way of making a little power go a long way. If that thing has a superconducting circuit, then its energy loss when idling would be minimal. It could take years to run down.'

'It's a good thought,' said Bernard. 'But did they have superconductors in the Stone Age?'

'Stone age?' Chris echoed.

'There's another conundrum,' John said. 'The site is a lot older than we thought it was. Nothing here fits any kind of conventional thinking.'

'Going back to our dreams,' Barbara said. 'Whenever the cylinder has appeared, it is in a building of some kind where the light level is low.'

'It was housed in a building,' John said. 'We can tell that from the carbon traces surrounding the area where it was discovered.'

Barbara's mobile phone sounded. She picked it up and left the room. A minute later she came back in and sat down. 'That was James Masters. He wants to take a look at the cylinder.'

'Well he can't,' John said.

'He's already here.'

'Bloody hell!'

16

James Masters was standing in the hotel lobby when the team left the room, their meeting over for now. He was a young man, smartly dressed and carrying a black briefcase. He had about him a somewhat raffish air, the mere sight of which made John bristle. On seeing Barbara, he stepped forward and smiled in recognition.

She greeted him and introduced him to the other team members. John decided to cut the ceremony short.

'I'm sorry,' he said. 'But I'm afraid you've had a wasted journey.'

'Oh?' He smiled. 'Barbara here informed me that you had found a cylinder or something made from some unknown material. I said I would take a look at it and maybe see what it's made of. Barbara and I are old friends. We were at university together.'

John wondered what to do next. He didn't want to appear unduly rude and risk offending one of Barbara's friends; that would have upset her, nor did he want this man poking around the cylinder and becoming affected by it. Somehow, he had to get rid of him. He decided to adopt the same ruse that he had used on Lynda.

'I'm afraid it's unsafe to examine it.' He said.

'Oh?' His eyes narrowed. 'In what way?'

'It appears to be made from some toxic material,' he said. 'Even close proximity may result in contamination.'

'I am equipped to deal with that,' he said. 'I frequently have to deal with hazardous substances. It's all in a day's work as far as I'm concerned.'

John felt himself boxed into a corner. He didn't know how to deal with this persistent stranger. He really wanted to tell him to bugger off, but that would appear too defensive and would be bound to arouse suspicion. Why, he wondered, had Barbara not called him off? A simple phone call would have done it.

'Look, I've got all the necessary equipment in the car. What say we go take a look at it? It'll only take a few minutes.'

John gave in. He hoped that the thing had become dormant again, having been covered overnight and through much of the morning, but he recalled what Chris had said at the morning's discussion and realised that it could well be as alive, if that was the right word, as it had been yesterday.

James followed them in his own car to the site of the dig, parking close to the road on a patch of hard standing and continuing on foot. Unlike the Land Rovers, his car was unsuitable for off-road driving. He joined them outside the shooting cabin, now dressed in a one piece protective suit with a hood. He had swapped his briefcase for a pilot's case and he carried a breathing mask in his other hand.

'You look like an astronaut,' Bernard quipped.

'Can't be too careful,' James said casually.

'It's in here,' John said, unlocking the door and unable to conceal the surliness in his voice. He turned to Chris and Lynda. 'Remember what I told you and stay outside.'

'Is there anything we can be getting on with?' Chris asked.

'Where were you working last?'

'Up in the north-eastern corner of the dig.'

'Carry on there, then.'

'OK.' They both withdrew.

'Right,' he turned to James. 'I'll go in first.'

'But you're unprotected,' James protested, 'I thought you said it was hazardous.'

John cursed silently. He was a lousy liar, he knew, but his bumbling carelessness here was unforgivable. A schoolboy might have fabricated a better excuse than the one he had invented. He stood back and allowed James to enter the cabin, then followed him in.

As soon as they entered, he knew that the cylinder was alive. To make matters worse, it had not been properly covered by the tarpaulin which had been hastily thrown over it in yesterday's panic and it lay, partly exposed and glowing slightly in the low light. Its energy filled the cabin. He could feel it.

Before John could stop him, James walked towards it and then froze. The pilot's case and mask fell from his hands and he rocked slightly, holding his head despite the protective hood that shrouded it. He staggered backwards and leaned against the stone wall of the cabin. 'Get me out of here,' he said thickly.

72

John helped him to the door and out into the air. 'It's stronger than ever!' he shouted to the others.

Barbara came over, followed by Bernard. There was no need for them to ask what had happened.

'What the hell is that?' James asked as soon as he had recovered sufficiently to find his words.

They looked at each other.

'This is what happens,' Barbara said. 'John, we've got to tell him the truth. He's a part of it now.'

'Part of what?' James queried. 'What the hell is that thing?'

John was crestfallen. The cat was right out of the bag now. He should have sent this interloper away instead of complying with his wishes and compromising the entire project as a result. Now he had no option but to tell him the whole story of the cylinder, just as he had just done with Chris and Lynda, except that with them he had made a carefully considered decision to do so. Now his hand had been forced by his own stupidity.

'We have all been similarly affected by it,' he began. 'That's why I wanted to keep you away. The story I told you of its toxicity was a clumsy effort to do that. I don't know what ever made me think you'd fall for it. It didn't fool anyone else.' He sighed. 'Now that you've been exposed, I might as well tell you what's going on here.'

'We still don't understand it ourselves,' Barbara added.

John told him the story of the cylinder from its discovery to the present moment. He reasoned that James possessed certain skills that could be of use to him. His initial hostility had faded and now, albeit reluctantly, he was prepared to accept the newcomer as a sometime member of the team.

James listened to the story, absorbing what he could of it with difficulty. His field was aeronautics and space exploration. He knew about satellites and spacecraft, but to him archaeology was another matter. Despite this, he had seen enough to know that the technology involved in that cylinder was far beyond anything ever achieved on earth.

'One more thing,' Barbara said. 'You will probably have vivid dreams. We all have and some of them are deeply disturbing. Be warned, we are still trying to come to terms with its effects.'

James looked at her and then looked back at the cabin. 'If I hadn't seen it for myself, I never would have believed it. It's unlike anything I've ever seen before. You know, if I didn't know better, I'd say its origin might be extra-terrestrial.'

'I no longer doubt that possibility,' John admitted.

Barbara raised her eyebrows. 'That's something coming from the arch sceptic.'

'Who else knows about this?' James asked.

'No one outside the team and I want to keep it like that for as long as possible.' John said.

'How safe is it to go back in there and have a closer look at it?' he asked.

'It's highly dangerous,' Bernard warned. 'It probably won't zap you like that again. Instead, it will work on a more subliminal level and I would strongly advise you against it.'

'Hmmm…' he thought about it for a moment. 'I'm going back in there to take a look. Time me. If I'm not out in three minutes, come and get me. Anyway, I left my instruments in there.'

'On your head be it,' Bernard said. 'Don't say we didn't warn you.'

'I'm willing to take a chance,' he insisted.

As he spoke, John noticed a peculiar look in his eyes – something he had not seen before in any other member of the team. It was an almost fanatical glint and it disturbed him.

James turned and went back into the cabin while the others stood outside.

'Is he mad?' Bernard asked.

'As a box of frogs,' John said, looking at his watch. 'We give him three minutes and that's it; we go in there and drag him out if we have to. That thing will fry his brains. You didn't see what I saw when I went in there. Bernard, you didn't cover it over properly. It's now glowing in the dark.'

Bernard looked awkward. 'Shit! I must have panicked when I had to pull you out.'

'It must be ten times more powerful by now. You can feel the energy field as soon as you walk in. It's practically crackling.'

'Then it's beyond our control,' Barbara said.

'I think it's beyond anyone's control,' he said. 'Perhaps it always has been.' He paused and then clapped his hands together abruptly. 'Right, that's it. We're pulling him out. I know his time isn't up yet and I don't care. Christ knows what's going on in there.'

John and Barbara entered the cabin and stopped. The cylinder had been completely uncovered and now James squatted in front of it, his face as calm as Buddha's. He held a small drill idly in one hand while his other hand rested on its glowing hull. His eyes stared fixedly, as if he was looking at something deep inside it. 'Don't come near,' he said. 'I'm all right. I wanted to take a sample of the material, but I'm afraid I might be hurting it. I can't hurt it. Anyway, it's hard, very hard. Not even a diamond wheel can mark it. Now it's talking to me. That's where you went wrong, you know. You didn't let it finish. Now leave me. I shall come out when it is ready.'

'You're coming out now!' John shouted.

'Leave him,' Barbara said. 'He knows what he's doing, I think.'

'Does he? Look at him!'

'Leave me,' James repeated. 'There is no danger here.'

'He's right,' Barbara said. 'There's no danger. I can sense it.'

'You too? Come on, let's get out of here.' He pulled her towards the door and out into the air once more.

'Why did you do that?' she said, a note of anger rising in her voice.

'That thing has got James and it nearly had you. If I hadn't pulled you out, it might have had all of us.'

'You fool, there was no danger.'

Bernard looked anxious. He had remained outside the cabin and so had not witnessed the bizarre scene. 'What's happening?'

John ignored him. 'No danger? No danger? Barbara, it has grabbed your mind, can't you see? If you think there's no danger in there, it is because it wants you to think there's no danger. Oh, Barbara, what do I have to do to convince you? You don't seem to hear yourself talking.'

'You saw James; he so reminded me of the girl in my dream who touched it and was transfigured. John, she was beautiful, so beautiful, and she was probably killed together with the others. Her bones are probably still here somewhere.'

Her voice trembled and he put his arm around her. 'We always destroy that which we cannot understand,' she moaned.

Bernard looked towards the cabin. 'Will someone please tell me what the hell is going on here?'

'It's that bloody cylinder,' John said. 'It has taken James and it nearly had Barbara. It might have had me as well if we hadn't got out of there when we did.'

'What!' He started towards the door.

'Don't go in there!' John shouted at him.

He stopped and came back. 'In case you've forgotten, there's a man in there having his brain frazzled by that thing. Damn it, if you won't get him out, then I will.'

'Stay out of there,' Barbara told him, having by now more or less recovered from the temporary spell that the cylinder had cast over her.

'Has everyone gone mad?'

'If you go in there you may not come out again,' John said. 'It's out of control.'

At that moment, James appeared in the doorway. With an almost casual air, he strolled over and joined them. 'There's nothing to worry about,' he said. 'I'm OK, see? I couldn't take any samples. It's made of some material that's harder than diamond. The tiniest sample would have been sufficient for analysis, but I couldn't even take that.'

The others stared at him in disbelief. Here was a man, who a few moments ago had been locked into some kind of telepathic conversation with the cylinder, now talking in the most matter-of-fact way about taking samples for analysis.

'You know,' he continued in the same conversational tone. 'Whatever substance that cylinder is made of, NASA would pay a fortune for it.'

'James,' John said. 'Do you remember anything else about the cylinder – how you were communicating with it?'

He shook his head. 'I just tried to get a sample from it, that's all.'

'You don't remember anything else?'

'No. Should I?'

'It's like hypnosis,' Barbara mused.

Bernard rolled his eyes and looked away.

'Well,' James said. 'I'm sorry I can't help you. You know, I'm as curious as you are to know what it is made of. It's a fascinating object...' He broke off. 'What?'

John realised that he was gaping at him. He shut his mouth and cleared his throat, but he could think of nothing to say. He had seen him held fast in the cylinder's thrall. Now he was standing there and talking away as if nothing had happened. How, he wondered, could anyone experience something like that and be so unaffected by it? Everyone else who had come under its influence could remember it in graphic detail. Barbara was right. It was like hypnosis. The reason why James could remember nothing of his communication with the cylinder was that it had told him he would remember nothing in much the same way as a hypnotist would. It was that simple. This left one important question unanswered: if there were no outward symptoms of psychological change, then what effect had it had on him and, more importantly, on his mind?

'I think you should stay at the hotel with us for a day or two,' Barbara said. 'Remember how we warned you about the adverse effects following contact with the cylinder?'

'You want to keep me under observation, don't you?' He smiled.

'Something like that,' Bernard said.

He sighed. 'OK, if it makes you happy.'

'It would,' John said.

'It will only be for one night, though,' he continued. 'I have to be back in London in two days time.'

'We shall see.'

'No, we shall not see. I have to be in London and that's that.'

'Do you think we should go in there and cover it up again?' Bernard said.

John looked wearily towards the cabin. 'Would it make any difference?'

'I doubt it, but we might as well try.'

'How do we ensure it doesn't hold us this time?'

Bernard flexed his muscles. 'We hit and run. In, pick up tarp, throw it over and scarper, right?'

'Right, let's do it. On the count of three; ready?'

On the count of three, they dashed into the cabin, ran to the cylinder and grabbed the tarpaulin. They straightened it as best as possible and threw it over the glowing object, then headed for the door. Once out, John slammed the door behind them and snapped the padlock shut.

'Let's get away from here,' He said.

17

That night the dreams came again, more vivid and graphic than before.

Bernard was less affected by them than either John or Barbara, having attempted to put his recent theory into practice and, prior to going to sleep, channelling his thoughts away from the cylinder and all to do with it. This was surprisingly difficult under the circumstances, since it had dominated his waking thoughts for most of the day. To help, he had lingered in the bar that night and, as a result, drunk more than he had intended. In an effort to steer his thoughts away from the cylinder, he had avoided the other team members and sought the company of other drinkers whom he guessed would have no interest in the dig. He had tried flirting with the barmaid first, then realising that she was not really interested, he had chatted to a group of visiting businessmen about football; a sport which held little interest for him, but it did at least help him to think of something else. When one asked him what he did for a living, he had lied and told him that he was a writer. That had settled the man's curiosity to his satisfaction.

He lay awake, trying to steer his thoughts into a realm where the cylinder would not intrude. First, he thought as hard as he could of a large, thick walled safe into which the cylinder had been put and the door locked. This had some effect. He then thought of the book he was currently reading and tried to place himself in the story as one of the main characters. This worked better.

Eventually he fell asleep and for once had a peaceful dream that was unconnected with the cylinder, but it was only a partial success. Another dream did feature it, but it was less violent than the horror that had invaded last night's sleep.

When he awoke he was disappointed to find that he could not quite remember it, so he did not bother to write anything down and went back to sleep again. He was too tired to write anyway. The rest of the night was dreamless.

Not so Barbara. She and John sat in the bar until late, talking; then they both went up to his room, undressed and got into bed together. There was little point in sleeping in separate rooms now, since they both needed the reassurance of each other's company and the close proximity of their bodies was comforting to both.

She stroked his chest with a finger while he stared up at the ceiling and brooded about the day's events. Things had gone badly and, to make matters worse, this James Masters character had jumped into the issue with both feet and emerged from it apparently unscathed. On top of that, Barbara had tried to defend his apparent folly. This had angered him. Now he regretted it.

He broke the silence. 'I'm sorry I was rough with you today.'

'Were you?' Her voice was distant and dreamy.

'You know I was. I felt that the cylinder had got a hold on you and was starting to control your thoughts. I can't let that happen. I love you too much for that.'

She propped herself up on one elbow and looked at him.

He took a deep breath. 'There, I've said it now.'

She leaned over and kissed his forehead. 'You're really sweet, do you know that?'

'No I'm not; I'm a grumpy old man. You said it yourself.'

'I did not! I said you were not the old grouch that some said you were.' She laughed. It was the first time she had laughed in days.

'Anyway, we'll have less of the old.'

She leaned close to him and whispered: 'I love you, grumpy or otherwise.'

'I'm not grump...' He broke off as she put her fingers over his mouth and kissed him. 'No more words.' She said.

Their lovemaking this time was almost violent in its intensity. She dug her nails into his back and kissed him so hard that it was almost painful, but he felt no pain against the pleasure of her body.

Afterwards, they lay together peacefully. She pressed his hand to her left breast as if afraid to let go of it. Eventually, they slept and, initially, it was a deep and dreamless sleep, soothed perhaps by the day's events and post-coital contentment.

Later, they woke up simultaneously, both having had the same dream and again, it was a terrible vision of indiscriminate slaughter, rape and mutilation. They each described what they had seen and were surprised by the similarity of their dream visions. As more grim details were added, they realised that their dreams had been identical. This could no longer be dismissed as chance. They both wrote their dreams down and went back to bed, but the fear returned of a repetition of the nightmare and they lay awake for some time. Finally, they made love again. This time it was less intense than on the previous occasion and, afterwards, they fell asleep.

John was awakened by violent movement from Barbara. Little cries came from her throat and her head rocked from side to side. She was gasping for breath. He switched on the light and gently stroked her forehead. She opened her eyes.

'You woke me up,' he said. 'You were dreaming again.'

'Oh God,' she said once she had gathered her senses. 'When will it end? It was horrible – horrible!' She got out of bed and, still naked, went over to the desk, picked up the pen and began to write. 'I've got to get this down while it's still fresh,' she said. 'God, I can hardly hold the pen.'

'Sounds like a bad one,' he said unnecessarily.

She swung around to face him. 'Bad is an understatement. It was worse than the last one.'

'Worse?'

'Worse,' she repeated. 'I can barely bring myself to describe it. This time I was in the dream.'

They were silent while she wrote. When she had finished, she put the pen down and said: 'It was awful. I was in the body of a warrior. I remember I had an axe and I was lashing out indiscriminately at anyone who got in my way. It was systematic slaughter. Whenever I faced someone, I just hit them and went on hitting them until they stopped moving, then I moved on to the next. We knew that we were to kill everyone there, regardless of age or sex, and so we did; old people, women and children – all were slain and their buildings were set alight. The town was to be utterly destroyed. Some begged for mercy, but it had no effect on us. We killed them anyway.'

John cut in. 'Who were "we"?'

'I'm not sure exactly. I'm fairly certain that the cylinder was the reason for the war, but in what way is anyone's guess. And this was a bitter war; a war of total annihilation. I now believe that cannibalism was involved in the aftermath, for a number of prisoners were taken alive, but these were not hostages – they were to be killed and eaten. All were young and they knew very well what we were going to do to them. Some were crying and pleading for their lives. Two of the girls even offered themselves to the warriors in return for their lives, but to no avail. One by one, they were stripped and slaughtered; then they were cut open and butchered like animals. I saw their insides being drawn from their bodies. Someone handed me the heart of one of them. It was truly awful and so graphic that it felt like I was actually there. God, I can still see the blood.' She came over and climbed back into the bed beside him, still shaking slightly.

'I've never had dreams like this before. Oh John, what's happening to us? I really am frightened now.'

He put his arm around her shoulders and drew her close. It made him angry to see her so frightened. 'It's that bloody cylinder.' He growled. 'We ought to dig a deep dark hole and bury it where it will never be found. It's sending us all round the twist.'

'We can't do that.'

'Why not? It's what I'd like to do.' He thought for a while. 'You know, I really believe now that the cylinder was the agent that sent these people mad. If what we are getting here are its recorded memories of the past, and these things actually happened, it would explain a lot.'

'You could be right. A lot of wanton slaughter took place around it. Do you think it really was governing people's behaviour and, if so, could it still be doing it?'

He lay back and gently guided her head so that it rested on his chest. 'It's a possibility. Now, try and get some sleep.

'I'm too frightened.'

'Hush, I'm here.'

All this time, James slept peacefully.

Elsewhere in the hotel, Lynda and Chris slept content in each others' arms.

18

They slept late again. John was the first to wake up. He looked blearily at the clock and read eight-thirty. Normally, this would have sent him into a panic, but this time he didn't care. Barbara lay asleep beside him. He decided to let her sleep on and got out of bed, washed and got dressed. Before he left the room, he picked up the *do not disturb* sign and hung it on the outside doorknob. She could now sleep for as long as she liked.

He went downstairs and found Bernard sitting with James Masters at the breakfast table. Bernard looked up as he approached. 'Good afternoon,' he quipped.

'No jokes, if you please,' John said. 'It's not at all funny. I've had a lousy night and Barbara has had an even worse one. I'm letting her sleep late.'

Bernard became serious. 'That bad, eh?'

'Worse.' He turned to James. 'How did you sleep last night?'

James shrugged dismissively. 'Fine.'

'You had no dreams or anything like that?'

He shook his head. 'I slept like a top.'

'I don't understand it. You were fully exposed to the cylinder for far longer than anyone else in our team, and yet you haven't been affected by it. The more I look at this, the less I understand it. Have you had any unwanted thoughts?'

'No.' He looked at his watch. 'Look, I've got to be going shortly. I have to get back to London, remember?'

John nodded. He might as well let him go. 'Very well, but I would ask you to treat this matter as strictly confidential. Tell no one what you saw up there.'

'If you do, we'll have to kill you,' Bernard joked.

'My lips are sealed.' He stood up. 'I'd better be going. Give my love to Barbara. Oh, by the way, I think I may have the beginnings of an idea as to what that cylinder might be made of and it is extremely complex; well beyond our current technology.'

Bernard looked up. 'What might that be?'

'It's far too complicated to explain in simple terms. I'm not sure if I fully understand it myself yet. Suffice it to say that it appears to be a kind of super-ceramic. Nothing like it exists on earth at the moment. If I can crack this, it will be the Holy Grail for every aerospace engineer.'

'So you think it may be extraterrestrial?' Bernard said.

'I wouldn't go that far, but it's a completely unknown substance to us. With its hardness and, I assume, heat resistance, it must have taken an extremely high temperature to form it. How did that happen in the Iron Age? They'd only just learned how to smelt iron. They couldn't possibly have made something like this. I'm not at all sure that we can do it now, even with our current technology.'

Bernard whistled. 'Blimey!'

'I must insist on absolute secrecy concerning this matter,' John said, aware that he'd already reminded him only moments before. Still, he strongly suspected that if the secrecy surrounding the cylinder was to be compromised, James would be the most likely source of any leak. Indeed, it was hard to imagine him or anyone else in his field keeping such a discovery to himself.

'Don't worry. I won't blab. Now I've got to go.'

They said their goodbyes and he left.

'Well,' said Bernard. 'Do you think he can keep a secret?'

'I hope so,' John said. 'I really hope so.'

Bernard thought for a moment. 'You know,' he said slowly. 'We thought it hadn't affected him, didn't we?'

'Yes...'

'Well, now he appears to have suddenly cracked the secret of the cylinder's composition, or at least he thinks he's somewhere near it. Where did he get that from? He never got a sample of it for analysis – he said he couldn't. The material was too hard, he said.'

'Now, suddenly and from nowhere, we have the dawning of an idea,' John mused. 'My God, it *has* affected him and he doesn't know it. *We* didn't know it! Now I'm beginning to understand how Stone Age people suddenly developed Iron Age technology. The cylinder... what exactly *did* the cylinder do, Bernard?'

'I can't really say, but it's beginning to look as if it was instrumental in some revolutionary shift in technology. The Stone Age suddenly jumps forward into a little Iron Age at exactly the same time as the cylinder appears on the scene. It fits!'

'And then it suddenly and unaccountably stops and we're back in the Stone Age again,' John reminded him. 'How did that happen and what did it do to make them so savage? This is what frightens me.'

Bernard thought for a while, then he said: 'They might have made technological advances, but how did they behave on a cultural and social level? Remember the Aztecs. They developed superb architecture and all the superficial trimmings of civilisation while ripping out people's hearts as a matter of routine, and all in the name of their religion. How civilised was that?'

'So you don't think the cylinder had anything to do with their violence?'

'I don't know. Perhaps it did make them mad, but you saw James; he didn't look like a madman to me. Outwardly, at least, he looked perfectly normal.'

'He might have looked perfectly normal, but was he normal? He might think so himself, but where did he suddenly get that idea from? And he's not the only one. Barbara has come out with one or two unaccountable statements as well, as if she was speaking an unconscious thought. When I asked her where she got it from, she didn't know.'

'Well,' Bernard said. 'We have all experienced something like that – you know: spontaneous thoughts that might be correct, but without any substance to back them up.'

'This makes us look like savants.'

'Perhaps we are.'

John decided to change the subject. 'Where are Chris and Lynda?'

'They finished their breakfast and went up to their rooms to do some work, at least that's what they said.'

'I wish I could get them more involved in the project. They're two brilliant young graduates and I feel as if I'm treating them as casual labourers. It's not right, but I'm scared of exposing them to whatever risk that cylinder presents.'

'I understand. But you have briefed them on the subject and they are grateful for that.'

'Are they?'

'They do understand your reasons for keeping them away.'

'How do you know this?'

Bernard smiled. 'They told me.'

John thought about this. It touched him that they had such faith in his judgement; something that he felt he could no longer trust himself. He resolved to no longer keep things away from them. Instead, he would give them more of a key part to play in the investigation of the site.

He had an idea. 'Do we know if there are iron ore deposits anywhere on or near the site? Only I wonder if the cylinder was found by these people after they settled there, or if they brought it to a site where they knew iron ore might be found.'

'I see; a chicken and egg question.'

'Something of the sort. They must have discovered that certain stones when heated to a sufficiently high temperature formed iron. Now, was this by accident or design? If it was the latter, then it is likely that they sought out the site because they knew that iron ore could be mined there. Do we have a geological map of the area?'

'We can get one.'

'I shall ask Chris to do that, and I shall give him my reasons for doing so. And I want Lynda to examine the soil and the local stone for evidence of iron. If it was mined locally, then it is highly probable that they settled there because of the iron. Were it to be otherwise, it would be too much of a coincidence for the cylinder and the iron ore to be discovered both at the same time.'

'It could still be a coincidence, though. Anyway, the magnetometer scan has already shown a high iron content in the soil. I don't know about ore deposits, though.'

'No, we don't, because we weren't looking for them. We made the initial mistake of assuming that the village was Iron Age, so we would have taken the presence of iron deposits for granted and anyway, iron is a common element. But something tells me that the cylinder instils technological advance according to the existing state of the technology it discovers. Look, James suddenly got the idea for this super-ceramic. This just happens to be on the very limit of our current ability, even if it can be done at all. With Stone Age people, the smelting of iron would be as much a progressive step as the one that just occurred to him with his ceramic.'

'But we think we already know that the cylinder induces wild ideas such as these.' Bernard countered.

'We *think* we do. What we now need is proof. This exercise may not provide us with absolute proof, but it would tip the balance strongly in its favour. On the other hand, it might prove nothing. Still, it's worth the effort and it will give Chris and Lynda something to do while getting them more involved in the project.'

Bernard grinned. 'Good thinking.' He was silent for a moment; then he said: 'You say Barbara had a bad night. How bad was it?'

'Very bad; that's why I'm letting her sleep as late as she wants.' He decided to confide in his colleague. 'You might as well know that a close relationship has recently developed between us. She is currently in my room where she spent the night.'

'I guessed as much,' Bernard said, clearly unsurprised by the news. 'I noticed the way she was looking at you yesterday. It's hard to disguise the signs.'

He pulled a face. This was typical of Bernard. Not much passed him by. 'She had a dreadful night and needed company because the nightmares kept coming. Do you think I was wise to allow her to sleep with me?' he asked.

'It's not for me to say, but I will say this: I'm delighted for both of you, though I'm not so happy to hear about the bad dreams. You know, I've wondered for a long time if you two would finally get together. More than anything else, you've seemed to me to be more like good friends than just work colleagues.' He laughed suddenly. 'Sod it, you belong together.'

John smiled. It was something of a relief to bring his relationship with Barbara out into the open. It would be only a matter of time before it became common knowledge anyway. He just hoped that she would see it the same way. 'Thanks,' he said, trying to sound as casual as he could.

Bernard sensed his unease. 'Look, if it's of any use to you, Lynda has guessed it as well. The only one who may not have noticed is Chris, and that's because his designs on Lynda have made him blind to anything else around him.'

'You mean Chris and Lynda are…'

'…An item? I don't know how you could have failed to notice. Look, the only unattached one left on the team is me, and I've got my eyes on that sexy little barmaid who was in here last night. There's just one problem.' He paused to wipe away a mock tear. 'She doesn't seem to fancy me.'

John laughed. 'You'll just have to keep trying.'

Bernard shrugged. 'Well, she's not the only one. Anyway, I've no plans for settling down – not yet at any rate.'

Barbara did not wake up until ten o'clock. She looked at the alarm clock, saw the time and reacted with a start. She had not intended to sleep so late. Where, she wondered, was John? It was obvious that he had let her sleep on and she felt angry with him for that, but then she realised that he had done it out of consideration for her loss of sleep and her anger melted.

She got out of bed and had a shower, then dressed and went downstairs. There was no point in rushing now. The morning was more or less over and she was too late, even for breakfast. She looked into the breakfast room and was not surprised to see it deserted. She tried the conference room next, and found herself face to face with a group of sales reps who were using the room that morning. She wondered where the rest of the team were. She fumbled in her bag, found her mobile phone and selected John's number, then remembered that if he was on the site, she would not be able to reach him. She could hear the ring tone – once, twice, three times, four...

'Hi, Barbara.' It was John's voice.

'Where are you?'

'We're out in the hotel car park, by my Land Rover. I let you sleep on. I'm sorry, I hope you don't mind.'

She opened her mouth to tell him off, then checked herself and smiled. 'Thanks. I'll join you shortly.' She flipped her phone shut and went outside.

In the car park, John stood with the rest of the team beside the Land Rover. The nearside door was open and Lynda sat sideways on the passenger seat with her feet dangling over the side of the vehicle. They looked up as she approached.

Bernard was the first to speak. 'I hear you had a bad night.'

She nodded. 'I don't ever want another one like it.'

'Might it help to talk about it?'

She looked at the ground at her feet. 'I don't know.'

John intervened. 'It was a particularly nasty dream this time, and difficult to talk about, but I'll leave it to Barbara to tell you if she wants to.' He looked at her. 'But only if you want to, Barbara.'

Barbara shrugged. 'What the hell? I might as well tell you if you think it helps. I know you like to keep a record of our dreams. Go on; get you pen and paper ready.'

Bernard produced his notepad and pen and, with the aid of her own notes, she proceeded as best she could to describe the awful dream that she had had that night. It was difficult, and in one or two places she faltered in her description of the butchery of the young captives, but she struggled through to the end, sparing none of the gruesome details, even to the fresh human heart that had been presented to her.

The others listened in near disbelief as she spoke and Bernard found much of it difficult to write. At one point, he wanted to throw his pen down and close the notepad, but he persisted, endeavouring to disconnect himself from its contents. John was less affected by the tale, having already heard it that night, but he still found it shocking. Lynda and Chris listened, open mouthed.

'Bloody hell,' Chris said when she had finished. 'I don't know how you keep your sanity with dreams like that.'

'We've all had them,' she said. 'At least all of us who have been exposed to the cylinder have had them.'

'All, that is, except James Masters,' Bernard pointed out.

She looked at him. 'How is he?'

'Fine,' he said. 'We saw him this morning and he seems to have suffered no ill effects at all. He's gone back to London now.'

'I don't understand it.'

'Neither do we. The thing had him in its power long enough to have given him a full dose of whatever-it-is, and so far he has had no dreams or unwanted thoughts – in fact none of the things that we have had.'

'That's not strictly true,' John cut in. 'He suddenly and unaccountably knows what it might be made of, remember? Now, where do you think he got that knowledge from? The technology required to make such a substance does not yet exist; he told us that himself.'

'I wonder why he hasn't had the nightmares,' Barbara said.

'We don't know,' John said.

She thought for a moment. 'Do you remember what he said while he was in the cabin? He said *you didn't let it finish*. Now, what do you think he meant by that?'

They looked at each other. 'No,' John said finally. 'I will not permit anyone to go near that thing again. Too much has happened already.'

Bernard tossed his head. 'And what do you propose we do with it?'

'For now, we leave it alone and get on with the rest of the project. We have wasted enough time already over these last three days. I shouldn't have to remind you that we are engaged in an excavation and time is pressing. We must get on with it. We have already made a number of astonishing finds; enough I hope to get an extension on the project, but if we go on like this, the faculty will pull the plug on the whole business, cylinder and all.'

'They would be making a big mistake,' Chris said.

'That's as may be. They won't see it like that. All they will see is their money going down the drain.'

Bernard had to agree. John had a valid point but the cylinder remained. It was not going to go away just because they chose to ignore it. It now dominated their thoughts, almost to the exclusion of everything else. It commanded their dreams, as awful as they were, and he had become convinced that it was by this means retelling its history and the history of the culture that had once surrounded it. It simply could not be ignored. It *would* not be ignored. It would see to that.

He tossed his car keys into the air and caught them with the same hand. 'Right, I suggest we get to work. The morning's nearly gone.'

John turned to Barbara. 'Have you had any breakfast?'

She shook her head. 'Too late, I'm afraid.'

'Then I suggest you get some now. You may have the rest of the day off if you like.'

'No,' she insisted. 'I'm not ill. I just had a bad night, that's all.'

'Still, I would advise you to get something to eat. Bernard, can you run Lynda and Chris up to the site and we'll follow on later. You know what to do when you get there.'

'Sure,' Bernard said and made for his Land Rover. The other two followed. 'We'll see you later.'

They watched the Land Rover as it left the car park and then headed for the High Street and the café where the team members normally went to eat when they were not at the hotel. There, John ordered coffee and a full English breakfast for Barbara. He had already eaten and was content with a toasted scone. They sat at a little table near the window.

When the food came, she stared at it and pulled a face. 'I don't know if I can tackle this,' she said.

'Give it a go,' he coaxed. 'You will need it if you're going to work today. You can still have the day off if you want to.'

'No,' she insisted, 'it would be better for me to get back to work and forget that dream, or at least take my mind off it. Look, John, I'm not an invalid and I don't want to be treated like one.'

'I'm sorry, but I am concerned about you. OK, I know we've all had bad dreams, but your one has been the worst of all so far. No one can have a dream like that and remain unaffected.'

She lifted a finger and smiled at him. 'Trust me, I shall be all right. Now, let's get on with our breakfast, shall we?'

Despite her initial protest, she finished her breakfast and John ordered another coffee.

'Shouldn't we be getting to work?' she said.

'Bernard's in charge and he knows we'll be late. He knows what happened last night and he understands the situation perfectly.'

She thought for a moment. 'Does he know we've been sleeping together?'

He nodded. There was no point in lying to her. 'He's guessed as much,' he said. 'In fact, the whole team has. You can't keep secrets here; it's like a village. Incidentally, did you know that Lynda and Chris are an item?'

'Yes, everyone does except you, it seems.' She paused, and then added: 'If our relationship has become common knowledge, then we might as well give up one of the rooms and simply move in together. After all, there is no point in paying for two rooms when one would do. What do you think?'

He took her hand and held it gently. 'I would love that.'

'Then let's do it. We need each other and, more than that, I need you. I want to live with you.'

He was silent for a long time as he tried to grasp the full implication of what she had just said. With one failed marriage already behind him, he was suspicious now of any long-term arrangement that might put him into the same situation again. He could not bear it if she tired of him and ran off with someone else as his first wife had done. After all, he reasoned, if it had happened once before, it could happen again. Against that, he could not deny that he was lonely at home and missed the company of a woman. He missed the quiet evenings at home that sadly had been too rare and he missed

90

the warm comfort of a female body beside him at night. He had now found it again in the form of Barbara, and there was no doubt that they needed each other, but how long would that need last? What would happen when the effects of the cylinder eventually wore off and the nightmares diminished, if, indeed they ever did wear off? Would she still need him then? He wondered if she regarded him as a lover or as a comforter. The difference was important, after all. He knew that he had fallen in love with her. They had grown together in the time that they had known each other and their relationship had developed slowly and naturally. It was no mere infatuation as far as he was concerned, but he was aware that working relationships could break down irrevocably once they transcended the confines of the workplace and strayed into the bedroom.

She looked at him and smiled. 'Which bit of that don't you understand?' she teased. 'Let me say it again, only slowly. I *love* you and I want to *live* with you. Now, what's so hard about that?'

He shifted in his seat and looked at the table. He wondered how he could confide his thoughts to her without offending her. In the event, there was no need.

'You are afraid, aren't you?'

He looked down at the table.

She squeezed his hand. 'There's no need. I'm not like her. I won't leave you like she did.' She chuckled. 'I know you better than you think.'

She could have been reading his mind. He looked up into her eyes which were fixed on his. He felt an unexpected tear sting the corner of one of them. He wanted to wipe it away, but was afraid that doing so might betray its presence. 'I'm sorry.' He said simply.

'Don't be. There's nothing to be sorry about. Just think about it. I don't want to put you on the spot and I don't want to coerce you in any way. I'll never hurt you.'

'I know.' His voice sounded thick and he cleared his throat. 'I know and I do love you. That's why I need time to think.'

'Then think about it. I'm not going to press you for an answer.' She laughed nervously. 'Now it's me who feels awkward. Have I pushed you too hard?'

'No, no. I...' He faltered and stopped, uncertain what to say. His face felt hot and he knew he was blushing. He hadn't felt like this for years. He could see the almost ridiculous situation in which they now found themselves. Here they were, seated across a café table;

mature adults acting just like awkward teenagers. It was ludicrous. He could see the funny side of it but felt disinclined to laugh. He pulled his thoughts together and endeavoured to start again, but she beat him to it.

'Let's call a halt to it here,' she said. 'I'm afraid I've moved too fast and put you on the spot, so let's take it one step at a time. I've made my feelings clear enough.'

He wanted to take her in his arms and kiss her. He squeezed her hand and the stinging tear reappeared, this time running down his cheek. 'Thank you,' he breathed. 'Thank you so much.'

She brushed the tear away with the tip of a finger. He had at last shown some sign of emotion and this pleased her. For the first time she had seen his vulnerable side and this too was pleasing. He was normally so immersed in his work that few people ever saw the real human being that hid inside a sometimes bluff outer shell. Now he was like a little boy; helpless. 'I shall always be there for you,' she said.

19

Work continued on the site at a steady rate, during which more discoveries were made. Many of them were familiar Stone Age tools and weapons such as hand axes and knives. Evidence was also found of iron which might have been the remains of weapons, but were so badly decomposed that they could have been anything. Traces of bone were also found, again surviving mainly as tiny fragments in an advanced state of decay. There was little further evidence of the technological revolution that had overtaken the place so long before the Iron Age had actually arrived. Chris's research duly showed evidence of iron ore in the area and a small excavation exposed a rich deposit of it, together with more stone tools and an antler that had probably been used as a pick. This was the evidence that they had been looking for. It now looked as though iron had indeed been mined here and this caused them to discuss the chicken and egg question of whether the cylinder had led the people to the iron rich area, or if it had been discovered in the same place as the ore. They decided that the latter case was too much of a coincidence and that the novel idea of smelting the brown stone to produce iron had drawn them to the spot to settle as proto-ironmasters. Just how they might have transported the cylinder with its extraordinary weight to this spot was a mystery, but they would almost certainly have had the manpower to undertake such a task.

John was successful in his bid to get an extension on the project after having convinced the university that important finds had been made. The discovery of the curious mechanism, whatever it was, had been instrumental in this and had led the combined forces of both the university and the British Museum to provide further funding. They even offered to send more help with the dig, but he refused, maintaining that he had sufficient staff to do whatever work was necessary. He told them nothing about the cylinder. Had they known, it would have meant an abrupt end to the project as far as the team was concerned, and he was not prepared to let that happen. It was not jealousy that made him so protective but a sense of continuity that would have been disrupted by the presence of outsiders tramping all over the site. Also, it would have only been a matter of time before government forces got involved and then it would be out of his hands altogether. Meanwhile, no one went near the cylinder. It remained locked in the cabin and no one was allowed even to approach the door.

The dreams persisted for some time and Bernard continued to record them; building what he hoped might one day present a brief history of the culture that had once surrounded the cylinder. It was still far from complete, but pieces were coming together to form a clearer picture, not much of which was pleasant. Not all the dreams were as nightmarish as many had been and gradually they diminished in frequency, but they were still present, as was the occasional nightmare. The more peaceful visions sometimes contained details of everyday life that Bernard felt was essential in understanding the culture of this ancient community. In one dream, he saw an instrument in use that resembled a quadrant. A priest or someone of the sort appeared to be using it to measure the angle of a star, much as a mariner would use a sextant. Someone standing beside him was drawing on a slate. This too was noted. No such instrument had been found, but that was hardly surprising. It was little short of a miracle that the geared mechanism they had unearthed had survived at all after so many millennia of interment.

John and Barbara's relationship grew and consolidated. They moved into the one room and started living together. Lynda and Chris remained in separate rooms, although it was customary for one to visit the other at night, usually not leaving until the morning. It was no secret that they were sleeping together and the others wondered why they continued with this pretence. It fooled no one. Gradually, things returned to some semblance of normality.

Barbara's attention turned back to the patterns on the cylinder. She devoted what time she could to analysing her photographs of them. They made no sense. Still, she noticed one common and repetitive denominator shared by all, and that was the number three. It appeared again and again, almost obsessively throughout all aspects of the diagrams or whatever those symbols were. She reasoned that this constant repetition of three must have some significance. Even the cylinder's physical dimensions had a ratio of three to one. She toyed with the idea of using not three but its square – that made nine, and nine, famously, was an indestructible number. No matter how many times it was multiplied, the resulting figures when added together always came back to nine. She toyed with this idea and then dismissed it. It worked well with the Arabic numerical system, but whoever made the cylinder may not have used numbers as such. No one could possibly know what system they employed. Even systems of counting on earth varied between one culture and another. Base ten was a convention in the West, but elsewhere, base five was often used. Then there was binary, octal, hexadecimal and God knows what else besides. Still, she noted her observation and filed it away for possible future reference, remembering that nine down the centuries had been a magical number by virtue of its indestructibility. She wondered if the cylinder had implanted a race memory into the descendants of the ancient people who had lived with it, but remembered that most of them had in all probability been killed in the mass insanity that had broken out around it. The more she thought about it, the more unanswerable it all became. In the end, she put her notes away. She would come back to them later.

She longed to examine the cylinder again. It dominated her thoughts throughout much of her working day. At times, when on site, she would look towards the cabin and know that it was in there, lying on the floor, covered up and probably inert again. After all, it had not been exposed to light for days and, if it really was light activated as was thought, its batteries or whatever power supply it had should be running low by this time. Consequently, it might be safe to handle and examine it again. She had indeed mooted this point to John, but he was adamant in his insistence that no one should go near it until he thought fit. As the leader of the project, there was to be no argument. If his word was not exactly law, it came pretty close to it and that was enough. No one went near.

Then there was another conundrum. James Masters had departed for London some days ago and no one had heard from him since. She had tried several times to contact him, but his mobile phone was switched off. This was unusual for a man who, like most young professionals, had numerous contacts and depended on the instrument for both office and social use. They had all supposed that he alone had not been adversely affected by the cylinder, despite his prolonged contact with it. Now she wondered if this really was the case. He had seemed fine at the time, but what of the long-term effects? This thought troubled her. It was inconceivable that he could have been left untouched by its influence, be it malign or otherwise. She recalled his words as he had squatted in front of it. He had told them that it was harmless and that they had not let it finish. It was talking to him, he had said with a face so serene he might have been the face of a saint. The more she thought about this, the more she came to realise that he had indeed been affected by it, but in a way that had manifested itself differently from the others. He might not have had the nightmares and the unwanted thoughts, but it had nonetheless affected him in a way so subtle that not even he knew.

One evening as they relaxed in the bar, she imparted these thoughts to John and Bernard. John agreed with her, but Bernard had some doubt.

'We saw him when he left,' he pointed out. 'He looked fine and said he slept well, which is more than we could say for ourselves that morning.'

'Yes,' she said. 'But that was on the surface. How did it *really* affect him? What I'm trying to say is that it has almost certainly affected him in such a subtle way that he doesn't even suspect it. How do you think he suddenly and unaccountably worked out the composition of that super-ceramic of his? It was not intuition, that's for sure.'

'We've already been through all this.'

'No we haven't,' she insisted. 'We've barely touched the surface. Didn't it strike you as odd that he alone was untroubled by the dreams and nightmares that have dogged us all ever since we discovered that thing? Now I'm beginning to worry that he has been adversely affected by it. I've tried to contact him, but his mobile seems to be permanently switched off. He hardly ever switches it off unless he's at a meeting or something of the sort.'

'It might be damaged.'

'He'd replace it,' she said impatiently. 'He depends on it.'

John shared her concern. It was inconceivable that anyone could have had such close and prolonged contact with the cylinder as James had had and not be affected by it in some way. Indeed, he *had* been affected by it. Both he and Barbara had seen him crouched in front of the thing and apparently communicating with it or, more precisely, it was communicating with him. He had said this much at the time. There was no doubt that it had captured his mind in some indeterminate way. It had nearly captured Barbara as well and in all

96

probability would have done so had he not pulled her out of the cabin when he did. He pointed this out to Bernard who was forced to agree with him.

His chief concern remained one of security. If the existence of the cylinder became known to a wider public and particularly the authorities, the whole project would be jeopardised. Furthermore, the cylinder clearly had powers over people that he felt would be as dangerous as an atom bomb if it ever fell into the wrong hands which, as far as he was concerned, meant the hands of anyone in a position of authority. He expressed this concern to the others, adding that if it had indeed driven those early people to murder and cannibalism, what might it do to a modern society equipped with modern weapons? It was a terrifying thought.

'How likely is James to talk about this thing?' he asked Barbara.

'Most unlikely,' she said. 'Remember, he works in the aerospace industry and has signed the Official Secrets Act. He's used to keeping secrets.'

'Hmmm…' This failed to convince him.

'Look, John, I share your unease, but I don't think he's a security risk. If I thought he was, I would never have brought him in on the project.'

'But something's wrong, wouldn't you agree?'

She decided to air her own fears about James. 'I'm afraid he might have been so badly affected by the cylinder that he might have suffered some kind of breakdown. God knows, we've been close enough to breaking down ourselves, and he was fully exposed to it for far longer than any of us have ever been. What did it do to him in that time?'

'What indeed?' He tapped a brittle rhythm on the table top. 'Keep trying to contact him, will you? I've got a nasty feeling about this.'

'So have I,' she agreed.

20

Days went by and still there was not a clue as to the whereabouts of James Masters. Barbara tried repeatedly to contact him without success and all the time her concerns deepened. She was becoming increasingly worried about his well-being, while John, although concerned for his health, also fretted over the possible security risk. He reasoned that if James worked in the hush-hush world of the aerospace industry, he would be known to MI5, possibly even monitored by them. If the cylinder's existence ever became known to the Security Services, then his entire project would be blown sky high and all his work would have been for nothing. The military would move in and take over and that would be that. He shuddered to think what the Army would make of such a mind-bending object, let alone how it might affect them if they were exposed to its influence. The thought of mad, armed soldiers was not a pleasant one to dwell upon.

One morning they arrived on the site and got to work as usual, noting the small finds and traces of human activity that remained and continuing to build up their virtual model of the ancient settlement. As more of it became evident, it was clear that the cylinder had occupied a central position in the village which turned out to be bigger than they had at first thought. It was almost a small town.

At first, no one noticed the cabin and how its door was gaping ajar. It was Bernard who first spotted it. Curious, he went over and eased the door open, noticing as he did so that it had been forced. The wood bore the deep marks of a screwdriver or something similar that had been used to lever it open and the padlock, together with its hasp and staple had been wrenched away. His first thought was that the cabin had been burgled, but when he looked inside, his apprehension turned to astonishment.

The cylinder lay in the same place on the floor, fully uncovered and there, squatting in front of it, was James Masters.

Bernard froze, unsure what to do or how to react. James did not even look up, but continued to stare fixedly at the cylinder.

'Oh, shit!' he muttered as he backed away from the cabin. He strode and then ran to the dig where the others were working. 'John! Get over here, will you?'

John was in the back of the Land Rover, working on his laptop. He looked up at the sound of Bernard's voice, closed the laptop and jumped down to see what was bothering him. 'What is it?'

'It's James,' Bernard gasped. 'He's in the cabin, sitting with the cylinder.'

'What!' John took off at a sprint and headed towards the cabin. He was furious as he reached the door and looked inside. 'What the fuck do you think you're doing?' he roared at the stationary figure, still squatting in front of the cylinder.

James ignored him. His face was impassive. He said nothing.

Bernard caught up with him and joined him in the doorway. 'What the hell is he doing here?'

'What does it look like?' He turned savagely back towards James. 'You, get away from that thing – now!'

Still James ignored him. This apparent act of dumb insolence incensed him even more. He wanted to drag him out of the cabin and thump him but he checked himself, afraid to go near the cylinder.

'What are we going to do?' Bernard said, more to himself than anyone else.

Before John could reply, James slowly got to his feet. He was dishevelled with untidy hair and what looked like three days' growth of beard darkening his face. His suit was crumpled and his shoes were muddy. This was not the James that had appeared so smart just a week or so ago. He looked like a derelict.

Slowly, almost casually he approached them. Before he could speak, John grabbed him by his lapels and dragged him away from the doorway with such force that the young man lost his footing and stumbled to the ground. As he started to pick himself up, John stepped towards him, his fists clenched.

'No, John. Leave him!' Barbara had joined them. She helped James to his feet. 'What happened?' She glared at John. 'Why did you hit him?'

'He didn't hit me,' James said quickly. 'I slipped and fell, that's all. I'm all right.'

'Are you sure?'

'Absolutely.'

'He broke into the cabin and was with that cylinder again,' Bernard said.

'You don't understand,' James said. 'I had to do it.'

'*Had* to do it?' John roared. 'What the hell are you blathering about?'

Barbara looked at him steadily. 'John, calm down. This is getting us nowhere.'

John took a deep breath and looked away. She was right, he supposed, but the act of breaking and entering the cabin against his explicit instructions to go nowhere near it had infuriated him. This much he tried to explain to her, but by now his spate was subsiding and he had to admit that he may have overreacted. Anyway, the damage, if damage it was, had been done. His anger would not change that.

She turned her attention to James. 'Where have you been? What's happened to you? We've all been worried to death.'

'I'm OK.'

'James, have you seen yourself? You look terrible. Where the hell have you been? I've been trying to contact you. We thought you must be ill, or worse.'

'Could I have a drink?'

She took his arm and led him towards the place where the Land Rovers were parked. 'Come on, there's a flask of tea in the Land Rover and bottled water. How did you get here? Where's your car?'

'I left it in town and walked up here. It's only about three miles.'

'You're not dressed for it. The weather up here can be quite nasty sometimes.'

'I took that chance.'

John watched them go. 'Cheeky little prick,' he muttered. 'I can't believe the sheer bloody nerve of the man; coming up here and breaking into the place like that.'

'I think he had no choice but to break in,' Bernard said. 'There's no point in being angry about this. We need to find out why he did it.'

'Oh, I'll find out. Don't worry about that.'

'John, you're angry; I've never seen you so angry. Now, please calm down and listen. Perhaps we'll understand more when we've had a chance to talk to him. We're not going to get anywhere by beating the crap out of him.'

John smiled. It was useless arguing with his unflappable colleague who, despite his frequent bouts of flippancy, was seldom wrong in his calm, methodical approach to such situations as this.

In the Land Rover, Barbara picked up one of the flasks and poured James a cup of tea. He took it in both hands and sipped the hot liquid.

'How long were you in the cabin?' she asked him after a while.

'All night,' he said. 'I got there yesterday evening and waited until you had finished work. Then I broke in. It gives off its own light you know, so I could see what I was doing.'

She pondered this. The cylinder had been covered over for several days now and in that time it had lost little or none of its acquired energy in the darkness. Either it was absorbing the few particles of light that must have filtered through the tarpaulin or it was so economical in its use of energy that it could hold its charge indefinitely, like some kind of superconductor. She made a mental note of this and returned her attention to James.

'Why did you break in?'

'I had to. I can't explain, but I had to see the cylinder again. I knew that you would never let me anywhere near it, so I took the law into my own hands and broke in. I know I shouldn't have done it, but I had no choice.'

'You could have stayed away.'

'No, no. Let me explain. You don't understand; I had to get something clear in my head. You don't really know that thing, do you?'

'I think we know it well enough to stay away from it.'

'Do you still get the nightmares?'

'Yes. They're less frequent now, but they still come from time to time.'

'They will.'

'You seem very sure of that.'

'I don't get them because I know what happened and why it happened. You only know a bit of what happened because you didn't let it finish what it was trying all along to tell you.'

She tried to make sense of this, but it was difficult. She concluded that either he had gone mad, or else he really did have a greater insight into the nature and history of the cylinder than the rest of them had so far gleaned.

The back door of the Land Rover opened and John and Bernard climbed in. John's temper had abated, largely as a result of Bernard's wise counselling and partly due to his curiosity. He wanted to know just what had driven James to break into the cabin in order to see the cylinder again. When he spoke, his voice was gentle.

'I'm sorry I lost my temper with you,' he said, 'but I had ordered no one to go near the hut, let alone the cylinder. Were you not aware of the danger you put yourself in?'

James looked at him. 'There's no danger.'

'No danger?' John felt a fresh resurge of anger. 'What the hell do you think we've been through since the discovery of that thing? Let me tell you we've suffered something close to hell since we first contacted it, and you tell me there's no danger!'

Barbara intervened. 'He was just about to tell me about it when you burst in. Next time, knock.'

John sensed the anger in her voice and backed down. 'I'm sorry, but you know the danger of that thing as well as I do. How can he tell us there's no danger?'

'There's no danger,' James repeated. 'That cylinder is not necessarily evil. It is a neutral force.'

'It wiped out an entire culture!' John snorted. 'How safe is that?'

'You only know part of the story,' James said. 'That's why you get the nightmares. You think it caused the destruction of those people, don't you? Well, I suppose it did in a manner of speaking, but that was because its purpose was misunderstood. It didn't destroy them; they destroyed themselves.'

'What do you mean?'

'They got too smart too quick. They outgrew their intelligence and ability by enslaving and subjugating the other people around them. The town and its fortifications were all built using slave labour. In doing this they sowed the seeds of their own destruction. They took the cylinder to be some sort of god and even sacrificed chosen victims to it. These were selected from the surrounding tribes who were peaceful and could offer no resistance. Their Stone Age technology was useless against the more sophisticated iron weapons of the People

102

of the Cylinder and any resistance was ruthlessly put down. They were divided into clans and disorganised, and this further weakened their ability to resist. They were starved and subjugated, forced to pay tithes of whatever they were able to hunt or glean and so they were driven to starvation. They barely had enough to feed themselves, so these tithes were insupportable. Eventually, the clans did unite and that was when they finally rose up against their masters. The result of this was the massacre that you see in your dreams. Although the city was fortified against these surrounding tribes, their fortifications were eventually breached and the defenders overrun. No one was spared. The city was utterly destroyed, together with most of its population, but the cylinder had nothing to do with that. It was just there, that's all, passively recording all that happened around it.'

'It did cause the massacre, though,' John pointed out. 'None of that would ever have happened but for the cylinder.'

'True, but the cylinder remained a neutral force. It could have benefited them, and to a great extent it did, but they failed to understand its purpose.'

'What purpose?'

'That's what I am still trying to find out.'

'Do you know where it came from?' Barbara asked.

He shook his head. 'That information is encrypted somewhere. I've yet to find it.'

'What about the cannibalism?' Bernard asked. 'A bit extreme, isn't it?'

'Remember the surrounding people were starving. They were desperate and so, after the final overthrow of the People of the Cylinder, a few of the younger ones were captured alive. These were killed and eaten, but it was an act of desperation and rage. These people were not habitual cannibals, just starved and angry at the way they had been treated. Remember, they had been enslaved and kept in a state of abject poverty while the People of the Cylinder lived a life of relative luxury. As if that was not enough, they had to suffer the abduction and sacrifice of some of their younger women. The People of the Cylinder didn't sacrifice their own. People can only stand so much of that sort of thing, you know, so does it come as any great surprise if they ate a few of their former masters' offspring?'

'I suppose not,' Bernard agreed. 'It still seems a bit of an overreaction, though.'

'They were driven to it. After that, I assume their lives returned to normal. I don't know, because after the destruction of the city, the site was abandoned. It's likely that they considered the place to be cursed and so it was shunned by generations to come until it was finally forgotten. The cylinder remained buried in the ashes of the temple and knew no more until you unearthed it. Anyway, at that point the story ends.'

John thought hard about this. James' story was indeed plausible. 'When you say that it knew no more until we discovered it, does that mean it now knows us?'

'Not properly,' James said. 'You won't give it the chance.'

'You talk of it as if it was a sentient being.'

'In a manner of speaking, it is. I don't know if it is alive or some kind of supercomputer, but it gathers information from all around it. That's why you felt that energy surge when you first contacted it. In that moment, it probed your brain and copied most of your knowledge and experience to its own files, like you might download a digital camera.'

'Bloody hell!' Bernard said.

John too was uneasy about the thought of the entire contents his mind being copied to that thing. It made him hate it even more. He wanted to smash it to pieces, but knew that he would be ill advised to even attempt it. Given the obvious intrinsic strength of its diamond-hard hull, it would probably turn a cannon shell. In addition, he reasoned that it might be equipped with some kind of defence mechanism and there was no knowing what it might do if its existence was threatened in any way. The problem was insoluble.

'You still haven't told us where you've been for the last few days,' Barbara said. 'Your phone was switched off so we couldn't contact you.'

'I switched it off.' He said. 'I needed a place to think. I thought at first that the cylinder hadn't affected me that badly, but I was wrong. Certain thoughts kept running through my mind; thoughts I couldn't begin to understand. Eventually, I took myself off to the Yorkshire Dales and stayed in a B&B for a few days, walking in the hills and trying to clear my head, but it didn't work so I came here – I had to.'

'Had to?' She raised her eyebrows.

'I can't explain. It became an obsession – a compulsion.' He laughed an edgy, nervous laugh that the others found unsettling.

104

'What about your job?' she asked.

'I saw the doctor and told him that I had been working too hard and that it was messing up my mind. He signed me off work and ordered me to rest for a few days.'

'So you came here?' Bernard said.

'Eventually.' He laughed again. 'Look at me. I've never had a day's illness in my life, and now here I am, pretending to be a nutter in order to recover my sanity.'

John sat back in his seat. He was in a quandary. It was clear that James had become mentally unbalanced by the cylinder and it was also clear that he could do little to prevent him from communicating with it again, short of imprisoning him. In any case, what difference would it make now if he did contact it again? The damage, if damage it was, had already been done. 'OK,' he said eventually. 'Since you have had more exposure to it than any of us, I am prepared to let you talk to your blessed cylinder as often as you like. You can act as a kind of liaison officer for us, if you like.'

The others gaped at him in astonishment.

'What difference does it make?' he asked, a note of despair rising in his voice. 'I can't prevent it anyway. I appear to have no more control over this situation than I have over anything else. Now, I'm going to get on with some real work.' He rose and got out of the Land Rover, slamming the rear door behind him; then walked over to where Lynda and Chris were working. The others watched him in silence.

Bernard shook his head. 'He's pretty stressed.'

'You can't blame him,' Barbara said.

'I'd better go,' James said. 'I've caused you enough trouble. I'm sorry.'

'I'll drive you back to town,' Barbara said. 'Where are you staying?'

'Nowhere; I came straight up here.'

'No wonder you look so rough. Do you have money?'

'I've got some cash and my credit card.'

'Where's your car?'

'I left it in the White Hart's car park. I didn't want to bring it up here because I guessed you would see it and be alerted, and I didn't want my presence here to be known too soon. I had to see that cylinder again.'

'*Had* to?'

'I can't explain. It's almost like an addiction. It's as if the cylinder is controlling me somehow. I get these ideas and I don't know where they come from. They just sort of pop up from nowhere. That's how I know the history of the People of the Cylinder. I don't know where it came from; it just formed in my mind.'

'Your story ties in well with the dreams we've all been having,' Bernard said. 'I've been keeping a record of them and they all fit the story you outlined.'

'So you believe me?'

'I have no reason to doubt you. I think we've all reached the point where nothing concerning the cylinder surprises us any more.'

Barbara thought of the beautiful girl who had touched the cylinder in her dream and wondered if she had been driven by the same compulsion that now drove James. The girl had appeared to be in the same sort of communion with the object as he had been when he had first knelt close to it. There were parallels here, she felt; parallels that disturbed her. She wondered if history was about to repeat itself with the same bloody consequences. She tried to dismiss the thought but it persisted and it was unsettling.

James had insisted that the cylinder was a neutral force, but so was electricity and from that neutral force someone invented the electric chair. It didn't matter one jot to the electrons whether they powered a life support machine or the chair. They had no say in the way they were used. So, she imagined, would it be with the cylinder. Its power had been misused once before with a result that was nothing short of catastrophic to the culture that had grown up around it, so it was only logical to assume that it could be misused again, possibly with the same gruesome outcome. She began to understand more clearly John's increasing antipathy towards the thing.

She wanted to voice her unspoken fear, but decided against it, deciding that this was neither the time nor the place to express her misgivings.

'Come on,' she said, 'I'll drive you back to town. You can stay in the White Hart with us until you are ready to go back to London.' She wondered why she had added that last bit to her sentence. It hinted of an almost indecent haste to be rid of him, but he appeared not to notice it.

He followed her to the other Land Rover and got in beside her. She started the engine and engaged first gear. At the sound of the engine, John came over.

'Where are you going?'

'I'm taking James back to town. I should only be half an hour or so.'

John said nothing. He turned and went back to the dig where Lynda and Chris had been joined by Bernard.

'I don't think he likes me very much,' James said.

Barbara tried to reassure him. 'Don't worry. He has a lot on his mind.'

He fell silent.

21

James did not join the group for dinner that evening. Later, when they adjourned to the bar, he was still absent. Only Barbara felt any concern for his well-being as she sat at the table next to a rather pensive John, having previously castigated him in the privacy of their room for his rough treatment of James and his rudeness to her. He had apologised, offering no excuse for his boorish behaviour. As her rage subsided, she had noticed that he was close to tears. It was only then that she began to fully realise the strain that he was under. He had lost control over what had turned into an almost impossible situation. She had failed to fully understand this. Her anger had then turned to regret and it had become her turn to apologise. This in turn had led to a welter of mutual apology and finally laughter, dissolving the tension between them that had been steadily growing throughout most of the day.

She now felt that the time was right to impart her renewed misgivings concerning the cylinder to the others. They listened as she outlined her worries to them. All were acutely aware of the inherent dangers concerning any sort of contact with it, except perhaps for Lynda and Chris who had never been allowed anywhere near it. Consequently, they found her concern more difficult to comprehend.

'What are we to do with it, then?' Lynda asked.

John shrugged. 'I'll give a hundred pounds of my own money to anyone who comes up with a practical solution. We just don't know. We can't handle or go near it without being affected by its mind-scanning, or whatever it is, so it can't be moved.'

Chris suddenly leaned forward. 'What about screening it with something like a Faraday cage? Something like a wire mesh net, earthed of course. It blocks all electromagnetic radiation, so it might impair whatever force radiates from that cylinder.'

'I wonder...' Bernard mused.

'It might just work,' Chris said.

'We are assuming that it works within the electromagnetic spectrum,' John cautioned. 'The trouble is we don't know how it works, so we don't know what we're dealing with.'

'It's got to be worth a try, though,' Chris urged. 'I mean, you said it yourself, we don't know how to deal with it.'

'Can we get hold of such a net?' Barbara said. 'Does such a thing exist, even?'

'I don't know,' Bernard said. 'I'm not an electronics engineer. Does anybody know someone who might be able to advise us on this?'

John thought for a moment. 'There are people back in the lab that might be able to lay their hands on something of the sort. The only thing is; I don't want any more people getting involved. We've got enough trouble already with James.'

'Does anyone know where he is?' Barbara asked.

'No,' John said.

'Only I haven't seen him since I dropped him off here this morning.'

'He's probably sleeping it off,' Bernard said. 'He looked like he'd had a rough night.'

'He looked as if he hadn't slept for a week,' Barbara corrected him.

'Maybe he hadn't.'

'That's a measure of the power that the cylinder exerts over people,' John said. 'And that's the reason why I forbade everyone to go near it.' This was directed towards Chris and Lynda. Everyone else at the table was only too aware of its effects for any explanation to be necessary.

'We're going to have to talk to him,' Barbara said. 'I really want to know what happened up there. He was with it all night.'

'And half the morning,' Bernard added. 'I didn't notice that the cabin door had been forced until I looked over and saw it. By that time it must have been ten o'clock.'

'It was,' John agreed. 'I can't imagine what it did to his mind in that time. By all the rules, his brains should be fried.'

'Still,' Barbara insisted, 'we have to talk to him. We must find out what took place while he was there with it. I mean, he knows its history and it's not exactly what we hypothesised.'

'There are a lot of parallels,' Bernard pointed out. 'If you look at my notes and refer back to your own dreams and nightmares, you will see that his story tallies with our own experiences. We didn't know the reason for the bloodbath, that's all. We thought the cylinder drove them all mad when in fact nothing did. If his story is to be believed, then the massacre was driven by anger and resentment, not the cylinder.'

'So you're saying that the cylinder is benign and that we've misunderstood it?' John said.

'Nothing of the sort, but it could be as he said; that it is neither benign, nor is it malign, just neutral, like any other force.'

'It'll be neutral all right if Chris's cage works,' he growled.

'There's an important difference,' Barbara said. 'He knows the history of the People of the Cylinder, as he calls them, but to him it's abstracted, like reading a book on the French Revolution. With us it's different. We have lived it in our dreams and we are conscious of the terror that these people suffered at the end. He is not conscious of that terror.'

'What are you trying to say?'

'I don't know, but is it not significant that we have been racked by vivid dreams and fear ever since we contacted that cylinder while he has not been affected in that way at all? Why? That's what I'd like to know. He's had more exposure to that thing than the rest of us put together, but he doesn't have the nightmares that we've had. Does that not strike you as odd?'

'Hmmm.' John thought about this. 'And yet he has been affected by it. You've only got to look at him to see that. Also, his mind is confused. He said he had to see the cylinder again, but he couldn't tell us why he had to see it. He had no answer for that. As for his apparent detachment from the slaughter of those wretched people, I don't know, but is it possible that the thing has desensitised him to violence and tragedy, so that he sees it only as a passive onlooker?'

'He is certainly not the James that I used to know,' she said.

All this time, Chris was doodling in his pocket note pad. He finally put his pen down and waited for a pause in the conversation. 'I don't see why we can't make our own Faraday cage,' he said. 'All we need is some wire netting; a roll of chicken wire might do and that can be bought from the local farm supply shop. All you need then is a length of flex and a steel spike for the earth and hey, presto! One improvised Faraday cage!'

John leaned over for a better look at Chris's rough drawing. It meant little to him.

'I can't promise that this will work,' Chris went on, 'but if we fold the chicken wire into three or four layers, it'll tighten the mesh. We then connect our flex to it with the other end connected to a clean iron spike driven into the ground. That should effectively screen the thing.'

'It might just work,' Bernard agreed. 'If it does, then we have a genius in our midst.'

'Just one thing,' John said. 'Who's going to wrap it around the cylinder, and what if it doesn't work?'

'It's worth the chance,' Bernard said. 'Let's face it, it's the best idea we've had so far, and if it doesn't work, what have we got to lose?'

'You don't need me to tell you that.'

'Well, I'm willing to take a chance on it. If we earth the mesh first, I can hold it in front so that it acts as a shield. I should quickly be able to tell if it works or not before I get too close.'

'That's it!' Chris exclaimed. 'I can make earthed shields for you. If you keep the shield between you and the cylinder, you should be safe.'

'OK,' John said. 'Let's give it a go. If it works, I'll stand by my word and you can have a hundred quid. It's the least I can do. Meanwhile, tomorrow morning I would like you to go round the town and pick up whatever stuff you think you might need. I'll give you some money for it now.' He handed him a couple twenty pound of notes. 'That should cover it.'

Chris took the money. 'This'll more than cover what I need.'

'Bring me back the change.'

Barbara got up, made a polite excuse and left the table. James's absence worried her. She had to see if he was all right. She made her way to the reception desk and asked to see the register. The receptionist looked at her suspiciously, but complied with her request. She was relieved to see his name in the book, having initially feared that he may not have even bothered to book himself in, given his strange state of mind. She checked his number and climbed the two flights of stairs to his room. She knocked on the door, gently at first, then more loudly. There was no answer. She knocked again and waited. Eventually, she heard a movement and the door opened a crack. James's face appeared in the aperture, bleary and unshaven. His hair was still tousled and he appeared to be naked from what little she could see of him through the gap. He stared at her through narrow eyes.

She searched hard for something to say. 'I wanted to see if you were all right.' She finally managed.

'I was asleep. You woke me.'

'I'm sorry. I was worried.'

'Why?'

'I was concerned for you. You looked ill.'

'I needed sleep. You woke me up.'

'I'm sorry.' She realised that they had entered into a circular conversation and apologised again, adding: 'I'll leave you to get some sleep.'

'Thanks.' He closed the door, leaving her to wonder if his thanks had been sarcastic or genuine. The edgy tone of his voice had suggested the former to be the case.

She turned and walked back along the corridor, relieved to know that he was in his room and alive, whilst smarting a bit from his apparent cold hostility towards her. This was atypical. She decided that his lack of civility was probably due to her having disturbed his sleep.

She descended the stairs and returned to the bar. The others were still sitting around the table. She rejoined them. No one asked where she had been, having assumed that she had left the room to go to the lavatory, and she chose not to tell them. There was little point in broaching a topic that had already been covered and she was aware of John's antipathy towards James, although she was uncertain why he appeared to dislike him so much. True, he saw James as an intruder who might put his beloved project at risk, but it was at risk anyway and had been since the discovery of the cylinder. James was incidental here. She was confident that he posed no security risk and that the biggest danger he posed was to himself. The way he looked now really frightened her. She had never seen him like this before and she had known him on and off since their student days when, as undergraduates, they had had a brief love affair, after which they had remained good friends despite the casual way he had dumped her for another, younger woman. She wondered if John suspected that they had once been lovers and that his animosity towards James might be due to this, but she dismissed the thought out of hand. There was no possible way that he could know of their previous liaison and even if

112

he did, what did it matter now? It was all in the past and she knew John well enough to know that he didn't bear grudges. True, he could sometimes be irascible, but he was never vindictive. In fact, his generosity of spirit was one of the things that she liked so much about him. No, there had to be another reason. She would find out in time.

The chief problem now was James's obsession with the cylinder; an obsession strong enough for him to journey up from London and break into the hut just to be with it. It was madness, but James was not mad; he was a highly competent aeronautics engineer with a first class degree in mathematics. He was not given to such irrational flights of fancy. Consequently, his strange behaviour troubled her even more.

That night she lay awake thinking about this. For once, she and John did not make love, both being tired and preoccupied with the day's events, together with the looming prospect of tomorrow and the possible hazards it might present if their efforts to screen the cylinder failed. She stared at the darkened ceiling for a long time until she finally fell into a sleep that was relatively untroubled.

22

The following morning after breakfast, Chris borrowed John's Land Rover and visited the local farm supply shop where he purchased a twenty-five metre roll of chicken wire, a fifty metre drum of insulated wire, a steel fencing stake, strong fencing pliers and a club hammer. Spade terminals, together with screws, nuts and washers he bought from the local garage and, thus laden, he returned to the hotel car park. He parked the Land Rover, noticing as he did so that the others were not outside yet. He had expected to see them in the car park waiting for his return, but the place was deserted. Then he noticed a note clamped under the windscreen wiper of Bernard's car. The message was in John's hand and informed him that they were in the conference room. He went indoors and, out of habit, knocked on the conference room door before entering.

The group was seated at one end of the large table. He noticed that James was not with them.

'I got all the stuff we're likely to need,' he said, taking a seat at the table and giving John the change from the forty pounds he had given him for the materials.

'Good.' John said, pocketing the cash and noticing as he did so that it was more than he had expected. 'Where did you leave it?'

'It's still in the back of the Land Rover.'

'Good. We'll attend to that later.'

'What about James?' Barbara asked.

John gave a little shrug. 'What about him?'

'He'll go ballistic if he can no longer access his precious cylinder. There's no telling what he might do in the state that he's in at the moment. He's like a drug addict without his fix.'

'That's not our problem. Anyway, where is he; has anyone seen him?'

Everyone looked blank.

Barbara stood up. 'I think someone should check to see if he's still in his room. I'm worried about him.'

Bernard joined her. 'I'll come with you.'

John looked up at them. 'See if he's all right, will you? God, I don't need this!'

Barbara made for the door, followed by Bernard. In the lobby, he turned to her. 'John's in a bit of a state over this, isn't he?'

'More than he lets on,' she agreed. 'He feels responsible for all of us, and now that James has got himself involved, he feels responsible for that as well. I'm afraid he might find the strain too much if things go on like this.'

He took her hand and gave it a gentle squeeze before letting go. 'You and John can always rely on me if things start to get on top of you; you know that, don't you?'

She bit her lower lip and fought back a sudden urge to cry. Bernard was a good and trustworthy friend in a crisis, unflappable and clear thinking with a ready sense of humour. It was hard to feel depressed in his company. 'Thanks.' She said. She wanted to add more, but further words seemed unnecessary.

She led him up the stairs to James's room and knocked on the door. There was no answer. She knocked again. Still there was no answer. Now she was getting worried. She tried to look through the keyhole, but the lock was a Yale and she could see nothing through the blind slot. 'I think we should get the manager,' she said, straightening up. 'He should have a pass key. I hope he's all right.'

Bernard's face was grim. 'I wonder if he might have taken himself up to the site again. Are you sure this is his room?'

'Absolutely; I checked on him last night. He was tired, but otherwise all right, or so I thought. He looked rough, though. Oh God, he might have died in there.'

'It's more likely he's gone out somewhere. Do you know what kind of car he drives?'

She shook her head.

'Never mind, let's find someone with a pass key.'

Eventually they found the manager and persuaded him to unlock the door. Inside, James lay on the bed, naked and still, staring blindly at the ceiling. The manager blenched and Barbara stepped back into the doorway with a gasp, fearing he might be dead. Bernard felt for a pulse and, detecting one, he stood up, relieved. He waved a hand in front of James's eyes. There was no reaction.

'James!' he shouted. Still there was no reaction. He turned to the manager. 'I think we should call an ambulance.'

The manager's face was pale. 'Is he... you know... all right?'

'He seems to be in some kind of coma. We need an ambulance urgently.'

Barbara flipped open her mobile phone and tapped 999. 'Ambulance,' she said quickly. There was a long pause while she was connected to the appropriate service. Once connected, she outlined the situation to the operator, remembering to give the address of the hotel. There was another pause while the operator spoke, confirming her message. 'Thanks.' She snapped her phone shut. 'They'll be here soon.'

Bernard took James's pulse again. It was weak, but there. 'He's in a bad way.' He said.

'What do you think is wrong with him?' the manager asked.

'I don't know,' he said. He could guess, but he wasn't going to say too much about James to this man. 'I'm not a doctor of medicine, just a PhD I'm afraid. We'll know more when we get him to hospital.'

In the conference room, John looked at his watch. 'What's keeping them?' he said, more to himself than anyone else.

Lynda and Chris looked uncomfortable.

'Something's wrong,' Lynda said.

He got up from the table. 'I'm going to find out.' As he spoke, his mobile phone rang and he answered it. It was Barbara.

'John, we've got a problem. It's James. He's unconscious in his room.'

'What's happened?'

'We don't know. We found him like this.'

'I'll be right up.' He ended the call and slipped the phone back into his pocket. 'Bugger!'

'What is it?' Chris asked.

'You two had better amuse yourselves for an hour or so. There's a problem with James. I'd better get up there and see what's going on.'

'I knew it.' Lynda said.

They followed the ambulance to the hospital where they waited until a puzzled-looking Indian doctor left the cubicle where James lay. 'You know this man?' he asked.

'He's a colleague,' John said quickly, aware that this was only a half truth, but it suited the moment.

There then followed a series of questions, most of which Barbara was able to answer, while the doctor made notes. 'We shall give him a brain scan,' he said when he had finished, 'but so far there seems to be no sign of stroke or haemorrhage and no outward sign of injury. Has he any history of epilepsy or anything like that?'

Barbara shook her head. 'Not to my knowledge.'

'Hmmm. We shall give him the full set of tests. In the meantime I'm afraid I am unable to give you any diagnosis.'

'We might as well get back,' John said.

Wait.' Barbara glanced at him and then turned to the doctor. 'May I see him?'

The doctor hesitated.

'I'll only be a minute.'

He gestured her through into the cubicle.

Inside, James lay on the bed, partly covered by a sheet. Wires were taped to his head and chest and these were connected to a machine that looked as if it had been built to monitor just about everything. His heart and breathing rate showed as regular waves on a screen, while what might have been brainwaves pulsed irregularly below. The sight distressed her.

She took his hand. 'James, what has that thing done to you?'

There was no reaction. His hand lolled, inert in hers. It was cool but not cold. She replaced it by his side, gently stroked his hair and turned away. There was nothing she could do. Quietly, she slid back the curtain and left the cubicle, closing it behind her.

Whispering her thanks to the doctor, she rejoined John and Bernard. 'Come on,' she said, 'there's nothing more we can do here. We'll just have to wait.'

They drove back to the hotel in silence.

It was lunchtime, but no one felt very hungry. They sat in the hotel bar and ordered sandwiches and coffee.

'Well,' John said eventually. 'I don't think anyone would call it harmless now.'

Bernard took a bite from his sandwich. 'I suggest we follow Chris's plan and screen that thing – disable it if we can.'

'I'd like to destroy it.'

'I very much doubt that we can,' Bernard cautioned. 'For one thing it's too hard, and for another, it might destroy us in turn. We don't know what it's capable of doing, do we? I mean, it has already destroyed an entire culture.'

'James said it did not destroy them. They did it for themselves because they misunderstood its purpose.' Barbara reminded him.

'Do we know that?' John said.

'Can we afford to doubt it?' she countered.

He nodded slowly. She might be right, but he remained unconvinced. What, after all, *was* its purpose? They could not even guess where it came from or why it was there. It just was, and that was all they knew. If it had come from another planet, which seemed increasingly likely, then it was the product of a culture so far in advance of their own that it was difficult to imagine the technology that could have built such a device and then sent it on a voyage that might have lasted for millions of years, perhaps for all eternity if it missed its target, even assuming that Earth had been its intended goal. Even if it had been deliberately placed there by visiting aliens, a voyage spanning hundreds, perhaps thousands of light years was simply unfeasible unless they had found some means of overcoming the time barrier involved in such a journey. Added to this, the selection of one small planet orbiting a common star – one of millions of similar stars, but one supporting life – was so improbable that the odds against such a thing happening were incalculable.

Barbara had told him while under its influence that it posed no threat and James had said the same. Now he was in a coma and it was by the grace of God that she had escaped its malign influence relatively unscathed. Nonetheless, it had left its mark on everyone who had come near it. Well, it would not get another chance, he would see to that.

He felt in his pocket and produced his mobile phone. 'Hello, Chris. Can you join us in the hotel bar? We're going to deal with that thing – now.'

'OK.' Chris's voice came back and the line went dead.

Barbara looked at him. 'John, you're angry. Be careful.'

23

James was in a strange place. He wandered under a milky sky and all around him were shapes – shapes that at the same time had no shape. They stood or else drifted silently around him, slowly changing, merging and dividing, drawing out what looked like protoplasmic threads along which tiny pulses of light darted as if they were communicating with each other. The ground on which he stood, although firm was ill-defined, as if covered by a thin ground mist that smudged the horizon, rendering it invisible. It was impossible to tell where the land ended and the sky began. The air was odourless and there was no sound. Indeed, he was hardly aware of any sensation at all, apart from a cool, bluish light that permeated everything. Although gravity or something like it was holding him down, he felt weightless.

He should have been alarmed, but he felt no fear in this hallucinatory landscape. Perhaps it was a dream. If it was, it was a vivid one. The shapes drifted like amoebae around him. One of the scintillating threads brushed against his hand and then bent away from him, arching high over his head like a rainbow bridge. It was impossible to tell whether these interlinked translucent creatures were individuals or parts of one infinitely complex super organism. It was clear that they meant him no harm. Had they done so, those fine threads could easily have wrapped him up like a moth in a spider's web, helpless in their bonds until he was engulfed by one or more of the drifting forms. Instead, the thread that had touched him had reacted by withdrawing instantly, either to prevent damage to him or, more probably, to itself.

He tried to call out: 'Hello? Where am I?'

There was no answer. His voice sounded muffled and distant, as if he was standing in an anechoic chamber. The very air seemed to be dead.

'Hello?' The word fell at his feet like a bag of dust. He gave up. There was no one here apart from the slowly moving shapes, whatever they were, and they were either deaf or blind to him, or else both. Yet they were aware of his presence. Those that came too close flowed away as if to avoid him. The few delicate threads that did accidentally brush against him stretched away in a graceful arc as the first one had done, so they were clearly not oblivious of his existence. He made as if to push one of the shapes out of the way and it reacted instantly, sliding to one side and skirting its neighbour with an astonishing degree of skill, thus avoiding a knock-on collision. Disorientated, he wandered aimlessly, not knowing where he was, where he was going or what he was doing here. He did not even know how he had come to this place. He was here and that was all. It was as if he had always been here. Time had lost its meaning. Indeed, time had ceased to exist. Perhaps if he stood still he would continue to move across the featureless landscape, drifting like some mythical ghost ship over a flat ocean. He tried counting seconds, reaching twenty. Well, that was twenty seconds accounted for, but it was meaningless. If he had counted to twenty thousand it would have been the same. The shapes that moved around him had always done so and, for all he knew, would continue to do so until he became one of them. Perhaps this was his destiny; to amalgamate with these timeless life forms – to flow together with them like a drifting spirit. Perhaps he was a spirit, he didn't know. His body did not feel right; in fact it was hard to feel anything at all. He had skin sensation, but little else. He pinched the back of his hand and felt the pressure, but there was no pain. Like most people, he was aware of his body and its natural functions, but here his body seemed to be missing something important, as if it no longer had any vital organs; indeed, he wondered if he still had a body. It felt too light and insubstantial, yet he was aware of a great strength and energy that surged through his limbs like hydraulic fluid. Perhaps this was why he felt almost weightless.

He had to be here for a purpose, he reasoned, but what was it, and how did he get here? There had been no journey that he could remember; no space flight along some intergalactic superhighway, no dark tunnel leading to a bright light, no pyrotechnics with stars shooting by – he was just here and that was all he knew or could remember. He tried to think of something that might jog his memory, but could not. In fact, he could remember almost nothing of his past life, assuming that he had ever had one; he could not even be sure of that any more. Yet there had been something. A few faces, vaguely recognisable came to mind, but he could no longer connect them with anything. He concentrated on this for a while before putting them to the back of his mind. He had time to worry about that later. For now it did not matter. He had to tackle the immediate problem of now, and now was a very important matter to him.

Like a newborn baby that in moments forgets its former life treading the womb's water to be faced with a new life of dry air and strange things, he knew he had to concentrate on his new environment. This was important, but still he could make no sense of it. The thought occurred to him that he might be dead and that this was some kind of afterlife. He was not religious and had no particular belief in such things, yet how else could he explain his sudden arrival in this timeless world, and why could he remember nothing of it? Nothing in whatever previous life he might have had had prepared him for this. It was perhaps too much to expect that he should understand it.

Something was happening. The shapes now appeared to be moving around him – forming a circle and then slowly flowing together, first with threads that grew thicker and more numerous before they finally merged into a seamless wall that surrounded him, arching over his head to form a large dome. He was now inside what appeared to be a translucent tent, or perhaps a sphere, he wasn't sure which. There were no corners or shadows to define its shape. He touched the wall. It was smooth and dry with a soft, yielding feel to it. It might have been a padded cell. This should have been alarming, but he felt no fear. This newly formed cell was not a prison and he was not a captive. He somehow knew that no harm would come to him in this place. It felt secure.

Something gently nudged him from behind and caused him to turn around. A flat protuberance like a ledge or a bed had appeared inside the empty chamber, growing out from the wall and apparently made from the same living substance that now surrounded him. He sat down on it. It supported his weight with ease, assuming that he had any weight to support.

'What am I doing here?' he said, more to himself than to any possible listener.

There was no answer. His voice sounded flat and distant, devoid of any normal interior acoustic.

He knew that he must lie down. He could just hear a faint whispering sound somewhere in the background. It was either the blood rushing in his ears or it was coming from the living wall that surrounded him, he did not know which and it did not seem to matter. He was tired. As his eyelids dropped he felt something like a soothing hand on his forehead, stroking him the way his mother had done so often when he was a child. It was warm and reassuring. He might have been a child. Perhaps he was a child.

Finally, like a child, he slept.

24

John parked the Land Rover near the cabin and Chris unloaded the roll of chicken wire, together with the flex and the necessary tools. Bernard jumped out and helped him with these while John and Barbara watched.

First, Chris cut two lengths of chicken wire off the roll and folded them four times into rectangular mats before firmly attaching a generous length of flex to each. Then he took the fencing stake and hammered it deep into the ground outside the door of the cabin, until only the head of it showed. He filed the eye of the stake so that the metal was clean and bright and with pliers he crimped spade terminals to the ends of the wire. These he screwed to the stake.

'Are you sure this will work?' John asked him.

'No,' he said truthfully. 'We'll know in a minute. It's nearly ready.'

John felt uneasy.

Bernard sensed this. 'Don't worry. If it doesn't work, we'll be out of there a bloody sight quicker than we went in.'

John smiled and nodded. If it did work, he thought, he would gladly part with a hundred pounds of his money to see that thing rendered harmless.

'OK, do you feel brave?' Bernard asked him.

'Not very,' he confessed.

'Keep the shields between you and the cylinder at all times,' Chris said, attaching the remainder of the flex to the roll of chicken wire. 'If you think it isn't working, back off immediately.'

'You don't need to tell us that,' Bernard said, picking up his shield. He threaded his fingers through some of the mesh and squeezed it so that it formed a kind of handle. It was not easy to hold in this way, but it would do.

John followed Bernard's example and, like two mythical knights entering a dragon's lair with shields outstretched, they stepped cautiously through the doorway. Meanwhile, Chris crimped a terminal to the free end of the flex, the other end of which was connected to the roll of chicken wire.

John peered through the small chinks in his folded chicken wire shield. He could see the cylinder ahead of them, lying exactly where it had lain when James had sat before it. 'Do you feel anything yet?' he asked Bernard.

'Not yet,' Bernard replied. 'I think it may be working.

They edged closer to it. 'By Jove, I believe it *is* working!' John said. He was close enough to touch it now 'Chris, one hundred pounds is yours, my boy. Right, let's get that chicken wire.'

They retreated to the door and picked up the roll of wire mesh. They then carried it back to the cylinder and unrolled it, a difficult task since both men had to work one-handed, with the other hand being reserved for their shields.

'Right,' John said. 'Give me a hand to roll the cylinder onto the wire.'

Between them they rolled the cylinder onto the free end of the chicken wire and began to roll it across the floor, wrapping the wire around it as they went. This too was difficult, since the extraordinary weight of the cylinder made it hard to manoeuvre in the confined space of the cabin. They continued to roll it until it bumped against the cabin wall. Then, with great effort, they walked it back across the floor and repeated the exercise until all the chicken wire had been used up and the cylinder lay near the wall, cocooned in wire mesh. They rested for a while, leaning against the wall. Their muscles ached from the effort of moving it while at the same time keeping their shields between themselves and the cylinder. It had taken a tremendous effort. John remembered that he had needed all four members of the team to carry it into the cabin. He now wondered how just the two of them had managed to move it at all.

Once they had recovered sufficiently from their joint exertion, they left the cabin and rejoined the others. Chris disconnected the shields and gingerly touched the crimp tag from the screen lead to the earth stake, half expecting to see a spark or some sign that energy from the cylinder was being discharged. Nothing happened. He screwed the terminal to the stake and stood back.

'Let's see if it works,' he said when he had finished.

Bernard cautiously entered the cabin, followed by John. 'It seems to be working,' he said.

'I do believe it is working,' John said and approached the cylinder. His initial caution had waned and he bent over it. 'Chris!' he called out. 'You're a bloody genius! It's safe!'

Chris stood in the doorway, reluctant to come in.

Barbara entered the cabin and looked at the cylinder, now almost concealed from view inside the roll of chicken wire. She stood beside John. 'You're right,' she breathed. 'I can't feel anything coming off it now.'

'I feel like an assassin,' Bernard said.

'We haven't killed it,' John reminded him, 'we've made it safe, that's all. It's still very much alive.'

He was right. The cylinder glowed coldly beneath its wire jacket.

Barbara wondered if safe was the right word for something that so far had defeated all attempts to suppress it. Still, she reasoned, Chris's improvised chicken wire screen had inhibited it, if only for now. Its influence had palpably diminished, but she still had reservations about John's assertion that it was safe.

'What sort of energy do you think it's emitting?' Chris asked from the safety of the doorway. 'It can't be electromagnetic, or I would have seen a spark or something of the sort as soon as I earthed it; yet it's effectively shielded.'

'I wish I knew,' John said.

Barbara thought of James lying in a coma and wired up to a monitor. She was in no doubt that the cylinder was responsible for this. She looked at it and felt a degree of loathing for the thing that hitherto had been john's preserve. She wondered if James would ever recover from whatever it was that had afflicted him, and if he did, how it might affect him afterwards. The whole project had been dogged by misfortune ever since the discovery of that accursed cylinder that now lay at her feet with its electric glow and its malevolence. She resisted a strong urge to kick it.

'Well,' Bernard said. 'Now that we've screened it, what do we do with it now?'

'We leave it and carry on with the dig,' John said. 'We've wasted enough time with this thing already. We can't afford to waste any more. Even with the extension we are getting into time trouble. If we lose much more time, I shall have the university down on my neck and we'll all be off the project.'

Bernard thought about this. 'If they knew about the cylinder they would understand.'

'They probably would, but we would be exposing more people to the dangers of that thing if we had all and sundry milling around it, trying to find out what makes it tick and having their brains frazzled in the process. I don't want to take that chance.'

'They're going to find out about it eventually,' he countered. 'You can't keep a thing like this secret for long, you know that.'

'Let's try and keep it secret for as long as we can, shall we? Look, we've been over this before and you know my feelings on the matter.'

Bernard gave in. There was no point in arguing with John sometimes. He was not going to change his mind and that was that.

'He is barely ticking over,' the first doctor said.

The second doctor scanned his notes. 'Have you ever seen this before?'

'No. His condition is symptomatic of a massive stroke, but the scan indicates nothing extraordinary. His brain looks perfectly normal. The nearest thing to it I can think of is catatonia, and he has no history of that. We have analysed his blood for evidence of poisoning or drug abuse, but so far there is nothing. The police are involved in the matter, of course, and they'll be making their own enquiries.'

'Do we know who he is?'

'A colleague of his gave me the essential details, but little else.'

'Hmmm, Pulse, breathing rate and body temperature are all stable. Well, we shall continue to monitor him and see if his condition improves overnight. Meanwhile, there is little we can do but wait.'

'One thing; his brain pattern fluctuates considerably. It's quiet at the moment – barely ticking over – but an hour ago there was a lot of activity; the monitor was going wild. Things have been happening in there.'

'It's a pity we can't see what. Who's next?'

The doctors moved on.

Do you see us?

Who are you?

Do you see us?

I don't know. Where are you?

We are here – with you.

This isn't happening.

No?

No. I can't believe in things I cannot touch, see and feel and I can't see you. I can't touch you. I'm not sure that I can hear you. Your voice is inside my head. My ears are not working too well – something wrong, see? Not been right since I got here – how did I get here? It doesn't matter. The thing is, I am here and I am alone with soft protoplasm. That much exists. I am aware of that. I have been out at sea all night, you understand, and things are a bit storm-tossed. I can see OK, but I can't see you. There's no one here apart from me and the shapes... the ever-changing shapes... the shapes that now surround me. What are they and what am I? I know what I am... I am, and that is enough, but what have I become? Do I have a body? I can't feel it and I can't see you. Are you there? What language is this? I don't understand what I'm saying. I don't hear you – I *can't* hear you. You're inside my head. That's it! You're inside my head and this is a dream. Ah, I've sussed you now, yes! This explains everything. OK then, give me your shtick. I'm listening.

Are you? Not ready yet. You will understand when you are ready.

Will I? Will I really? Hello?

(Silence)

Hello? Hello? Nothing there. There was nothing there. Fever, that's what it is. I must have caught something nasty while I was out there wandering and this is the result; a fevered dream. I have come a long way, or so it feels, but now I have my room. It is safe in here. I don't want to leave. Perhaps if I dream – did I dream? Have I dreamed? Did I dream all this and am I still dreaming? Don't know… I don't know. Perhaps I should sleep again and then maybe it will come clear. I feel rough. Something's wrong, I know that, but what is it? I *was* all right, but now… now… I don't know. Why did I say I was out at sea? I'm safe in here and I'm dry. There is no sea, or perhaps I am at sea and have been all night – tucked up safe in my life raft. There was this murmuring sound. I remember that, but there is no movement and no sound any more. Where did it go? Hello. Are you still there?

(Silence)

Any…

Sleep.

27

Barbara showered and quickly towelled herself. She sat on the edge of the bed and brushed her hair before drying it. Then, almost idly, she took James's mobile phone from her bag where she had secreted it before the ambulance had come to take him to the hospital. She switched it on and checked it for missed calls and text messages. There was a large number, but the phone was security protected and she was unable to gain access to them without knowing his password. She switched it off and put it back in her bag. She wanted to cry. The sight of him lying there, wired up to the machine and looking so helpless had affected her deeply.

She blamed herself for this. She had after all invited him to examine the cylinder. But for that his mind would never have been ensnared by the accursed thing. John had seen the danger inherent in such a venture and had vehemently opposed it, but in the end he had given in. That had been a mistake. The other mistake had been to underestimate James's fascination with the object and no one could have predicted the kind of hold that it would exert upon him. Yet they should have foreseen it. *She* should have foreseen it. Instead, they had allowed him to be with the cylinder for far longer than anyone had ever been and this was the result. She tried to console herself with the thought that it was as much James's fault as anyone else's. After all, he had been warned, yet this thought brought little comfort to her.

The hospital had taken both her and John's mobile numbers and had promised to contact her if there was any change in his condition, but so far no news had come through. For the third time in an hour, she checked her phone for missed calls but there were none.

Snapping her bag shut, she got dressed and left the room. The familiar sight of the corridor reminded her again of James's illness. It had only been hours ago that they had gained access to his room and discovered him lying there on the bed, naked and unconscious. She remembered with a chill the shock of seeing him like that. She tried to put it out of her mind as she went downstairs to the dining room where the rest of the team had already assembled.

Chris was looking pleased with himself. His improvised Faraday cage had worked against expectation and the cylinder had been deactivated, if only temporarily. Still, he had scored a valuable point. John and Bernard too were looking satisfied with their work. She was sure that if smoking had been allowed in the dining room they would have passed around the cigars to celebrate.

Lynda was not quite as buoyant as the others, having not been involved in the deactivation of the cylinder. John had given her the rest of the day off and she had used the time to catch up on some work of her own. Therefore, she had been on the outside of the day's events. Barbara chose a vacant seat beside her and sat down.

'Any news of James?' she asked John, trying to sound casual.

John shook his head. 'I checked my mobile just a minute or two ago and no one's been in touch. I take it no one's contacted you either.'

'No.'

'Look, if you like, I'll drive you to the hospital after dinner if you'd like to see him. I don't mind.'

She smiled. 'Thanks, but there's nothing I can do for him until they call. There's nothing any of us can do at the moment.'

'What do you suppose happened to him?' Lynda asked.

'I wish we knew,' John said. 'I'm only sure of one thing – that bloody cylinder has something to do with it. I said it would scramble his brains.'

'He seemed to be addicted to it,' Bernard said. 'What else could have driven him to break into the cabin just to be with it?'

'And walk up there in the dead of night,' John added. 'Three miles of unlit country road in unpredictable weather; it's the act of a madman, or else an obsessive.'

'James is not mad, nor is he an obsessive,' Barbara protested. 'He is a very balanced man with a rational mind. The cylinder made him act like that, I'm certain.'

'We're going to have to get rid of it.' Bernard said. 'On top of everything else, it's jeopardising the entire project.'

'We can't simply get rid of it,' John said. 'Right now, we can't do anything with it; it's too dangerous.'

'We screened it successfully,' Chris reminded him, still pleased with his idea.

'It's safe for now, but for how long?' John said. 'We simply don't know the power of that thing. To be honest with you, I don't know what to do with it. Even screened, it might still be dangerous, we don't know.'

'Do you think the Army might be able to deal with it?' Bernard suggested.

'They might, but what if they can't? You know perfectly well what happened to the people in the settlement. I wouldn't like to see the same thing happening to modern soldiers equipped with modern weapons, would you?'

'James said that the cylinder had nothing directly to do with the violence,' Barbara pointed out.

'Does anyone want to risk it?

No one spoke.

'Look, I'm sorry Barbara, but James was not the most rational person in the world at the time, regardless of whatever he might have been before. Right now, I'm not prepared to take his word for it and I'm not prepared to risk the lives of others getting involved.'

'Then what do we do?' Chris asked.

'I wish I knew.'

Barbara thought about this. The whole project had turned into a sticky mess; one from which they could not escape, nor was it possible to progress further with ease while the cylinder dominated everything. John was right. It was too risky to involve others at this stage, yet it was going to be hard for the team to go on as before. In the days following the cylinder's discovery, normal work on the site had all but ceased and now James, whom she had brought in on the project, was in a coma. They were stuck. They could neither go forward nor back. There was no answer.

That night she lay in bed beside John, but she was thinking of James. She could not get his plight out of her mind. Her phone lay on the bedside table, switched on and ready to receive the expected call from the hospital, but it remained stubbornly silent. She looked at the clock. The large green digits read 1:26 and then the six became a seven. Sleep was eluding her again. She reasoned that if the hospital had not contacted either her or John, then James's condition must be stable, but this did little to make her feel better.

She examined the possibilities of what might have happened to him and wondered what, if anything might be going on inside his unconscious brain. What if he was trapped in the sort of nightmare of systematic mass murder that she had experienced, but without the possibility of escape into wakefulness? The thought was indeed a terrible one. No one could endure a continuing horror like that and come out with their sanity intact.

John stirred beside her and she wondered if he was entering into a dreaming phase, but he settled down and his breathing became steady again. Their dreams of that ancient past had become less frequent recently, but they still occurred from time to time. Nothing like her nightmare of the slaughter and butchery of the young prisoners for meat had returned to torment her sleep, but every night she still feared its recurrence. This too contributed to her sleeplessness. The memory of that dream still haunted her and sometimes its awful images would invade her thoughts unbidden. Then she had to get up and write or do something in an effort to clear her mind. Tonight these thoughts stayed away, but the image of the unconscious James remained; lying naked on the bed and later in the hospital cubicle, wired up to a machine.

Eventually, she did sleep and a dream came, but this was unlike any other dream that she had had so far. In it, she saw an ill-defined human figure wandering through a formless landscape with no horizon, surrounded by curious biomorphic shapes that drifted or floated around it. Somehow, she knew that this wandering figure was James, although he was not recognisable as such. He seemed to be as translucent as the indefinable things that surrounded him and he moved or glided with the same apparent ease as they did. The dream was brief, barely a glimpse in fact, but like many such fleeting images it stuck in her mind. She thought about writing it down and then decided against it for fear of disturbing John who was sleeping peacefully. She was not likely to forget it anyway.

This led to another sleepless period, during which she was haunted yet again by images of the unconscious James and the vision of his soul or whatever it was drifting through that Limbo-like landscape. Again, the thought that she had inadvertently sent him there returned to torment her and all the what-ifs returned with them. What if she had not invited him to inspect the cylinder, and what if… The exercise was useless. She turned over onto her right side and closed her eyes in an effort to sleep in a different position but still sleep eluded her. Eventually she sat up, muttering 'Damn, damn, damn!'

John stirred and half woke, mumbling something unintelligible. Then he realised that she was sitting bolt upright beside him in the bed and he woke up properly. 'What's the Matter?'

'Nothing,' she lied.

'Have you been dreaming?'

She nodded. 'This one was different.'

'Different?'

'Yes.' She then proceeded to tell him about it, keeping her description as brief as possible. The dream having been so short, there was little to tell other than to describe what she had seen. She then went on to tell him about her sense of guilt over James's present condition. She was close to tears.

Sensing her heightened emotional state, he sat up and gently put his arm around her waist, drawing her close. 'You are not to blame,' he said softly. 'Any one of us could have stopped him – *I* could have stopped him but I didn't even though I was against it, so if anyone's to blame, it's me. Besides, he revisited the site and broke into the hut without our knowledge and it is that which led directly to his collapse. You had nothing to do with that.'

'He was driven to do it,' she said. 'The cylinder had him in its power.'

'So the cylinder is responsible. You are not. Now hush and try to sleep.'

'I can't sleep. These thoughts keep going around and around in my head and they won't let me sleep. And I'm afraid of the nightmares returning.'

'Have you had any recently?'

'No.'

'Then why…'

'I suppose this new dream started me thinking along those lines again. That might be enough to restart the process.'

He drew her closer and kissed her forehead. 'I am here for you.'

She put her arms around his chest and kissed him. 'I'm glad you are. I don't know what I'd do without you.'

He lay back and she snuggled up to him, her head resting on his chest. Despite all his higher motives, he felt the first stirrings of an erection. He tried to control it, but could not. He desperately wanted to

134

resist this most basic and unbidden urge, feeling that it would be inappropriate to make love to her at this particular time.

'Your heart is thumping,' she said.

'Huh?'

'Yes. And...' she slid her hand down his body. 'You seem to be standing to attention for me.'

'I'm sorry.'

'Sorry; why?'

'I don't want to appear to be taking advantage...'

'Shut up. You're not taking advantage, you silly goose.' She stroked his erect penis and whispered: 'It might help me to sleep.' The truth was she wanted to make love. Sex has its own way of discharging pent-up anxiety and right now she felt that she needed it badly, after which they would sleep. If anything, she was taking advantage of him. She knew he was tired, but she contented herself with the thought that a good set-to would benefit them both.

He was fully awake now, all thoughts of sleep suspended as he ran his hands over her body, feeling the sensuous contours of her breasts and buttocks, the soft, undulating plain of her belly; slowly working his way down to the small triangular patch of hair that led his exploring fingertips to the moist cleft of her vulva with its innermost mysteries. There was no stopping either of them now. She spread her thighs and willingly allowed his fingers to enter and explore her. His gentle finger movements coursed through her nerves like bolts of electric current, causing her to lose all sense of reason and control. This was what she needed; it was not just comfort and pleasure, it was a necessity. She gasped as if in pain and lay back, rolling her head from side to side, breathless and ready to receive him while all the time his fingers kept working, sending out tiny sparks that set her body alight, causing her to thrust her hips forward involuntarily, willing him to enter her. She pulled him closer, grasping his flesh with a strength that was surprising for a woman of slight build. He grimaced with something like pain as she clutched and held him with a power that was as new to him as it was savage. It was the power of desperation and a total surrender to love. She would hold nothing back.

'Come into me,' she gasped. 'I want to feel you inside me now.'

They made love with a new, almost ferocious intensity, after which they lay close together in a state of post-coital half sleep until a deep and natural slumber eventually overtook them.

There were no more disturbing dreams that night.

28

No one speaks. It is silent now. It has always been so, but no, there was something – a voice, what did it say? I don't remember; it was inside my head and in a language I don't speak and yet which I could understand. How was that? Now it is silent; silent as it ever was. This is now but when was then? Was there ever a then? Let's see, I am here, placed in a small point in time – infinitely small – and yet it stretches away to all eternity. This much I can understand. I have an infinite lifetime in which to understand all this and so much more besides and yet there is no time at all. How's that for a riddle in a place where time does not exist? How do I know that? I slept, I think, safe in my room – this room that lives; that holds me here – enfolds me, perhaps.

But why am I here? It must be for a reason otherwise nothing makes sense so there must be a reason or else I am not here. Perhaps I am not here and all of this is just a figment of an overactive imagination. I will not ask how long I have been here. Such a question would be immaterial where there are no normal dimensions. That's profound. I should write that down, but there is nothing here to write with and even if there was I don't think I could write it and still make sense. Language fails me and yet I still have my thoughts and I am aware of what surrounds me. It is here and now and that is what matters. I wish I knew why it matters.

Something occurs. It is faint and far off like a half-forgotten memory of a soothing hand and a soft voice, but it's all mixed up in my head and far away; too far to come close. And I thought I saw her as I wandered in my dream – if I did dream, that is – a dream within a dream, now there's a thought like a Chinese box; one inside another and another, deeper and deeper, it goes on, of course it does. We are dealing here with many dimensions so if I slip through one and into another it shouldn't really surprise me. That seems to be the way things work here.

But who was she and why do I say she? How can I be sure of that? Someone from my past, perhaps; that's if I can have a past in a place where the past does not appear to exist. Try and equate that. It's a complete contradiction but there are many contradictions here, perhaps that's why I feel confused by what should after all be simple. Someone half seen like the shadow thing that moves on the periphery of vision to vanish when you look; that's what she was but why do I say she? It might have been anything and yet I said she and not he or it. I wish I could remember. It is almost as if I knew her. Maybe she was a false perception that vanishes as soon as you become aware of it, like *déjà vu*. There is so much that is peripheral and half seen and maybe that's how I miss the point. Perhaps if I search I might find the answer to that one. There are no limits here; I can see that much. Maybe if I could reach her she might help me with the answer to my question, but what is that question? My mind seems to have blotted it out. Anyway, there is more than one question; many more than I can count. So many...

'The EEG is quiet now, but take a look at this,' the first doctor said, drawing a section of graph paper from the machine. 'It's wild.'

The second doctor examined the chart. 'Something's been going on in there, that's for sure. This recording is recent.'

'It happened just a few minutes ago. I switched the machine on as soon as I spotted the rise in brain activity. I wanted a hard copy of this.'

'It's quiescent now. His heart and breathing rate is steady, it's just the brain patterns that are fluctuating so wildly. Otherwise, his condition is stable.'

'No change, in fact.'

'No, but those brain patterns are crazy.'

The first doctor thought for a moment, then said: 'Do you know what this patient's condition reminds me of?'

The second doctor looked blank.

'Unconsciousness brought about by extreme shock. The brain sometimes shuts down as if to block out whatever caused the trauma.'

'Have you ever come across such a case?'

'No, it's very rare and I'm not a psychiatrist. They deal with that sort of thing.'

'Interesting. Well, we shall continue to monitor him for now. There's something odd about this case. Nothing quite fits here.'

'No suggested treatment, then?'

'It's hard to know what to do when we don't know what we're supposed to be treating, isn't it?'

'Hmm.' The doctors moved on.

'How did you sleep?' John gently brushed the hair away from Barbara's face.

She slowly opened her eyes and gave him a little smile. 'Fine, considering...' She yawned and stretched, then yawned again. 'I'm tired, though.'

'I made you a coffee.'

'What time is it?'

He glanced at the clock. 'Seven thirty. There's no rush.'

She collected her thoughts and, remembering James, she sat up quickly. 'Has the hospital been in touch yet?'

He shook his head. 'I'll drive you round to the hospital after breakfast and you can see him. I'll leave Bernard in charge of the dig.'

She stroked his cheek. 'Thanks.'

Breakfast that morning was a rather sombre affair with little conversation. John let Bernard know of his intention to take Barbara to see James in hospital and Bernard nodded in mute agreement, understanding the situation and her concern. He knew what to do anyway. Chris had by now recovered from his previous day's euphoria and sat silently wondering if his scheme to screen the cylinder had worked as well as he had originally hoped, or if the whole issue had melted down or blown up overnight and his dream to outwit the thing had come to nothing. He contented himself with the thought that he would soon know. Lynda made a small joke about something in an effort to enliven the conversation, but it did not work and so she fell silent with the rest of them. It was clear that the aftershock of James's breakdown, or whatever it was that had laid him so low, had affected them all in different ways and that this matter was now uppermost in everyone's mind.

As soon as breakfast was over, they left the table and went out together. After a brief exchange of words, Bernard drove Lynda and Chris out along the narrow country road that eventually led to the site while John drove Barbara to the hospital. What they would do when they got there neither of them knew. They would worry about that when the time came.

On arriving at the hospital, John parked the Land Rover and they headed for the main entrance and the reception desk where they were directed to the private ward where James lay, presumably still unconscious. Here they were intercepted by the ward sister who forbade them to see him immediately. Instead, she asked them to wait while she called the switchboard and paged a doctor. This unexpected reception served only to heighten Barbara's worries. Now frightened and pale, she obediently took a seat and waited. There was nothing else to do.

John sat down beside her. Neither of them spoke. There was little to say that was worth saying. It was just a matter of waiting.

Time dragged by while they sat there, reading and rereading the posters on the wall that advertised for blood donors or else plugged the essential wash-your-hands-to-avoid-infection message, neither of them taking any of it in. It was just wallpaper.

They waited for about fifteen minutes, each alone with their thoughts before a doctor appeared and spoke in hushed tones to the ward sister. At one point they paused and looked towards Barbara and John before continuing their conversation. Papers were examined and then put down.

Finally, the doctor came over and stood before them. He carried a clipboard under his arm.

'Doctor Barbara Sedgwick?'

At the sound of her name, Barbara looked up. 'Yes.' Her voice was strangulated with tension.

The doctor tried to smile reassuringly. 'You were here yesterday when James Masters was admitted. Now, his condition is stable, but he has not yet regained consciousness. We are trying to treat him, but we still cannot ascertain his condition with any certainty. Until we can, you must understand that it is difficult for us to treat him. Meanwhile, I need to ask you one or two questions. Do you mind?'

'No,' she replied meekly.

The doctor raised his clipboard and produced a pen before turning his attention to John. 'And you are...'

John stood up. 'Professor John Black. I was here yesterday with Barbara.'

The doctor noted this down. 'And you also know him?'

'Not as well as Barbara,' he admitted.

'I would like to know exactly what happened yesterday.'

'We don't know,' Barbara said. 'I found him like this in his hotel room yesterday morning. I immediately called for an ambulance and... well, you know the rest.'

The doctor looked at her. 'What is your relationship to this man?'

'He is a colleague.'

'And what do you do?'

'We're archaeologists. James came in to help us with something – a technical problem.'

The doctor wrote some more. 'So James is an archaeologist as well, is he?' he said when he had finished writing.

John felt a tingle of fear. The doctor's probing questions and Barbara's answers were getting too close to the subject of the cylinder for his liking. If it went on like this he would have to intervene and draw him off the scent.

'No,' Barbara said. 'He's an aerospace engineer. We brought him in to look at something that we'd just dug up.'

At this, John looked at the floor, clutched his hands together and fought hard to control himself. He wanted to stop her there and then before she spilled everything over the side about the discovery of cylinder and all that followed, but he could do nothing to stop her without drawing even more attention to it.

'We weren't sure what it might be made of and we thought he might be able to help us here,' she continued. 'We often bring in specialists from outside areas of study when we're stuck.' She paused for a moment and then turned to John who was still staring at the floor, afraid of what might be coming next. 'Do you remember that Saxon bracelet? You must do. We had to call in a metallurgist to decide what it was made of.'

At this John looked up, relieved. The bracelet, if fictitious, was a masterstroke; a perfect red herring. It served its purpose. The doctor moved on.

'OK,' he said. 'I just need some more details for our records; his home address, next of kin, employer – that sort of thing.'

Barbara gave him what information she could and the doctor noted it. Finally, to her relief, he lowered his clipboard and addressed them both.

'You may see him now, but I must tell you that he is still unconscious and we are continuing to monitor him. He's not in danger, but we are concerned and it's still too early to say when he will come out of his coma. So far, we are unable to diagnose his condition, so I'm afraid I cannot give you any prognosis.'

He led them through into the ward where James lay with electrodes wired to his head and chest. Beside him, an EEG machine traced erratic lines on a slowly moving chart while above it a monitor traced his heart and breathing rate, beeping rhythmically with each heartbeat. What might have been brainwaves squiggled erratically below these lines. His eyes were closed and his face looked peaceful.

Barbara took his hand and held it. 'James,' she said softly. 'James, can you hear me? It's Barbara.' There was no response. She gently touched his forehead, taking care not to dislodge the electrodes. 'James, we've come to see you. Can you hear me?'

Again there was no physical response, but John made a sudden noise. 'Look at this!' He indicated the EEG machine and the doctor came over to look. Two of the pens were scribbling wildly on the graph. The others still waved lazily as before. 'Something is happening,' he said.

Barbara continued to talk to him while the doctor and John watched the EEG. The doctor signalled to a colleague who joined them while she went on talking. The two doctors exchanged glances.

'I think you can leave him for now,' the first doctor said after she had been talking for three or four minutes. 'We don't want to overexcite him at this stage.'

She slowly removed her hand from James's forehead and said: 'We shall see you tomorrow.' As she spoke, she looked at the doctor who nodded in reply. She stood up from the bedside and joined John and the two doctors who were watching the graph. The pens were still scribbling their erratic lines.

'Well,' the first doctor said. 'He seems to be responding to your stimulus. Can you try again later? I want to see if we can repeat the test.'

'We'll come in this evening,' she said.

'Could you make it tomorrow morning? I should be off duty this evening and won't be on again until the morning. I'd like to be here to see what happens.'

'OK.'

They left James with the doctors and left the ward. As they walked across the car park, John leaned over and kissed her on the cheek. 'Barbara, that was brilliant!'

She looked at him, surprised. 'What was?'

'He really responded to your voice. I'm sure he did. That machine had been quiet until you spoke.' He really wanted to tell her how delighted he was with her quick-wittedness in skilfully avoiding any mention of the cylinder whilst directly answering the doctor's questions, but he decided against it. Somehow, it seemed inappropriate at this time. That would do for later. Her invented story of the Saxon bracelet had successfully halted all further questions concerning the dig. It had been a difficult moment, though.

His sudden concern for James's condition puzzled her. Up to now, his feelings towards James had been, to say the least, cool if not downright hostile. She wondered what might have happened to change his attitude like this and she thought of asking him. Instead, she just said: 'Do you really think he heard me?'

'I'm certain he did.'

'I still feel responsible for all this, you know.'

'You shouldn't. We discussed this, remember?'

'Yes. But if I hadn't invited him to examine the cylinder, none of this would have happened.'

John turned and faced her. 'Now look, it's only by the grace of God that it's not one of us lying there instead of him. Any one of us could have become as obsessed with it as he did. It's just pure luck that we realised in time the dangers inherent in the thing. You nearly succumbed to it yourself, need I remind you, so stop beating yourself up about it. It's not your fault.'

She tried to smile but his words did little to ease her sense of guilt. She knew that he meant well, but it would take time for her to rid herself of the blame. She would feel better when James was well again; if indeed he ever was well again.

He gave her a little smile. Let's go for a coffee. I don't know about you, but I could use one.'

'Shouldn't we be getting to work?'

'Who's the boss here? Come on.'
They drove back into town.

31

I cannot leave here yet. There's something important I have to do but what is it? I shall know in time whatever that may mean here. She was here again, trying to get me out, but I can't leave. I couldn't tell her that. There were words but I couldn't understand them. Odd, that… It's as if I can't understand language any more and yet I still get the drift of it, but what is language anyway? Communication, that's what it is. She was communicating. I couldn't fathom her words and yet I understood just the same as I understand why I must be here; something has let me know that. Perhaps that's why I have no fear. This life is new and at the same time I can't remember it ever having been different. Yet it was different once; I can't remember when and it doesn't matter much anyway, yet I still wonder about it. Perhaps it's just idle curiosity. That's it. I must have another life somewhere, but it's a parallel one. Two lives running parallel; now there's a thought. Like book leaves, they all run together simultaneously, the first page and the last with all the others in between; any number of pages and any number of books all running in parallel; it makes sense. Perhaps time is like that with all periods in history and all that came before it and all that are yet to come running in parallel. Therefore there is no beginning and no end. It is; that's all. Can it really be that simple? This is big. I must think this one through. Well, I have time. There's no effective limit.

She was here and there were words; soft and comforting, but I don't really need comforting. No one can see that, I suppose. No one can see what I see or feel what I feel – what *do* I feel? That's a strange one. I don't know. And how do I know she was here? She could not have been here physically; that would be preposterous. No, she must have been outside somewhere or else inside my head. It's hard to know what is real or imagined in this topsy-turvy world which is why I don't know if I'm dreaming or not; I can't be sure any more. Perhaps this is reality and all else is a dream – that other half-forgotten world that lurks somewhere in the back of my mind – the bit that sometimes tries to break through. Perhaps she was trying to break through, but who is she and what does she want with me? Is she real or just a half forgotten memory?

Are you still there? Hello?

Nothing. Well, I'm still here, of that there is little doubt. It's odd that I've not actually met anyone, though. Yet there was someone else… when was that? It doesn't matter and I didn't see anyone, but someone was here; I heard a voice or at least I thought I heard a voice. In that case, if someone was here it follows that they will be here again. I have only to turn back the pages of time or else turn them forward to know. Now here is power. This way I can see into the future or look back into the past, in fact I can go anywhere should I so desire. Perhaps I can command it, but not now – no. If I could only find the words, not that words have much meaning any more; in fact they have no meaning so I don't know why I use them. I suppose it's just force of habit and it's convenient. It is language and language is one of my tools. I don't think I understand this language and yet I understand exactly what I'm saying and what is said. Where's the intellect in that? That's something else I must think through.

Well, I have time…

32

Bernard parked the Land Rover off the road in the usual place and he, Lynda and Chris collected their equipment and got out.

Chris immediately headed for the cabin to inspect his brainchild and was relieved to see that everything was still intact. The cylinder hadn't exploded during the night, nor had it melted down, in fact nothing had happened at all as far as he could see. For a moment he was tempted to test his hypothesis further by going in there, but he remembered that he and Lynda were under strict orders to stay away and, just in case he had forgotten, he was promptly ordered away from there by Bernard who spotted him standing in the doorway.

In fact the order had been quite unnecessary. He had already decided not to enter and Bernard now felt somewhat abashed at having told him so brusquely to get away from there. After all, he knew perfectly well what and what not to do, having been told so often. Bernard realised this almost immediately and was quick to apologise for his unusually high handed manner. It was as if the stress of the last few weeks was beginning to affect everyone concerned. Chris accepted his apology with good grace and the team was spared further stress.

Bernard was glad of that. Things were fraught enough already without adding to them. He approached the cabin with caution and peered through the doorway. The cylinder lay on the floor, still shrouded in chicken wire with its earth cable still attached. Emboldened by this, he entered the cabin and slowly walked towards it. He touched it with his foot. It appeared to be as inert as it had been when it was first discovered. It now looked as if Chris's idea really had worked and they had successfully disarmed the contraption, if disarmed was the right word for it. He left it and went outside. Chris and Lynda were already at work on a section of the dig and things were beginning to look normal again; normal that is if one disregarded the fact that a man was lying in hospital in a coma that almost certainly had been induced by the cylinder. He tried to put the thought out of his head and turned his attention to the door of the cabin that had been damaged by James when he broke in. He would have to repair that in an attempt to discourage any further unauthorised entry. He soon found the wrenched-off hasp and staple, still with the padlock attached. They had been bent by the force of whatever James had used to lever them off, but they were salvageable. He would try to straighten them, or else he would wait until John and Barbara arrived when he could drive back to town and buy a replacement. He put them in his pocket and walked over to where Chris and Lynda were working.

'How's it going?' he asked them as he approached.

Lynda looked up. 'We think we've found some more bone fragments here. We don't know yet if they're human or animal. I think that'll have to be decided in the lab.'

He smiled approvingly. This was getting back to what they were here for.

33

John and Barbara sat facing each other across the café table. Neither had spoken for some time. Barbara thought about the way James had appeared to react to her voice. There had been no physical reaction at all, but the machine had shown heightened brain activity, indicating that her words had had some effect. She tried to remember what she had talked about but could not. She had just talked, that was all. Anything would do.

John stared out of the window, watching the people outside as they went about their daily business. He liked to do this. Here he could watch normal life going about its daily business, unaffected by alien cylinders or anything like that. These people knew nothing of the effects that alien contact, if that was what it was, could have on human beings. They knew nothing of the disruption that it could bring down on the heads of normal, rational people to turn their lives inside out and upside down as they shopped and thought about what they would have for dinner that evening. The young woman leaving the estate agent's shop was oblivious to the extraordinary thing that dwelt in a humble shooting cabin just three miles away from where she was. The youth pedalling his BMX bike neither knew nor cared about it. Thank God for normality, he thought.

Barbara broke the silence between them. 'I saw your face when the doctor started asking questions concerning James's connection with the dig. What were you thinking when he asked?'

'I was bricking it,' he said truthfully. 'You fended him off beautifully with that story of the Saxon bracelet. That was really quick thinking. I wanted to congratulate you on that, but it was inappropriate at the time. Well done. It was brilliant.'

'I had to think of something to draw him off the scent.'

'It worked. It was a nasty moment, though.'

'What will you do when the news about the cylinder finally does leak out? It can't be kept secret forever, you know.'

'I do know, but I would like to keep it secret for as long as possible. Quite honestly, I don't know what to do about it. If I disclose its existence, it means the end of the project as everyone crawls all over the site and runs the risk of being infected. I don't like to think of what would happen then.'

'And if you don't?'

He shook his head. 'I don't know. I really don't know. I wish it had never been found. It's caused us nothing but trouble since it was unearthed and it will go on causing trouble for as long as it is there. Quite honestly, I can't see an end to it, except that it will probably be very messy.'

'It already is.' She thought for a moment and then she said: 'Do you think we ought to rebury it? Now that it has been screened it should be safe to handle it again. We could do it.'

'I would like to.'

'But...?'

'But... I don't know. It goes against everything I believe in. I'm an archaeologist and archaeologists don't bury their discoveries, especially one as important as this. We're dealing here with what is probably the most significant find of all time. Once it comes out into the open, it will overturn everything that was ever believed to be true about our early history. All the books will have to be rewritten. You can't simply bury that. Besides, someone else can always dig it up again.' He paused and then continued. 'Barbara, we have opened Pandora's Box. We can't ever close it.'

'We're going to have to think about it, whatever happens.'

'I wish I knew what to think. The thing's got me between a rock and a hard place, it really has. I don't know which way to move from here.'

She reached across the table and touched his hands. His face reflected much of the constant turmoil that dominated his thoughts by day and by night. She understood his dilemma. Any decision he might make would probably be the wrong one. She thought hard for something that might help to put his mind at rest, but nothing would come. He was right; the problem was insoluble.

Now, on top of everything else there was the matter of James to add to their troubles. It was sheer good fortune that the police had not been called as soon as he had been admitted to hospital. That was what usually happened when normally healthy people were taken ill. There was no knowing how long it would be before they came looking for him. It was probable that he had already been reported as a missing person and, since his occupation as an aerospace engineer sometimes engaged him in work involving matters of defence and national security, they would lose no time in searching for him. For all she knew to the contrary, they could be looking for him now. When they eventually found him, questions would be asked – awkward questions. She thought of mentioning this to John but decided against it. He had enough to worry about already without her adding more troubles to the still growing list.

He looked up suddenly. 'When our work is finished, I shall announce the cylinder's discovery to the faculty. It'll then be their problem and not just ours.'

She looked at him. 'How do you think they will deal with it?'

'I don't know. We shall have to stress its dangers to all concerned. I don't like to think of what might happen if it affected them as it did us and James in particular.'

'That may not be necessary,' she observed. 'The danger is now becoming all too obvious.'

'James evidently didn't think so.'

She sighed. It was James again. Something had compelled him to revisit the cylinder; he had said as much, and that something had almost certainly been the cylinder. Here was a danger indeed. If it worked on people's minds like that, then it was more dangerous than a bomb. At least a bomb could be defused or otherwise disposed of; with this they could do nothing. She remembered the girl in her dream and wondered if she might have suffered the same fate. Had she been a kind of human sacrifice, or had the outcome been entirely different? In James's case, time would tell.

'I wonder what he will be like when he recovers – *if* he recovers,' she said.

'He probably will recover; they say his life is not in danger. What do you mean?'

'I don't quite know, but I have a feeling that he may be undergoing some kind of metamorphosis, rather like a chrysalis. If this is the case, then what he will be like when he emerges?'

'That's an odd thought. What brought that on?'

'It's just a suspicion. It sounds silly I know, but I have a feeling that something is about to happen.'

152

'Concerning James, you mean?'

'Yes. I think we could be entering a new phase in this story.'

John pondered this idea. He was now familiar enough with these occasional spontaneous and outwardly irrational thoughts to be unsurprised by them. In any other circumstances he would have dismissed them as nonsense, but normal circumstances had been suspended and rationality stood on its head. If she was right and James really was undergoing some kind of metamorphosis, then it would be anyone's guess as to what would happen when he recovered. This thought worried him. If anything was likely to blow the gaff on the cylinder, it would be a new and transformed James. Even if he said nothing about it, the change, in whatever form it might take, would in all probability be noticeable and likely to draw attention to his contact with it. That alone would arouse suspicion.

He swore under his breath. 'This is not the time for further complications.'

'I think we should be ready for them. The way things look at the moment, anything might happen.'

'If it does it'll scupper the project; you know that, don't you.'

'Yes, and I wish none of this had happened. However, it has happened and now we must try and make the best of it.'

'Make the best of a bad job, you mean.'

'Think of it as a salvage operation.'

He was already thinking of it as such and he told her so as he listlessly stirred his coffee and turned his attention back to the scene of everyday life outside the café. He knew that they ought to be joining the others on the dig, but thinking of it as just a salvage operation gave him a sense of futility to which he was unaccustomed. He tried to shake this feeling off with the thought that they had already accomplished a lot and had made some astonishing discoveries, not the least of which was a highly developed culture that was millennia ahead of its time. That in itself was something that would shake to its foundations the received knowledge of his fellow academics. If nothing else had been discovered, the mysterious and still unidentified mechanism would be proof positive that certain Stone Age people were far more highly developed than the hairy cavemen that popular imagination still supposed them to be. This thought lifted his spirits and helped to return to him his sense of purpose.

'Damn it,' he said suddenly, fighting off the bout of gloom that had descended over him. 'I am not prepared to see it turned into a mere salvage operation. There is still important work to do; we are making some invaluable discoveries with the prospect of more to come and I will not see the project abandoned without a fight.'

She smiled, relieved to be off the emotional rollercoaster, if only for a time, and glad that his mood had become positive again. She knew that her words had depressed him; she had read it in his face and she felt bad about that. She had not intended to affect his thoughts in such a negative way; just to prepare him for the worst that might happen. Now he was fighting back.

'Good on you, Tiger,' she said. 'Let's get back and see how they're getting on without us. There's work to do.'

34

The rest of the day passed without incident. The newly discovered bone fragments were mostly identifiable as animal bones, although what manner of animal was an open question. Associated with these were shards of broken earthenware and these represented a significant discovery. Their presence was another anachronism since Stone Age pottery from this era had been hitherto unknown. Together with the mechanism, this discovery added further value to the project. From this evidence they deduced that this particular spot might have been a rubbish dump or midden. All manner of bone fragments were found, differing in size and they guessed that these were probably the detritus of many different meals of different kinds of animal. Once more, the lab would decide what kind of bones these were. As far as they could see, there were no human bones amongst this assortment.

Bernard decided that the hasp and staple from the cabin door had been damaged beyond hope and duly drove back to town to buy a replacement set, plus other bits he thought he might need for the job. When he returned, he had bought an additional padlock and an extra strong hasp and staple.

'Right,' he said when he had finished fixing these to the door. 'Now try to break into it!' He snapped both padlocks shut and gave the door a playful kick. 'It won't be so easy next time.'

The others looked on approvingly and even gave him a ripple of applause, relieved that the cylinder had, at least for now been securely incarcerated.

Everyone was in a light-hearted mood as they finished a successful day's work and returned to town for the evening; all except Barbara who was still worried about a number of things, not the least of which was James. She understood the team's euphoric mood; their relief at having achieved a good day's work without any disruption and having rendered the cylinder harmless, but she could not entirely share in their relief.

She felt that something was about to happen. It was nothing tangible and had little to do with her earlier fears concerning the likelihood of police involvement – she could deal with that when or if it came – no, it was something else; something that she could not adequately define. It was more of an intuitive and serious doubt that the situation had been even temporarily resolved. She remembered her words to John that morning when she had expressed her feeling that the story was about to enter a new phase. She wondered where this idea had come from and why she had said it. It was completely without substance. There was not one scrap of evidence to support such an idea and yet she had said it. What was more; she had said it without having first thought it through. This was not the act of an educated woman. It was as if she had been uttering a hitherto unspoken fear. She examined the possibility of the thought having been implanted into her, either by the cylinder or the unconscious James. Neither of these seemed likely, but then, the idea of dreams of a distant past being implanted by the cylinder had at first seemed so unlikely as to appear ludicrous, and yet it had happened and was still happening. Even if the dreams had become less frequent, they still came from time to time as did other unsubstantiated thoughts and ideas. This was another such thought.

She scribbled it down on her notepad and turned her attention back to the group. They were sitting around their accustomed table in the hotel bar and the feeling of relief at having returned to some semblance of normality was tangible. Chris was in a particularly buoyant mood since John had promptly kept his promise and given him a hundred pounds for having had the brilliant idea of deactivating the cylinder in such an ingenious and simple way. Thanks to his makeshift idea, the problem of the cylinder had been resolved, if only temporarily.

John was in a less buoyant mood. The cylinder still dominated his thoughts and, despite his having rewarded Chris's ingenuity, he shared Barbara's sense of foreboding. The cylinder had only been suppressed; it had not gone away and it was not going to go away just because they had wrapped it up in a roll of chicken wire. It would remain until some means could be found either to effectively deal with it and render it safe once and for all, or else have it removed, assuming that such a means could ever be found. Meanwhile, it was still very much alive and a potential threat to all concerned for as long as it remained on the site. He was resigned to the thought that eventually someone, the Government if necessary, would have to be brought in to deal with it, but that would have to be a problem for later. He was not going to call anyone in until the project was finished, and that was still some way off. For now, it was to remain where it was: a constant caged threat in the background. He was not happy with this situation, but there was little he could do about it other than bring the project to an abrupt halt as others came in to investigate it.

He considered Barbara's strange comment that the story was about to enter a new phase. What the hell did that mean and where had she got such an idea from? Up to here there was not a scrap of evidence to support her statement, apart from James of course, but he was effectively out of the game, at least for now. What would happen when he recovered was an open question. She had used the analogy of a chrysalis metamorphosing into a different creature; the imago emerging from the larval stage – a new life – a new James – now there was a thought. He had never much liked the man for reasons he could not exactly define. Probably he considered him to be an intruder who had come in late, knowing nothing and ready to sort things out without a thought for the background story, much less the nature of the beast that he was to deal with. Well, he was paying for that now. Since then, his attitude had softened towards the unfortunate young man but, even though he had been forced by circumstance to include him as an honorary member of the team, he still saw him as an interloper. Despite this, he felt a certain responsibility for James's wellbeing, the same as he felt responsibility for the others. After all, he was responsible for everyone on the project. That was the nature of his job as team leader. True, he could not be blamed for James's irresponsible and compulsive action, but when questions were asked – and it was likely that questions would be asked – he would be expected to supply the answers. Well, he would cross that bridge when he came to it. Meanwhile, James was in hospital, turning into God-knows-what if he was to believe Barbara's extraordinary theory of metamorphosis. This was not the time for levity.

'John… John.'

He interrupted his reverie. Barbara was leaning across the table, addressing him.

'It's time for bed. You look tired.'

'I think I am tired,' he said. 'It's been a long day.'

Upstairs in their room they undressed and got into bed. For a long time they lay there in silence, each with their own thoughts. Both were preoccupied with the prospect of seeing James in the morning. This was going to be a tense time, particularly for Barbara who despite everything still felt responsible for his present condition. She knew that this sense of guilt was unfounded and yet she still blamed herself for having invited him to investigate the cylinder in the first place. She tried to discount the thought. But for so many things, so many other things might never have happened. Had the Titanic sailed an hour later, it would in all probability have crossed the Atlantic without incident. Against that, no one had actually placed the iceberg in its path, so that particular analogy was invalid. She tried to find another one: Abraham Lincoln having a migraine and missing the theatre that night... so many possibilities, so many variables; the list was endless and it did not work. Nothing matched this particular case.

John viewed it differently. In his opinion it was entirely James's own fault and no one else was in any way to blame for his present condition, but then he had not invited him to look at the cylinder. He did not fear for James's chance of surviving whatever it was that had laid him low. The doctor had said that he was not in mortal danger and consequently he was not concerned about the possibility of James dying. He thought of the transformation of an insect from larva to pupa, when all the former body's organs dissolve and reform themselves to present the perfect insect. It was a marvel of Nature and he wondered what kind of marvel James might present when he emerged from his mental pupation. This thought was disturbing, but then, it could be wrong. It was only Barbara's theory based on what was after all a hunch, and yet there was something about it that sounded right. Just why it sounded right he was not sure, but it did, and this was what disturbed him. None of this would stand up to analysis of course, and here was a rather nasty paradox. He had been trained to deal in hard facts and here he was being forced to take into account what amounted to little more than a gut feeling. It was atavistic. It was wrong, yet it could not be discounted.

He put his hands behind his head and stared at the ceiling.

Barbara moved beside him. 'Finding it hard to sleep again?'

'Yes.'

'Me too. I just can't shut my mind off.'

'You're thinking about James, aren't you?'

'Yes.'

He put his arm around her shoulders. 'You shouldn't worry. He's in safe hands.' He was aware as he spoke just how empty these words sounded. He had wanted to sound reassuring. Instead, what he heard sounded like a bloodless platitude. He groaned inwardly, trying to think of something that might sound less hollow and more reassuring. 'I'm sorry,' he said after an uncomfortable pause. 'That didn't work, did it?'

'No,' she replied. 'John, you can't make me feel better with words. Quite honestly, I don't know what will make me feel better.'

'I wish I could do something.'

She stroked his chest with a nervous hand. 'Just be here for me. That's the best you can do right now. You don't have to say anything.'

He continued to stare at the ceiling. He could feel a slight tremor in the small hand that stroked his chest and wished that he could do something that would take her mind off James, the cylinder and all, if only for the remainder of the night.

He looked at the clock. Ten thirty-seven. He had thought it was later than that, but they had gone to bed early, having felt tired and then, once in bed the tiredness had gone and the concerns of the day had taken over. This was now becoming a familiar pattern. The next thing to come would be the nightly fear of a recurrence of the nightmares. Often at this point they made love. It helped them to relax and so induce sleep. This was more than mere comfort sex, although as such it usually worked. It may have started as such, but it had now become a lot more meaningful than that, for a strong bond had formed between them; a bond that had been forged long before they ever slept together. Since then, they had shared so much in their nights together that this bond had strengthened to go far beyond the mere need for physical contact. Their minds had, sometimes literally, come together. They had even shared the same dreams, although this might have been by way of the cylinder's dubious agency rather than by some kind of lovers' telepathic link.

Her fingers moved lower and stroked his stomach, tracing little circles on his skin. She rested her head on his chest and listened to his heartbeat. 'I like being with you,' she said. 'You're sometimes grumpy but always reassuring, like a big, growly teddy bear.'

He smiled at this and put his arms around her.

She kissed his left nipple, causing him to shudder; then she looked into his eyes. 'You're so good to me and I don't deserve it.'

'Yes you do, and never say that again. I know no one more deserving than you. You're a beautiful person and that is your trouble. You care too much.'

She stopped stroking him. 'How can you care too much?' Despite the slight edge to her voice he could feel that she was beginning to relax.

He searched for an answer but could not find one.

To his relief, she did not pursue the question. Instead, she kissed his nipple again, causing him to take a sharp intake of breath as a wave of pleasure surged through him.

'You like that, don't you,' she said.

'Yes, I like it. Do it again.'

She did it again and he arched his back, holding her closer. He slowly ran his fingers up and down her back, touching each vertebra from the nape of her neck to the base of her spine, as if counting. She slipped her hand between his thighs and fondled his balls. He resisted a strong urge to enter her body then and there. Instead, he kissed and stroked her fine hair, breathing its fresh, honey-like scent. He wanted this to last.

Their worries shrank into the background as they touched and traced the contours and outlines of skin, feeling the muscles beneath the skin and learning the hidden mysteries of each other's body. Fingers and lips sought and relished the secret intimacies of taste and smell, celebrating the body's natural secretions and scents and the small, deep pains and fires that bring so much pleasure to the senses. They knew that in this they were hiding, if only for now, from their personal demons. These demons would not go away; they would still be there, waiting, but at least for now they could be kept at bay by these fierce and uninhibited naked pleasures; the pleasures of all the senses kept under control by the warm, overwhelming weight of breasts and limbs as they stroked, probed and explored each other with no part of the body denied.

Eventually, she arose and sat astride him. Gentle fingers guided his penis into her and they made love. He resisted the instinct to ejaculate for as long as he could, but after what was probably only a matter of minutes, he could delay his climax no longer and he surrendered to it. She seized his hands and pressed them to her breasts, tipped her head back and groaned aloud as she felt the springing of his seed inside her.

Finally they slept, at peace in each other's arms. Their protracted lovemaking on top of the day's events had exhausted both of them, but it had had the desired effect and, as they drifted into sleep he recalled her final drowsy words whispered in his ear with a gentle kiss: 'I love you. I shall always love you.'

35

Around James, things were moving again. He was oblivious of this as he slept, dreamless in his now dissolving chamber. The things that had fused around him to form this chamber were now separating and once more becoming discrete organisms, slowly moving and reforming into new shapes. Fine threads darted between them as signals were exchanged and he was gently lowered to the soft ground, or whatever surface passed for it. The amorphous creature that had provided him with the bunk bed on which he slept now divided into four individuals, three of which began to drift with the others. The fourth flattened itself and, very slowly, covered his reclining form like a blanket. He could sleep on while all around him a great hall was forming as more shapes joined the others and fused together again. Others remained discrete and moved around him, ghostly in their silence. Slowly, their shape and colour changed as they developed heads and limbs and became bipedal, like people.

In the centre of the hall, something bulged from the floor, slowly growing like a large fungus. It continued to grow upward as if extruded from some invisible pore beneath it. Finally, the pore closed and the extrusion lay on its side.

It was a cylinder.

36

In the morning, John drove Barbara to the hospital while Bernard went to the site with Lynda and Chris. But for this division of duty it might have been a normal day.

Sitting beside John in the Land Rover, Barbara stared straight ahead, her face expressionless. He could well guess what was going through her mind as he drove, going through the gear changes automatically, his eyes fixed upon the road. He too was preoccupied with the prospect of seeing James and he wondered what reaction Barbara's words would produce when she spoke to him again. Well, they would find out when they got there.

'Thanks for last night,' she said, finally breaking the silence between them.

John smiled but said nothing. Words were unnecessary. What had happened last night had happened of its own accord. There was no need to thank him for it. Indeed, he was mildly surprised that she had mentioned it at all. They had needed each other and, quite naturally, had sought mutual comfort in each other's body, fulfilling a need that was both physical and psychological.

'I really needed your love last night,' she continued. The worries… you know…'

'Yes, I know. I just hope it helped you to relax.'

'Did it show?'

'You were shaking.'

'Was I?' She paused. She had not realised that her nervous tension had been so visible at the time. 'Anyway, thanks.' She paused again and then continued: 'I really do need you. You put me at my ease when the fears come.'

'And you do the same for me.'

'We really do need each other, don't we?' She laughed. 'I never thought that this would ever happen to me. We always used to be so independent. Now look at us!'

'You're beautiful,' he said.

Their talk continued in this vein, becoming more intimate in the privacy of the car until the hospital came into view. They fell silent again. Words were of no more use to them here. John knew that whatever happened in the next hour would be out of his hands.

He parked the Land Rover and they made their way to the main entrance, thence to the ward where James lay. Here, they introduced themselves to the ward sister whom they had not seen before but who seemed to be expecting them.

'Would you mind waiting for the doctor?' she said, looking at a handwritten note on the desk in front of her.

Barbara stared at her, her face pale.

The sister flashed a reassuring smile. 'He's OK, don't worry. The doctor simply wants to see if he responds to your voice. I'll just page him for you.'

They sat down and waited. Eventually, the doctor whom they had seen the previous day arrived and, after apologising for having kept them waiting, he ushered them to where James lay, still wired to the monitor which continued to trace its numerous wave patterns across the screen. The EEG machine had been switched off. Barbara noticed with some unease that he had been put on a drip feed. She had always associated these things with serious illness, even though she reasoned that it was not possible to feed him by any other means while he remained unconscious.

'Here he is,' the doctor said in a hushed voice. 'He is much the same as when you saw him yesterday. No change, I'm afraid.'

'Still no clue as to what might be the matter with him?' John said.

The doctor shook his head and switched the EEG machine on. The paper chart started to scroll slowly across the platen. 'OK, you can talk to him now.'

Barbara moved to the bedside and gently touched James's forehead. 'Hello James,' she said. 'We've come to see you again.'

There was no reaction.

She looked at John and the doctor who nodded his approval.

'James, can you hear me? We've come to see you.' She continued like this for some time while the doctor watched the traces

164

on the EEG. Still there was no reaction; then there was. One of the pens twitched and started to move erratically, and then another pen began to jerk.

'Something's happening,' John observed.

The doctor looked at the chart and then at Barbara who faltered for a moment before continuing. It was hard for her to think of things to say to someone who appeared not to hear a word of what was being said, but something was registering, the instruments agreed that, so she kept on talking about anything that came into her head: anecdotes about their time together at university when they were undergraduates, the drinking parties, the professors and lecturers, fellow students – anything, in fact. All the time the pens showed activity.

John looked at the doctor. 'What do you think?'

'I think there's no doubt about it. He's responding to her voice.'

They continued to watch the moving chart while Barbara talked and all the time the pens registered some sort of brain activity, though no one could even guess what might be going on in his mind. His face showed no movement, not even the flicker of an eyelid to indicate that he was hearing anything. Still she continued to talk to him until, all topics exhausted for the time being, she quietly concluded the one sided conversation with a softly spoken goodbye.

She stood up and joined the two men standing by the EEG machine. 'I think that's all we can do for now,' she said.

'I would appreciate it if you could come in again tomorrow,' the doctor said. 'I'm in little doubt now that he really is responding to your voice. Meanwhile, we shall continue to monitor him around the clock and we'll let you know as soon as there are any developments in his present condition. Oh, and thanks for coming in today.'

'We were coming anyway,' she said, surprised that he had thought fit to offer his thanks.

They left the hospital and got back into the Land Rover. For a while they sat in silence. John put the key in the ignition lock and, instead of turning it, he left it there. He felt that Barbara might like to talk to him about her feelings after having seen James, but she said nothing. He started the engine.

'Coffee,' he said.

They drove back into town.

They sat at the same café table as they had done the day before. For a long time neither spoke, each alone with their thoughts. Barbara slowly stirred her coffee and tried to think of what could possibly have happened to James, while John stared out of the window, for once not taking in the scene outside. His mind was on James too, but in a different way.

Barbara still felt some guilt at having invited him to examine the cylinder, although this feeling was now diminishing as she began to accept that she was not entirely to blame. James had taken fool risks with it and was now paying the price for his carelessness. True, the cylinder had to a great extent compelled him to act in such a way, but he should have realised the inherent danger of prolonged contact with it. After all, they had quickly understood the risks involved with such close contact as soon as they had first felt its effects. He had chosen to ignore that warning.

She also accepted now that he was not in grave danger and would sooner or later emerge from his coma, but what would he be like when he did come round? She was becoming increasingly convinced that he was undergoing some kind of metamorphosis and this thought disturbed her. Whatever the outcome, she somehow knew that he would be a very different person when he woke up. She had no idea why she felt this, she just did and that was all. She decided to voice this feeling to John. She leaned forward and gave a little toss of her head as if to clear it.

'I wonder what will happen when he comes round.'

John looked up, surprised.

'James, I mean. I still think he's going through some kind of change.'

'We shall have to wait and see. So you don't think he's in danger any more?'

'No, I don't think he's in danger, but I have this feeling... I can't explain it, it's as if he is trying to communicate something to me; something important. The trouble is I'm not sure just what it is he's trying to say.'

He tried to make sense of this. Then he remembered the dream that she had imparted to him of a human figure wandering in a strange landscape and surrounded by curious biomorphic shapes that drifted around him like amoebae. This had been shortly after James's collapse, and he wondered if there really was some kind of telepathic link between them. In normal circumstances he would have laughed

166

such a cockamamie idea to scorn, but recent events had forced him to keep a more open mind on the subject. It could still have been a crazy dream, of course. Anything was possible.

'Do you mean telepathy?' he asked.

'Something like that. It's a tenuous link, you understand, but I sometimes get the feeling that he is trying to reach me – I can't explain it.'

He decided to take this seriously. 'Perhaps you should not ignore these feelings. God, I can't believe I'm saying this, but I'm prepared to believe that something paranormal is going on here. Tell me more.'

'There's little else to tell you at the moment.' She looked at him intently. 'You really believe me, don't you?'

'I believe you.'

She made no reply to this, but relief showed on her face. Secretly, she had feared that he might laugh at such an outwardly screwball idea. Instead, he had taken her thoughts seriously. Perhaps this should not have been surprising after all that had happened since the cylinder's discovery. After all, most of their previously held beliefs had been overturned by recent events. Still, she felt relieved that he had listened and not pooh-poohed the very idea of such a thing.

She reached across the table and took his hands in hers. 'Thanks.'

'Thanks? What for?'

She smiled. 'Thanks for listening to me.'

'It's what I'm here for.' He looked at her with something like tenderness. 'We've been through a lot together recently and if I can't listen to your ideas and take them on board, then I'm in the wrong job. Never be afraid to tell me your thoughts, no matter how daft they might sound. I won't laugh.'

'There was a time when you would have done.'

'That was before the cylinder.'

37

What's happened? Things have changed and I didn't notice. I must have slept while it was happening, but what has changed? My mind is blank.

Someone was here again – I heard a voice. I wish I could remember what was said but I can't. It's my head, you see; it's not quite right at the moment... feels like it's been shot through with something; a bullet perhaps, but no, it's intact as far as I can tell; no holes or anything like that, no blood or leaking brains – I'm quite intact or at least I think I am so where am I then? I've asked this question before without getting an answer and I don't know what's going on except that I'm here for a reason, but how do I know that? Something tells me so, that's how I know, but what? What is it that tells me so? There only seems to be me here. Maybe that's why I feel so woozy in the head; too much time alone, that's it. I'm going crazy for lack of company. It's supposed to happen to prisoners that have spent too much time in solitary but I'm not a prisoner, I'm here for a purpose whatever that purpose may be. I suppose I shall find out in due course. It is after all one of the great philosophical questions: why are we here? Why indeed!

Do you hear that? Why am I here?

There's something funny about the sound here – it's dead. Hello? No one can hear me and yet there are people or things that look like people. I wonder how I failed to notice. Look at them. They're walking around and yet they don't seem to be aware of my existence. It's as if I don't exist. Do I exist? Am I here?

You see, they drift on by without so much as a glance in my direction but then why should they look at me? What makes me so special that they should stop to look at me? Am I not one of them? Perhaps if I stand up I might join them, maybe challenge someone to tell me what I want to know. Now there's a thought. There's something odd about them, though – not quite right – what is it? They're put together like people: two arms, two legs equipped with feet that walk; hands that move at their sides and heads with eyes that look ahead. Maybe that's it: they look straight ahead – not to the left or right – not at me. There's something wrong with that. People don't do that, do they?

Hey, I'm over here!

It's as if they're all deaf; just so many articulated tailor's dummies or computer generated images that never quite look like real people. Well, they don't fool me. I've sussed them. Amoebae, that's what they are; overblown protoplasmic blobs. Why didn't I see that straight away? OK, they look like people but they are not complete – not all there in fact. Something's missing. That other one was real though; speaking things I couldn't understand but could appreciate even if it meant nothing to me. I feel as if I know her, but who is she? My mind has blotted it out. She actually touched me which is more than these blob-things could ever do, at least in their present state. That's why I believe she was real. She was complete even though I don't remember seeing her. Still I know she was here. She's not here now, though. I wonder if she was here at all. I can't remember, in fact I don't remember having been here before and yet it looks familiar somehow.

I wonder if she'll come back. I miss her in an odd sort of way. There's a link here that I can't quite reach; something in the background that makes me look, but when I look I see nothing. Perhaps there is nothing, just a vivid dream that seems so real at the time that it stays with you long after you wake up to a different reality. That's most probably what it is. After all, nothing should surprise me in a place like this.

Hey, you dummies, can't you see me?

Evidently not. They're just wandering around aimlessly. Why can't they see me; don't they know I'm here? Something's wrong with them. They're like robots – perhaps they *are* robots. They don't look mechanical, though. They're more like zombies. They're not wearing any clothes, but neither am I so we're even there. I must get up and walk with them. Perhaps this will bring me up to their eye level and they will see me. This blanket is soft and warm. I don't remember it before but here it is, covering me with its smooth texture; not like any blanket I have ever had before, but why should that surprise me? It's odd that nothing ever surprises me here. It's strange and at the same time it's familiar as if I have lived here all my life. Perhaps I have lived here all my life. No. There was another life before this. I don't remember it too well, in fact I don't remember it at all but I know that there was something before my life here. All the same, I feel as if I have always been here. Why won't they look at me?

Anyway, get up. This lying around will never do. It all seems too easy. That's because I have no weight so there's no effort involved. There. Now I'm on their level.

They still don't see me but it doesn't matter now. Why should I care if they see me or not? They are all very similar to look at and they appear to be asexual. There's nothing to distinguish them as men and women, in fact I don't know what they are. They're only half formed, I see it now; they're incomplete. They don't have navels or nipples and their faces are not clearly defined. Their bodies all look the same, without genitals or even pubic hair. That's what's odd about them. I don't know how I failed to notice that.

This floor – it's like Freemason's Hall with its black and white tiles and classical pillars that I can't see the top of and the cylinder taking pride of place in the middle... now what's that doing here and why does it look so familiar? I think there was one like it before I was here – in that other life – the one I don't remember and yet I do remember a cylinder like that one, but it was smaller, I think, or was it the same? Come on, brain, do your stuff and think. It's all a muddle with bits stuck anywhere and no order; that's what makes it so difficult to put things together logically, I can see that. Things have to be sorted but that takes time, same as it will take time to complete these people. That doesn't figure in a place without time, but then, perhaps it does. Remember the book leaf theory. If it takes a million years it will still take no time at all. That might be an oversimplification but it'll do for now.

Perhaps these people are waiting to be born. I assume they can see because they don't collide or bump into things, but nothing registers yet. They are incomplete, that's why; the same as I am incomplete. But things are slowly coming together for me and for them and soon the time will come for us to be born. What will happen then? Will it be the beginning or the end? *In my beginning is my end...* where did that thought come from? Something from that other life, perhaps. I don't think I could have made it up, not with my head in its present state. It sounds like poetry – I wish I could remember but it will not come. Never mind, I shall remember it in time, whenever
170

that time comes, but I have time. That's one thing that I have plenty of. I like that.

That cylinder must be here for me. Why else would it be here? Not for these half-formed creatures, that's for sure. They don't even know it's here so it must be for me. I long to touch it but something's preventing me from doing so. I don't even know how big it is. When I look it is huge and then it becomes tiny in the same instant. That doesn't make sense but neither does anything else here. I should be able to estimate its size by measuring it against the tiles, but I can't. That's something else that's odd about this place. Even the tiles don't conform to normal physical laws. They at least should be constant, but they're not. Perhaps it is me that varies in size, or else it is me and everything else around me. Phew! Try calculating that one.

This is too disorientating. I can cope with things being constant, but where nothing is fixed I find my head spinning. I am not equipped to handle it, you see. I come from some place where things are quantifiable, not big and small at the same time. I'd better lie down again before I fall down. I haven't experienced this before. That's better. I suppose I ought to expect this effect where there are so many different dimensions. I am conditioned to living with – how many; three, I think. It's obvious that here there are many more – I don't know how many.

These walking dummies seem to be more or less constant in relation to my size, even if they're still only half formed. I wonder if they will ever learn to speak.

38

The group sat around the table in the bar that evening, satisfied with another productive day's work unhindered by the cylinder or its influence. Things were going normally again and John felt particularly pleased with the day's work, during which a number of significant finds had been made, including a finely crafted brooch that appeared to have been carved from bone or something similar and a red oxide stain that might have been the remains of a dagger. It was scarcely surprising that the site had originally been presumed to be an Iron Age settlement. From the outset, everything had indicated this to be the case. An aerial photograph had shown what appeared to be the worn down remains of ancient earthworks and it was this that had drawn attention to the site in the first place. From this superficial evidence the site had been assumed to be a fairly typical Iron Age hill fort. No one would ever have guessed its true age.

Their talk was centred on their recent discoveries and for once the cylinder did not get a mention. It was as if things were getting back to normal again, but this was an illusion. Little was normal where this project was concerned. The site was out of time and there was little doubt now that it had met with a violent and bloody end, instantly sending the world straight back to the Stone Age. The whole episode had been an aberration – a hiccup in time. At the heart of this, of course, was the cylinder. Everything revolved around it; a cult had grown up around it, it had tasted the blood of innocent girls sacrificed to its supposedly divine power, it had initiated others into its inner mysteries and heard the chanting of its devotees. Finally, it had witnessed the destruction of the culture that it had created. It had controlled everything from beginning to end and now it threatened to do the same thing to those who had awakened it after its age-long sleep.

Bernard went to the bar to get himself a drink. He was in a good mood and glad that things were getting back to some semblance of normality. It was while he was at the bar that a man approached and began to engage him in conversation.

'What do you reckon to the beer here?'

Bernard looked at his full pint and at the stranger's half. 'It's not bad. At least they know how to look after it, which is more than I can say for the Five Bells down the road. If it's not keg or lager they're clueless.'

The man laughed. 'I take it you're a real ale man.'

'Bloody right I am. I won't drink anything else if I can help it.'

'Me too.' He took a sip from his half pint. 'Are you staying here?'

Bernard nodded. 'Yeah.'

'Here on business, I suppose.'

'In a manner of speaking,' he said. Somewhere inside him a mental alarm bell rang. He was not at all sure that he trusted this stranger, as affable as he appeared to be. He was certainly not going to entrust him with any information concerning the nature of his work and he decided to be as non-committal as possible.

The man chuckled. 'I suppose everyone staying here is on business. There's not much in this backwater to attract the tourists, is there?'

'Not a lot.' He took a drink and edged away from the bar. 'Sorry, but I must rejoin the others or they'll think I've deserted them.'

'You're here with friends, are you?'

'Colleagues,' he corrected him.

'OK.' The stranger turned back to the bar and Bernard returned to the table.

'I see you've made a new friend,' John said with a smile.

Bernard made a wry face. 'I wouldn't say that exactly.'

'Who is he?'

'I don't know.' He leaned forward and lowered his voice. 'Quite honestly, I get the feeling he isn't quite kosher.'

'What do you mean?'

'I'm not sure, call me suspicious if you like, but I think he was trying to pump me for something – information, perhaps.'

'Concerning the dig?'

'Not exactly, but I think he was working up to it.'

John looked in the direction of the stranger at the bar and rubbed his chin. 'Hmm, I think we ought to watch out for that one. You didn't tell him anything, did you?'

Bernard recoiled at this. 'Of course not.'

'I think he's watching us in the mirror.' He looked away from the bar and turned his attention back to the table, trying to look as casual as possible. 'Don't look.'

Bernard thought for a moment and then he said: 'Of course, he could be perfectly innocent and just trying to make conversation. I'm only assuming that he might be snooping. Perhaps I'm getting paranoid.'

'Well, we shall watch him for now.'

Barbara looked at the stranger at the bar, which was easier for her since she was already facing him. In this position with her head slightly turned away she did not appear to be watching him. She decided it was time to voice her earlier thoughts concerning James's apparent disappearance.

The others listened to her with increasing concern. The possibility of police involvement was a very real one given the sensitive nature of James's work in the aerospace industry. It was probable that much of what he did would be connected in some way with defence, so his apparent disappearance would be likely to trigger a nationwide search, particularly if that disappearance was thought to be a matter of national security.

'Fuck it,' John mumbled. 'I should have thought of that.'

'There's no need to panic,' she said. 'If anyone does come looking for him we tell them the simple truth that James has collapsed and is in hospital, that's all. We don't have to tell them the whole story, do we? For one thing they'd never believe it and anyway, what is it to them? They're only interested in finding a missing person, not some funny old cylinder that has been buried in the dirt for thousands of years.'

Bernard turned to him. 'She's right. If they come looking for him, and I accentuate the *if*, then that is all we need to worry about. As far as they're concerned, the cylinder is irrelevant.'

'But it isn't irrelevant,' John protested. 'It is instrumental in causing his disappearance and his present condition. How long before they find that out?'

'We'll worry about that if and when it happens,' Bernard said. 'Hopefully, by that time the matter will be out of our hands anyway, so let's be calm about it. This is not the time to panic.'

'Right,' Barbara said. 'So if anybody does ask, we tell them all they need to know. We don't have to say anything about the cylinder or even the project. Anyway, I think he's leaving.' She watched as the man left the bar. 'OK, he's gone.' She also noticed that as he left he paused by the door and looked in the direction the group, but she decided not to mention this.

John sat back in his chair, somewhat relieved by the stranger's departure. It seemed as if he was the only one to feel any sense of panic at the prospect of being questioned by the police. This, given his other concerns, was perhaps a natural reaction since he felt responsible for the future of the project and was terrified of the risk of the cylinder's existence becoming known before he was ready to make it known. Now that the man was gone he could relax. He smiled to himself. It was good to have such a loyal and clear-thinking team.

Detective Sergeant George Gallagher of the Special Branch sat across the desk from his boss, Inspector Dennis Fox. 'I've found them,' he said. 'They're sitting in the bar at the White Hart. I think they might be staying there.'

The inspector raised his eyebrows. 'Did you speak to any of them?'

'I spoke to one of them, but only briefly. He seemed a bit cagey to me.'

'Well, we know where Masters is. What I want to know is why he disappeared and how he came to be in hospital.'

'You think they have something to do with it?' Gallagher sounded surprised.

'I wouldn't dismiss the thought. You heard what the chief told us; if someone like that vanishes without explanation and then turns up in a coma right out in the sticks, it stands to reason that something dodgy might be going on.'

'They looked harmless enough to me.'

'So might Osama Bin Laden. That doesn't mean a thing.'

'But the hospital told us that the woman and one of the men brought him in. They left their names. Why would they do that if they had anything to hide?'

Look, they are most probably innocent. All I want to establish is a connection between him and these archaeologists or whatever they are. We'll bring them in for questioning just to clear matters up. Get your coat.'

Barbara yawned and looked at her watch. 'I think I'll go up to our room. I want to get on with a bit of work before bed. Don't be late.'

'Right.' John looked at his nearly full pint. 'I'll be up later.'

She stood up and headed towards the door to the reception area as two men entered the bar and without hesitating, made straight for her.

'Doctor Barbara Sedgwick?'

She turned to face the speaker and immediately recognised the man who had spoken to Bernard. 'Yes,' she said cautiously.

The man produced an ID card. 'I'm Detective Sergeant Gallagher, Special Branch. I wonder if you would mind answering a few questions.'

'Concerning…? She looked at the two men. Gallagher was a stocky man with short cropped hair and a smart suit. His companion was the taller of the two and also smartly dressed. Both looked like hard cases.

'I understand you know a man by the name of James Masters. We are currently making enquiries concerning his disappearance and we believe you can help us.'

She thought quickly. There was no point in trying to duck the issue. 'I'll do what I can.' She said. 'He's currently in hospital. We don't know what's wrong with him.'

The taller man spoke. 'Would you mind accompanying us to the station? We won't detain you long.'

John came over. 'What's the matter?'

The taller man turned to face him. 'And you are…?'

'John Black. This woman is a colleague of mine. Now, what seems to be the trouble?'

'I'm Detective Inspector Dennis Fox and this is Detective Sergeant George Gallagher, Special Branch. We are making enquiries concerning the disappearance of James Masters. We would like you to help us with our enquiries.'

John scowled. 'Don't you know what time it is?'

'I'm sorry sir, but we would like to clear matters up as soon as possible. We shall try not to detain you too long.'

'I bloody hope not. We have to get up in the morning. We were about to go to bed.'

'I'm sorry sir, but this is important.' Fox insisted.

'So is sleep.'

Barbara touched his arm. 'We'd better do as they say.'

'Excuse me,' John said to the two detectives and went over to where the others were still sitting. He touched Bernard on the shoulder. 'Sorry mate, but Barbara and I have to go to the police station with these two gentlemen. They're asking questions about James.'

Bernard recoiled. 'What?' He turned and saw Barbara with the two officers. 'Christ, that's all we need!'

The interview with Barbara did not take long. She told them all she knew about James while carefully avoiding all references to the cylinder in much the same way as she had done with the doctor at the hospital; in fact it was practically the same story. This seemed to satisfy the two detectives. Then it was John's turn. He faced Fox across the desk. Gallagher stood to one side.

'What is your connection with James Masters?' Fox began.

John shrugged. 'No connection; I barely know him. We brought him in to look at something that we found on the dig. We didn't know what it was made of and we decided that someone like him might be able to help us.'

'What led you to call for the assistance of an aerospace engineer?'

John recalled Barbara's story of the Saxon bracelet. 'We often call in experts to clear up a point. Barbara knew James from their days together at university and so we called him in to help us. He was available and he joined us for a day. He was more than qualified enough for what we needed.'

'Do you know that he has been absent from work for two weeks? His employer says he reported sick, and that was the last anyone heard of him until now.'

John swore inwardly and tried to think of an answer to this. 'He did come back. He said he wanted to take another look at the object in question. It was after this that we found him unconscious in his room.'

'Did he say anything about being off sick?'

John felt boxed into a corner. He sat back in the chair and tried to look as casual as he could manage. 'He did say he'd been feeling a bit grubby, but I thought he meant he just had a bit of a cold or some minor infection. None of us paid much attention to it, I'm afraid. Now I wish we had.'

'Hmm.' Fox doodled something on his notepad.

There was a brief silence during which John reflected on how it had gone so far. Not telling the whole truth was easier than he had dared to hope. He was not lying, just leaving out certain details; that was all.

'Do you know what happened to him?' Fox fixed his eyes on John's.

He shook his head. 'We found him unconscious in his room.'

'We?'

'Barbara and I. We had to get the hotel manager to open the door and we found him unconscious on the bed. It gave us a nasty turn, I can tell you.' He deliberately omitted any mention of Bernard's presence at the scene. The fewer people involved in this investigation the better, he reasoned. They did not comment on this, so it was likely that Barbara had done the same thing, at least he hoped that this might be the case.

'The manager was with you at the time?' Fox sounded surprised to hear this.

'Of course. How else do you think we got into the room? He had a master key.'

'Why did you not report this matter to the police?'

John was unprepared for this. He thought for a moment; then he said: 'I honestly don't know. It seemed more important at the time to get him to hospital as soon as possible. It was a shock finding him like that and we were all a bit frightened. We thought at first he might be dead. When we realised he was unconscious we called an ambulance and had him rushed to hospital. We didn't think to call the police.' He could feel himself sweating under his clothes.

'How did you find him?' Gallagher asked. He had been silent all this time.

'How do you mean?'

'I mean what condition was he in when you found him?' Were there any signs of violence – bruises, stuff like that?'

He shook his head. 'No. He was lying on the bed, that's all. He was naked and lying on his back as if he was sleeping. There were no signs of violence that we could see. He certainly wasn't cut or bruised.'

Fox casually tossed his pen down on the desk. 'OK, that'll be all for now. How long will you be staying in town?'

'I don't know. It all depends on how much work there is left to do.'

'Very well, Professor Black, we shall be in touch if we need to talk to you again.'

'I think I've told you all I know,' John insisted, noting as he did so that Fox had addressed him as Professor. He had not introduced himself using his title. It occurred to him from this that they might know more about him than they were letting on, unless of course Barbara had mentioned it in the course of her interview. All the same, he wondered what else they knew about him and the other team members. These were not ordinary coppers; they were Special Branch and probably linked with Military Intelligence. He would have to be careful.

He got up and headed for the door which Gallagher had obligingly opened for him. Gallagher accompanied him along the corridor to where Barbara sat waiting for him.
She got up as they approached.

'It's OK, we can go now,' he said to her.

They left the police station and headed back to the hotel. Barbara was the first to speak. 'Well, that wasn't too hard, was it?'

'I don't know,' he said. 'I don't think they're quite finished with us yet.'

'How did they know we knew James?' she asked.

'It was the hospital. They must have informed the police. Now Special Branch is involved and, if we don't watch it, we shall be up to our necks in the brown smelly stuff.'

180

'They're only interested in James though, aren't they? I mean, they're not likely to be interested in the cylinder. They don't even know about it.'

He hoped not.

Back at the police station, Gallagher rejoined Fox in the office after having escorted the interviewees to the door. 'Well,' he said. 'What do you think?'

Fox made a wry face. 'They seem to be genuine. I certainly don't think they've been up to any dirty work, they're too head-in-the-air for that.' He paused and drummed his fingers on the desk. He coughed and then he continued. 'I think tomorrow morning we shall visit the hospital and have a look at our friend Mister Masters. I would like to talk to that doctor and the hotel manager as well.'

Gallagher nodded. 'Do you think it would be of any use to take a look at this site of theirs?'

'Probably not, but it might not do us any harm to take a look.'

41

The next morning after breakfast, John drove Barbara to the hospital in what by now was becoming a routine. Both were tired, having found it difficult to sleep that night. Their interview with the Special Branch officers had confirmed Barbara's worst fears and, even though neither she nor he had given them any information regarding the cylinder, they both knew that their involvement with the police was not finished yet. John was particularly worried. Sooner or later those two would come snooping around the site and he mentally prepared himself for such an event. He contented himself with the thought that it would not be difficult to hide the cylinder from their prying eyes and in any case they would not be looking for it. There was no reason why they should. It had nothing to do with the case as far as they were concerned. It was secure inside the cabin but it would only be a matter of time before James eventually came round and then they would want to talk to him. They would be very interested to hear anything he might have to say about his recent involvement with the project. If he broached the topic of the cylinder then the secret would be out and that would be that.

Bernard, Lynda and Chris must have decided on an early start, for they had been absent at the breakfast table. Therefore John and Barbara were unable to tell them of the night's proceedings and give them a suitable briefing, should they in turn be interviewed.

In the hospital, they were joined by the doctor who was treating James and Barbara took her usual seat by his bedside. As on previous occasions, she talked to him about anything that came into her mind while John and the doctor watched the moving pens on the EEG machine. Sure enough, they began to wave erratically, indicating a degree of brain activity that had not been evident before she started talking. There was no doubt now that he was responding to her voice. The doctor noted this approvingly.

After about ten minutes she arose from the bedside and joined the two men standing by the machine. 'How is he?' she asked.

'See for yourself,' the doctor said. 'He is definitely responding to your voice. There's not much doubt about it now. Concerning his overall condition, there's little change, but he's stable and we no longer consider him to be in any real danger. We must wait for nature to take its course, but with luck he should regain consciousness sooner rather than later. I stress that it may still take some time, though.'

Barbara was relieved to hear this and she thanked the doctor for his trouble, then she turned her attention back to the EEG. The pens still scribbled their crazy lines, though by now they were beginning to return to their former quiescent level of activity.

A figure appeared in the corridor, saw them grouped around the machine and immediately withdrew. It was Detective Sergeant George Gallagher. He had been trained to maintain a low profile and he did not want them to know that he was pursuing his investigation as far as James's bedside. He found a convenient waiting room, picked up a magazine and began to read, keeping his back turned to the corridor. He could wait.

Back in town, John and Barbara sat at their usual table in the café, recounting their separate interviews with the Special Branch officers. Both were relieved to note that their accounts of the discovery of the unconscious James tallied in almost every detail with only minor variations, sufficient to be put down to the vagaries of memory. They had been too tired the night before to accurately compare notes, so this was a good time to do it. As John had hoped, Barbara had also omitted any mention of Bernard's involvement in the discovery of the comatose James in the hotel room. He was glad of this, since a single omission would have inevitably resulted in further questions. This to some extent put his mind at rest. The rest of the team were now less likely to be interviewed as a result, although it still remained a possibility.

The cylinder, they reasoned, should be easy to keep secret since the police would most probably show no interest in it, any more than they would be interested in any other object found on an archaeological dig. As far as they were likely to be concerned, it would be just another piece of ancient detritus of no more significance to their investigations than a hand axe; just a piece of irrelevant junk. The only reason for their presence was James and, since he was not

183

the victim of foul play or espionage, they should soon be eliminated from the enquiry, after which they could be left to continue their work in peace. This gradually eased John's anxiety concerning the possibility of the cylinder coming to their notice. The only hole in this theory was the possibility of James disclosing its effect on him when he came out of his coma. That would blow the whole thing wide open but by then, he hoped, the project would be over and the cylinder's discovery could be made known. It would then be someone else's problem.

This thought made John somewhat uneasy with himself. It was wrong to hope that James's illness would be a long one, at least long enough for them to complete the project and he wondered what his sense of responsibility for the project's security was doing to him. This was not a normal human reaction to another person's misfortune and he wondered what was happening to his innate humanity. His preoccupation with the project's security and the cylinder in particular was beginning to look like an obsession. He wanted to voice this personal doubt to Barbara but decided against it. It would have upset and probably angered her to know that he could take such a cavalier attitude towards the health of a friend of hers. Such anger would be entirely justifiable. In addition to this, he felt that he had burdened her enough with his troubles; therefore it was better for him to keep his thoughts on this matter private. Nonetheless, it worried him to be so apparently unfeeling towards the plight of a fellow human being. It was as if he was beginning to attach more importance to the cylinder than to human life. This was the very attitude that had ultimately led to the destruction of the society that had placed the cylinder above all else and he wondered if it was now beginning to affect him in a similar manner. He hoped not.

Their conversation ended and, with time pressing, they finished their coffee and left the café for the site. When they got there, they found the others in a state of excitement.

'Come and have a look at this,' Bernard said, leading the way to the freshest part of the dig. 'If this isn't a significant find, then I don't know what is.'

They went over to where Lynda squatted on her haunches, holding in both hands a finely crafted and elaborately patterned dagger. John looked at it. The steel, or whatever the blade was made of, was bright and there was not a trace of rust or corrosion, while the ornate hilt appeared to be made of the same material. It was decorated

184

overall with abstract patterns of an unknown style. The straight, double edged blade was about twenty five centimetres long and broad, tapering gradually to a sharp point. As a weapon it was ferocious, although its purpose may have been purely ceremonial. It looked too elaborate and expensive for a fighting or hunting knife. Earth still clung to it in places and filled the complicated patterns on the hilt. Otherwise, it looked nearly new.

'Where did you find this?' he asked.

'Just down here,' Lynda said, pointing to the floor of the pit where the dagger's imprint was still visible in the earth. 'Isn't it amazing? It looks almost new, but it must be old. There's no sign of recent soil disturbance so I don't think it's a plant.'

'Look at this.' Bernard took the dagger and turned it over. 'Where have we seen this before?'

The flat of the blade had been engraved with a cartouche-like pattern, similar if not identical to the one that they had first noticed on the body of the cylinder. 'Wow,' Barbara breathed.

John looked at it closely. 'It looks brand new,' he said. 'What the hell can it be made of? These people had only just learned how to smelt iron.'

'They did have other metals,' Bernard pointed out. 'Remember that clock or whatever it was? That seemed to be made of brass or some kind of bronze. They knew all about metals.'

'Far more than we give them credit for, it seems,' Barbara said. 'I doubt if we could make a knife like this now. Just look at the workmanship; it's fantastic.'

John shook his head. 'It's beyond belief that they could produce a weapon like this, however clever they might have been. The British Museum will think it's a hoax when they see it. They'll never believe me.'

'They will when they've examined it,' Bernard said. 'I'm in little doubt that it's genuine. As Lynda pointed out, there's no sign of recent soil disturbance and, if it really is a hoax, how do you explain that pattern on the blade? Whoever planted it would have to have copied it directly from the cylinder, which means that they must have had access to it. It can't be a hoax.'

Barbara went to the Land Rover and returned with her briefcase and camera. She then set about photographing it from every angle; first, exactly where it was found, and then placed on the ground with a rule positioned alongside it to provide a scale. She paid particular attention to the pattern on the blade. Finally, she photographed the weapon's imprint in the soil. When she had finished she opened her briefcase and took out the prints that she had made of the patterns on the cylinder. The cartouche pattern on the blade matched the cylinder almost exactly with only a minor difference in its overall proportion.

'Proof, if proof were needed, that it is genuine, I think,' she said, showing the picture to John, who placed it on the ground beside the dagger. After comparing the designs he stood up.

'They match,' he said.

'Bernard followed suit. 'There's no doubt about it,' he said. 'They're more or less identical. I wonder who owned it. It must have been someone in a pretty exalted position; a king or something of the sort.'

'Have you found anything else?' John said.

'Not yet,' Lynda replied. 'But we're going to excavate some more around here. This may be part of a hoard.'

'Well, keep looking. This is a major find even if we find nothing else.' He gave her an encouraging smile. 'Well done.'

'It might well be the find of the century,' Barbara said and then added with a slight shiver: 'I wonder what it was used for… could it be a sacrificial weapon?' She remembered again her dreams of human sacrifice – the throat slitting and the blood. It was clear from the design on the blade that it must have been connected in some way with the cult of the cylinder. She wondered if it might be the very weapon that had slit the girl's throat in her dream or if its use had been purely symbolic – more of a spiritual weapon than an actual one. Again, it might have been purely a status symbol; an expression of wealth and power, marking its owner as someone of importance in the community. After all, the use of such elaborate ceremonial weapons was something that had persisted throughout history up to the present day. The Swords of State were just such an example. She tried to content herself with this thought. Still, she could not forget that dream.

John was convinced that its use must have been entirely ceremonial. He guessed that it might have been the product of a mistake in the smelting of the iron. It was conceivable that the ore used might have been accidentally contaminated with a high proportion of nickel or some other element, thus producing a form of stainless steel. It was unlikely that these early workers in iron would have known exactly what they were doing. Alternatively, they might have experimented with the iron by adding other things to the crucible just to see what they might do, like proto-alchemists.

'We may never know,' he concluded. 'The lab might be able to analyse it. In the meantime, we can only guess.'

Bernard grinned. 'Anyway, your getting an extension on the project has been vindicated.'

42

'Excuse me Sir, but do you know this man?'

Gallagher looked up from the motionless figure of James Masters to see the doctor standing behind him. He produced his identification card and introduced himself.

The doctor examined the card and looked at him. 'Special Branch?' he queried. 'What has this man done?'

'Nothing, as far as I know,' Gallagher said. 'He has been reported as a missing person and, due to the sensitive nature of his work, we were called in to investigate his disappearance. The hospital authorities reported his admission to the police and they contacted us. We had already alerted all forces to his disappearance.'

'How can we help you?'

'I'd just like some details on how he came to be here, who brought him in and what you think might be the matter with him.'

'Come with me.' The doctor led him to a vacant office. 'I don't know how much you already know,' he began, 'but he was brought in by a couple who found him unconscious in his hotel room. As to what is wrong with him, we simply don't know. We have tested him for drugs and other toxins, and he is clean.'

'So you don't think he's been got at?'

'He has certainly not been poisoned, if that's what you mean, and there are no physical injuries. As far as we can determine, there are no suspicious circumstances surrounding this case. I'm afraid I can't tell you any more than this. The truth is we don't know any more about him than you do and I am not at liberty to give you any more personal details concerning this patient. To do so would constitute a breach of professional etiquette, I'm sure you understand.'

'We already know who found him and brought him in. Can you verify that no one else was involved?'

'As far as I know, no one else was involved. I'm sorry, but I cannot tell you any more than this.'

'That is all I need to know for now, thanks. If anything else comes to mind, please let me know. I will remind you that there is such a thing as withholding evidence.'

The doctor bristled at this. 'Don't try to threaten me, Sergeant Gallagher. I have told you all you need to know. Now, if you'll excuse me, I'm very busy.' He got up and opened the door. 'Goodbye, Sergeant Gallagher.'

Gallagher backed down. 'I'm not threatening you, Doctor, and I apologise if I gave you that impression. We shall be in touch if we need to talk to you again.'

He left the hospital with the doctor's brusque dismissal still ringing in his ears. The doctor had been quite correct in withholding certain details from him, he knew that, but he was unhappy with the way he had been so summarily brushed off like some tabloid journalist. Damn it, he had the authority and every right to enquire as to how Masters had come to be in hospital unconscious after having gone missing without any adequate explanation for his absence. Well, he would wait until the man regained consciousness. Then he would learn the truth.

He was quite willing to believe that the whole business was probably one of chance; that masters had suffered a minor stroke or else some kind of nervous breakdown. Indeed, this was the most likely explanation for his apparent disappearance. He simply had to verify this and satisfy the authorities that he had not been the victim of some terrorist organisation or other hostile power. Once this had been cleared up, everyone would be satisfied and the whole matter closed. Then he could go home.

'Well, did you get anywhere at the hospital?' Fox asked him over a cup of coffee.

He made a wry face. 'I got my balls chewed by an officious doctor and that's all I got. They don't appear to know any more about this case than we do.'

Fox leaned back in his chair. 'Hmm... well, we shall go through the motions, but I think there's not much more we can do except close the case. I'm satisfied there are no suspicious circumstances, but just to be sure, we shall hang around here for a bit longer.'

'Did you speak to the hotel manager?'

'Yes. He told me that three other people discovered Masters in his room, not two as we were told.'

'So, we were not given the whole truth then?'

'We were not. It's a minor detail and probably due to an oversight, but I think we'd better follow it up. I want another word with those two.'

43

I keep drifting from here. It seems that every time I come back something has changed. These beings, whatever they are, seem to be evolving or, more precisely, developing. They now look more like real people; more natural in their movements and more intelligent, not like the standing, walking dummies that they were. I wonder if they know I'm here yet. They don't seem to be aware of me but are they looking? If they see me at all they show no apparent signs of curiosity. I might as well not be here. They might notice me in time, whatever that may mean in this place. They have definitely changed. I can now tell that they are men and women, not the asexual things that they were before. They are still unclothed; quite naked in fact but so am I so that much hasn't changed. What's more, it doesn't seem to matter.

Why do I keep sleeping like this? When I wake up it always feels like I've had my brain removed, scrubbed and pushed back in so that I have to keep reinventing myself and all around me as if I'm seeing everything for the first time even if I've seen it all before, it doesn't seem to matter. Every time it's new. These people are new but there are others elsewhere, I know. I am vaguely aware of their presence somewhere outside here in another world where I have, or perhaps had another life. Why do I keep thinking that? The only life I seem to be aware of is this one and yet this thought keeps popping up that there is or was another life somewhere out there just out of reach – somewhere out there, wherever that might be. It's like believing in an afterlife or else its opposite: a perceived life once lived before in a previous time and place that cannot be substantiated or proved in any way. If asked, you say: *it's just a feeling* and leave it at that and then nobody believes you.

But there is someone else. She comes and goes like everything else here, but I am aware of her. It's as if she's trying to reach me in some way but I am out of reach now. I cannot be reached but I may reach out when the time comes. It is up to me. I choose and that gives me power over that other world. If only I could remember who she might be, and she is definitely female; of that I am convinced. She is my contact with that other world – my spirit guide – my medium. If I could extend my thoughts out to her then we might build a bridge between our two worlds. I must try that some time, but for now, and now is all I have; I must concentrate on where I am and why I am here.

I wonder what she looks like. Perhaps one of these women might give me a clue. They do look familiar in an odd sort of way. It's as if I know them but I don't know them. How can I know them? They're all brand new; created from protoplasm or whatever those things are made of. If I was to touch one then we might be able to talk or at least communicate in some way but I feel that the time is not right for that. I would like to jump forward in time – I could probably do that now that I know how it works, but it feels inappropriate somehow, like opening a present too soon and spoiling the surprise. They will let me know when the time is right and then we will touch, but why do they look familiar? Perhaps they are images of people from that other world that have been dredged up from my subconscious. If so I should recognise them but I don't. Do they know they're naked? They are almost fully formed now. They now have hair, nipples and genitals; they even have navels but they are still incomplete. See, they still don't have fingernails or toenails and their ears have not yet fully formed. They are unfinished so it's no use trying to talk to them. They won't hear me; they cannot. I wonder how complete they will be when they have finished growing, if that's the right word for it. Will they have warm blood and internal organs, hearts and brains like real people, or will they just be semblances of what they imagine people to be; superficially correct but with nothing inside? In other words, will they ever be *real* people? Will they be sentient with feelings and emotions, thoughts that are their own and the ability to love? Will they ever see and hear me, perhaps recognise me, or shall I always be different from them? After all, I come from somewhere else. I may be here but do I belong here? I feel as if I do but feelings cannot be relied upon – I should know that.

That girl with the dark hair – she saw me, I'm certain. Her face showed no sign of recognition but her eyes lingered upon me so something is happening. It will be soon, I know that now. See how she pauses in front of me. Why does she show no expression or any sign that she sees me here? She is still incomplete, that's why. She's very near to perfection with all the defining parts of a woman in all the right places. She has breasts and pudenda; legs and arms fully formed with almost perfect feet and hands, eyes that appear to see, but what is behind those eyes? Is there anything there? Does she know that there is more to a woman than just physical attributes? Maybe she does, or maybe she will, perhaps I shall know, but not yet.

And then there is the cylinder. It is still there but I cannot touch it – the vertigo – it's too disorientating. If I stand up I am afraid I might fall because nothing here is to scale. I can't get used to that. The people or whatever they are seem to be unaffected by it. I wonder why. I suppose the answer is obvious. They don't know anything else because this is their world. They don't need to adjust to it. I do, and that probably explains a lot. For instance, that previous world of three dimensions – it must be real; that's why I have difficulty with this one. There are too many dimensions here and I haven't yet got used to that. Perhaps that is why I keep thinking about that other place. *Do* I keep thinking about it? Probably not if the truth be told but it is always there in the background, lurking like a half-forgotten memory. Well, if that is the case, this cannot be my real home. I am beginning to understand it better though; in fact there is much here that I have already learned and I am still learning.

For instance, these people – they are too perfect; that's why they look slightly wrong. They all resemble models: idealised forms devoid of blemishes and flaws. Maybe it's the fact that they are so new that they are still not fully formed and are consequently blemish free but there could be another explanation and that is that they have been extracted from my mind, or rather their images have been. That would explain why they all look vaguely familiar. They are people from my dreams; I see it now. My, my; someone's being very clever. My mind has been probed. By all the rules I should be alarmed by this but for some reason I am not. What's more, I'm not at all surprised. That's because I know it's for a reason. How do I know that? I just do, that's all. This knowledge must have been implanted by whatever it is that took these people from my mind. It makes sense.

The dark haired girl is looking at me again. Do you know me? You must have seen a naked man before. After all, you're surrounded by naked men and women so what's so special about me? If I waved my cock at you would you scream and run away? I doubt it. Her face looks innocent enough but there's something else there as well;

193

something other than innocence. She seems to be the only one to see me. The others show no apparent interest. Why are they here? Why are you here, looking at me like that? There must be a reason for all this. I shall stand and face her. Standing is easy. It's remaining standing that is the tricky bit. I wonder if my body is as perfect as hers. I don't know. There are no mirrors here. My body still feels light – too light for its apparent mass but that's something I can live with.

Hello. Do you know me? May I touch you to see if you are real?

I don't think she understands me. Don't rush it. She gave me a quick little smile, though. I'm sure she did. Now she's backing away from me. I won't hurt you. Please come back. I'm taking things too fast. Slow down. You frightened her. Remember, if she is new then everything here will be as unfamiliar to her as it was to me when I arrived, but is she new? She's new in her humanoid form, but she is not new to this world, is she? Not long ago she was a shapeless blob flowing around with the other shapeless blobs; an organic and integral part of this world. I only want to know if she feels like a living human being. I mean, can those amorphous shapes change their texture as well as their shape: become hard and soft? Can they change their temperature to match the body heat of a human being? They can change their colour to match stone or flesh – what is their natural colour? I can't define it. Whatever their colour, I'd like to know what they feel like. I could touch one of those pillars to feel if it is hard like stone but I still have difficulty judging distance and size. That's my main difficulty. I don't know if that one is three feet away or thirty or even if it's exactly where I see it. I still can't get my head around that one. I think I understand the principle, but understanding the principle and having to live with it are two different things. The vertigo – this is what happens when I try to get to grips with this funny perspective. It makes me dizzy.

What's that? Did she try to say something? It sounded like 'Aaaah,' only faint, but I'm sure she made a sound. Did you try to speak? She did, I'm sure. She's still looking this way. Perhaps she's trying to communicate with me. Yes, yes, I'm listening. It's good to hear a voice, even with the strange acoustics here. Why do the others still ignore me? So far it's only this dark haired creature that seems to acknowledge my presence here. I would love to talk to you but I don't think you understand me, do you? It's odd that I am the only real human in this place and yet I don't feel lonely. I keep getting the feeling that there's someone else here with me all the time; not just these humanoids – something else – something I can't define. There was a voice once that said I wasn't ready – ready for what, I wonder. That will come in time, I suppose. Meanwhile, I shall have to wait and see what happens. One thing's certain; someone somewhere has plans for me and that's for sure. After all, there's little point in my being here if it's not for a purpose; that stands to reason. All the facts are in my favour. I only have to wait to understand what's going on here.

She's reaching out to me with her arms and that little smile. She wants me to come to her but do I dare? I want to but I am, well, frightened to approach her. The last time I tried she backed off and I don't want to frighten her again. I don't want... Oh shit, the vertigo ... I'm falling... falling ... slowly...

44

Further excavation of the area where the dagger had been found revealed little else of such significance. A few small bone fragments were unearthed together with faint traces of what might have been carbon deposits – possible evidence of the burning of whatever had housed the weapon. Its proximity to the area where the cylinder had been found suggested that it had been housed in the same building. A quick reading of the recorded ground penetrating radar scan proved this to be the case.

It was while John was looking at this on his laptop in the back of the Land Rover that a car pulled up behind the parked vehicle. The doors opened and two men got out. He immediately recognised them as Fox and Gallagher. He swore under his breath and put the computer down on the seat.

'Do you mind if we have a quick word?' Fox called up to him.

'I've told you all I know,' he said with some irritation in his voice.

'Not everything,' Fox said. 'We just want to clear something up, that's all.'

He jumped down and stood in front of the two detectives, his eyebrows raised in an expression of puzzlement. 'What?'

Fox looked around slowly. 'So this is what you do, is it?'

'Yes, and it keeps us very busy. We have a tight schedule. Now, did you come here to just have a look around, or is there a specific reason for your visit?'

'I shall come straight to the point, Professor. I have spoken to the hotel manager and he tells me that there was a third member of your team present when you entered Mr. Masters' room. Is that correct?'

Fuck it, John thought. He had assumed that they might be satisfied with his and Barbara's account of what happened that night.

He tried to look casual. 'Yes,' he said after a brief pause. 'Bernard was also present in the room. I must have forgotten to mention it because only Barbara and I went to the hospital. We spoke to the doctor; I think I told you that.'

'Do you mind if we speak to him?'

'You mean Bernard? Is it absolutely necessary? He's very busy at the moment, as are we all. We have just made an important discovery.' He decided that the unearthing of an old dagger would hold little interest for them so there would be no harm in mentioning it, should he be asked.

Fox let it go. 'We only want to ask him one or two questions,' he insisted.

John gave in. 'Very well. He's over there.' He indicated the area of the dig where Bernard was working with Chris and Lynda.

'Who are the other two?' Gallagher asked.

'They know nothing about it at all,' he said quickly. 'They are in no way involved with this matter.'

'Are you sure?'

John flushed with anger. 'Do you doubt my word?' He resented the presence of these two men on the site and would have liked to have ordered them off, but he knew that they held a certain authority over him. He resented that too.

Barbara had seen the arrival of the officers and she came over. Her presence calmed him down somewhat. 'Speak to them if you like,' he said, 'but they won't be able to tell you anything.'

'Thank you, Professor.' Fox wandered over towards the dig, followed by Gallagher.

'Be careful where you put your feet,' John called after them.

Barbara touched his arm. 'What do they want?'

'They've discovered that Bernard was with us when we discovered James in his room,' he huffed. 'They want to interview him now.'

She ran her fingers through her hair. 'Christ, can't they leave us alone? What did you tell them?'

'I couldn't very well refuse their request. Anyway, Bernard's got nothing to hide.'

'Neither have we. Should we wander over there and join them?'

'Better not. I don't want them thinking that we're influencing him in any way. They're a suspicious bunch. Anyway, you know Bernard. If he can't spin them a convincing yarn, then nobody can.'

Bernard was crouched in the pit with Lynda, inspecting the partly uncovered flank of what appeared to be a nearly intact earthenware vessel of some kind. He recognised Gallagher immediately and stood up as the officers approached.

'Doctor Savage?' Inspector Fox began.

Bernard grinned. 'I'm afraid so.'

'We understand you discovered James Masters unconscious in his hotel room.'

'That's right.'

'Who was with you at the time?'

He scratched his head. 'Barbara Sedgwick who I believe has already spoken to you; oh, and the hotel manager. He had to unlock the door so we could get in. We got suspicious when he didn't answer.'

'How did you find him?'

'Well, after the manager opened the door we found him spark out on the bed.'

'Did you go to the hospital?'

'No. I wasn't really needed there. John and Barbara went, though.'

Fox nodded. He was satisfied, but Gallagher, who had seen the cabin, asked: 'What's in there?'

He felt himself flush at this unexpected question. 'Nothing much,' he replied as casually as he could manage. 'It's just an old shooting cabin we used to use as a store for tools and that sort of stuff.' He spotted the improvised earth lead snaking out from under the door, thought quickly and added: 'We also keep a spare generator in there.'

'What do you do when the shoot wants to use it?'

'They don't use it. Anyway, it's the close season. They can have it back any time if and when they want it.'

Gallagher seemed to be satisfied with this, but Fox asked: 'Would you mind if we take a look inside?'

Bernard felt a sudden surge of panic. He searched his mind for some way to fob them off. 'I don't think we have a key with us at the moment. There isn't much in there, see? Now that the heavy digging has been done, we've taken the tools away. We are storing them in a
198

lock-up garage in town. You know what it's like; we have to think of security, especially in a remote area like this. There are a lot of tea-leaves about.'

'All the same…' Fox insisted.

'I'll see John.' He hurried over to where John and Barbara stood. 'John, you're not going to like this, but they're asking if they can look inside the shed.'

'Well they can't!' John snorted.

'I've tried to put them off, but they're now insisting on it.'

Barbara smiled. 'We don't have a key with us, do we? Leave this to me.' She went over to the two men and spoke to them. Eventually, after what looked like some sort of agreement and a further brief exchange of words, they headed back towards their car. She gave them a friendly wave as they got in and drove off; then she rejoined her two companions.

John gaped. 'What did you tell them?'

She gave him a knowing smile. 'There are some things a woman can do that a man can't,' she said mysteriously. 'I persuaded them that we no longer use it for anything at all now and that we no longer have a key for the door.'

He hugged her. 'I don't know what we'd do without you. You've done it again.'

She became serious. 'I hope so. I really do.'

In the car, Fox and Gallagher were silent for a while. It was Gallagher who spoke first. 'What do you reckon?'

Fox tapped the steering wheel. 'I'm not convinced about that shed,' he said. 'I think we'll come up here when they're not there and have a look around.'

45

Blurred... I feel blurred. Something's wrong. I can't think straight any more. What happened back there? I remember falling – vertigo, that was it, now I feel hot and confused. Nothing here is what it seems so it's no wonder I fall down. Did I black out? I suppose I must have done. I feel odd – not right. Someone's covered me up; I wonder who might have done that; my memory fails me. The dark haired girl was standing before me and then I fell – I remember that but the rest is a fog. Someone's hand is on my head, trying to ease whatever it is that's happening to me. It is her. She is sitting beside me like some ministering angel trying to soothe my mind; that is if I have any mind left to soothe. Her hand is cool and comforting. I need that. I'm glad of it but who is she? I wish I could remember. It's been a rough night all right but we're back now and safely tied up in harbour, or is this all just so much delirium? The amoebae have taken over – they are running the show now. Well, they are people too, aren't they? After all, I have seen them as people. Not many have seen that but I have. I have been privileged enough to witness the event. How many others can say that they have seen the metamorphosis of amoeba to man? You're just an amoeba, aren't you, my sweet? I wish you could speak. Perhaps you can, but prefer not to. Maybe you talk through your hands, now there's a thought; communication by touch, but that's ridiculous. They must have some way of communicating, though – something other than speech. After all, where do these thoughts and ideas come from? Some of them are things I have never considered before, relating to time and space – stuff that relates in many ways to this no-place wherever it is in the general scheme of things or not, as the case may be. It must be the mind probe. If they can read my mind then I must assume that they can implant thoughts in a reciprocal way. That would make sense. It's a logical assumption but who are *they*? Amoebae, that's what they are, but are they individuals or parts of a much larger individual – a super organism? I remember interconnecting threads between some of them transferring pulses; tiny points of light between one and the other. My God, they remind me of brain cells. Is that what they are and what this is – the cortex of some super intelligence? That would be an oversimplification of the fact, but it will serve for now.

No wonder my head's in a mess. How can I be expected to handle this? I don't have a super brain so what am I doing here? How can I be expected to understand all this and what is it that I am supposed to understand? I wish you could tell me, my sweet amoeba, but you can't tell me anything yet, can you? I wish I could talk to you but I'm not sure that you would understand me. Everything's so quiet here. No one speaks or makes a sound. Perhaps that's another reason why my head feels funny – too much silence – not the silence of simple quietude, no, this is a dense silence; a silence that I can feel – that wraps itself around me like a thick blanket. It's unnatural and that's why it's odd; it's too intense. I wish you would speak to me but still it's nice to feel your hand upon my forehead. Why don't you speak? I would like to pull you down on top of me and fuck some sort of conversation into you, but that would be a betrayal of your trust and your care and anyway I don't think I have the strength to do it. I wonder why I have such a brutal attitude towards you. Is it because you don't speak or because you're just an amoeba? I have had these thoughts before and I hate myself for that. You really don't deserve it, do you, my sweet? You don't deserve me. You are a creature of love and I am not. How do I know that? What is it that makes me assume such a thing without a shred of evidence to back it up? Just a feeling, that's all, like so many thoughts and feelings that arrive unannounced and for which I'm not prepared. Perhaps I ought to get used to it; I should be by now. Goodness knows I've been here long enough. How long? It doesn't matter. It's not important. What matters now is what happens next and that's the vital thing. Always remember you must look forward. Never look back. That is a pointless exercise.

Those hands, they feel real. I can sense the soft skin and the finger bones that lie beneath. She feels real or nearly so, not some kind of animated dummy as I might have supposed. I would like to touch her – to feel that too-perfect body of hers – I would know then just how real she is but I don't have the energy even to lift my arms. I'm not well. My strength is gone and I feel muzzy. This is wrong, or maybe it isn't. Maybe it is just a natural stage in my development if I only knew what it is that I might be developing into. You can't tell me, I know. I wish someone could but even then would I understand? I shall call you Angel. Perhaps then my thoughts towards you might be less unkind. I wish I wasn't so unkind to you. I don't deserve you. Inside I am still a man and you – what exactly are you? Not a real angel, that's for certain. At the same time you're not exactly human so I'm left wondering. Soothe this fever with your comforting hands, my angel. I wish I was worthy of your care.

Very gently, Angel brushed a tear from his cheek.

46

That night, Fox and Gallagher drove along the country road to the site of the diggings. They parked their car on the soft ground and, in the combined light from the headlights and their hand torches, they made their way to the shooting cabin. They checked the door and noted the two recently replaced padlocks. It was Gallagher who discovered the wire and the earth spike. In the dark, he snared his foot on it and nearly tripped.

'Bollocks!' He kicked his foot free, breaking the wire in the process.

'What is it?' Fox asked.

'I don't know.' Gallagher shone his torch on the ground and saw the wire. His trip had torn it away from the spike. 'I nearly went arse over head on that bloody wire. Watch where you put your feet; there may be more hazards around here.'

Fox remembered Bernard's statement. 'That'll probably be their generator. They said they keep a spare one in there.'

'Well, they might have put their cable in a better place. I nearly broke my bloody neck on the thing.' He thought for a moment. 'Didn't Barbara Sedgwick tell us they no longer use the shed now? If that's the case, then what might a generator be doing in there? That wire must be connected to something. The cabin can't be empty.' He bent down and gave the wire a tug. It resisted his pull. 'It must still be connected to something. I suspect someone's not been telling us the whole truth.'

'Really?' Fox went over to the small, dirty window and shone his torch through it. At first, he could make out little through the grime; then he became aware of something. He switched his torch off. Take a look at this, will you?'

Gallagher shone his torch through the window. 'What?'

'Switch your torch off and then look.'

He switched off his torch and saw immediately what had alerted his boss. The interior of the cabin was lit by a pale bluish glow. He looked at fox. 'What do you reckon?'

'I don't know. Can you see where the light is coming from?'

Gallagher craned do see a possible source of the light. 'No,' he said after a moment. 'Let's try the other window.'

They walked around to the other side of the cabin and looked through the other, somewhat larger window. It was as grimy as the first one, but it was clear enough to see in better detail the interior of the cabin and its apparent light source. In the corner, something vaguely cylindrical and apparently wrapped in chicken wire glowed bluish white. The brightest light came from the just visible domed ends of the object where the wire did not quite cover it.

'What the hell is that?' Fox said.

Gallagher shone his torch on the object. 'Buggered if I know,' he said. 'I think someone's been hiding things from us, don't you?'

Fox looked at it. The chicken wire wrapping was plainly visible in the torchlight. From it a wire trailed to the door where it passed beneath it. 'That's what tripped you up,' he said. 'I think we should ask them what exactly is going on here. This looks highly suspicious to me. They could be storing radioactive material here, the way that thing's glowing. That makes it our business.'

'Bloody hell,' Gallagher said. 'You're not suggesting they might be terrorists or something, are you?'

'What do you think?'

'It's a possibility although I very much doubt it,' he said. 'One thing's certain. They've been hiding this lot from us. I thought they were being cagy about something. I've a good mind to break in and get a better look at that thing in there.'

Fox nodded. 'Well, we have the authority, but I think I shall talk to them first. Besides, we don't know what level of radioactivity there might be in there. It could be hazardous. Better to wait.'

'Do we pull them in now?'

'No. We shall watch them for a while. Keep a low profile and see what they do next. There may be others involved.'

47

The next morning Bernard drove up to the site with Chris and Lynda, while John and Barbara went to the hospital to see how James was progressing.

On arrival at the site, Bernard, Chris and Lynda set to work on the area that they had been excavating the day before. No one noticed the broken earth lead.

John and Barbara went straight to the ward where James lay. This time they did not see the doctor, but one of the nursing staff intercepted them and told them that his condition had deteriorated somewhat. This was disturbing news for Barbara, despite the nurse's insistence that he was still stable and that there was no real danger. They went straight to his bedside where Barbara started talking to him as she had done before. John watched the EEG, but this time there was no apparent reaction to her voice. Despite this, she continued to talk to him as before, but her voice betrayed a renewed sense of desperation and urgency. Still the machine registered no reaction. Eventually, she gave up and, in a mood of some despondency, they drove back into town for a coffee.

Neither of them noticed the silver Audi that followed them back into town and which parked around the corner from where John parked the Land Rover.

In the café, they sat at a different table away from the window. Barbara seemed close to tears. Her sense of guilt had returned to torment her, triggered by James's deterioration and his lack of response to her voice. There was little that John could do or say to ease this sense of guilt. She sat opposite him with her fists clenched.

'We've killed him,' she said.

'He's not dead,' he replied.

'He might as well be. Damn it, you saw him lying there. His body may be still functioning but he is dead to all intents and purposes, and we killed him.'

'We haven't killed him. We cannot be blamed for his actions. No one forced him to revisit the cylinder and expose himself to its forces for longer than any of us would ever have dared. If anything is responsible for this, it is the cylinder. It turned him into a slave to its power to the detriment of his health. The cylinder did this and no one else.'

'And who exposed him to the cylinder in the first place?' she countered.

'OK, we did, and I'll admit that we started the process. But I won't accept responsibility for his later actions, and I won't have you blaming yourself for it either. No one's to blame. I don't know how many times I have to say this.'

'What if he dies?'

'He's not in mortal danger. There's been a set-back, that's all, but he's not about to die; far from it. I knew someone once who was in a coma for six months following a motorbike accident. He was in a far worse state than James, but he made a full recovery and if you met him today you would never guess that he had ever been so close to death. James is in no way as seriously ill as he was.'

'How do you know that?'

'If he was that ill, the doctor would have told us and his next of kin to prepare us all for the worst. No one has done any such thing; quite the opposite, in fact.'

'So he's fine and well, is he?' She got up from the table. 'I can't believe you can be so blind – so uncaring. I'm going for a walk. Don't try to follow me.'

He watched her leave the café with a heavy heart. He understood her concern, but could not understand her all-consuming guilt. It was out of proportion. James had got himself into this mess and no one else was to blame, yet she was blaming herself for everything that had happened. He was willing to admit that it had been rash to have ever allowed him to go anywhere near the cylinder, but it had largely been at James's own insistence. He should have forbidden all further contact with it. After all, he was supposed to be in charge of the project. Still, Barbara's accusation stung him. He was deeply concerned for the young man's fate and to be called uncaring had hurt him. He felt personally responsible for the safety of all members of the team, and to have this happen to a visitor worried him more than he could express. He understood that her words had been spoken from a mixture of fear and anger and that these emotions had clouded her judgement. Still, he felt saddened by what she had said. It saddened him too to know that she was suffering as a consequence of James's foolhardiness.

He thought of following her out, but decided against it. She obviously needed time to be alone and a space to think. He would not deny her this. He decided to go alone up to the site. She could have the rest of the day off. He poured himself another coffee, rummaged in his pocket and found a notepad and pen; then he began to write.

> *Dear Barbara,*
>
> *I have gone up to the site on my own. I understand that you are distraught about James and that you need to sort things out on your own. Therefore I am giving you the rest of the day off.*
>
> *Please forgive my seemingly uncaring attitude towards this unfortunate situation. I do care, more perhaps than I can say, and it hurts me to see you so upset by this business as it hurts me to see James in his present condition. Believe me, it hurts.*
>
> *I hope to see you this evening when we get back.*
>
> *I love you.*
> *John   X*

He folded the note and carefully tucked it into his pocket. He wondered what she would do with the rest of the day and if he was wise to let her have her way like this. He would see.

He finished his coffee, paid the bill and left the café. Then he walked to the hotel where he went straight up to their room and knocked on the door. The chambermaids were vacuuming the corridor and he assumed that they had already tidied the room. Therefore, there was little chance of his note being picked up as waste paper.

There was no reply, so he took the note from his pocket and read it once more before sliding it under the door.

On arriving at the site, he was met by Bernard who had nothing new to report.

Bernard looked first at him and then at the Land Rover. 'Where's Barbara?'

'She's feeling a bit off colour today, so I've given her the day off. You'll be all right without her, won't you?'

'Sure.' Bernard looked at him quizzically. 'What exactly is the matter with her?'

He decided to tell him the truth. 'She's a bit upset about James. He's suffered a relapse and she blames herself for all that's happened to him. I tried to tell her it's not her fault, but I can't convince her otherwise. She's beating herself up over it and all the time it's the fault of that bloody thing in there.' He gestured towards the cabin.

Still no one noticed the broken earth lead or that inside the cabin the cylinder was heating up. The cool glow was becoming hot and the chicken wire roll that surrounded it was beginning to smoke.

Back in town, Barbara wandered around the high street for a while before returning to the café in the vague hope that John might still be there. It did not surprise her to see that he had gone. She looked at her watch. Half past ten. She decided to go back to the hotel to see if he was there. She wanted to apologise to him for her harsh words. She had not meant to attack him like that; it was unfair and unjustified. He had just provided her with a convenient target to vent her anger; that was all. Knowing that James had relapsed had made her angry – more with herself than anyone else and John had acted as a channel for that anger. She knew that she had hurt him with her words.

Back at the hotel, she collected the key from the reception desk and went up to their room. Almost immediately, she saw the folded note on the floor and at the same time noticed that the room had been tidied and the bed made. She picked up the folded paper and read it, shaking her head slowly.

'Oh, John,' she mouthed. 'You fool. Why do you have to be so bloody nice?' She threw herself down onto the bed and began to cry.

48

'They didn't see you, then?' Fox leaned across the desk.

Gallagher shook his head. He was dressed in a blue anorak with faded blue jeans, beneath which an old and rather scruffy pair of Nike trainers projected. His hair was tousled and he was unshaven. He looked nothing like the well dressed man that had first presented himself to Barbara and John just two nights ago. If not exactly a master of disguise, he had certainly made a passable attempt at making himself look as anonymous as possible. 'I took great care to see that they didn't.'

'And...?'

'Well, they spent some time by his bedside before returning to town. The Sedgwick woman seemed to be upset about something, so I sat in the corner of that little café in the high street where they sometimes go and tried to eavesdrop on their conversation. I couldn't hear everything, you understand, but they seemed to be having words.'

'Words?' Fox raised his eyebrows.

'Like I say, I couldn't hear it all, but she seems to be blaming herself for Masters' illness. The professor was trying to reassure her, but it wasn't working. Eventually, she got up and walked out on him.'

'Did she, by God?' Fox chuckled.

'I think this was more than just a lovers' tiff.' Gallagher's face was serious. 'She seemed to be very upset.'

Fox produced a letter. 'I took the liberty of checking them out with MI5. They have nothing on them apart from the usual flirtation with radical politics back in their student days, and that was only one of them. All the others are clean and have no connection with any political group as far as is known.'

'So no luck there, then?'

Fox tossed the paper down on the desk. 'No, but something's going on, I'm certain of it.'

'I'm sure of one thing,' Gallagher said, 'and that is that they've got something to do with Masters' disappearance and his present condition; and what about that thing in the shed?'

'What indeed? We'll continue to keep tabs on them for now. I'm not going to approach them yet, but be ready to pounce on them at the first sign of trouble.'

'I'll be ready, don't worry.'

49

James lay inert while people gathered around him. The dark haired girl looked at him and then at the others as wordless messages flashed between them along the fine filaments that interconnected their bodies.

He is changing. There is no direct cause for concern. This is normal. When he returns we shall present him and then he shall be yours to guide. Guide him well.

I shall. He is for me. I hope I please him well.

Let it begin.

The dark haired girl knelt beside the horizontal man and put her hands on his head. Threads darted from the others and attached themselves to her skin as she gripped his head tighter. Her fingertips appeared to merge with his skin. A fine silvery thread shot in a straight line between her head and his, attaching itself to his forehead and tiny nodes of light began to travel along it. The process took an indeterminate time, after which she broke away and the connecting thread dissolved. The other threads withdrew from her as she stood up and turned to face the others.

It is done.

Let him rest. He shall be weak for a while. You will know when he is ready. We shall know. No person has been here since the ones that came aeons ago. This shall be significant for us.

How shall he be treated when he returns to his own kind? Will they kill him as they did the others?

We shall take that chance. They are creatures of another world of time.

That time has changed them. I have learned that much.

Good. Then we shall see how they react to the experiment. We can wait and see. Other beings have reacted well, so why not this one?

I shall be with him until his return. No harm shall come to him while I am here.

Be careful he does not harm you.

He shall not.

No. He shall not. We are here.

You are always here. I for now shall be a person and that will make me different for a while. My body is nearly complete and soon I shall know what it is to be human. My organs are now fully formed. A network of nerves runs through me and I can feel as he feels, hear as he hears and see what he sees. Soon we shall lie together and I shall know what it is to experience the life of one such as she who is with us still. My body is hers and it is his to do with as he desires. We shall learn this way.

We shall learn, but we need to be careful and must not lose sight of the fact that people are at times violent and unpredictable. They can kill that which they fail to understand. It is their way.

It is in our power to destroy them. We choose not to. This is our way. That makes us different. When he awakes we shall learn. He too shall learn, but we must fear for his return when the time comes. Therefore he must be taught to hide his knowledge.

He shall be taught.

The men and women linked hands and surrounded James and the girl who sat beside his reclining form. Their thoughts became silent. Still small signals passed between them along the fine threads that connected their bodies together, intermittently sparking tiny pulses of energy. The girl was now independent of the others and she slowly ran her hands over her body, sensing new muscles and nerves beneath her skin. It was good. She was satisfied that her replication was complete and that for now at least, she was fully human.

50

Barbara arose from the bed and went over to the dressing table, pausing to look out of the window. She wanted to get on with some work, but she had left her laptop and briefcase in the back of the Land Rover that John had now driven up to the site. In her heightened emotional state she had forgotten it and it was clear that he had forgotten it as well, leaving it in the vehicle.

She picked up her phone, intending to call him, and then she remembered that the site was in a blind spot and that he was out of reach. She flipped the phone shut with a silent curse and looked at herself in the dressing table mirror. Her eyes were red and puffy. She shook her head as if to clear it and let her hair fall free around her neck. It had been a silly and pointless argument, but seeing James in what appeared to be an even deeper coma had upset her more than she was willing to admit, even to herself. She read John's note again and put it down on the dressing table, this time resisting the urge to cry that welled up inside her again.

She opened the drawer and took out a sheet of the hotel's notepaper and found a pen in her bag. Then she began to write:

Dear, Dear John,

Sorry I was so rotten to you. You don't deserve it, I know, but I was distraught and...

She screwed the paper up and threw it in the bin before starting again on a fresh sheet:

Dear John,

I have gone down town for a while. I don't expect to be long, so don't fret.
I'm sorry I was so horrid to you. You didn't deserve it and I feel quite rotten about the things I said. I really didn't mean them. You are a kind person and not at all uncaring – I know that and I really am sorry. I do love you.
I shall see you for dinner.
I love you.

Barbara   XXX

She folded the paper and wrote John's name on it; then she placed it on the bedside table on his side of the bed where she guessed he might be most likely to see it.

She had a shower and then got dressed, feeling somewhat better. Then she went downstairs and left the key at the reception desk before going out into the high street again.

Through the café window, Gallagher watched as she walked along the pavement and disappeared into a dress shop. He finished his coffee, paid the cashier and went out, merging with the shoppers. He stood in the doorway of a nearby charity shop and waited, feeling all the time that he was engaged in a pointless exercise. He was following a woman shopping. Still, Fox had said that he wanted her followed, so he would follow her as far as decency permitted. He had dealt with terrorists before and he knew well enough that they mostly lived quiet lives – at least outwardly. He would see and make notes of who she spoke to in the course of the day. He would miss nothing.

In the event, she spoke to no one as she browsed the shops and sat over a coffee in the café where she had sat with John that morning, reading a paper that she had bought in the local newsagent's shop. She was bored with having nothing to do except view the local shops and kill time, and she wished to God that she had not left her laptop and briefcase in the Land Rover.

Gallagher too was getting bored with having to watch her. Nothing he saw aroused even the slightest suspicion that she was engaged in anything other than a quiet day's window shopping. His
214

time would be better spent up at the site where, for all he knew to the contrary, the rest of the team were up to goodness knows what with that radioactive thing in the cabin. This was just a waste of time. Still, he stuck to her tenaciously, managing to remain unobserved as he pretended to window shop while watching her reflection in the glass. He was careful wherever possible to avoid looking at her directly. He had been well trained in surveillance methods, for all the good that these were doing him now. One thing was certain: he would have little to report to his superior at the end of the day.

In the end she returned to the hotel, went up to their room and lay down on the bed. She decided that she might as well sleep for an hour. She slept for two, waking up at one thirty.

She got up and washed, then went downstairs to the bar for a drink and a light bar meal, taking her paper with her. She could catch up on the news while she waited for the team to finish work. That would not be for another four hours at least. It was going to be a long afternoon.

Gallagher meanwhile had given up and returned to the police station. It had been a wasted morning and he was fed up. He said this much to Fox who glumly accepted it while insisting that the surveillance operation continue. It might be boring but it was necessary. Gallagher acknowledged this, despite a growing feeling that they were not going to discover anything out of the ordinary. So far he had seen nothing that might incriminate anyone involved in the case, apart from that glowing thing in the cabin.

She finished her meal and went out again. This time she shunned the high street and walked out of town into the country, deciding that a long walk would help to clear her head of the morning's events. To some extent it worked. It did not lessen her deep sense of concern at James's condition or her unease with the way she had treated John that morning. It was very untypical of her to behave like that, but she was better able to see it in its true perspective. It had been a minor storm, but the resultant damage could be repaired. She would see to that.

51

The team returned to the hotel at about five thirty after a fairly uneventful day. John went straight up to the room to have a shower and change for the evening. He had hoped that he might see Barbara and was disappointed to see that she was not there. Then he saw her note on the bedside table. With some trepidation he unfolded it and read the message written in her neat handwriting.

'Oh Barbara,' he murmured. 'I'm so sorry.' With a sigh he put the note back on the table, then got undressed and showered. After he had changed, he sent her a quick, conciliatory text message on his mobile phone and went downstairs to the bar. He was the first one in there. He bought himself a pint of bitter and sat down at a table. Soon, Bernard came in and joined him.

'Hello mate. You lost no time getting here.'

'I feel as if I need a drink,' he said moodily.

'No sign of Barbara?'

He shook his head. 'She left me a note saying that she would be back shortly. She's somewhere in town.'

'Probably shopping,' Bernard said. 'What do they call it; retail therapy?'

'Something like that.' He looked at his beer. 'Anyway, it's her money. I hope it does her good.'

Bernard smiled and took a long drink. 'Men like beer – women like shopping. That's one of Nature's immutable laws.'

'Not always,' John corrected him. 'There are no strict rules here.'

'That's true.'

Lynda and Chris entered the bar. She sat down with John and Bernard while Chris bought the drinks. 'I somehow guessed that you two might be the first ones in the bar,' she laughed. 'Where's Barbara?'

'In town, shopping, I guess,' John said.

Half an hour went by before Barbara entered the bar and looked around. She saw them at the table and came over. 'Did you get my note?' she asked John.

He stood up. 'Yes. Let's go somewhere and talk. I want to say something, and I suppose you do as well.'

'We'll go up to our room.'

They excused themselves and went upstairs. Once the door had closed behind them, she put her arms around him. 'John, I'm so sorry. I know I hurt you. I really didn't mean to behave like that, but seeing James there… it… well, it hurt me so much.'

He returned her embrace. 'It's me who should apologise. I should have known that and understood it better. I'm afraid I was a bit heavy handed in my treatment of you. Do you forgive me?'

She kissed him. 'There's nothing to forgive. We were both unreasonable and I was a cow. I shouldn't have sounded off at you like that.'

'Enough,' he said. 'Let's forget it and go to bed.'

She backed away from him and smiled. 'Later, I promise. You left your beer in the bar and we'll be late for dinner.'

'Bugger dinner.'

She took his hand and led him towards the door. 'We'd better join the others. I'll make it up to you tonight and that's a promise.'

They went downstairs and rejoined the others at the table.

Bernard leaned towards Barbara and asked: 'Have you seen anything of our detective friends today?'

She shook her head. At no time during the course of the day had she had the slightest suspicion that she was being watched.

'Hmmm,' he mused. 'I wonder what they're cooking up for us now.'

She looked at him. 'You don't think they've finished with us, then?'

'I'll bet they're not.'

52

James awoke slowly from a fevered sleep in which he had dreamed of sticky threads attached to his body like spider silk. How long he had been asleep he could only guess. His body ached and when he moved his head it felt as if it was coming off. Something touched his forehead. With an effort he opened his eyes and saw the girl looking down on him. He closed them again. She was there.

'Angel,' he mouthed, remembering the nickname he had given her.

A light hand brushed his forehead. 'Rest now; you will feel stronger soon.'

He opened his eyes wide. 'You spoke!'

'I now have a voice. I can speak, but you must rest. You have undergone more than most people will ever experience in their time. It's too much to expect you to understand what is happening at this stage.' Her voice was soft and soothing to his confused brain, and she spoke in a language that he could understand. He wondered if it was his language. He could not remember.

'Who are you? Who are these people?'

'We are here to guide you. I am here for you.'

'I don't understand...'

'You will.'

'Are you real? Do you breathe; have flesh and blood and bone? Can you feel as people feel or are you just a figment of my imagination? I want to know.'

She smiled. 'I am real enough.'

'I have seen them – they change shape. They were all around me. I saw them – creatures of mind; that's what they are. Are you one of them, or are you human?'

'For now I am human. Here...' She took his hand and pressed it to her side. 'Do I feel real to you?'

He felt the warmth of human flesh, the softness of skin and the firmness of the muscles beneath the skin. He felt a living body. He smiled weakly. 'You feel real.'

She put his hand up to her head and let him feel her hair. It was soft and it felt natural to his touch. Then she placed his hand back down by his side and gently covered his eyes. 'Be quiet now. You will know more when the time comes, but for now you must rest. You have been through a lot and there will be more to come.'

He closed his eyes. Her voice was soothing after so much silence. He felt an upsurge of mental energy that seemed to emanate from her fingertips, as if she was injecting his being with a fresh knowledge of the things that surrounded him and that lay outside the immediacy of where he lay. How foolish he had been to have imagined that this was all when all infinity lay beyond the confines of the great hall, but could he grasp it? It was beyond anyone's power to comprehend the vastness of it all and he was a person from a three dimensional world that might be a billion galaxies away for all he knew to the contrary. If he did not even know where he was, what chance had he of understanding something like this? It was more than big, it was unimaginable.

He tried to lift his hand to touch the girl again. To feel her would have been comforting to him, but he lacked the strength to do it. The contemplation of something on such a scale gave him an overwhelming sense of loneliness. He might have these people and the girl in particular to accompany him on this journey, but he knew that essentially he was alone. He would always be alone. It was a terrifying thought and it filled him with dread.

He groaned and felt her hand again on his forehead, soothing him. She spoke, but he did not hear what she said. He felt as if his brain had turned to liquid in his skull, but still the thoughts kept coming; thoughts that he had never had before. He did not know if this was a delirium or if it was a part of the changes that were taking place in his mind, and what if it was not only his mind that was changing? What of his body; was that changing too? His strength had gone, but that might have just been the effect of the fever or whatever it was that had laid him so low. Perhaps the mental agony and the sense of loneliness that now gripped him was also a product of this malady.

He wished for sleep to intervene and give him rest, but sleep would not come. Instead, he drifted through a state of semi consciousness, not knowing what was real and what was imagined.

The cylinder, or one like it, drifted into and out of his vision, always just out of reach. He knew that this was a key to his further understanding of the time and space conundrum in which he currently found himself. A complex circular design, familiar to him in a way he could not quite remember, appeared before him and he was falling into it, or perhaps through it and into another identical pattern and then another – on and on through successive patterns that opened up to receive him. It was like falling down a bottomless well. This did not alarm him. He knew that this was not an infinite progression, but a corridor that led to something else that might shed light on where he was and why he was here. He had to know.

Stars appeared in countless numbers and he was through, drifting in a void; moving through space at speed towards something indefinable – a patch of light that, despite its brilliance, he could see without discomfort although its light should have blinded him. He knew that this was his destination and that he had nothing to fear from the tremendous heat and mass that normally would by turns first burn him and then crush him to a speck. You cannot burn or crush a vision. The light got bigger until it filled his field of view. Despite his proximity he felt no heat and still he could look at it without discomfort. He was decelerating, drifting down through the bright, corona-like atmosphere towards a smooth surface of light. Drifting – drifting – down…

Angel's voice came, whispering cool in his ears. 'I am here for you. Do not fear.'

He opened his eyes and saw her leaning over him. Her face was only inches from his; so close that her hair brushed his cheek. With some difficulty he spoke. 'I have been on a journey. Did I arrive?'

Her reply was cryptic and told him little. 'You have travelled far. You are here now and we are together. I shall always be a part of you; a part that shall not die. Do you understand?'

'Yes,' he said slowly. 'I am beginning to understand many things.'

'You will.'

'I am not the first to make this journey, am I?'

'No. There are others who have done it.'

'Where are they now?'

'They are here.'

'Why can't I see them?'

'You will, but not yet. Your journey is not over.'

'There is more?'

'Yes.'

He closed his eyes and tried to contemplate this, but could not. He had seen enough for now. More would come, but that would be in its own time and his, when he had gained sufficient strength to absorb it, but for now he was tired. His strength was slowly returning, but still not sufficiently for him to raise his arm more than a couple of inches. A sense of peace descended upon him.

She stroked his forehead again. 'You can sleep now.'

'I shall sleep. Stay here with me, Angel.'

'I shall stay with you.'

53

That night in the shooting cabin all was still. On the now scorched earth floor in the corner, the cylinder lay once more exposed, its chicken wire wrapping burnt away. No longer effectively screened, it had by now accumulated sufficient energy to circulate a massive eddy current through the wire jacket which had rapidly heated up until it had become incandescent. It had started to melt and then finally it had burned with a brilliance that for a while illuminated the cabin's interior with a searing white light. White hot sparks had showered the cabin's interior and started a minor fire which, owing to the damp conditions in there plus a deficiency of combustible material, had gone out of its own accord, but sufficient damage had been done to blacken the walls and leave an acrid smoke stench that permeated everything. This process might have depleted the cylinder's energy resources, but it had reabsorbed the heat and light that the burning steel had generated, so very little energy had gone to waste. It had been designed that way.

The screen had not been particularly annoying or even inconvenient to the cylinder; it was incapable of such feelings, but it had sensed that its force had been inhibited by its wire cocoon. It was therefore beneficial to lose it.

Now, once more free, it lay on the scorched floor, or rather it hovered just above it, glowing with a cool, pale light, unaffected by the smoke and once more waiting. It had waited a long time, but time meant nothing to it. It mattered not whether it waited for minutes or aeons. It had slept for seven and a half thousand years, but this was of no importance. It was only aware that it had been uncovered recently and, as a consequence, reawakened. It could now return to the task that it had been sent here to do: to act as a bridge between the intelligence that had created it and whatever life forms it might encounter. It could sweep and search for whatever central nervous systems these creatures might possess and instantly determine whether or not they were intelligent. If so, then they could be assessed as to their suitability for possible liaison with its creator. If not, then they would be left to continue their lives in peace. It meant nothing to the cylinder if it found intelligent life or not. It would have lain dormant on a completely uninhabited planet for all time or until such time as it sensed something that it deemed to be a life form and then it would be activated. For this one, that time had come.

Its first efforts had been unsuccessful. The first creatures to encounter it had been driven by blind instinct and consequently they were left alone. Later, more intelligent creatures had found it and it had got to work on them. This too had only been a partial success and had ended in a disastrous war, destroying the culture that it had created and leaving few survivors. This had not been the fault of the cylinder, but of these new creatures, most of whom had failed to understand its purpose. They had worshiped it as the manifestation of a god and it had been powerless to correct them on that matter. By the same token, had it understood them better it might have expected this to happen. Instead, it had simply recorded all that had taken place around it and gone on waiting for another contact. It was, after all, only a machine.

Despite their flaws, its first worshipers had shown promise. Under its guidance, their technology had progressed. Unfortunately, the mental development of most of them had not kept pace with this and, as a consequence, the experiment had failed. Perhaps these new discoverers would fair better. So far, only one of them had got close enough to it to be absorbed. That one showed real potential and might make the experiment worthwhile, pending further tests. The others had been suspicious of its motives and so far had stayed away. This had not happened before. Once it had been the focus of everyone's attention; now it was imprisoned and shunned. An attempt had been made to deactivate it and that showed a degree of intelligence and technological understanding that indicated a considerable advance over its earlier discoverers. Even their suspicion was a good sign. It indicated a degree of scepticism that distanced them from the blind faith that had been so ineptly demonstrated by their predecessors. It measured their behaviour against that of their ancestors and found so many differences that they might have been another species, even if the body scan had shown them to be practically the same.

All it had to do now was wait to be discovered again. After millennia of waiting, time was of no consequence. It was now once more free to make contact with whoever came close.

It would finish what it had started.

54

Barbara awoke to see that John was in the shower. She had dreamed that night of James, and this dream had burned itself into her memory. In it she had seen him lying on the floor of a large chamber or hall, surrounded by men and women and tended by a dark haired girl. All appeared to be naked, but she had barely noticed that. What she had noticed about the girl in particular was her face that seemed to radiate love. There was no other word for it. It was the face of a mother caring for her new baby: tender and devoted. In the background, the cylinder or a replica of it lay on the chequered floor, apparently unconnected with the scene.

As if by a jump cut, she was travelling through space towards what appeared to be a star or a large planet. Its outline was hazy. Somehow, she knew that this was the place where James lay.

She had woken up at this point and lain awake for a while, pondering this dream. For no obvious reason, she felt more reassured about James – that he was not in mortal danger and that he would eventually return. What she did not know was what he would be like when he did return. She wondered briefly if she was receiving a message from him, but she dismissed the thought as ridiculous. Still, something in her had changed and she slept again, this time peacefully and untroubled by further dreams.

This feeling remained with her as she lay there, listening to John in the shower. They were going to see James again this morning and this time she would not feel as anxious as she had felt the day before.

She got out of bed and wrote her dream down. She was not likely to forget it anyway. Despite this, she wrote it as a matter of course. It had now become a habit of hers to record all dreams, no matter how vivid or fantastic they were. When she had finished, she remembered the earlier one she had had of James in which she had seen him wandering through a formless landscape, surrounded by curious drifting shapes that moved around him. Somehow, she knew that these images were linked.

Later that morning she sat at James's bedside and stroked his forehead as she had done before. This time, though, she felt that he was safe, wherever he was. She told him this much in her monologue as she relayed her dream to him.

John listened to her as he watched the trace on the EEG machine. She had told him already of her dream and he was pleased to see that if nothing else it had put her mind at rest. Certainly, her mood had become more optimistic than it had been the day before. There was another good sign too. James seemed to be responding once more to her voice. The EEG was showing definite signs of brain activity again and this was encouraging. Had the doctor been present, he would have noticed that this renewed level of brain activity was abnormally high. The pens were dancing all over the chart.

They left the hospital feeling more buoyant than they had felt for some time and went to the café as before. Neither of them noticed the untidy man seated with his back to them at a small table in the corner, dressed in a navy blue anorak with faded blue jeans and reading The Sun. Right now, neither of them was thinking about Gallagher as they talked in hushed tones, but he was listening. What he heard made little sense.

Bernard, Lynda and Chris arrived at the site, ready to recommence work on the dig. Lynda was the first to notice something wrong with the cabin. Her eyes narrowed as she saw what appeared to be smoke darkened windows. It had not been like that yesterday. Her face showed a mixture of shock and surprise as she pointed to the cabin with a small, inarticulate cry.

'What is it?' Bernard followed the direction of her gaze. 'Oh my God...' He jumped out of the Land Rover and ran over to the cabin. He fumbled in his pocket for the keys and undid the two padlocks. In the same instant he noticed the broken earth lead. 'How did this happen?' he called to the other two, who came running over to him.

'What?' Chris looked baffled.

'Look – here.' Bernard pointed to the broken wire.

Chris picked up the broken end of the wire and looked at it. 'It seems to have been pulled away,' he said. 'Well, it wasn't one of us. None of us went near it yesterday. I reckon someone else has been here.'

Bernard opened the door and immediately stepped back. The cylinder was there, surrounded by grey metallic ash and the charred remains of a chair. The acrid smell of stale smoke assailed his nostrils. 'Fuck!' He slammed the door shut. 'Get away from here, all of you!'

Chris and Lynda backed away.

'What's happened?' Lynda looked frightened.

'The cylinder's burnt the place out!'

'What!' Chris took a step forward.

'Don't go near it,' Bernard said. 'The thing's back and it means business.'

'What about the shield?' Lynda said.

'It's all burned away. There's nothing left.'

'Bugger!' Chris muttered.

'Who could have disconnected the earth lead?'

Chris looked again at the end of the lead, and then at the metal stake. 'I reckon someone's either pulled or kicked it away. Look, part of the wire is still attached to the stake. Someone's been nosing around here.'

Bernard thought for a moment. 'Those bloody detectives! I bet it was them.'

'What are we going to do?' Lynda said.

'For now there's nothing we can do except wait for John and Barbara to get up here. He'll go bloody berserk when he sees this.'

'Are you sure it was those Special Branch men?' Chris asked. 'I mean, it could have been some kids from town mucking about.'

'It could have been, but my money's on those nosey coppers. Meanwhile, I suggest we carry on with the dig until they get here, then we'll see what John says. You'd better expect some profane language; I'll warn you now.'

Gallagher was not in a good mood. As far as he was concerned, the morning had been a complete waste of time. He had followed and observed the two archaeologists for half the morning and so far he had not seen or heard anything above the mundane and the trivial. True, there had been some reference to James Masters, but what he had overheard in the café had been little more than the usual concern expressed by people who know the patient in question. They might have been talking about anyone in hospital. The rest of their conversation had made little sense to him and signified nothing that might incriminate them in any way.

As on the previous day when he had tracked Barbara's movements around the town, there was little or nothing to arouse suspicion in these people. He said this much to Fox as he sat in their temporary office in the town's police station.

Fox listened to his account and smiled. He produced a sheet of paper and waved it at Gallagher. 'This'll cheer you up,' he said. 'I have obtained a warrant to search that cabin. We're going to pay our friends a visit and see what's really going on up there. Coming?'

55

She was here again; I heard her voice. She is still here, I sense it. I don't see her, but I know that she is still here. She can't quite reach me from her world, but I can reach out to her, it's getting easier now. I can also understand what she is saying. That's good. That means I can speak to her if I wish and bridge the gap between her world and mine.

Angel still tends me. How can an amoeba be so patient? I chose your name well, Angel. In all my life I have never known anyone like her. She tells me she is here for me – I wonder what that means. It could imply that she's my guide. If so, I certainly need one; or it might mean something else – something that for now I can barely bring myself to think about. That would debase her apparent love for me. This transcends the mere physical; it feels almost sacred. That's good coming from me, the unbeliever. My lack of faith is being tested, I can see, but what does all that mean in this place where the things that I have seen exist? All of this is impossible and yet it exists. It surrounds me and for all I know I have become an integral part of it as well: an impossible being. That's a laugh. It's also wrong. I definitely do exist, therefore I am more than just possible – I am. I am here and Angel is here and the people that surround me are here, even if they've been synthesised by whatever it is that made them and everything that surrounds us all. That makes us different. I am not a manufactured being in the sense that these people are manufactured. They were taken from my mind, therefore they are forgeries. They have never actually existed except perhaps in my dreams. It should follow then that they know everything that I know, but I doubt if it's that simple. True, they will possess my knowledge, that makes sense, but they may also possess the knowledge of whatever it is that made them. That could add up to a formidable intellect – far beyond anything that I could imagine. That leaves me as little more than a creature that grubs around in the dirt, barely aware that it even exists. Is that what I am to you, Angel – an amusing little pet to be kept in a cage or a fish tank? Should I grovel to you and perform amusing tricks – crawl across the floor and roll on my back for you – perhaps make funny noises? Gooblygooblygooblygooblygooblygooblysnortsnort! Would that make you laugh? You don't look like the kind of person who would treat someone like that and I don't like to think of you as such. It is wrong, but what if I am right? Am I right? I don't know. I try to think of the purest kind of love and then I pollute it all with thoughts like these. I am not worthy of love if that's what it is; I don't even know that much. I fail in so many ways. It's clear from this that we are different. You are like a creature of spirit and I am… what am I? What exactly am I and what am I doing here? I still don't know why I am here and no one will tell me. Apart from Angel no one speaks and yet there was a voice or was it inside my head: my imagination fooling me into thinking I am not alone inside my head and perhaps this is all inside my head and I am not here at all.

What was that vision I had of travelling through space towards a star – was it a star? There was this light and I was travelling towards it – flying into it in fact, but I don't know what happened next. Nothing happened next, that's what happened, or perhaps didn't happen as the case may be. I was there and then I was back here, so what was it about, then? Does it have a meaning? Perhaps that star-thing is where I am now. Maybe something was trying to tell me that. Maybe it has been trying all along to tell me things like that and I have lacked the ability to understand it. It's hazy. Everything's hazy.

She told me I had travelled far. I wonder what that meant. She told me that my journey is not over. That means there must be more and what is that cylinder doing here? It reminds me of that vision – I will not call it a dream – where I passed through it and tunnelled through space to one particular star, if star it was. I was falling towards it, or perhaps into it – falling slowly, gently falling, drifting down to something, but I don't know what. She was there or perhaps here whispering 'I am here for you. Do not fear.' I did not fear and yet in many ways I am afraid of what might happen to me. I suppose this is a natural fear born of the self-preservation instinct and yet it seems misplaced. I do not feel threatened here, so why should I be afraid? If they were going to hurt me they would have done it by now and somehow I know that they will not hurt me so where's the danger? It must be fear of the unknown. I know I am on the brink of something –

something that they have planned for me and that is most probably why I'm afraid. I am poised on the edge of the high diving board and I am frightened to step off it into the – what exactly…? What will I step into? Perhaps this is another cause of my unease. I simply don't know what is happening to me or why it is happening and why it should be happening to me in particular. It really shouldn't be surprising if I do feel apprehensive under such circumstances.

Perhaps Angel might help me here. She is here for me; she told me so.

I have not been well. It was a fever, I think. Perhaps I am still not well. I feel better but I am still not right. This may be a convalescent period, but what am I convalescing from? Did I fall ill after contracting some alien disease, or was it something else? I was all right to begin with, I remember that, in fact I felt fine and then it hit me with vertigo and I was falling. How long have I been like this? I have no idea and it doesn't matter anyway; I understand that much. I have got used to being outside time's boundaries. What I have difficulty with is having nothing to scale. That's what caused the vertigo. The simple act of standing up becomes difficult because the normal rules of perspective don't seem to apply here. When I tried to walk towards the cylinder it seemed to get further away from me and I couldn't judge its size. When I tried to measure it against the tiles I found that I couldn't measure the tiles either. They were both large and small at the same time as I was large and small and everything around me became variable – that's when I fell and I have not been right since then. Maybe it was the fever that made things difficult to measure, or else it was being unable to measure that engendered the fever – brain overload – couldn't handle it and I simply shut down in order to process this new information. I may never know.

I feel like a child again, learning by trial and error. Children can't judge distance too well, can they? That's why they fall over and bump into things as they learn to walk. Well, that's where I am now: learning to walk all over again. I'm a toddler, that's what I am; bumbling around and discovering new things with each new day. If I think of it like that, it's exciting. After all, everything is exciting when it's new, but it can also be frightening and perhaps that is why I feel frightened. Maybe that answers my question. Once I understand the source of my fear I have mastered it and I can then proceed since it can no longer hold me back. Now there's a thought to hold on to. That puts me on top. I shall do my best to hold on to that. The trouble is things like that slip away from me, but then I have had the fever to contend with. That cooked my memory for me. It should improve now as I get better. I will get better. I am getting better. Do you hear me, Angel? I am getting better. She cannot hear me, of course. These are only thoughts in a time of thoughts. The time for talking is not yet. I can talk as can Angel now that she is whole. The incomplete one now is me. Now there's a turnabout for you. How funny is that? The irony doesn't escape me and that's good. If I can appreciate a small joke I must be improving. Everything is in my favour.

56

John and Barbara arrived at the site and were immediately met by Bernard who came running over even before John had properly parked the Land Rover. John opened the door. 'What's up?'

'Have a look at this.' Bernard pointed towards the cabin.

'Why, what's the matter?'

Bernard swallowed hard. 'Someone's damaged the earth lead. Now the cylinder's back, as large as life and twice as ugly.'

'What do you mean?'

'It's burnt the shield away.'

'What!' John jumped out of the vehicle and strode towards the cabin, followed by Barbara and Bernard. He picked up the broken end of the lead and looked at it. 'How did this happen?'

'We don't know, but I can guess. It's probably those bloody coppers. I suspect they may have been snooping around here.'

John threw the wire down on the ground. His face was livid.

'We don't know that it was them,' Barbara pointed out.

'Who else could it be?' John said. 'It certainly wasn't one of us. I know for a fact no one went near the cabin yesterday. In fact, as best I can remember, no one's been near it since we put the screen around the cylinder.'

'Chris said it might be kids from the town mucking about,' Bernard said. 'Personally, I doubt it, but it's a possibility. Take a look at this.'

He pushed the door open and John looked inside. The cylinder was there, glowing in the dim light of the cabin's smoke-darkened interior. He could see at a glance that its power had increased to something like its full potential, whatever that was. The field of its influence was now tangible from the doorway and it was obvious that the power required to burn away the chicken wire must have been tremendous. The acrid smell of smoke still hung in the air. He stepped back from the door. 'We're lucky it didn't set fire to the whole cabin,' he said. 'The shield has completely burned away. Well, that's put paid to all our hard work trying to make it safe.'

Bernard pulled the door shut. 'What the hell do we do now?'

'Be buggered if I know,' John said. His buoyant mood had evaporated and now he felt despondent. Since effectively screening the cylinder, the project had returned to something like normal. Now all this had been undone, most probably by a prowling, snooping, clumsy policeman. He was furious. What worried him more was the thought that Fox and Gallagher had in all probability seen the cylinder through the cabin window. If so then the game was up. He could no longer keep its discovery a secret.

He turned away from the cabin and started walking back towards the Land Rover. Barbara and Bernard followed him.

'Where are you going?' Barbara said.

'Back to town,' he called over his shoulder. 'When I see Fox I'm going to choke the life out of him!'

She caught him by the shoulder. 'John, calm down. For one thing, we don't know if it was them, and if it wasn't them, you'll give the whole thing away by revealing it to them. Now think! What are you going to do?'

He turned to face her. His shoulders slumped and he shook his head. She was right.

'We're going to have to think very carefully about this before we do anything,' Bernard said. 'I suggest we leave them to make the next move. If they did come up here snooping, they'll sooner or later want to speak to us again.'

'And...?'

'Well...' He thought for a moment. 'I'm afraid we may be forced to disclose the cylinder's existence to them.'

John turned away from him and took another step towards the Land Rover.

'John,' Bernard persisted. 'John, listen. If they have discovered it for themselves we can hardly deny its existence to them now, can we?'

'I suppose not,' he admitted. 'Well, I suppose that does it. We might as well abandon the project here and now and turn it all over to them. We're finished here.'

'John, don't be despondent,' Barbara said. 'They might not have seen it.'

'And if they have?'

'Well, then that's it I'm afraid,' she admitted. 'Come on, John. We're not criminals. They're hardly going to send us to jail for finding it, are they? They might not be too pleased with us for withholding it from them, but that's their problem, not ours.'

'If we have to abandon the dig at this stage, then it is our problem. We have made the most important discovery of all time – far more important than Tutankhamen's tomb, and we shall be forced to abandon it for the sake of that cylinder. I feel sick. We have discovered a culture many centuries beyond its Mesolithic origins and now we have to face the prospect of abandoning it in midstream.'

'We may not have to,' she said. 'I suspect that once the matter of the cylinder has been cleared up, they'll go away and leave us to finish the project in peace. It's an object of great antiquity and it will probably be of little interest to them. Their business is catching terrorists and criminals, not archaeologists.'

'It's an object that glows in the dark and hits you on the head if you get too close to it,' he pointed out. 'What do you think they'll make of that? We might as well be caught in possession of a bomb. We all know what it did to James.'

'Well,' she said after a moment's pause. 'If they have discovered its existence, then I suppose it's out of our hands. We shall just have to wait and see what happens next, but it will have to be their move, not ours. Meanwhile, I suggest we use whatever time we have left to get on with the job in hand. Worrying about it is getting us nowhere.'

'She's right, you know,' Bernard said.

John gave in. She was right. She usually was.

It was mid afternoon when the silver Audi pulled up behind the Land rovers and Fox and Gallagher got out. Fox went straight over to where John was working, while Gallagher wandered over to the cabin. No one noticed him at first.

'Professor Black.'

John looked up and saw Fox standing above him on the edge of the dig. 'Yes?' His voice was icy.

'I would like to speak to you if I may.'

John dropped his trowel and stood up. He guessed what was coming next, but said nothing.

'Where can we talk?'

He climbed out of the pit and stood facing Fox as the others watched. 'What's wrong with here?'

'Suit yourself. I have come to ask you what is in that hut over there.'

'I think we told you once.'

Fox smiled. 'Now, what is *really* in the hut? We have reason to believe that it is being used for something other than tool storage.'

John suddenly felt hot. He was cornered.

'I'm waiting for an answer.'

He searched for an answer but his brain felt paralysed.

Fox took a deep breath. His annoyance was beginning to show. 'Very well, then I shall tell you. We have reason to believe that you are storing radioactive materials in there. Now I am going to demand that you let us have a look inside that hut, or we shall be forced to break and enter. Now which is it to be?'

'You can't do that!' he stormed.

'We *can* do that, Professor. I assure you that we can. We suspect that it is being used to store illicit radioactive materials and that makes it our business. I have obtained a warrant to search that cabin so if I wish to break into it, I can. Do I make myself clear?'

There was no way out. His attitude softened in the manner of one who knows that the game is up and he might as well come clean. His voice became more reasonable and he spoke slowly. 'You can't go in there because there is something in there that we believe is highly dangerous. We don't know what it is. What we do know is that it has an adverse effect on anyone who comes close to it. Do I make myself clear? I cannot allow you to go near that thing. James Masters did and that's why he's in hospital now. It has affected us as well, but to a lesser extent.'

'This sounds to me like bullshit.'

'I assure you that it is not bullshit. I will tell you now; you approach that thing at your peril. I can't stop you, I know, but I urge you to stay away from it until we know how to deal with it.'

'I'm taking a look at it.' Fox insisted and headed towards the cabin. John followed him. Neither of them knew that Gallagher had already entered the cabin and was now squatting in front of the cylinder. In the heat of the moment, Bernard had forgotten to lock the door.

57

Gallagher noticed straight away that the padlocks were not in place and, seeing his chance, he cautiously pushed the door open. Since all eyes were on Fox, it was easy for him to enter the cabin unobserved. Almost immediately he became aware of some kind of energy field inside the building that made his skin prickle. It was obvious too that there had been a small fire in there. The windows had been dimmed by smoke and the charred remains of a chair stood near to a bench which had escaped the worst of the flames, being only slightly charred. In the corner, the curious cylindrical object appeared to float just above the ground, emitting a bluish white light. This was different from the thing that he and Fox had glimpsed through the window that night. It was brighter now and its light was even, not brightest at the ends as it had appeared to them before. The chicken wire wrapping had gone, apparently burnt away.

He took a step towards it, aware that his heart was pounding and that his hands were sweating. If the thing was radioactive, he knew that he could not stay in there for long. He may have already picked up a dangerous dose for all he knew to the contrary. It was while he was thinking this that a loud note sounded inside his head and all thoughts vanished momentarily as he staggered back against the wall. He put his hands up to his head and grunted as he leaned against the wall and tried to regain his composure. His first thought was to get away from there and he took a step towards the door. Then he stopped.

He looked at the cylinder again. He had to. Something compelled him to do so. In the same instant he lost all fear of the thing. He was no longer aware of its energy field and he somehow knew that it would be safe to examine its glowing hull. He wanted to see more of it – to get closer to it – to *understand* it. Slowly, he approached and knelt before the object, curious as it slowly rotated and the patterns presented themselves to him; first the cartouche-like design and then the circular pattern. This one caught his attention and held it. The cylinder stopped rotating and hovered as if inviting him to touch it. This he did. Almost immediately, thoughts came into his head that he had never had before. The cylinder's smooth surface pleased him. It was beautiful. He wondered how he could ever have feared the thing or even thought that it could be at all sinister. It was wholly benign.

He was aware of a multiplicity of thoughts and emotions that flashed before him in quick succession and still he held on to the cylinder, his eyes fixed upon the circular pattern that seemed to grow as if enveloping him. It was turning into a vertical shaft down which he was falling. This might have been alarming, but he had no sensation of depth or fear of what might be at the bottom of the long fall into he knew not what, but he was aware of circles within circles that overlapped and inverted to become other shafts and tunnels down which he hurtled at an ever increasing rate. It looked like the beginning of a long journey in which time would be suspended.

58

'Christ!' John saw and immediately recognised the figure of Gallagher hunched over the cylinder. He stepped back a pace and groaned: 'Oh, you bloody fool.'

Fox paused in the doorway and stared at Gallagher who appeared to be oblivious of his presence. 'What the hell do you think you're doing?' he barked.

Gallagher ignored him and continued to gaze at the cylinder.

'Gallagher, get away from that thing – now!'

Still Gallagher ignored him. He took a step towards the sergeant, but was forcibly restrained by John.

'Don't go in there. That thing will have you as well. This is what I was trying to tell you if only you'd listened to me.'

Fox glared at him. 'Then tell me what the hell else I'm supposed to do. What is that thing?'

'We don't know. What we do know is that this is what it does. James Masters was taken by it in exactly the same way. We nearly were as well, but we were able to see the danger in time. That's why none of us will go near it and that's why I'm asking you to not go near it. It will take you as well.'

'Then what am I supposed to do?' He raised his voice to a shout. 'Gallagher!'

'He probably can't hear you. That thing's got him.'

'Then let me through!'

'No!'

Barbara and Bernard came running over. 'What's up?' Bernard asked.

'It's Gallagher. The cylinder's got him.'

'Shit!' He looked through the open doorway. 'I must have forgotten to secure the door with all the kafuffle we had this morning.'

'That reminds me,' John said, turning to Fox. 'I want a word about that.'

'Leave it for later,' Barbara said. 'In the meantime we have another one in there getting bombed out by that cylinder.'

'There must be something we can do,' Fox said, a note of desperation rising in his voice.

'There's nothing we can do. It's too late,' Barbara said. 'Believe me; if you go in there you'll end up like him. Now, for once in your life, listen. We have all suffered adverse effects from contact with that cylinder. The truth is we don't know how to deal with it and that's why everyone is under strict instructions to stay away from it.'

'Then we've got to get him out of there if it's as dangerous as that,' Fox said. 'For God's sake do something. He's a good officer.'

'Well, I'm afraid that that may change,' John said. 'If you hadn't broken that bloody wire, none of this would have happened. We had that thing under control until you two came snooping around. It was screened and effectively safe, at least for the time being. By breaking that wire you buggered it all up and nearly set fire to the cabin too.'

'How the hell were we supposed to know that? You wouldn't have told us.'

John nodded. That much was true. In a manner of speaking, he was as much to blame as anyone else. He moderated his tone. 'I'm sorry. I'm sorry that this has happened, but really there is nothing we can do for him now. I just hope that he doesn't end up like James Masters. This is exactly what happened to him before he went into a coma. At first he seemed perfectly OK. The coma came only after a second, more prolonged exposure to it.'

'Why did you let him do it a second time?'

'We didn't even know. He broke in under cover of night while we were off the site. We didn't know anything about it until the morning when we found him in there.'

Fox looked at him incredulously. 'Why didn't you tell us this before?'

'Would you have believed me?'

'I suppose not,' he admitted. 'I can scarcely believe it now.'

'Whatever happens,' Barbara said, 'do not let him anywhere near that cylinder again. He may have a compulsion to return to it. James did. He even broke and entered the cabin just to be with it and that is why he's in hospital now. If necessary, lock him up, but don't

240

let him anywhere near here again. That's the best advice we can give you. There's nothing we can do for him now except give you this advice.'

As she spoke, Gallagher arose and slowly, almost casually, walked over to the doorway where they stood. 'What's wrong?' he said.

'What's wrong?' Fox echoed. 'What the hell do you think you're doing, going in there without my knowledge? I should bust you back to the beat for this, you stupid flatfoot. Do you know what you've done?'

Gallagher looked puzzled. 'What?'

'He doesn't know,' Barbara said. 'He will probably have no memory of what happened in there. James was the same.'

Gallagher looked at her. 'I don't know what you're talking about. What is that thing in there?'

'We don't know,' she said. 'We dug it up.'

'And we've never been the same since,' Bernard added.

She ignored his flippant remark and turned to Fox. 'Are you satisfied now that you know what's in there?'

'No,' Fox said, 'I am not satisfied. If that thing is as dangerous as you say it is, it should be removed.'

'And who would remove it, and how?' John said. 'We can't go near it now. The field is too strong.'

'It's perfectly safe,' Gallagher said. 'I've seen it – I've even touched it and it's harmless.'

'Don't you remember?' Fox stormed. 'Don't you remember anything about what happened in there? Damn it man, you were captivated by it. I shouted your name and you didn't hear me.' He stopped and looked at him. 'You really don't know, do you?'

'Come with me,' Barbara said and led him away from the others. A short distance away, she stopped and turned to him. 'Look,' she began. 'Shouting at him isn't going to help. He has no recollection of what happened in there. This is exactly the same as what happened to James. He came out looking as if nothing had happened and he was all right the next day, and for some days after that. He only went AWOL later, and that's when he developed his compulsion to get back to the cylinder. I'm telling you this because what's happening here is almost a carbon copy of James Masters' story. Now do you understand why we didn't want you to go near it? We don't know what we're dealing with here. That thing may possibly be of extraterrestrial origin; we don't know. What we do know is that it employs a technology that is unknown to us and that it is extremely dangerous to go anywhere near it. It may trick you into thinking it's safe, but we've experienced nightmares and vivid dreams ever since we first contacted it. Gallagher may well suffer the same thing, I'll warn you now.'

Fox was lost for words. He looked at the ground at this feet and then at Barbara. 'You mean it's going to screw his head up?'

'I wouldn't put it in those words exactly, but yes. This is why we have been trying to contain it so that the fewer people know about it the better. We don't like to think what might happen if its effect spread any further than it already has done.'

Fox was in a quandary. In his entire career he had never encountered a situation like this and he had dealt with some odd ones. Dealing with something that might have come from another planet and that had the power to alter peoples' minds was almost past belief and consequently he was not equipped to deal with it. No one was. 'I will admit I don't know what to do about this,' he said.

'Neither do we,' she admitted as they walked back to rejoin the others.

'What happens now?' Bernard asked as they approached.

Fox came to a decision. 'For now, we shall seal off the area surrounding the hut and no one, I repeat, no one will be allowed to cross the cordon or they will face the consequences.'

'How will that affect our work on the project?' John asked.

'As long as no one crosses the cordon, you can carry on as before.'

Gallagher shook his head but said nothing.

'I must ask you for the keys to the door,' Fox said.

Bernard fumbled in his coat pocket and produced the keys. Fox took them.

'What are you going to tell them back at the station?' Bernard asked.

Fox gave him a quizzical look.

'I mean, are you going to tell them that you've discovered an alien machine that's been buried for seven and a half thousand years and that alters peoples' minds if the get too close to it? I'd like to see their faces when you do.'

'I'll think of something,' he said. 'Let me worry about that.'

Bernard shrugged. 'Good luck.'

'So you're not going to arrest us then?' John said, unable to conceal the sarcastic tone in his voice.

Fox glared at him. 'I would like to, but as far as I can see you've done nothing wrong here.' He turned to Gallagher. 'Come on. Let's get this door locked and head back into town.' He turned back to John. 'I repeat; no one is to go near this shed. Do I make myself clear?'

John said nothing. Fox's order was unnecessary as far as he was concerned.

Fox closed the cabin door and snapped the two padlocks shut; then he and Gallagher headed back to the car. The team watched them go.

'Pompous prick,' John growled.

Barbara touched his arm. 'He's only doing his job.'

'So was Hitler,' he retorted.

59

James opened his eyes and saw Angel beside him. Her eyes were closed and he wondered if she was asleep. Indeed, he wondered if she ever slept – if she was capable of sleeping. After all, she was not truly human. Just how human she was he could only guess. He wondered if she ate and drank and had the normal bodily functions common to all living beings. Did she hunger and thirst and sometimes feel the sexual urge? He did not know.

At the same time he realised that he had neither eaten nor drunk since his appearance in this world; neither had he felt the need to do so. He wondered if he was being fed and watered by some osmotic process of which he knew nothing. Perhaps he could obtain sustenance through his skin from the air, rather like some plants did. It was an interesting question for which he had no answer.

He moved his right arm and found that movement was no longer difficult. This meant that he was getting better. He felt better.

'Angel,' he whispered.

She opened her eyes and looked at him. 'Are you better?'

'A bit; I feel stronger.'

She smiled and brushed a stray hair away from his eyes. 'Good,' she said. 'Soon you will be strong again.'

'I will need to be strong.'

'We have much to learn from each other.'

'Don't you already know me?'

'Not as much as you think we do,' she said. He noticed that she often referred to herself in the plural and he wondered if she was indeed referring to herself, or to herself and the other beings that surrounded them and which inhabited this world. Perhaps that was to be expected from a collective intelligence. It stood to reason. He wondered why she and the other humanoids had been created, if that was the right word. Perhaps synthesised would have been a more apt description for these beings. He assumed that they had been put there to make him feel more at ease in this alien environment. He looked at her again. She was familiar in an odd sort of way. He could not remember where or even if he had seen her before. Perhaps he might have known someone like her in that previous life of which he was only barely aware, or perhaps she was a composite of the various women he had known in that life. Another possibility was that she was the product of a fantasy with her perfect body and immaculate skin; he did not know, but still she looked familiar. He looked at the others arranged around him, now in attitudes of rest. Some sat, others lay down and appeared to be sleeping, none of them spoke; in fact, he had never heard any of them speak apart from Angel. He wondered if they possessed the power of speech or if they had been created as mutes; put there purely for effect and for no other reason. He wondered if they looked as familiar to him as she did. They did, but again he could not remember where or even if he had actually met them before. They, like Angel, also had perfect bodies, almost too perfect, and this was why they did not look real. Few people in his experience had bodies as flawless and as perfectly proportioned as these.

'Why am I here?' he whispered.

'Soon you will know.'

This did not answer his question. This vague reply to a valid question angered him, but he suppressed it. He felt that the beautiful, if synthetic creature that hovered over him and who had tended him through his illness was a creature of pure love which was why he had nicknamed her Angel. He could not express anger towards her. She seemed to be too pure for that. Looks could deceive, he knew, especially in a place where everything seemed to be an illusion, but in his present circumstances he was forced to suspend his disbelief and simply take things as they appeared. He had no reason to doubt the reality of the things he saw, no matter how fantastic they seemed. As in a dream, he saw everything as real, no matter how impossible it might appear to be, but this was not a dream. If it was, then it was the most protracted dream he had ever had, and the most vivid. He had been told that other humans had been here before him and he wondered if they too had had similar experiences to those that he was now undergoing. He wondered if this was a normal process for those in his position, common to all new arrivals, or if he was unique.

He wondered about those others and if they were still here. He had asked Angel and she had answered him, affirming that they were, but for some obscure reason he was not able to see them yet. He knew that he would always be here, or at least a part of him would remain to occupy this particular point in time, even if he eventually had to return to that other world. It stood to reason that in a place where time lines ran parallel, part of him would always remain. Perhaps that was what she had meant. The same would be true of them. He wondered how many of these others there were and how long they had been here, as if it mattered in a place without time. He still had difficulty understanding that, but he was beginning to find his comprehension of such things getting easier as he got better. His illness had fuzzed his thoughts for a while and yet he felt that his thought processes had not diminished as much as he might have supposed. Concepts that were once hard to understand were becoming clearer to him. Perhaps Angel, with her constant light hand pressure to his forehead, had been altering his consciousness in such a subtle way that he was barely aware of it. After all, she was not human. He had to keep reminding himself of that fact. She looked human, she felt human; she was warm and alive, but the fact remained that she was not human. She was a good replica, but she was a creature or perhaps a part of a creature that was not of flesh as he would know it. This was a being of pure intellect and she had been created by that intellect.

He felt a sudden urge to discover just how human she was. With astonishing boldness he raised his right arm and touched her face. 'Kiss me.' He said.

Without a word she bent over and kissed him on the mouth. Her lips were moist. It was a light kiss and yet it made him tingle in a way that he had not experienced before or if he had, he had forgotten the sensation. He put his arms around her and felt the warmth of living flesh. Before he knew what he was doing, he cupped her left breast in his hand and felt its firm softness and the steadily hardening nipple. She was real.

She broke away from him and sat up again.

He let his arms drop back, feeling ashamed of what he had just done. 'I'm sorry,' he said. 'I didn't mean to…'

She lightly brushed his cheek with her hand. 'Don't apologise,' she said. 'The time is not right. We are not ready for this yet.'

He wondered what she meant by *we*. Was she referring to them both, or was she once more referring to herself in the plural? All too often he found her statements cryptic and ambiguous. As a consequence they were frequently difficult to understand.

He was aware that he had an erection and he tried to force himself to lose it. He hoped that she had not noticed.

'I understand how you feel,' she said. 'You are human after all.'

'And you are not, I suppose?' He thought he might test her with this question.

'That was unkind.'

He knew he had gone too far. 'I'm sorry,' he said. 'I didn't mean to hurt you.'

She spoke to him in the first person. 'I have feelings, you know. Does that make me human?'

He felt an upsurge of sadness at this and fought hard to control it. He wanted to draw her close and express his regret, but he resisted the urge for fear that it might be misinterpreted as another clumsy attempt at sexual contact. He felt that he had done enough harm already with his carelessness and acid tongued cruelty to one who had done nothing to deserve it. His throat was tight and his eyes burned with suppressed tears.

He attempted a smile. 'Yes it does. It makes you very human.'

Perhaps, he thought, her capacity to forgive and understand made her more than human.

She touched his forehead again. 'Your anger will leave you as you improve. We are not strangers to it. There has been anger before, as you will learn.'

'There was a massacre.'

'You know of it. Mistakes were made. That too makes us human.'

It surprised him to hear through her that this super intelligence had the modesty to admit to having made mistakes. This knowledge was reassuring. She had told him that they had much to learn from each other and this too had amounted to an admission of an imperfect knowledge of humankind. It also implied that the forthcoming learning process in whatever form it took would be more than just a one-way affair.

'We are a dangerous species.' He said. 'Do you not fear us?'

'We do not need to fear you. We fear nothing.'

'Nothing?'

'Nothing.'

'You are a creature of love and we are not. We fight wars, commit murder, lie, cheat and steal, even from those we may love. We are untrustworthy and duplicitous. As a result we suspect everyone else of being the same, even those whose motives may be genuine. We flatter ourselves with the thought that we are capable of love, but we don't really understand the meaning of the word. That is why I say we are a dangerous species – and you do not fear us?'

She smiled at him. 'You are not all bad. We know that much. You have a rather dim view of yourself, don't you?'

'I'm not talking about myself.'

'Are you sure?'

He was not at all sure. He would have to think about this. The possibility that he could be projecting his own faults onto others occurred to him. If that was so than she was right and he really did have a poor view of himself.

He looked into her eyes and saw that she was looking at him intently, as if she was reading his thoughts. He could not lie to her. 'I...' he began and then hesitated. Those eyes held him in thrall. He started again. 'You've read me well. Perhaps here is where my journey begins.'

The eyes smiled.

60

Fox and Gallagher drove back towards the town in silence. Normally it was Gallagher who did the driving but in view of recent circumstances Fox felt that it would be safer if he drove. He was still quietly furious with Gallagher for his foolhardiness in entering the cabin unprotected against radiation or any other possible hazard and without his knowledge or consent. If that thing in there was radioactive, then he would have picked up a heavy dose of it. Goodness knows he had been exposed to it for long enough, the stupid bastard. He decided that it would be best to have him scanned for possible radioactive contamination, just in case. Gallagher's insistence that it was perfectly harmless had convinced no one, him least of all. He made a decision.

'I'm running you to the hospital,' he said.

Gallagher looked surprised. 'What for?'

'A full check-up, just in case.'

'There's nothing wrong with me,' he protested.

'You'll bloody well do as you're told.'

They fell silent again as Gallagher tried to recollect his experience with the cylinder. He could remember little of it. He recalled seeing it in the corner of the cabin and hearing the loud noise in his head that had knocked him staggering before he had crouched in front of it and reached out to touch its smooth, glowing shell. There had been a sensation of falling into it and then nothing more until he stood with the others by the doorway. What had happened in between was blank. Despite this, he was aware of odd fragments of thought that seemed to enter his head for no obvious reason and then disappeared just as suddenly as they appeared, rather like mini hallucinations. Perhaps Fox was right after all and he really did need a medical check-up. He was still smarting from the way his superior officer had spoken to him. He was not used to people talking to him like that. Although he resented Fox's brusque attitude towards him, he had to admit that he was probably right to insist that he visit the hospital. He still did not believe that the cylinder was in any way dangerous, although he had no sensible reason to suppose that it was safe either. It was just an unaccountable feeling; that was all.

He yawned. Whatever had taken place during his time with the cylinder had tired him out. He felt that he needed a long sleep. This was unusual, since he was not in the habit of afternoon sleeping. Perhaps that thing really had screwed his head up. At the same time he felt that he had to see it again. He tried to put this urge out of his head by wondering how Arsenal would fare against Leeds on Saturday, but still the cylinder kept intruding into his thoughts.

They arrived at the hospital and went straight to the Accident and Emergency department where Fox presented Gallagher to the triage nurse, stating possible radioactive contamination as the reason for his visit. The nurse gave him an odd look at which he felt obliged to produce his ID badge and introduce himself with his full title as Detective Inspector Dennis Fox, Special Branch. This changed her attitude and she immediately picked up the telephone and spoke to someone, stating that this was an emergency.

They sat down and waited for someone to come.

'I don't know what I'm doing here,' Gallagher said moodily.

'You're here because you're a prat,' Fox reminded him. 'If you hadn't gone charging in there without my knowledge, we wouldn't be here.'

'I'm sure the thing isn't radioactive.'

'How do you know?'

He did not know.

Eventually they were met by a doctor and Fox concocted some story about possible exposure to a source of radiation and maybe other contamination as well in the course of his duty. Once more, he produced his ID badge to verify this unlikely sounding tale. The doctor explained that the hospital was not properly equipped to deal with this, but he admitted Gallagher anyway for observation. They would collect saliva, blood and urine samples and send them to the Physics Department at a nearby university where they could be checked for the presence of radiation. They had the equipment there to detect it. Meanwhile, they could check him for symptoms for the onset of radiation sickness and conduct tests to see if any known toxins were present in his system.

Fox was satisfied with this while Gallagher maintained that it was a lot of fuss for nothing. He felt fine, or so he said. The truth was he felt very tired.

As a precaution, Gallagher was put into an isolation ward and left there, still protesting that he was not radioactive. Fox then returned to town, intending to file a report and get the police to fence off the area surrounding the cabin, after which he would speak to those archaeologists again when they had finished work and got back to town. Although he no longer considered them to be a risk to internal security, he was still not happy with the situation as it stood. Despite his hardboiled scepticism, he was convinced that they were holding something which, even if it was an ancient artefact, was still potentially dangerous. He had no idea what it was, but he had witnessed its effect at first hand, first on Masters and now on Gallagher. This was evidence enough as far as he was concerned. It was then that he made a surprising decision. He would sue for peace with Professor Black and his team. Alone, he was not equipped to deal with the cylinder. He needed advice from those who had had some experience of it and the peculiar effect it seemed to have on those who came into contact with it. He had noticed Gallagher's uncharacteristic tiredness and this concerned him. No matter how Gallagher might have denied it, that cylinder had affected him.

Meanwhile, overcome by tiredness, Gallagher slept, accompanied by fitful dreams and visions of the cylinder. Once more he was falling into the circular pattern, going faster and faster, accelerating towards something, he knew not what. He awoke and slept again. This time he dreamt of people from another time, performing some kind of esoteric ceremony that was centred on the cylinder. He heard a rhythmic chant and a brittle five note tune that was repeated over and over again with small variations occurring from time to time, but always consisting of the same five notes. He could see some of the people reaching a kind of ecstatic climax as the chanting continued while the cylinder remained in the centre, coolly glowing and hovering just above the ground as he had seen it in the cabin. He knew that he was witnessing a scene from long ago. The simple clothing of the people and their unintelligible language suggested this.

He awoke from this second dream with the arrival of a doctor who had come to take swabs from his mouth and a blood sample for analysis. He wanted to tell the doctor about the cylinder and the effect that his recent contact with it seemed to be having on him, but he decided against it. For one thing, the doctor probably would not believe him and for another, if he did, then that would alert more people to its existence and that would never do. He was still professional enough to know when to keep a secret, so he kept all details of the possible cause of his supposed illness to the barest minimum.

The doctor left and once more he was alone, believing now that Fox had been right to admit him. That thing in the hut had definitely had some effect on him. He picked up the headphones and tried out the radio. It worked, but it failed to take his mind off the thing in the cabin. Still he listened to it and once more he fell asleep, listening to pop music interspersed with the friendly chatter of the hospital radio DJ telling him more about the cylinder.

61

The team returned from the dig and, after parking the Land Rovers in the hotel car park, went up to their rooms. They met later in the hotel bar as was their custom before dinner and here they were joined by Inspector fox who had been patiently waiting for them. He stood at the bar, watching them in the mirror as they entered. Bernard came in first, followed by Barbara and John. It was Bernard who spotted him first. Instead of avoiding the detective, he walked over to him and enquired about Gallagher's health.

'I've admitted him to hospital,' he said. 'Did none of you ever think that that thing might be radioactive?'

'No,' he admitted.

'Look,' Fox began. 'I'm off duty at the moment, hence this,' he indicated his three quarters full pint, 'so this is a purely social chat. I want to make it clear that I don't suspect anyone involved in this case, so you can relax. I'm not here to arrest anyone. I just want to clear one or two things up, that's all.'

'We wouldn't mind clearing one or two things up ourselves,' Bernard said. 'Look, we don't know any more about that thing up there than you do. It's a mystery object.'

'But you've had more time to study it than we have. That's why I want to talk to you about it.'

John and Barbara joined them. John was not happy to see him there, but he said nothing. He ordered drinks for himself and Barbara without a glance in Fox's direction. He gave the barman a ten pound note and waited for his change.

Fox ignored this deliberate snub and came straight to the point. 'Professor Black, I'd like to have a chat with you if you don't mind.'

John turned to face him. 'What is it now?'

Fox attempted a smile. He did not want a confrontation with this irascible man. He began apologetically. 'I'm sorry to bother you again, but it seems now that we find ourselves in the same boat.'

'In what way?'

'It's that cylinder thing. It's put one of your men into hospital and now I've got one in there by the same token.'

'You?' John's eyes narrowed.

'Detective Sergeant Gallagher. They're holding him for a day or so for observation. He reckons he's all right, but I'm not sure about that. Something in him has changed.'

'In what way?'

'I don't know exactly. He looks tired and this is not typical of him. We've worked together for two years now and I think I know him well enough to know his ways. They're conducting tests on him for radiation poisoning and other toxins that might have got into his system. Have they tested James Masters for the same thing?'

'I really don't know. I imagine they probably would as a matter of routine, but I don't know. The doctor has told us nothing about it.'

Fox nodded. 'That's reassuring. If they'd found anything, they would have told you by now – or us,' he added.

'That's if they tested him,' John pointed out. 'Like I say, I don't know.'

'Listen,' Fox began. 'I'm here off duty and I can tell you now off the record that I don't know what to do about this situation. I'm out of my depth here.'

'You and me both, mate,' Bernard said.

Fox continued: 'I'll come straight to the point. I would like us to work together on this case. I know we got off to a bad start, but I'd like to offer you a truce. I am satisfied that there has been no skulduggery here, but that cylinder has got a lot to answer for. I would be interested to know how it has affected you since your exposure to it.'

John looked at him incredulously, but Barbara stepped in. She was as anxious to make peace as Fox appeared to be, having realised that further confrontation would only serve to hinder both parties involved in the matter. She looked at John who was about to say something and held a finger up. 'Pax,' she said.

John held his peace.

She turned to Fox. 'OK, I see no point in us remaining at loggerheads, but I would like you to grant us the freedom to continue our project in peace. First...' and here she looked at John... 'Is it absolutely necessary to cordon off the cabin? I mean, wouldn't the presence of police tape simply draw attention to it?'

Fox thought about this. She had a valid point. At the same time there was the constant danger of a possible break-in, either by vandals or someone like James Masters who had already broken in once before. 'I'll think about it,' he said.

'Believe me; none of us is likely to go in there. We know only too well what happens if we get too close to the cylinder, remember. I have no wish to relive some of the dreams that I have had since I handled that thing.'

'And what about Masters and Gallagher, what's to stop them from breaking in?'

'Tying a cordon around it will do nothing to prevent that, will it?'

'I suppose not,' he admitted. 'I would have to post a guard on the door. I do have the authority.'

'But wouldn't it put an extra strain on your resources? This is a peaceful town with only a few available officers, is it not?'

'I could draft extra officers in from London.'

She was in no doubt that he could. 'How would you explain the cylinder to them? I mean, we can scarcely believe the thing ourselves, so how might you explain it to a bunch of sceptical policemen?'

He held his hand up. 'Ok, you've got me there; but I shall make no promises. I shall think about it, that's all.'

'Good. Now we shall talk of other things. What exactly do you want to know?'

'You said that it affected you psychologically. What exactly did you mean by that?'

'Dreams,' she said simply. 'We have all had them, and they were all centred on the same thing. It might sound crazy, but we have reason to believe that they were implanted by that cylinder and that what we were seeing were images from its past. Now I want your assurance here that you will not divulge to anyone what I'm about to tell you. Do I have that assurance?'

'Trust me.'

'Right, the reason for all this secrecy is the size of the discovery we have made. When the news breaks, it will shake the world of archaeology to its foundations. We thought at first that the site we were excavating belonged to the Iron Age. It does not. Put simply, the site dates from the Mesolithic period, some seven and a half thousand years ago. It is middle Stone Age, but it possessed a technology far in advance of anything belonging to that era. Are you with me so far?'

Fox looked doubtful. 'I think so.'

'Well, we think, in fact we're sure that the cylinder had something to do with that. It did something to those people that accelerated their technological development to a point where they were millennia ahead of their neighbours. The trouble was that their cultural development did not keep pace with this.'

'How do you know all this?'

'We built up the story from our dreams. I know it sounds crazy, but they became like jigsaw pieces from which we were able to build up something like a history of the culture surrounding the cylinder. Before James went into his coma, he reeled off a potted history of what he called the People of the Cylinder, and his account matched what we had seen in our visions almost exactly. It is almost certain that the cylinder was instrumental in turning them from Stone Age people to developing iron tools and weapons and becoming an elite civilisation, enslaving those around them and demanding tithes that they could not afford to pay. This drove the neighbouring tribes into starvation. On top of that, they practised human sacrifice and young women were taken from the surrounding clans to be slaughtered in the name of the cylinder. Because the People of the Cylinder were well armed and organised, all resistance was ruthlessly put down. Eventually, there was a mass uprising and the People of the Cylinder were overthrown in what I can only describe as a bloodbath. Most if not all were killed and the culture died. After that, the cylinder was forgotten until we rediscovered it.'

He listened to her account with interest. 'You mean to tell me that that thing created an entire culture?'

'It would appear so, albeit a small one. It might be argued that it was also instrumental in its destruction. That's another reason why it should be considered dangerous. I'm still not convinced that we're ready for it yet.'

Fox took a drink.

'Another thing,' she continued. 'After his first contact with it, James said he was on his way to working out the cylinder's composition. He said it was some kind of super ceramic, but we don't yet possess the technology to make it. Now where do you think he got that idea from?'

'From the cylinder, presumably.'

'Exactly. You might notice something similar with your colleague.'

'George? He has enough bright ideas already. He's one of the best in his field, or he was.' He was silent for a moment. 'I hope he's OK. What possessed the daft sod to go in there?'

'He couldn't help it. Once the cylinder had him he had no choice. If any of us had seen him, we'd have hauled him out of there double quick. But by the time we discovered him in there it was too late.'

'What will happen to him now? Will he end up in a coma like James Masters?'

She shook her head. 'We shall have to wait and see.'

62

Eventually, Fox departed and the team, now joined by Lynda and Chris, went to the dining room for dinner.

'Well,' Bernard said after they had ordered their meal. 'What do you think of our new colleague?'

'I'd like to know why he wanted to declare a truce,' John said.

'He explained that,' Barbara said. 'He was honest enough to confess he was out of his depth and he wants our assistance.'

'And he thinks we are able to give it? What makes him think we might help him? It's not long ago he wanted to lock us all up for possession of a mysterious object.'

'Oh, come on John. You know he never intended to do anything of the kind. He was here to investigate James's apparent disappearance.'

'Well, now he's found both him and the cylinder. How's that for a bargain?' He thought for a moment. Perhaps he was being unfair to Fox, but he mistrusted the man and doubted his motives for wanting to work together with the team. He was aware that he could be wrong, but he was also aware of the fact that Fox was a policeman and not an archaeologist. This was an important difference and it mattered.

'Let's give him a chance,' Bernard said. 'I have no reason do doubt his sincerity in this matter. His sergeant's in hospital and could end up in a coma like James. He has every right to be concerned and it's lucky for us that he didn't stop the project on the strength of that alone.'

'He still could,' John said.

'He seems to have chosen not to. No, I say we give him a chance.'

John backed down. He was outvoted on the matter. He understood that it was better to have Fox on their side than against them, but he could feel his authority slipping away from him and this rankled. Still, he was in no position to argue. Fox had him by the balls and he knew it. At least Barbara had the knack of managing him. Her skill in handling people was remarkable and her negotiating ability had probably helped to save the project. He admired her for that. Without her, the police might have taken over and the project would have foundered.

'OK,' he said at length. 'We'll give him a chance. The way I see it, we have no choice. I could still wring his bloody neck for breaking that earth wire, though.'

'It was an accident,' Barbara pointed out.

'An accident that has sent us straight back to square one,' he said. 'We had it under control. Breaking that earth lead freed it to destroy the screen and capture Gallagher. Have you any idea how much power that thing has now? I very much doubt that we could ever get close enough to screen it again, even with our earthed shields. Chris's screen was vaporised and that must have taken a tremendous surge of power. I'm not prepared to take the risk of attempting it again. There's no knowing what it might do to anyone approaching it now.'

'It didn't vaporise Gallagher,' Bernard pointed out.

'True,' he admitted. 'But it has ably demonstrated that it could have done and that's enough for me.'

Bernard pulled a face. 'I'm out of my depth here.'

'We all are,' Chris said.

'The man's right,' Bernard agreed. 'This whole bloody situation has gone out of control. Whether we like it or not, that thing has taken our lives over. Perhaps this is where Inspector Fox comes in. An extra head might think of something to bring it under control. We can't.'

'Then it is agreed that we take Fox on board,' John said, even though it was still against his better judgement.

'Agreed,' Bernard said amid a murmured consensus of approval from the others. The matter was decided.

The next matter for discussion was Gallagher. There was no doubt that Fox had done the right thing in taking him to the hospital for tests. John reflected that he should have done the same thing with everyone who had come into contact with it, himself included. However, none of them had shown any physical symptoms and he was satisfied that they had not been exposed to dangerous levels of radiation. Had this been the case they would almost certainly have started to show the first signs of sickness by now, if not sooner. Still, he should have thought more about the physical risks than he had done. Goodness knows, the cylinder's psychological effects should have alerted him to the possibility of physical damage as well, but he simply had not thought of it. That had been careless, but he had not considered the possibility of the thing being radioactive. For the first few days, even after it had become active, it had not aroused any such suspicion. It should have done as soon as it started to glow and its energy field became tangible.

He made a mental note to ask the hospital if James had been tested for possible radioactive contamination and then he thought against it. It would be likely to arouse further suspicion and anyway, Gallagher was to be tested for that. He would know when the test results were made known and then he could act if necessary. Besides, one of the doctors had told him that James had been tested for the presence of toxins and possible drug abuse – that was now standard procedure in a case like this and nothing had been found. That was one of the reasons why they were so baffled by his condition. There seemed to be no physical cause that they could determine, so the possibility of poisoning or even radiation could be eliminated. This, to some extent, put his mind at rest.

He wondered now how Gallagher would react to his prolonged exposure to the cylinder. He had spent as much if not more time in its power than James had done the first time and he had reacted in much the same way, displaying little or no memory of what had happened while he was there. Added to that, the cylinder had now reached a new level of energy even higher than it had been when James had handled it, so there was no knowing what the outcome might be. In short, it was all a bloody mess.

Eventually, the meals arrived and everyone fell to eating. The conversation then turned to more general matters, but still John saw further trouble ahead. It was bad enough having had one man hospitalised by the cylinder; two was becoming too much to contend with. He began to think that if Fox wanted to mount a police guard on the cabin door, it would be a good thing. He would do nothing to prevent it.

63

Gallagher awoke from a strange dream in which he was wandering across an alien landscape amid what appeared to be living creatures, but these were unlike anything he could have imagined. They had no shape that he could define and they seemed to be interconnected by fine threads along which tiny pulses of light travelled, as if they were all communicating with each other in some kind of super network. Although the air was clear, there appeared to be no horizon and the sky had about it a milky appearance. The ground was indistinct.

He lay awake for some time, pondering this peculiar vision. It was unlike anything he had ever dreamed before. He tried to remember what had happened before he had arrived in that strange landscape, but he could not. Again he thought of the cylinder in the cabin and he remembered the circular pattern that had held his attention for so long. He had half forgotten that. Now it appeared before him again as a tantalising design – one that seemed to draw him in and engulf him as if swallowing him whole, but this was not an alarming experience. He felt that it was the beginning of a fascinating journey. What did alarm him was the fact that these visions were invading his mind uninvited. He rearranged his pillows and sat up in bed. It was night and the ward lights were dimmed. He had no idea of the time. He could not see a clock. Some insidious voice told him that the cylinder was not finished with him yet and that he would see it again soon. He thought of getting up and leaving the hospital, but he lacked the energy to do it. Whatever else the cylinder may have done to him, it had sapped his strength and left him unaccountably tired. This was unnatural for a normally fit and energetic man who regularly worked out in the gym, liked running and boxing, and who had to keep fit as a necessary part of his job. Perhaps he really was ill after all.

He thought of James Masters. At the same time another thought came to him. The archaeologists had told him that James had been brought in to look at something they had found. Supposing that thing had been the cylinder. It occurred to him that James's coma might have been the result of prolonged exposure to it. Although he had not been told the full story, he reasoned it was likely that James had done much the same thing as he was supposed to have done and now he was lying in a vegetative state, probably not far from where he lay. If that was the case then it was almost certain that the cylinder had put him into that state and now he, a professional police officer attached to Special Branch and a man who should have known better, had put himself into a similar position. What had he been thinking of? True, he had not known the risk involved at the time, but surely he should have been aware of other possible dangers such as radiation. Damn it, both he and Fox had initially thought the thing to be radioactive and still he had gone in there, unprotected and forgetting all those original suspicions. Because of his stupidity, he had exposed himself to the risk of lapsing into the same condition as Masters, and yet he recalled having felt a sudden compulsion to get closer to the cylinder. He had not been able to resist it.

He tried again to recall what happened when he had first entered the cabin. Something had hit him – a pulse of energy or something of the sort – he remembered that, after which he had become aware of the cylinder's presence. It was then that he had felt the need to examine it more closely. In that instant he had lost all fear of it and all his natural caution had evaporated as he approached the object and – and here he now found his next action hard to believe – he had actually touched the thing. What had happened after that he could only recall in fragments. Initially, he had remembered nothing of it, but now small fragments of the experience started to return to him. The pattern returned yet again. He felt that this was a key to something important, he could not guess what, but it was crucial to better understanding the cylinder's purpose. The cylinder had stopped rotating with the pattern facing him and then he had entered it, hurtling down a tube or a tunnel towards he knew not what. Now he had the still fresh memory of the dream of a landscape so unlike anything he could have imagined that he was forced to wonder if there was a link between it and the cylinder. He had no knowledge of the dreams that the members of the archaeological team had had since their initial contact with it. Had he known, he would have had no doubt about the connection. As it was, he could only speculate.

He wondered what the time was. He wanted to sleep again, but the threat of further dreams forced him to try and stay awake. These dreams had not been unduly disturbing, but they had unsettled him in a way he could not quite define. Again, he had no prior knowledge of the blood-soaked nightmares that had so tormented Barbara and the other members of the archaeological team that had had previous contact with the cylinder, but still he had an uneasy feeling that a considerable amount of bloodletting had been involved in its history. This seemed wrong for something that he was convinced was essentially benign. He could not know that the early people who had first contacted the cylinder had performed human sacrifices to it and that ultimately it had witnessed a bloody uprising with indiscriminate slaughter. Despite this lack of knowledge, he felt uneasy about the prospect of further dreams invading his sleep, fearing that something nasty lay in wait for him and so he sat awake, contemplating his next move. As best he could see he had only one option. There were too many questions still unanswered concerning that cylinder and he resolved that as soon as he was discharged from hospital he would try to get back to it at the first opportunity. Fox would try to stop him of course, but he would get around that particular problem if it arose. Fox could not watch him all the time. He began to work out ways of getting back to it, unaware that he was succumbing to the same obsession that had so gripped James Masters.

64

That night Barbara had another dream about James. In it she saw him inside the same large hall, surrounded by the same people and attended by the beautiful dark haired girl who still sat beside him. No one spoke and at first she thought he was asleep, but she saw that his eyes were open and fixed upon something that she could not see. She tried to attract his attention by calling his name, but he appeared not to hear. Then she heard his voice although he did not appear to speak directly to her.

I know you, you have been here before.

'I am Barbara.'

Barbara...   There was a pause.   Barbara, I think I remember you now; I hear your voice but I'm not able to see you. You are somewhere else which is why I cannot see you. Here things are different.   There was another pause.   I feel I know you but I don't know where you are. Do you understand?

'Yes, I understand, but where are you?'

I don't know, but I do know I am safe here and that you are worried. I can feel that. You needn't worry. When the time is right I shall return.

'When will that be?'

There was a long pause.   Here time as you know it does not exist so I cannot say. The matter is not in my hands but I know I must return to the world of your people. It may be soon but I cannot measure time here.

'Who are those people with you?'

They were made for me.

'Made for you?'

They were made for me. I don't know why, but they are here for me. Angel is here for me... Angel... Angel...   His voice faded and returned.   You needn't fear for me. Do not fear... do not fear... do not... fear...

'James... James!'

Silence. The image faded and she awoke with it fresh in her mind. She switched on the bedside light and got out of bed. She had to write out a transcription of the conversation before she forgot it. Already it was fading. John stirred and turned over, but he did not wake up. She found a pen and paper and wrote what she could remember of their conversation. On reading it back, it looked disjointed, but the essence of what had been said was still there. She put the pen and paper down and returned to bed, feeling reassured. It was irrational, but she now felt that James was safe, wherever he was. She tried to get back to sleep but sleep eluded her. No matter which way she looked at it, she was convinced that she had somehow been in direct contact with James and that this had not been a mere dream. It had been too vivid for that. She saw again in graphic detail the great hall with James surrounded by people and attended by the exquisite girl he called Angel. He had said that she was there for him. She wondered what he had meant by that. On reflection, their entire conversation had had about it a vague quality, revealing little or nothing of what was actually going on in that ethereal place. She did not know why he was there. She might never know. What she did know was that he did not belong there. His place was with his own people, not in some celestial Nowheresville devoid of time and out of place. He had told her that he was safe and that there was no need to fear for him, but how true was that? It was, after all, only his word, or words that may have been fed to him by the mysterious people that surrounded him. On the rational side it was possible, indeed probable that the whole vision might have been just a dream, but it had been so vivid that she found it hard to dismiss it as such. She wondered if he might have established some kind of telepathic link with her. She had spent more time with him than anyone else outside the hospital since he had gone into his coma and they had been friends for a long time. It therefore made sense that if he was going to attempt any sort of contact with his own world, he would do it through her.

It was a distinct possibility that the things she had seen existed inside his head and that she had had a glimpse of his fevered imagination running through an alien world of his own invention. This was most likely, but it still retained the possibility of a telepathic link having been established between them.

She resolved to discuss it with John in the morning over their now customary coffee after their visit to the hospital. Slowly, she drifted off to sleep, recalling James's words: *Do not fear...do not fear...* She would try not to fear for him.

65

The next morning after breakfast, Barbara and John visited James again and once more she spoke to him, but this time her topic of conversation was different.

'Hello, James,' she began. 'Thank you for talking to me last night; it was reassuring to hear that you're keeping well.'

John listened to this, scarcely able to believe what he was hearing. Had James sent her a postcard or some kind of spectral voicemail from beyond? This was verging on madness, but then so was the whole preposterous situation.

She went on, speaking slowly and evenly, as if every word had been rehearsed beforehand. 'I believe you really did talk to me and I spoke to you. We're still thinking of you, you know that, don't you? We want you to return to us as soon as possible, but it'll be in your own time, I understand that now.'

John listened with increasing incredulity. She had not yet told him of her vision of James that night and consequently he could make no sense of her words.

Eventually she finished her monologue and they left his bedside. As they walked back along the corridor, she thought it might be a magnanimous gesture to visit Sergeant Gallagher, but John was against the idea. As far as he was concerned, Gallagher deserved everything he had got for his stupidity. In any case, he pointed out, he was being kept in isolation and visitors would not be permitted to see him until he had been cleared of any possible risk of radioactive contamination.

They drove back into town and went to the café where they sat at their usual table.

'OK,' John began after they had ordered their coffee, 'what was all that you were telling James about having spoken to him?'

She smiled. 'I don't expect you to believe me, but I think James was in touch with me last night.'

'What?'

'I know it sounds daft, but I had a really vivid dream last night in which he spoke to me. It was so graphic in its detail that it didn't feel like a dream. It was more of a vision, but he spoke to me.'

'Spoke to you?'

'Yes.' She produced the paper with the notes she had written that night. She unfolded it and then proceeded to tell him of her dream, describing the place where she believed James was and the girl he called Angel. She went on to recount her conversation with him in as much detail as she could muster.

John listened to her story with more than a degree of scepticism. After his earlier experiences of shared dreams, he was prepared to believe in the possibility of telepathy, but James was in a coma. They had seen him only a short while ago and it was undeniable that he could hear her voice when she spoke to him; the instruments agreed that, but the idea of him projecting images of some fantasy world to her while she slept seemed a bit too farfetched to be believable. Her next statement only served to reinforce his initial doubt.

'This is the second time I've seen him there,' she said. 'The last time he didn't speak to me but the setting was identical – I can describe it now. The same people were there, including the dark haired girl who seems to be in constant attendance on him; the hall was the same, with pillars and a chequered floor, and there was the cylinder, or one like it.' She took a deep breath. 'OK, you might think I'm losing my marbles, but I know what I saw and I believe that James, or at least a part of him, is somewhere... well, I don't know exactly where he is, but he said I was not to worry and that he would return when the time is right.'

'Barbara, James is in hospital. You saw him there only twenty minutes ago.'

She sighed. 'His body is in the hospital, I know that, but where is his mind?'

He thought about this for a moment. 'You are suggesting that this is some kind of out-of-body experience? It's possible, I suppose, but is it likely?'

'Is any of this likely?' she countered.

'No.'

'Yet unlikely things have happened, haven't they; so why not this?'

He had no answer for that. It was time to moderate this argument. 'Barbara.' He spoke softly, almost gently. 'I don't doubt your word; I just suppose someone has to play devil's advocate here and it might as well be me. Damn it, I'm as well aware as anyone else involved in this matter that anything seems to be possible where the cylinder is concerned. Like you, I have encountered phenomena that not long ago I would have laughed to scorn, so I have no reason to doubt you.'

'Then you believe me.'

'I believe you.'

'What do you think he will be like when he returns?'

'I don't know, why?'

'I think he will be changed. I don't know, it's just the things he said; they were cryptic but he seems to understand a lot about where he is. For instance, he says it's a place without time as we know it. There were other things too.'

'Such as...?'

'I don't know. Reading between the lines, I get the feeling that he has transcended time and space as we know it. Another thing; he told me that those people were made for him and that the girl he calls Angel was also for him, whatever that might mean.'

He chuckled. 'I might hazard a guess. She was naked, you say?'

She gently kicked his shin under the table. 'John, you have a dirty mind. You're almost as bad as Bernard sometimes, making jokes about everything. Seriously, I think she might be there for him as a guide, or perhaps a tutor of some kind.'

He became serious again. 'You mean he is there to learn?'

'What have I been trying to tell you all along? He's already acquired extensive knowledge of where he is and I get the feeling he's only just begun. It'll be interesting to see what he'll be like when he returns.'

'The thought might be a terrifying one, think of that. I mean, we know what happened the last time this started, don't we?'

She thought about this and remembered her earlier dream of the girl who had been initiated into the cult surrounding the cylinder. She wondered if that girl might have undergone the same process as James now seemed to be experiencing; if she had lapsed into the same comatose state and emerged, transformed and doomed to die in a bloody revolt. She shuddered. 'I don't like to think about that.'

'I think we shall have to think about it. I'll be damned if I know what to do if he does emerge as some kind of superman, but if that does turn out to be the case, then we'll have to be ready for it when it happens.'

'There won't be much we can do if he does, short of killing him.'

'We can't do that.'

'Of course not. That really would be history repeating itself and we're not going back to those dark days.' She looked at him. 'What are we going to do? We've lost control of this situation, haven't we?'

'We were never in control of it,' he grunted. 'The cylinder now has total control and there's nothing we can do about it, except pray that reason will prevail and what's the chance of that happening where people are concerned?'

'Can't we destroy it?'

'I doubt it very much. It burned away Chris's wire netting shield as easy as striking a match. This indicates it has some kind of inbuilt defence mechanism, so what might it do if we tried to blow it up or posed a similar threat to its existence? That's one of the reasons I don't want the Army getting involved. If they decide to play soldiers with it – well, I'll leave it up to you to fill in the rest.'

'Then it's got us over a barrel.'

'Unless we can outsmart it, it has.'

'I doubt that we can do that.'

'We did it once before,' he said. 'It was safe until that bloody clumsy flatfoot broke the cable. I could have killed him for that.'

'I don't think we'll get another chance to do it. It has learned that trick now and it'll suss us out if we should try it again,' she said.

'Do you think it's intelligent?'

'Whoever controls it is.'

'Controls it?'

'I think it may be controlled by the same intelligence that has James, whatever and wherever that may be.' She leaned forward. 'It stands to reason if you think about it. Now, we know that it records everything that happens around it. It almost certainly knows about us by now. In addition to recording, it also replays these events as we know from our experience of recent weeks.'

270

'So can a camcorder.'

'A reasonable analogy, I suppose. But unless someone controls the camcorder, it is inert. It can neither record, nor can it play back. Do you get the idea?'

John thought about this for some time. What she said made sense, but its full implication was disturbing. It meant that if it was still active, then so was the hand, if hand it was, that controlled it. Furthermore, that hand was guided by an intelligence that no one could even begin to comprehend.

'Oh my God,' he said slowly. 'What have we done?'

She smiled, but there was no humour in it. 'We have opened Pandora's Box.'

66

I did it. I spoke to her, or at least communicated with her. That's a start, but it took some effort. I feel drained.

Barbara... I remember her now. Bit by bit, the pieces of the life I had are starting to return to me. How did I forget? Perhaps there was no point in remembering it initially. After all, it has little significance here where everything is different. Perhaps that's it – I was cleansed of my previous existence in order to forget the three dimensional world and come fresh to this multidimensional one. That way I would be less disorientated by it. But I was disorientated when I fell ill. I wonder what it is like now if I try to stand. Will I fall over like I did the last time, or shall I swim through the dimensions without let or hindrance? I shall know soon and Angel shall guide me this time – perhaps catch me if I fall. No, I shall not fall. I shall be stronger. I shall need to be strong for what is to come. I don't know what is to come, but do I know I shall need my strength to face it, and face it I will. The cylinder... it involves the cylinder. Everything involves the cylinder. No, not everything; after all, no one here is using it – has ever used it as far as I can see, so not everything involves the cylinder. Therefore it must be there for me. It is still there. I see it still some distance away. I don't know how far because I don't know how big or small it is and I can't judge distance so therefore I don't know how far it is away from me.

Perspective bends here. The creatures that inhabit this place don't seem to have eyes and therefore they probably don't have the binocular vision and perception that I have. They see things differently. I can't imagine how they see or if they see at all in the conventional sense of the word. Yet the people here have eyes, don't they? Angel has eyes with which she sees me, that's if she does see me, of course. I don't know if she sees me in the way that I see her; but then, the same might go for all other people. Even the fact that I can see myself in a mirror is at odds with the way others perceive me because the image I get is laterally reversed, in fact wrong.

She is silent at the moment. She is often silent and I wonder if she is communicating without words with whatever it is that made her. Perhaps that is her purpose: to liaise with that intelligence from time to time – filing a report, so to speak. Perhaps I should be angry with her for talking behind my back, but I must rise above that. This is the first step of my journey – to explore my inner space – that unexplored dark labyrinth of my being and this is dangerous. There are monsters lurking there. They have lived there for a long time and they will not leave without a fight. That's why I must be strong.

I am learning to recognise some of them; for instance, my all too often unkind thoughts towards Angel who has nothing but love for me and she is not the only one I have been cruel to. There have been many; just how many I have no idea, but I know that I have hurt many people in my time, sometimes unintentionally, it's true, but there have been times when I have knowingly hurt people and here is a real monster to contend with. Then there are the other monsters and demons; those that have been implanted by the circumstances of life in general; the cut and thrust of daily existence and the stamping on the hands of those beneath me in order to consolidate my position in industry. Once it didn't seem to matter, but it always will to those whom I might have damaged in the process. God, what a jumped-up little prick I was then. I remember it now in parts and it hurts – oh God, it hurts. The beast inside is gnawing at my entrails and that beast is me. I shall need to be strong. I must be strong to withstand this pain – the pain of others that I have hurt and now I feel it. I really feel it. It is karma – bad karma, grey in its sickness and red in its rage. It is blue in grief and black in despair, hot and cold and it runs through me – runs me through like a rapier.

Still she doesn't move. It is as if she is asleep. Oh, Angel, if ever I needed your love it is now. Can you feel my pain? I have been unkind to you and I am sorry, so sorry. You give me love and I reward you for it with contempt, calling you an amoeba and suspecting your motivation when I can only feel unconditional love radiating from you. I am the beast. I am the monster. I have hurt so many, from the little quiet one I bullied in the primary school to the girl who loved me that I threw over for another, prettier one without a thought for her feelings and careless of her pain. I know how much it hurt her and I didn't care. All that mattered was the moment and the sensation of the new and I was cruel. Now I feel that cruelty. It has become my torturer, here to show me what pain is really like, devoid of pity and without mercy. I suppose I shouldn't expect mercy and yet I do. I expect forgiveness and mercy and I don't deserve it. I have done nothing to deserve it. What can I do to deserve it?

This is so painful I don't think I can tolerate it for much longer. Will nothing ease it for me – take it away? Please take it away from me. Oh, take it away take it away, take – it – away!

I must get up from here and try and walk it off. Perhaps then I'll feel better. My body feels better; it's my mind that's screwed up now. If I could cry I might feel better but I can't cry. I can't cry for those that I have damaged, even though I feel their pain but I can't cry although I want to and even if I could it would change nothing. I cannot undo all that I have done to harm those around me and this is out of proportion.

I wasn't ready for this. It came upon me suddenly. I suppose I should have expected it. I knew I had to face it sooner or later, but I didn't expect it to feel like this or hit me so suddenly and so violently and I didn't expect it to hurt so much. I shall try to walk it off. I must. My strength has returned to a great extent and I can do it if I don't fall again. My limbs feel light and I can stand, so it should be easy to walk from here to there, or maybe to the cylinder. Perhaps it holds the answer but everything's skewed. Even now I don't know how far away it is but I might have some idea if I take a step and a step and another step that brings me closer to it and I cannot lean against the wall because I don't know where it is and the pain is going to bring me down before I get there which means I cannot run away and my feet don't have skates and the faces of those I hurt are all around me now and I want to shout sorry I'm sorry but I can't... I can't because the words will not come and someone has caught me from behind so that now I am afraid of what it is that holds me so tightly and will not let go...

'Let me go. Let me be with my pain. I have to be with it to fight it and come to terms with the beast that might devour me. Let me go!'

'Come back with me. I feel your pain. Let me ease it for you.'

'Angel?' She must have come up behind me. 'How can you ease my pain? Hold me. I'm afraid. I'm afraid of what I am.'

'Come with me and do not fear. There is nothing to fear. I shall take you somewhere safe. Hold on to me. There.'

274

'It came suddenly. There was no warning. I see myself now as a monster.'

'Do not fear. I am here for you.'

'Cruel. I am cruel to people. I have been cruel to you with my unkindness and my anger and invective. I'm sorry. Oh, Angel, I'm so sorry. You've done nothing to harm me and yet I've been an absolute bastard to you. Forgive me. Please forgive me. Forgive…'

'What is there to forgive? I understand you spoke in fear and uncertainty and that you are afraid.'

'I am afraid. I am afraid of myself.'

'You mustn't be. Come, I shall lead you to where you will be safe. You are still new to our world and there is much you have to learn, starting with yourself. You must be strong to overcome your inner beast, but you will overcome it.'

She led him outside the circle of beings to a seemingly solid wall that was made indistinct by the false perspective of the great hall. A slit in the wall opened as they approached and they passed through it into a small, dome-like chamber, rather like an igloo. The aperture closed behind them without a sound. There she let him lean against the wall. It was warm and yielding and, like the floor, it felt alive.

She looked at him. He had not noticed until now that her eyes were deep chestnut brown and flecked with gold. She reached out and touched his face. In that instant he saw again the faces of those that he had hurt and that had hurt him and once more he was overcome with grief for them all. He could bear it no longer.

Like someone wounded he sagged and fell to his knees. She knelt beside him and cradled his head to her breasts. 'You must let go,' she said.

He could not hold it back this time. The tears flowed and he began to sob.

'It's been building up for a long time,' she said. 'Now you must let it out. There.'

His sobs became uncontrollable and she held him closer, rocking him like a baby as his tears trickled in rivulets down the front of her body. He could not remember having ever cried like this before.

She gently stroked his face as if she was washing it with his own tears. 'This will cleanse you of your guilt and self-hatred,' she said. 'Your journey has begun at last.'

In the ward where he lay, the monitor indicated an abnormal level of brain activity as every pen scribbled erratic traces across the chart and small tears appeared in the corners of the unmoving eyes of James Masters.

No one noticed.

67

That evening, the group was joined in the bar by Inspector Fox who sat down with them, looking uncomfortable. He felt out of place among these academics, but he accepted the necessity of working with them if he was ever to crack a problem for which he had no answer and no way to deal with it. He had come to this place to investigate a disappearance, not to deal with a mysterious object that a bunch of archaeologists had dug out of the ground in some Godforsaken spot that wasn't even on the map. However, this object was now his business whether he liked it or not. His unease was not helped by the constant feeling that he was regarded by the team as an intruder into what was in effect a private club. Worst of these was Professor Black whom he sensed barely tolerated his presence among them. He felt that he did not belong here. He had no knowledge of archaeology other than the occasional popular TV programme he had seen on the History Channel with some celebrity presenter and consequently much of their conversation was so esoteric as to be incomprehensible to him. His only interest in the project was the cylinder and the effect that it had had on James Masters and now on George Gallagher.

Despite this, he listened attentively as Barbara went over the conversation she and John had had that morning.

'Well,' Bernard said when she had finished. 'This puts us into something of a spot, doesn't it? If that thing has been gaining strength all the time, even with the shield on, then that gives it the upper hand. Quite honestly, I doubt that anyone can handle it.'

'Not safely,' Barbara said. 'We have thought of this from many different angles and it seems to have us in a corner. It is simply not safe to go anywhere near it.'

'James Masters could,' Chris said.

'If that's a joke, it's in very bad taste,' Barbara said.

Chris was serious. 'It's not a joke. When he comes out of his coma, he will have already been fully exposed to it. Therefore it can do nothing more to him than it has already done. He will to all intents and purposes be immune to its effects.'

'It makes sense,' John agreed. 'There's just one problem. He loves that cylinder. I can hardly imagine him conspiring with us against it, can you?'

'It's unlikely,' Chris admitted.

'What about Sergeant Gallagher?' Fox said. 'I mean, he's been exposed to it as well, hasn't he?'

'No,' John said. 'I won't allow him anywhere near it. He's already in danger of finishing up like James Masters and I will not take the responsibility of putting him in any further danger.'

'I could shoulder that responsibility,' Fox said, but John was adamant.

'I will not expose anyone to that thing,' he insisted. 'Damn it man, you've seen what it can do – you've seen what it has done. Add to that its strength which seems to be growing at an exponential rate and you might as well tell him to defuse a bomb with a club hammer. For all we know, the power level in that thing could kill him. If it could vaporise a roll of chicken wire, what could it do to a human body?'

'It didn't vaporise him though, did it?'

'It didn't, but it could.'

'What makes you so sure about that?'

John sighed and looked up at the ceiling in an expression of exasperation. 'We have seen a sample of its destructive power demonstrated on that roll of wire. You might be right, I will admit, but I believe it may have an inbuilt defence mechanism that is triggered if it senses it is in danger. We now know that it possesses the potential to blow a man into the next world. It may not do that, but are you willing to take that chance with Sergeant Gallagher?'

'No,' Fox said. 'Well, I'm at as much of a loss for ideas as you are. The way I see it, we're going to have to bring in an expert to deal with this.'

'Who do you suggest? We don't know what that thing is or where it comes from. One thing is certain; the object is alien in the sense that it doesn't belong here. James Masters said it employed a technology unknown on earth. If that is the case, then who on earth can deal with it?'

278

Fox looked crestfallen. 'I don't know. In that case I'm afraid it leaves us with only one option and you're not going to like it.'

John was immediately put on guard. 'What might that be?'

'We get the Army to fence off the area around the cabin and declare it off limits.'

'What?' John's voice was icy.

'No!' Barbara protested. 'It will impinge on the excavations. If you do that, we might as well pack up and go home. Don't you realise that that site is the most important archaeological find of all time? As a result of our discoveries there, all the textbooks will have to be rewritten. I thought this had already been made clear to you.'

'I'm sorry,' Fox said. 'But I'm afraid we have no option. That thing presents a clear danger to the public and I would be failing in my duty if I was to leave it lying there unprotected. No one can go near it and the thing can't be handled. You told me that yourself. I'm afraid it leaves us with no option. I'm sorry.'

'Fuck this!' John got up and went over to the bar.

'You've upset him,' Bernard said.

'And not just him,' Barbara added. 'Christ, I really can't believe I once thought that you were on our side. How could I have been so stupid?' She paused and then went on, slowly. 'You had this idea all the time, didn't you? All that guff about burying the hatchet and joining forces was just a charade to lull us into a false sense of security.'

Bernard was white with rage. 'When we were kids we used to say a lot of disparaging things about policemen, but I never really believed them until now.'

Fox was unmoved. 'I'm sorry, I really am, and I'm sorry if you and your colleagues are upset by this, but as I have already pointed out, I have a duty to protect the public and that cylinder represents a clear danger to public safety; possibly even a danger to national security and that's my department. I have no option but to take this action. And for your information,' he added, turning to Barbara, 'I had not planned this from the outset. This really is the last resort. I really do wish that we could have worked together to find a solution to the problem.'

'I've heard enough of this,' Bernard said, half rising. 'Just get out of here, will you?'

Fox stood up and left without a further word.

'Well,' Bernard said when he had gone. 'That drops us nicely in it.'

'What happens now?' Lynda said who had been silent all this time.

'I wish I knew.'

Barbara got up and went over to the bar where John stood, leaning on the counter. 'You can come back and join us now,' she said. 'He's gone.'

'Well,' he said, 'that's it. We might as well pack up and go home. In a couple of days or so the site will be crawling alive with soldiers and their equipment, digging holes and ploughing up the whole area. It's over.'

'John, I'm so sorry. I really believed him.'

'You needn't blame yourself. I believed him too. I think we all did. God, I could murder him.'

'Never mind.' She tried to sound consoling. 'We have made several significant discoveries; enough to make you as famous as Howard Carter, if not more so.'

'I wasn't thinking of that,' he said.

She touched his arm. 'I know. Believe me; I am as upset about this as you are. We all are. Bernard's absolutely livid; I've never seen him so angry, Lynda and Chris look shattered but there's nothing we can do. It's out of our hands now.'

'And into the hands of people who don't know what they're doing. If they think that erecting a fence around it will solve the problem, then they must be more naive than I thought they were. They don't know what they're dealing with.'

'Come on, let's rejoin the others.'

They returned to the table where Bernard, Lynda and Chris sat. The look on the faces of those assembled reflected all that John felt. Lynda looked close to tears.

Bernard looked up and forced a smile as they approached. 'Never say die,' he said in an effort to sound cheerful, but it didn't really work.

John sat down heavily. 'I feel gutted.'

'We all do,' Bernard said.

'What can we do?' Lynda asked.

He looked at her with a sense of pity. She had worked on the project since the first spade cut and this was the reward for her diligence. 'I'm afraid we can do nothing,' he said. 'Fox has all the big guns in Whitehall lined up on his side. We can't fight him.'

'Then it's over,' she said, almost in a whisper.

'Yes,' he said and she began to weep. She could hold it back no longer. Chris put his arm around her shoulders in an effort to comfort her. John too felt close to tears. His project was on the scrapheap, thanks to Fox's intervention. True, they could carry on with it until the Army arrived, but he knew that no one's heart would be in it any more. For the first time since the project had begun he felt broken. Whatever authority he possessed was about to be overruled by the combined forces of Special Branch and the Ministry of Defence. He could not fight that.

'I'm going to bed,' Bernard said, getting up and leaving his beer on the table.

Barbara looked at his glass. 'What's happened to the Beer Monster?'

'I've lost my appetite for it,' he said. 'I'll see you in the morning.' He wandered out of the bar.

'I think we should go as well,' Chris said, rising. Lynda got up too and they left, leaving John alone with Barbara.

'John,' she said, 'do me a favour, will you?'

He nodded.

'Get me a large brandy.'

He went to the bar and ordered a large Martel and large single malt whisky for himself. He felt he needed it. He returned to her and put the drinks down on the table.

'Are we going to see James tomorrow?' she said in an effort to resume some semblance of conversation.

'I don't see why not,' he said. 'There's little else we can do.'

'Sod them,' she said. 'We shall go up to the site and carry on as usual until the Army boots us off it. We still have important work to do.'

He looked at the floor. 'I could weep, both for the project and for the team. That bastard Fox has got me over a barrel. I'd like to take him by the scruff of the neck and pitch him into the cabin together with the cylinder and then see how he likes it.'

She squeezed his hand. 'Let's not accept defeat. We shall go on working up there until the bitter end. Don't give up.'

He tried to smile. 'You're right as usual, I suppose. I just feel betrayed. I knew all along I should never have trusted him.'

She swirled her brandy around the glass. 'Don't remind me. It was me who believed him and persuaded you to do the same. You shouldn't have listened to me.'

'He had us all fooled, not just you.'

A thought occurred to her. 'How far is the cabin from the dig?'

He thought for a moment. 'I guess about two hundred yards from where we are working; why?'

'Well, it would have to be a big fence to surround a radius of two hundred yards, wouldn't it? That means we can still carry on outside the perimeter.'

'It's a possibility,' he agreed. 'It all depends on what the Army has to say about it.'

'Can they stop us working outside the area?'

He took a sip of whisky. Despite the anger he felt against Fox, he began to feel better. 'We shall see.'

68

Gallagher had a dream in which he was a passive witness. In it he saw people gathered around the object and chanting rhythmically in a language that he could not understand. He knew that he was witnessing a scene from long ago and that this was some form of ancient sacrament. A girl was led into the centre of the circle, stripped of her robe and forced to kneel before the cylinder. Her face was expressionless with terror. Someone stepped forward, pulled her head back by the hair and drew a long, broad bladed knife across her throat, slicing it from ear to ear. Blood splashed the cylinder and sprayed the wall behind it as she slumped to the floor, the blood still flooding from the hideous wound. The chanting grew in its intensity as the dying girl's body was dragged unceremoniously out of the building, leaving a trail of blood to the doorway.

He awoke from this dream with a start. He had had nightmares before, but he had never had a dream quite so ghastly or as vivid as this one and he wondered if the cylinder had anything to do with it. It had certainly been central to what he had seen. It had been so real that he felt as if he had actually been there. He could still see the interior of the hut with its earthen floor and the people in a circle around the cylinder and the girl whom he knew must have been a sacrificial victim. What he could not know was that his dream was identical to the one that Barbara had experienced shortly after her first exposure to the cylinder.

He lay awake for some time after this, afraid to sleep in case the dream recurred. The cylinder already dominated his waking thoughts and now it was invading his sleep. He decided that if it continued like this, he would ask to see the hospital psychiatrist. Such dreams and thoughts were abnormal. Given the predominance of the cylinder in his recent dreams, it was possible that the thing had implanted these visions into his mind. He toyed with this idea without really believing it. It was ridiculous to suppose that an inanimate object could do such a thing, and yet it had held him in its power while he had been in the cabin and, most certainly, he had not been the same since it had happened.

Eventually, he slept again and in due course he entered another dreaming cycle. This time he saw the sacrifice in context as a part of a series of ancient rites that had once surrounded the cylinder. It had been central to an entire culture that had grown up around it. He saw this now and understood that its purpose had been misunderstood by those who had adopted it. In a later dream he witnessed the bloody downfall of this culture and knew that this had been the end result of this misunderstanding. It had not been the cylinder's purpose to be worshipped, nor had any such thing been the intention of the intelligence that had created it and sent it to Earth in the hope that it might find intelligent life forms. What he had witnessed in his dream had been a perversion of its intended purpose. Earth had not been the only planet to receive a cylinder. A very large number had been scattered like seeds on other Earth-like planets throughout the galaxy with most finding nothing at all, but with a few, such as this one, encountering the intelligent life that it had been put there to find.

He understood this now and the terror that had come with the first nightmare vanished. The cylinder had been a passive witness to human sacrifice because it could do nothing else. It had attempted to create a sophisticated culture, but things had gone badly wrong and it had learned a valuable lesson from this failed experiment. Its fundamental error had been to suppose that the people who first discovered it would be more culturally developed than they actually were. It was little wonder then that the experiment had failed, but it had not been a total failure. The civilisation it had created, although bloody and mistaken, had advanced in certain areas beyond merely developing a superior technology. The people, under its guidance, had discovered the rudiments of mathematics, astronomy and medicine as well as developing artistically. They had invented a primitive form of syllabic writing, although none of this survived the final holocaust, and had developed high art forms including painting and sculpture. Their metalworking skills advanced to a point where they were millennia ahead of their time. Neither was all of this culture completely lost, for a handful of survivors had managed to escape the massacre. Therefore, it was likely that a fragment of this culture might have survived its supposed annihilation and begun a more gradual
284

process of human development that in all probability would have happened anyway. Thus it was an open question as to whether or not the cylinder had had anything at all to do with humanity's advancement. In that sense it had failed.

He pondered this in the half light of the isolation ward and marvelled that he could have learned so much about a vanished civilisation from apparently nothing. Surely the cylinder could not have taught him all this, but he could not think of anything else that could have done it. This knowledge was both exciting and frightening. It was exciting to know that he was one of a privileged few to have seen and understood a pivotal point in mankind's development, if pivotal point it was. It was also exciting to be poised on the brink of something huge into which he felt he would soon be launched, but it was also frightening. He did not know what lay ahead of him, but he knew that something had been set in motion that would irrevocably change his life. He wondered if James Masters had undergone a similar experience before his final, fateful encounter with the cylinder and if that was the reason why he was now in a coma. In all probability, his condition had been induced by the cylinder, and yet he could not imagine it as being anything other than beneficent. True, his initial reaction to it had been one of extreme caution, but that had evaporated as soon as it had spoken to him. He reflected that this was a curious phrase to describe an exchange of information that had not employed words, but that was what had happened.

The cylinder – he had to get back to the cylinder. Whatever it took; if it meant he had to walk there he would do it to satisfy a need that he felt was mutual. He felt that the cylinder needed him as much as he needed it and he began to work out possible ways to get there unnoticed. He knew that Inspector Fox would not allow him anywhere near it and neither would anyone else involved, so it would have to be a covert operation. Also, once there, he might have to get past the guard, assuming that Inspector Fox had posted one on the door. That might be difficult, but it would not be insurmountable. He would think of a way to deal with that should the need arise.

He wondered if he could leave the hospital now under cover of the night, but he decided against it. It would be foolhardy to abscond and trigger a manhunt that would inevitably lead to the cabin the very moment he was missed. They would in all probability be waiting for him when he got there and he would be arrested on the spot. No, he would be a model patient and a good policeman. No one would be allowed to know what was on his mind but he would get there, no matter what it took.

He stared at the ceiling and smiled. He would get there.

69

Just how long James wept he did not know, but it felt like a long time. All this time in the small antechamber Angel held him, cradling his head to her breast. Gradually, his grief subsided and his sobs became more intermittent as he recovered. He felt drained, as if he had cried all his energy away and there was a buzzing noise inside his head. He had never before felt or even considered the feelings of others and it had been a bitter experience. His former lack of empathy had turned round and bitten him, and it hurt.

Angel smoothed his untidy hair with a gentle hand. 'It had to come.' She said. 'You have carried this guilt for a long time, we can tell. It had to be cleansed.'

'Am I clean?'

'You will be.'

He rubbed his eyes and the words began to tumble from him unbidden in a torrent of confession. He had to discharge it. Had she not been there, he would have been driven to spill it anyway, if only to himself. 'It feels like I've been at war with myself for most of my life. I wounded myself in all those battles. Perhaps that's why a lot of people didn't like me, because I lacked all feeling for them and I didn't care who I hurt in the process of gaining status and consolidating my position. I treated women like toys and thought nothing of their feelings and I was unkind to you. What I didn't know was that for everyone I wounded, I wounded myself as well. I see that now.'

'Then you've learned that much. You've been washed with your own tears. Now you can wash yourself with clean water. Come.'

She arose and led him to a washstand with a bowl and a ewer from which she poured water over his head before filling the bowl. He had not noticed it before and it struck him as incongruous to see an old-fashioned washstand in a place like this. She poured some of the remaining water over herself and ran her hands over her body, washing away the tears that had flowed so freely down her front. He too washed himself and allowed the cool water to soak his skin. His face was hot and his eyes were swollen. The water soothed him. His throat was dry. He picked up the ewer and took a drink from it. The water had no taste at all and he deduced from this that it must be distilled. At least it was pure, even if it lacked any kind of taste. He decided that, like the washstand and everything else around him, it must have been synthesised for his benefit and that consequently it would be in its purest form.

He forced a smile. He could not imagine any other circumstance in which he could be bathing in the company of a naked woman and not be sexually aroused, but for some reason he was not. It was natural for them to be naked. They had never been clothed while they had been together. He watched her as she washed and he could see that she in turn was watching him. Her face showed no sign to indicate whether or not she had any sexual feelings towards him. Despite this, he could not deny having sexual feelings towards her. Her supple, almost willowy body fascinated him. It was the body of a teenage girl and it took him back to a time in his life that he thought he had forgotten when he was still tentatively discovering the mysteries of sex. He tried to put these thoughts aside. Somehow, it did not feel right to have such thoughts at this particular time. He decided that if she was capable of feeling any kind of sexual urge towards him she would make it known in her own time.

At the same time another thought occurred to him. The triggering of this memory of his schooldays indicated that, bit by bit, some memory of that elusive former life of his was returning. The greater part of it was still lost to him, but small fragments like these were enough to establish that he had indeed lived another life before this one. The still painful memory of those whom he had hurt was evidence of that alone.

He took another drink of distilled water. It tasted horrible because it had no taste, but his mouth was still dry and he had not drunk anything since he had arrived here, just when, he could not remember. This did not surprise him, nor did it surprise him that until now he had not felt the urge to drink. This was not a normal place; therefore it stood to reason that normal rules did not apply here. If, as he had already surmised, he could absorb all necessary nutrients through his skin by way of some osmotic process, it stood to reason

288

that he would not feel the urge to eat and drink. By crying, he had lost a larger than usual amount of water from his body that a small measure of water from the jug would replace.

Angel took his hand. 'Do you feel better?'

He did not know. It was too early to tell.

The gold flecked eyes looked into his. 'I understand,' she said. His silence had told her all she needed to know. 'You have undergone a lot. You must rest.'

'Will you lie down with me?' The words had left his mouth before he was aware of what he had said.

She drew him close. 'Our love must be honest, you understand.'

He had to speak the truth. 'Your love might be pure but mine is not. Your love is true and unconditional while I can't be sure if I am driven only by lust for your body. I'm afraid I may not ready yet.' His unexpected honesty triggered a fresh upsurge of emotion which he fought hard to suppress.

'Come, I shall down lie with you.'

He looked at her. 'What?'

She smiled. 'I shall lie down with you. Your honesty tells me that you are beginning to know yourself and your failings. Now come and we'll lie down together.'

She led him by the hand to the place where they had lain before and he lay down on the soft floor. She lay down beside him, drew herself close and rested her head on his shoulder. Despite his desire to make love to her, he felt that it would be wrong to do it, as if the sex act might debase her love. He also suspected his true motive for wanting to make love to what still appeared to him to be an innocent young girl. Even if she had been created as a sexually mature woman, her true desires remained an unknown quantity and this served to heighten his sense of impropriety. He felt that he would be taking advantage of her apparent innocence.

'Let's just embrace,' he said.

She kissed him and he held her close, feeling the slow rhythm of her breathing and the tiny muscular movements as she adjusted her position next to him. Somehow, this close contact felt more intimate than it might have done if they had made love.

'You are good to me,' she said.

He stroked her back. 'I want to be good to you.'

'You must rest now.'

He hugged her, enjoying the warm feeling of her body against his. Her skin was soft and smooth. Although she had been manufactured by the intelligence that had made everything else that he could see, she was to all intents and purposes a real human being. She had flesh and bones, she lived and breathed and she had a heart that beat like his. If he placed his hand beneath her left breast he could just feel it beating. He had already decided to suspend his disbelief in her reality and accept her as a living, breathing woman, not just a replica but someone with thoughts and feelings. At the same time he wondered how this intelligence had gained such a perfect knowledge of human anatomy and psychology as to create this creature – to synthesise her from the same protoplasm-like substance that constituted the things that he had seen on first finding himself in this world. Again he marvelled at an intelligence that appeared to be able to create anything it wished, animate or inanimate.

He wondered if she was asleep. Her eyes were closed, but he was not sure. He was still not sure if she slept at all. He had seen her sitting beside him when he was ill. Sometimes her eyes were closed, but they appeared to be closed in concentration rather than repose. In that sense she was not human. No human could stay awake for so long and not suffer from exhaustion and eventual mental illness. From this he deduced that whatever being it was that controlled all of this never slept either. This surprised him, since he had always assumed that all living things slept, from the most primitive to the ultra complex super organism of which he now seemed to be a part.

'Angel,' he whispered.

She opened her eyes.

'Does anyone ever sleep here apart from me?'

She gave him a smile. 'We do not sleep as you do. One part sleeps while another part remains awake.'

He tried to make sense of this, but it was difficult. Again she was using the plural. It was often *we* with her. Then a realisation came to him that was as sudden as it was startling. She was part of this super organism – a cell in a vast, complex body composed of billions of cells, perhaps subdivided into billions of subsidiary cells. When she spoke for herself she spoke for all. She was effectively the voice of this vast super organism. He thought again of the shapeless beings that had surrounded him when he had first arrived. They were cells or, to be more exact, they were super cells in a body with a brain so vast he could not envisage it. The interconnecting threads had indeed been exchanging signals as he had originally suspected. He remembered that they had arched away from him as he had passed so that he might not damage them. This thought, if it was right, was too big for him to comprehend. He could not imagine a being so huge that it surrounded him and encompassed all that he was and all that he would become. No wonder it had the power to copy a human being to the smallest, most intimate detail exactly as it had forged everything else around him down to the very water that had washed him and which he had drunk to quench his thirst. To a pan dimensional creature such as this, the cylinder would be nothing more than a simple tool, as basic as a screwdriver.

She gave him a little hug. 'Why do you call me Angel?'

'Because that's what you are to me.'

She smiled and rested her head on his shoulder. In that moment he felt a new warmth burn within him. It was the warmth of a love that he had hitherto never known. He could not doubt that she loved him now. She *was* love.

70

Sleep eluded John that night. He lay beside Barbara's sleeping form, staring up at the dark ceiling and damning Fox for his treacherous U-turn. He felt betrayed. He had allowed himself to be persuaded that an alliance between his team and Special Branch might have certain advantages, perhaps even assist with the project's security. Now it had all gone to hell and he had to face the uncomfortable fact that everything would soon be out of his hands and put under the command of the Army. He had little doubt that there were still many more valuable finds lying undiscovered and that these would be priceless treasures from a unique and vanished civilisation. Now, in all probability they would be left beneath the soil for all time if the Army did not destroy them first with their heavy equipment as they erected their security fencing around the cabin. Soldiers were not known for their care and sensitivity when it came to dealing with such delicate matters as archaeology.

Barbara had tried to console him with the thought that they could continue their work outside the security fence, but he was not convinced that this would be the case. Once the Army arrived they would take over and no one would be allowed to come near. That was the way they usually conducted their business.

The effect that Fox's duplicity had had on the other members of the team angered him as well. He recalled Lynda's tears and Bernard's rage. Bernard was well known and liked for his cheerful and informal manner and John had never seen his second in command so angry before, or so depressed.

Again, Barbara had tried to console him by recounting the valuable finds that they had already made, among them the peculiar geared mechanism and, most recently the stainless dagger. True, these had indeed been astounding discoveries, enough to rewrite all the history books and shake the world of archaeology to its foundations which they would most certainly do when he published his findings, but this did little to offset his sense of frustration at having to terminate the project after only recently having successfully obtained an extension for it. The Faculty had willingly granted this extension once they knew what had already been discovered, from the debatable evidence of cannibalism to the fine mechanism that seemed to be out of its rightful time. The discovery of early pottery and the dagger would have more than vindicated their decision to grant the extension. Now it was over, thanks to an overbearing policeman who wouldn't know a significant discovery if it jumped up and bit him on the arse.

He turned over onto his right side and tried to sleep, but without success. He hoped that Fox was having a similarly uncomfortable night, but he doubted it. It did not matter one jot to a man like that whether the work and labour of weeks might continue or not. That was not his department.

Barbara had been right about many things and one thing in particular. The project would continue until they were forced off it by the Army. He would put this to the team in the morning and to hell with Fox.

He turned over and lay on his back once more. Barbara stirred beside him but did not wake. Whatever happened, he decided that when this was over they would continue to live together, if she was willing. Their relationship had been cemented by a combination of proximity, circumstance and need and forged in the fire of the distress that had been induced by the cylinder. That was a funny one. The object of their mistrust and loathing had actually brought them closer together. He owed it a debt of thanks for that if nothing else, not an eternity of incarceration behind a fence. For the first time since its discovery he began to wonder if he had misjudged it.

He cast his mind back to what James had told them after his first prolonged contact with it. *You didn't let it finish*, he had said. Finish what? What had they not let it finish? Well, it had most certainly finished James, or at least the James that was. Barbara too had been nearly captivated by it at the time and now her emotionally charged words returned to him: *we always destroy that which we cannot understand*. He recognised that this was in all probability a spontaneous thought induced by the cylinder, but on reflection it might have had more significance than he had at first thought. He wondered if all along he had failed to understand its purpose. Only James could answer that question and he was in no condition to talk.

He had scorned with some justification James's insistence that it was harmless. It had, after all, put him into a coma and might in all probability do the same thing to Gallagher. That much remained to be seen, he thought and then something else that Barbara had said came back to him. The idea that James might be undergoing a metamorphosis was a possibility that had to be considered and he wondered again what he would be like when he returned to consciousness.

He began to wonder if he might have been too harsh in his initial assessment of the cylinder, but it had given him every reason to be harsh in his judgement. Its mind-altering quality was enough to arouse suspicion in anyone who did not wish to have their mind altered. In that sense he had been right to declare it dangerous. It might not have been responsible for the madness and slaughter visited upon the culture that it had created, but it had caused them to sow the seeds of their own destruction. If James's account of what had happened was true, they had enslaved the surrounding clans and captured selected young women to be sacrificed to their new god, and all this time it had done nothing to prevent or put a stop to this barbarous practice. This gave the lie to its being harmless as James had insisted.

He looked at the bedside clock. One forty seven and sleep was as far away from him as ever. Whichever way he looked at it, the problem was insoluble. He had wanted to be free of the cylinder. It had disrupted the dig and affected the lives of all who had gone near it, but now that he was about to lose it he was also losing whatever remained of his control of his project. Indeed, it looked as if he was about to lose the project itself. It was being taken out of his hands and handed over to the Army's not too tender mercies, thanks to Fox's heavy handed interference. He wondered who might help him to regain control of the situation but could think of no one. The University could do nothing against the combined forces of the Government. James, who knew the cylinder better than anyone else, was out of action and likely to remain so for the foreseeable future; in fact, there was no one able to help him. He had lost the battle.

Another thought emerged as if from nowhere and it was frightening in its implications. After all that had happened since its discovery and from the way that it had so dominated his life with its plethora of unanswered questions, he realised that he was beginning to revise his former opinion of the cylinder. It fascinated him. It had fascinated him all along and now that it was about to be taken away from him he was reluctant to let it go. He was sure that Barbara felt the same way about it as well. It was their cylinder and not Fox's. They had discovered it; it had affected their lives in various ways and brought him and Barbara together as a consequence. Now that he was about to lose it he felt that it really had been the victim of an injustice committed upon it by all concerned and Fox in particular. He felt that instead of hating it and all that it had done, he should be defending it, particularly from an interloper like Fox who did not know or care what he was doing as long as it was in the line of duty as he saw it. This may have been a case of 'my enemy's enemy is my friend,' but somehow he had to get Fox off the case, if only to finish the project in peace. The trouble was that Fox was not likely to be moved on the subject, so once more he was stymied.

It was then that the full significance of what he was thinking struck him like a blow. Rather like an old adversary that one has learned to admire and respect, in his heart he was beginning to love the cylinder.

71

The next morning John slept later than he had intended. Not until Barbara brushed his ear with her finger did he open his eyes and see that she was up and fully dressed.

'What time is it?' he mumbled.

She looked at the clock. 'Eight thirty.'

'Shit! I've overslept.' He sat on the edge of the bed. 'Why didn't you wake me?'

'You looked as if you needed the extra sleep. Did you have more dreams last night?'

He shook his head. 'I couldn't sleep. I just kept thinking about the future of the project. Now that Fox has dug his oar in, it has no future.'

'Don't be despondent,' she said. 'We shall do as I said last night and carry on until the Army kicks us off the site, even if they do.'

'They probably will,' he said.

'Oh, come on, John. Lighten up. It's not over yet.'

'No?'

'No.'

He went into the bathroom, wishing that he could share her optimism. He knew that she was right, but he could not evade the fact that Fox had him in a corner.

Once he had dressed, they went downstairs to the breakfast room where Bernard, Lynda and Chris sat. Bernard looked up as they entered. 'Hi, you two; have a good night?'

John shook his head. 'Not particularly. You look more cheerful than you did last night.'

'I've had time to think,' he said, 'and I'm not going to let Fox spoil the party. I suggest we just carry on regardless for as long as possible until we're ordered off.'

John and Barbara exchanged glances. 'You've been reading my mind,' she said. 'This is the easiest meeting I've ever attended.'

'Then it is agreed,' Bernard said. 'We go on for as long as possible.'

All agreed.

After breakfast and a short visit to the hospital to see James who showed little change in his condition, John and Barbara sat in the café at their usual table. John was still preoccupied with his thoughts of last night. Barbara read his face and took his hand.

'You're in a bit of a brown study this morning,' she said.

He looked up and decided to confide his thoughts to her. 'I've been thinking,' he said. 'I lay awake last night and a lot of thoughts came to me besides Fox and his devilish machinations.'

'Go on.'

'Well,' he began. 'Do you think my judgement of the cylinder has been too harsh? I mean, we don't really understand it, do we?'

'That's an understatement,' she said. 'We don't understand it at all.'

'Exactly; and by that token it's possible that we might have misunderstood its purpose, wouldn't you agree?'

She gave him a funny look. 'What are you trying to say?'

'I know it sounds crazy, but you said it yourself: "We always destroy that which we cannot understand." Don't you remember?'

'Did I say that?'

'It was just after James made his first contact with the cylinder and I had to pull you out of the cabin. You said...'

'That was the cylinder talking through me,' she said. 'I was not in my right mind. If you remember, the cylinder nearly had me the same way that it had James. If you hadn't pulled me out of there, it would have taken me as well.'

'Quite, but it started me thinking last night. We don't understand it, in fact we know nothing at all about it and we're never likely to if Fox has his way. The thing will be incarcerated forever and no one will ever be allowed to go near it again. Now, up to here we have assumed it to be malevolent, but what if we're wrong? What if we have misunderstood its purpose? You suggested that James might be undergoing some kind of metamorphosis. Now I'm beginning to wonder what he will be like when he regains consciousness, and what will he have to tell us about the cylinder? Through him, we should understand its purpose a lot better than we do now.'

She stared at him, incredulous. 'I do believe that you are beginning to like that thing. How can this be?' She smiled as a realisation hit her. 'It's Fox, isn't it? He's threatening to take your favourite toy away and you're going over to the enemy just to spite him. John, think very carefully about what you're saying.'

'I spent a long time last night thinking about it and I can't escape the truth that we still know nothing about it. We have acted mainly out of ignorance and blind instinct, assuming for want of better knowledge that the cylinder poses a threat to us, but does it? What evidence do we have that it poses a threat to anyone? I don't know about James, but you have become increasingly convinced that he is not in danger and that he will return to us in some altered form. This thought is alarming, perhaps, but what are we frightened of? We don't know, do we? We are afraid of the unknown.'

'I can't believe I'm hearing you say this,' she said. 'After all that's happened, you are now trying to defend the cylinder. Need I remind you of the dreams and nightmares that have tormented us since that thing first hit us?'

'James didn't have them because he saw the cylinder's history in its entirety. We did not. What we got were isolated snatches of that history taken out of context as a series of loosely connected dreams and nightmares which, although they revolved around a common theme, were otherwise unrelated. We only had a fragment of the story, not the story itself. As such it is meaningless. James had the full story and he understood. It was not the cylinder that caused the slaughter; it was the people because they failed to understand.'

'That still makes it dangerous,' she pointed out. 'Anyway, what has brought about this sudden about-turn in your attitude towards it? Up to here you have hated it with a passion.'

'I did, but at the same time it has always fascinated me. How could it fail to fascinate anyone with an enquiring mind? I had hoped to one day understand it better. Now as it stands, Fox has effectively taken it away and I may never get the chance.'

She stroked his hand. 'Poor John, you really are in a state over this, aren't you? Well, we're not beaten yet. Something tells me this story hasn't quite finished.'

'What do you mean?'

'I don't know. It's just a feeling, that's all.'

'Hmm.' He was silent for a while and then he began again on a different topic. 'I had another thought last night.'

'About the cylinder?'

'No, about us. Once this business is over, I'd be happy for us to go on living together if you are willing to live with an old grouch like me.'

She looked into his eyes. 'Of course I'm willing. I've wanted this all along. You're not such an old grouch, actually. For a start you're not old and your occasional grumpiness comes with a soft centre. I've seen that and I love you, grumps and all.'

He smiled for the first time that morning as the despondency that had hung over him lifted like a cloud. Perhaps they would outwit Fox after all.

72

They arrived at the site where they joined Bernard and the team and set to work on the dig. They were still excavating the area where the dagger had been found. A metal detector scan had shown no other metal objects, but they decided to investigate further just in case there were other non-metallic objects there. Their persistence paid off.

It was Lynda who first spotted what looked like a small pedestal protruding from the floor of the pit. Carefully, she dug around it with her small trowel and, bit by bit a small statuette came into view. It was heavily encrusted with soil and, as she carefully cleaned it with the aid of a dental probe and a small paintbrush, she began to see just how finely it was carved. She called the others over to take a look at it. They gathered round as she cleaned more soil away from it.

It was an effigy of a standing naked woman. Barbara examined the finely crafted statuette. It was carved from some alabaster-like stone and parts of it still bore the smooth finish of its original polished surface. The figure was well proportioned and anatomically perfect in every detail, down to the fingers and toes with their delicately carved nails.

Bernard whistled. 'Say what you like about them, but they knew how to carve. This looks like it ought to come from Greece at the height of the Classical Period.'

Barbara took out a hand lens and examined it more closely. 'It's beautiful,' she said. 'I've never seen anything like it dating from this era. The female characteristics are not exaggerated, so I don't think she's a fertility goddess. Like so many other things here, it's millennia ahead of its time.'

'Here, take a look at that.' Lynda pointed with her dental probe at a small pattern on the pedestal.

Barbara examined it through her hand lens. It was a tiny replica of the cartouche-like pattern that they had first noticed on the cylinder. 'These symbols seem to permeate everything.' She said.

'It just shows how much the cylinder dominated their culture,' Bernard said.

Lynda continued to clean away the soil and gradually another pattern was revealed on the pedestal. This time it was the now familiar complex circular pattern. 'We've seen this before as well,' she observed.

Barbara took a closer look. 'The cylinder,' she mouthed.

'I wonder who she is meant to represent,' Chris said.

Barbara continued to study the little figure. 'She could be one of their deities, but she is not like any normal representation of a goddess from this period. I don't know…' Her voice trailed off as she recalled her vision of James and the girl who had appeared to be tending him. The effigy bore a striking resemblance to that girl. 'She is beautiful,' she continued, more to herself than anyone else.

She looked at John. 'John, can I have a word?'

'Sure,' he said.

She got to her feet and walked a short distance from the dig while he followed. She stopped and turned to him. 'Please don't laugh,' she began, 'but do you remember that vision I had of James in that strange place, surrounded by those people and accompanied by a beautiful dark haired girl? Well, that statuette reminds me of her.'

John stared at her. 'Are you sure?'

'Of course I'm sure. If it's not her, then it's someone who looks a lot like her. John, I know what I saw.'

'I'm sorry,' he said. 'I don't doubt your word, but that statuette is about seven and a half thousand years old, assuming it's genuine.'

'I know how old it is, but does that matter in a place without time? James told me that time as we know it does not exist where he is. John, it looks so like her.'

'Blimey,' he said. 'Give me some time, will you? I need to think about this.'

'We both do.'

He thought for a moment. 'You understand the implication of this, don't you? First, let's say she really is the girl you saw in your vision. If that is the case, then James is indeed in another place, or at least a part of him is. It also indicates that others have been there before him. That's if she is the girl you saw. There still remains the possibility that the statuette merely looks a bit like her.'

'It looks a lot like her,' she corrected him. She thought again about the girl she had seen in her dream who appeared to be undergoing an initiation into the cult of the cylinder and she wondered how many others had gone through the same experience as James now appeared to be going through. Perhaps some had even been tended by the same girl. This was too much for her to fully comprehend and she brushed the thought aside. Such thoughts were pure speculation anyway, but the fact remained that the statuette bore more than a passing likeness to the girl in her vision.

They returned to the dig where Lynda was still patiently cleaning the statuette. She looked up as they approached.

'I wonder if there are others around here,' she said.

'Where there's one, there's likely to be another,' Barbara said, 'possibly a male counterpart.'

Lynda giggled. 'That would be nice.'

Bernard heard the sound of an approaching car. He looked up from what he was doing and saw a car slowly driving over the soft ground. It pulled up behind the Land Rovers and Inspector Fox got out. 'Oh, fuck,' he muttered and stood up. 'Oh guys, we've got company!'

They all stopped what they were doing and turned to face Fox as he approached. John stepped forward. 'What do you want?'

'I'm interested to see what you're doing,' Fox said in an effort to sound amiable.

'Don't give me that,' John said. 'I know you well enough to know that you don't make social calls.'

'OK,' Fox said. 'I'll come straight to the point. I have with me a declaration of secrecy under the Official Secrets Act concerning that cylinder. I want you all to sign it. As of now, that cylinder doesn't exist and you never saw it, do you understand?'

'And what if we refuse to sign it?' John challenged him.

Fox shook his head. 'You will still be governed by the Official Secrets Act. If you talk to anyone about the cylinder while held under the Act, you will be liable to a term of imprisonment. Do I make myself clear?'

'Fuck off,' Bernard muttered.

John ignored Bernard's comment. 'In that case we have no choice, do we?' he said wearily.

302

'No.'

'Is it absolutely necessary to invoke the Official Secrets Act?' Barbara said. 'I mean, we've not mentioned it to anyone outside the group so far. What makes you think we're going to go blabbing about it now?'

'It's just in case,' Fox said, taking a sheet of paper from his inside pocket and unfolding it.

Bernard scowled. 'Stick it up your arse.'

'Very well,' Fox said and proceeded to read the contents of the page to the group. When he had finished, he said: 'I shall now sign this sheet to testify that I have read this undertaking to you. As of this moment you are governed by the Official Secrets Act.'

'Bollocks,' Bernard said.

'That's all. Good day to you.' Fox turned and walked back to his car as Bernard waved two fingers after him.

'The pompous, jumped-up turd.' Bernard's face was livid.

For once it was John who was conciliatory. 'Bernard, calm down. I'm as angry as you are, but there's nothing we can do. He's got us by the balls.'

'I'd like to see his balls on the end of my trowel.'

This made Barbara laugh, even though she was in no mood for laughing. Fox's highhanded attitude had angered her as much as anyone else, but she shared John's philosophical view of the situation. Against the power of the Official Secrets Act they could do nothing.

'Don't you think we should be getting on with the dig?' she said. 'Forget about Fox. He's nothing.'

'A nothing that could bring us all down,' Bernard snorted.

She touched his arm. 'Bernard, I'm as angry as you are, but we've just made a highly significant discovery – one of many. The archaeological importance of this site cannot be overstated. The cylinder still could be our ace in the hole.'

'In what way?'

She thought for a moment. 'If he wants to gag us concerning the cylinder, then he'll have to gag us concerning everything else to do with this site. The cylinder is integral to that. Now, if he wishes to gag us about the site and all the other things we've found here, he'll have to gag the university, the British Museum and everyone else outside the team who've been involved, one way and another. Can he gag them all? I don't think so.'

'Who else knows about the cylinder, apart from us?'

'Just after its discovery, I contacted Lars Ericsson of Uppsala University, telling him about the object and asking if he could identify the language of what we took to be words inscribed on it. Now he knows of its existence and he's in Sweden, outside Fox's jurisdiction. I also thought of emailing Professor David Emmett of Princeton University, but when Lars came up with no suggestion, I didn't.' She paused. 'But I could.'

Bernard smiled as the realisation hit him. 'Yes, you could.'

John banged his fist into the palm of his hand. 'By George, she's got it! Once it is known in America, then Fox won't be able to do anything to stop it. That'll spike his guns.'

Bernard chuckled. 'You could say Fox's goose will be cooked, and serve him right. The game's not over yet. But he said we are held under the Official Secrets Act as of now. How are you going to let him know?'

She smiled. 'As far as he is concerned, I already have, so it's too late.' She turned to John. 'Can we get back to town? I want to email him now.'

John nodded. Up to here, he had been keen to keep the cylinder's existence as secret as possible. Now, thanks to Fox's interference, he wanted to make it known. 'Come on,' he said. 'It's only a narrow window, so we'd better move fast.'

73

Back in their hotel room, Barbara set up her laptop and began to compose an email to Professor David Emmett. 'There,' she said when she had finished.

John looked over her shoulder and read:

Dear David,

I am attaching some photos for your perusal. They were taken just after the discovery of an unidentified object and show the object itself, as well as some curious inscriptions inscribed on it. I wonder if you could identify the writing. I tried Lars Ericsson of Uppsala University and he could not, so I thought perhaps you might be able to help.

We don't know anything about the cylinder's origin, but it's beginning to look as if it could be extraterrestrial. It is certainly not Mesolithic, and that is the age of the site that we are excavating. A number of other interesting and unique finds have been made as well that are far ahead of their proper time, more of which I will tell you later. Meanwhile, study the photos and let me know what you think.

For the record, this email was sent ten days ago. Don't ask why. Also, if the cylinder really is extraterrestrial in origin, I must insist on the strictest security regarding this matter. However, if your colleagues should know about it then I won't mind.

I should also tell you that since we unearthed it, it has developed certain psychotropic powers that are hard to explain, so that now it cannot be approached without becoming psychologically affected by it.

I know you'll find all this difficult to believe, but I assure you that this is not a hoax. You know me well enough for to know that I wouldn't try to fool you over something like this.

I look forward to hearing from you in the near future and hope that you are keeping well.

Barbara Sedgwick.

'That should do it,' John said.

Barbara attached the relevant photographs and clicked *Send*. 'That's it,' she said. 'They've gone. We'll see what he has to say about that when he reads it.'

'I just hope he believes it.'

'He will. I know it reads like a sci-fi fantasy, but David is a good friend and has no cause to doubt me. We have a mutual respect for each other.'

'Well, the cat's out of the bag now. Fox will go potty when he finds out.'

'He won't find out until the news breaks, by which time it'll be too late. Just a minute...' She started to type again, this time addressing her email to Lars Ericsson.

Dear Lars,

Do you remember the photos I sent you of unidentified writing on a mysterious cylinder that we discovered recently? Since then, we have come to believe that the cylinder may be of extraterrestrial origin, which would explain why you could not identify the script.

The cylinder is made from some unknown material and has the ability to affect the minds of all who get too close to it. We believe that it advanced the culture that we are currently investigating and which we originally thought belonged to the Iron Age. We now know it to be Mesolithic. This is a potentially earthshaking discovery and I urge you to keep it as secret as possible, particularly from the Press. The last thing we want is them nosing around. However, feel free to divulge it to your colleagues. Perhaps they might help you to shed some light on this mystery.

I would ask you to delete this message from your file once you have read it. For the record, I sent this email ten days ago. Don't ask why.

Best wishes from Barbara.

She sent this one off as well. 'That should really do it,' she said when she had finished. 'Lars could never keep a secret.'

'I hope he reads the bit about keeping the Press away,' John said. 'I really don't want them nosing about.'

'The Government will probably gag them,' she said. 'It'll be like the Roswell Incident all over again, only this time it's the genuine article.'

'You mean the rumours?'

'Precisely.' She closed her laptop with a flourish. 'That should put Inspector Fox in his place. I've wanted to do that all day.'

'You're a genius. I just hope it doesn't backfire on you. I don't want to see us all in jail and Fox will go ballistic when he discovers that the secret's out in the open.'

'By that time it'll be too late,' she said. 'In fact it's already too late. After all, the secret was already out before he warned us, wasn't it?'

'Of course it was.' He smirked. 'After all, your friend Lars has known about it ever since it was first discovered, and that's the truth.'

74

James awoke to see Angel still lying beside him. She was awake and her eyes were fixed upon his. He closed his eyes again.

She brushed his cheek with a finger. 'Are you feeling better?' Her voice was soft, almost a whisper.

He nodded. 'Yes.'

'You slept for a long time.'

'How long?'

'It doesn't matter.'

'Why are we here, away from the others?'

'We expected you to be distressed. We felt it would be better for you if no one witnessed it.'

'You witnessed it.'

'Are you angry that I witnessed your distress?'

'No. I needed you here with me and we have grown so close. I feel that we have become closer than lovers. I can't hide anything from you. I am naked before you in body and spirit.'

'You have grown to love me.'

He thought about this. In so many words he had already declared his love for her, but for some reason he felt unable to say it directly. Perhaps he feared her rebuttal if he dared to do so. He did not know.

She smiled. 'You needn't answer that. I understand your feelings. The love that I have for you is unlike any love that you have ever experienced, except for the love your mother showed you long ago in your world.'

'When was that? I still can't quite remember. It's like a dream of another time.'

'It will return. This is your world for now and we shall guide you as you grow to know it. You have learned a lot – more than you know, but there is still much more to learn and some of it will be difficult. We have only just begun.'

This was another vague, Delphic answer of the kind that by now he was getting used to. He often felt that she was talking over his head in riddles and normally this would have annoyed him, but he felt no anger towards her. He could not. He suddenly wished that they could unite in the ultimate copulation, coming together both physically and mentally, their minds and bodies merging in a whirlpool of flying thoughts, dreams and fantasies. He wanted to make love to her while at the same time he was afraid to do so. The very thought felt like a violation of her love and of the trust that she had placed in him, and yet he still felt the desire to be more intimate with her than he had so far dared to suggest, even to himself. He was aware that these thoughts, assisted by the close proximity of her body had given him an erection. Again, he hoped that she had not noticed.

Her hand travelled down his body and gently closed around his penis. 'This is the instrument of human love,' she said.

He felt a sudden surge of embarrassment. 'I'm sorry. I can't help myself. Please believe me, I love you on more than just the physical level, but sometimes my basic natural instincts take over and... well...'

'You don't have to apologise. You are human.'

'I... I...' He did not know what to say. His emotions were out of control.

She placed a finger over his lips. 'Don't talk. Relax.'

He tried to relax, but it was difficult. Her hands moved up and down his body as if she was examining the texture of his skin for the first time and marvelling at the many intricacies of the human form. Although willing to accept whatever she might do to him, deep inside he was apprehensive, as though this was to be his first sexual encounter. Something came back to him; it was the hazy and distant memory of a pretty young girl in an empty house and his tentative, clumsy fingered fumbling as he explored the new and hidden delights of her body. He remembered the confusion of different emotions as her nervous fingers moved inside his trousers and the electric sensation as she fondled his already erect penis. That time there had been no serious attempt at sexual intercourse. They were still too young and inexperienced for that, in addition to which there was the ever-present risk of their being discovered by an early returning parent. It had been purely a matter of exploration as bit by bit they loosened each other's clothing until eventually they were naked, revelling in the newly revealed secrets of each other's body and thrilled by the many new sensations that such intimate contact had brought to them, but it had gone no further. They had both been too anxious to do any more than simply touch and explore those parts of the body that were supposed to be forbidden to them. He felt like this now.

She continued to run her hands over his body. He spread his arms and let her explore him until he could no longer be just a passive recipient. He pulled her close. He cupped her breasts and felt his way down her belly until his fingers found her crotch. She shuddered and emitted a throaty little groan as he found her clitoris, leaving him in no doubt that she was indeed now fully human and still he continued, fingering her and caressing her nipples so that they hardened and stood erect, willing his mouth to encircle them and taste their imagined sweetness. Her hand travelled down to his penis and fondled it with a sense of increasing urgency.

'Now,' she whispered. 'It has to be now.'

She gasped as he entered her body and pulled him close, gripping him as he thrust deeper into her. Her hands clasped his head and drew his face up to hers, kissing him with an intensity that was surprising as it was new.

In that instant he saw himself swimming over a primeval seabed inhabited by curious invertebrates, most of which he could not identify. There were tubeworms and what might have been arachnids walking over the sandy floor, leaving behind erratic tracks with their many tiny feet. Small jellyfish drifted around him together with other swimming things, so bizarre that they defied any attempt at identification. One large swimming creature grasped a jellyfish in two extraordinary frontal appendages and swam away with it, its paddle-like feet beating the water in rhythmic waves. Now he was in a different sea. This one was inhabited by creatures that he recognised as trilobites as well as other things that were less easy to identify. A trilobite was seized and engulfed by a large, squid-like animal with a long, tapering body and numerous tentacles surrounding its big-eyed head.

More scenes of a similar nature appeared before him, with primitive fishes and sharks. Then he was on land where slow, browsing millipedes were preyed upon by centipedes and scorpions, and where spiders preyed upon primitive insects. Further images
310

appeared in rapid succession: images of amphibians and reptiles, followed by what must have been mammals. Then he saw ape-like creatures that might have been the first humans. These were replaced by other, even more humanoid animals, walking semi clothed in a subtropical landscape and now clearly recognisable as people. These were hunters and gatherers. Although armed, they appeared to be peaceful. Then he was in a large, communal building with what amounted to a congregation of these people. The cylinder dominated the central portion of this building and he saw that some of them took turns to hold it as he had once held it. Next he saw some of them in this world that he now inhabited and in the same position that he now occupied. Each was tended by a companion as Angel now attended to him. It struck him that one of the female companions that he saw bore a striking resemblance to Angel, if she was not exactly the same.

The scene dissolved and was replaced with something that he could not comprehend; a vast, brilliant star-like body that grew in immensity and radiance as he approached it, falling into a web of complexity that defied description and then its brilliance burst around him as he came inside her and he cried her name aloud as her fingers tightened on his back, holding him close, gripping more tightly than before.

Eventually, they relaxed their mutual embrace and lay back together. He had never made love like that before; nor had he expected to see the things that he saw during the course of their lovemaking. He wondered what these images had been about and then it occurred to him that the creatures that he had seen had been the most advanced animals of their particular time, and all had been at the top of the food chain. This was the position now occupied by Mankind. The final part still puzzled him, though.

He kissed her on the cheek.

She looked at him. 'Do you still doubt that I am human?'

'No,' he said simply. He could not doubt it now and yet he had envisaged things during their lovemaking that he could not account for. He could only assume that these images had been induced by the intimacy and heightened emotion engendered by their sexual union. If so, this was superhuman. No normal human being could have induced such images by mere dint of the sex act. Still he wondered what these images had been meant to convey to him. The history of life on earth was something that he might have read in any book on the subject or watched on the Discovery Channel, but this had gone beyond that with the final image of that quasi-stellar object. Perhaps this was to be the destiny of his people. He did not know. He wanted to ask her, but he feared another answer that he might not understand so he contented himself with the thought that he would come to understand in time, and time here was a commodity in plentiful supply.

He wondered if they would ever make love like that again and he turned over to face her. Her eyes looked into his and she touched his cheek so lightly that he barely felt it. It was like the faintest breeze upon his face.

'How do you feel now?' she said.

He smiled into her eyes. 'I feel better than I've ever felt before.'

He did.

75

That evening the team held a meeting in John and Barbara's room, since the nature of what was to be discussed was of the most secret nature and no one wanted to risk any of it being overheard in the bar.

John and Barbara sat on the bed while the others sat where they could. Lynda held in her hands a shoebox in which the statuette lay, carefully wrapped in layers of bubble plastic. Her search to find a companion statuette had so far proved fruitless. Bernard sat on a chair by the dressing table while Chris leaned against the wall.

'Well,' John began, 'it looks as if the project will be coming to a premature end in the near future. I'm sure you're as pissed off about it as I am, but it seems there's nothing much that I or anyone else can do about it. Once the Army moves in, it's likely that we'll have to move out and that's that.' He paused and looked at the despondent faces before him. 'However,' he went on, 'the story is not over yet and the cylinder will not be buried quite as easily as Fox would like to think.'

'The secret's out,' Barbara continued. 'I took the liberty of informing Lars Ericsson of Uppsala University and Professor David Emmett of Princeton. This is in deliberate contravention of the Official Secrets Act so, for the record, I didn't do it today but ten days ago, long before we were warned. I want you all to agree to that.'

The others voiced their agreement and Bernard's face had a wicked smile. No matter what they thought about the cylinder, they all wanted to see Fox outwitted on this matter. His recent actions had turned everyone against him.

'So,' John said, 'they will know of its existence in Sweden and the United States, but not here where it was discovered. Before long it will be known around the world; everywhere, in fact, except here.'

'That'll make Fox look rather silly,' Bernard said and clapped his hands together. 'Ha! I love it!' He became serious. 'I just hope he doesn't take it out on you. He won't be very pleased.'

'Let him try,' John said. 'I would look forward to humiliating him in court.'

'It'll be all right as long as we all agree on the story already being out before he tried to silence us,' Barbara said. 'It is vital that we all stick to this story. In fact, Lars Ericsson already knew about it, so that's no lie.'

Chris had a thought. 'I just hope that Fox doesn't impound your laptop and read your sent emails.'

'Shit!' John said as the realisation hit him. 'I hadn't thought of that.'

Barbara had not thought of it either. Her face went pale. 'I can delete the incriminating ones,' she said.

'They might still be able to recover them,' Chris said. 'Here, give me your computer. I'll see what I can do.'

She passed her laptop over to him and they got to work on it.

'That concludes the day's business for now,' John said. 'I repeat, I must insist on the strictest security regarding everything that's been discussed in this room. Those emails were never sent and the two gentlemen in Sweden and America already knew of the cylinder's existence. Is it agreed?'

They all agreed.

'I'll see you downstairs in the bar,' Bernard said, standing up.

Chris and Barbara were concentrating on the computer as Chris accessed the relevant files and deleted them. He then searched the system for traces of any such message having been sent and found nothing.

'I think it's clear,' he said, but he continued to scour the system for some more minutes, just to be sure. Eventually he passed the laptop back to her. 'The boffins might still be able to recover them, but I can't. Let's just hope they don't think to look.'

Barbara looked relieved. 'Thanks, Chris. I don't know what I'd have done without you. I'll buy you a drink for that.'

'You don't have to,' he said.

'Oh yes I do. If Fox ever discovered that I'd sent those emails, he'd have us all in jail in five seconds flat.'

'And he'd enjoy doing it,' John added.

Lynda handed Barbara the shoebox containing the statuette and she put it on the dressing table, alongside the box containing the dagger.

She turned to John. 'Tomorrow I want to take these to the University. They're sure to be fascinated by them, especially when I tell them they came from the same site as the mechanism and the other stuff we found there. It's a long drive, so I'll probably stay overnight and come back the day after.'

'It's a pity you can't mention the cylinder while you are there,' he said.

She smiled. 'I think they already know about it.'

76

Barbara sat in the study of William Reynar, curator of the university's museum. The dagger and the statuette were on the desk before him, together with the pieces of Stone Age pottery that they had recovered. He had just examined these artefacts with something approaching disbelief. Finally, he leaned forward and looked at her. Had he not already known her and John, he would have dismissed it all as a hoax. In fact he was still not sure whether or not they had been the victims of some student prank. He was aware that some remarkable discoveries had been made on that particular site, but up until now he had not actually seen them. The other finds had been sent directly to the British Museum as would these, very soon. Until now, the university had only seen photographs and reports of the discoveries that had been made since the beginning of the excavation. This time, however, she wanted William to see these objects at first hand since it was now important to all concerned that the university should know the true value of the project.

He picked up the statuette and looked at it again. 'I cannot believe that these objects date from the Mesolithic period,' he said. 'They are so out of time and so well preserved they could be modern, apart from the potsherds. They at least look genuine. Are you sure this is not a hoax?'

'I'm certain,' she said. 'These are not the only anachronisms we have found. These people had a highly advanced culture. You'll already be aware of some our other discoveries; and take a look at that dagger. It doesn't appear to belong to the period, I know, but this is the sort of stuff we're finding, like that clock or whatever it was. Now, sadly the whole project is under threat for reasons I'm not at liberty to divulge.'

William's eyebrows rose. 'What?'

She leaned forward and lowered her voice. 'Promise me that you will not breathe a word of this, will you? I want none of what I'm about to tell you to leave this room.'

He frowned. 'This is all starting to sound a bit cloak and dagger. What's the big secret?'

She indicated the statuette and the dagger. 'Look at the design on the pedestal. The same design appears on that blade. This is no coincidence. A similar design appears on something else – something we haven't divulged to anyone other than those immediately involved in the project. No one here knows of its existence.'

He examined the patterns on the dagger blade and the statuette's pedestal with mild interest before replacing them on the desk. 'What's so remarkable about this other thing that you have to keep it so secret?'

She began hesitantly, aware that her story of the cylinder's discovery and the subsequent events surrounding it, including the dreams and visions, sounded so fantastic as to defy belief. Despite this she persisted, outlining the story of James and finally bringing in the intervention of Special Branch and Detective Inspector Fox.

'Now,' she concluded, 'the whole project is threatened with closure as soon as the Army moves in and takes the site over.'

'You say the Army is getting involved?'

'Inspector Fox said he would have to call them in to fence off the entire area since it is now considered too unsafe to go anywhere near it.'

He nodded. 'I see his logic. If that thing really is as dangerous as you say it is, then it's probably best that it is fenced off. Why are you telling me this anyway?'

'I want to try and save the project. Even if the Army doesn't boot us off it, they're likely to damage the site beyond repair with their heavy equipment and fencing gear. Bill, we've made some earth-shaking discoveries up there and, in all probability there will be more to come. That statuette was unearthed only yesterday. These objects are seven and a half thousand years old. It's just sheer good luck we found them when we did.'

'What do you want me to do?'

'There's not much you can do, to be honest. The matter is completely out of our hands. John Black is in overall charge of the project and he can do nothing to prevent what is about to happen, so no one else here can help; but...' she lowered her voice, 'if the university already knew of the cylinder's existence, Fox and his cohorts would have a much harder job keeping the lid on it, wouldn't they?'

He smiled knowingly. 'You're letting the cat out of the bag.'

'Me? For the record, this conversation never took place and I haven't been here. I'll leave you with the photographs of the cylinder and the other artefacts, and that'll be your evidence. Officially, as of yesterday the cylinder doesn't exist and I risk going to prison for telling you about it, but if it was already known here then it would be Fox's fault for being too late.'

'I understand,' he said. 'We already know about the cylinder and have done for some time. I shall put out a discrete word or two. I can think of one or two people who would be very interested.'

'Thanks,' she said. 'I know this sounds vindictive and perhaps it is, but I resent the way that Fox has just steamed in and taken everything over. This is the most important archaeological discovery of all time and to have it taken out of our hands and covered up is just too much. I will confess that we don't know how to handle it. We did once, but no one is prepared to risk it a second time. Nonetheless, we have another case here of Whitehall digging its oar in and interfering with our research and, to be honest, we've all had enough of it.'

He got up and looked out of the window across the quadrangle. 'I'll find a way to leak it,' he said. 'I shall say I already had the photographs of the cylinder on file, but I'd paid them little attention until now when the pictures of the dagger and that statuette arrived by post. It shouldn't arouse undue suspicion, so for the record, I've known about it for some time.' He smiled. 'All that's left to do then is gently start the rumour mill. Does Fox know you're here?'

'No,' she said. 'At least I hope not and you…'

'I haven't seen you. I know.'

'Thanks. May I use the computer? I want to write a letter.'

'Of course.' He indicated the office computer which stood on a wide shelf in a corner of the book and box file lined study.

She sat down and composed a covering letter to the British Museum, avoiding all reference to the cylinder, but stressing the importance of the dagger and the statuette. She finished the letter and printed it out.

'I shall send these by Special Delivery to the British Museum,' she said, carefully wrapping the items in the bubble wrap and placing them back in their respective boxes. 'At least Fox won't keep the lid on these.'

After thanking him for his assistance and bidding him farewell, she left the curator's study and descended the stairs to the quadrangle, hoping that no one there would recognise her. She knew that she was taking a terrible risk, but she also knew that William would be discrete as he quietly spread the word. He would be careful to tell only a few selected people about this sensational discovery and not blab it to all and sundry. She had confidence in his ability to keep their meeting secret, for he was a quiet man with only a small circle of friends, but some of his friends were quite influential.

By the time Fox discovered that the cylinder was not a secret, it would be too late for him to stop the rumour from spreading and he would be faced with a damage limitation exercise. He might not like it, in fact he would be furious, but if she had covered her tracks as carefully as she hoped, then as far as he was concerned, the word had already leaked out long before he ever got involved with the cylinder. He just did not know yet. How could he? No one had told him.

She found her car and unloaded her briefcase and laptop into it. Then she took the boxes with their covering letter to the Post Office where she carefully wrapped and sent them by Special Delivery to the British Museum, ordering that extreme care be taken of them and insuring them for the maximum amount. Soon, she thought, the British Museum would be in possession of two unique treasures plus samples of Stone Age pottery, hitherto unknown from that era. They might not know about the cylinder; they would not need to. The mere existence of these objects, as well as the fine, if highly corroded mechanism, would be proof enough as far as they were concerned that something extraordinary had happened long ago in a remote Mesolithic settlement, lost to history until now. Fox could not change that.

77

Bernard drove John, Lynda and Chris up to the site and stopped, open mouthed as the place came into view. The Army had already moved in. Soldiers were at work with a posthole borer, erecting large concrete fence posts in a ring with a radius of about twenty five metres around the cabin. This area included part of the site that John had designated as being part of the settlement under their investigation.

For a moment they sat there in the Land Rover, trying to take in what they saw.

Lynda broke the silence. 'Oh, no,' she breathed.

John and Bernard jumped out and went over to where the soldiers were erecting one of the concrete posts. One of the men looked up as they approached. 'Sorry mate, you can't cross the line.'

'Who's your Commanding Officer?' John demanded.

The soldier indicated a group of men standing nearby. 'Colonel Fraser.'

Ignoring the soldier's request for him to stop, John approached the officer who was talking to a sergeant and a lance corporal. 'Colonel Fraser?'

The colonel looked at him. 'Yes. And you are…?'

'Professor John Black. I'm in charge of the archaeological dig here. Now, what exactly is going on?' He corrected himself. 'No. you don't have to tell me, I can see perfectly well. This is Fox's doing, isn't it?'

Colonel Fraser smiled apologetically. 'I'm sorry, but I'm not at liberty to tell you who ordered us here. This area has been declared unsafe and we have been ordered here to erect a ring fence around this cabin where I believe the hazard lies. I'm sorry if this is inconvenient to you, but we received our orders directly from Whitehall. Now, I'm afraid I must order you to evacuate the area.'

'Do you know exactly what this hazard is?'

'We were told that it is an extremely dangerous object; a large bomb or something of the sort that would be too dangerous to defuse and is best left untouched.'

'That's what you were told, is it? Well, I know what's in there and it's not a bomb. You're right that it's dangerous, but it doesn't need to be fenced off over such a large area. A radius of ten metres would be more than sufficient to render it safe. Look, you're damaging an archaeological site that is unique in its importance to the history of Mankind.'

'I'm sorry Professor, but we have our orders. We were commanded to erect a perimeter fence around the cabin with a radius of thirty metres and that's what we're doing. Now I'm afraid I must order you to leave the site at once.'

John bristled at this, but checked himself. 'Very well,' he said. 'But I want to make it known that I strongly object to being treated like this. We have been engaged in work of the highest archaeological importance and I resent the presence of soldiers with their bloody big boots tramping all over months of our hard work.'

The colonel looked genuinely sympathetic. 'Come with me, will you?' He led him away from the site of the perimeter fence, towards where the Army had parked their heavy lorry. John noticed that its tyres had already sunk two inches into the soft ground. Here they stopped.

'Right,' the colonel began. 'First, let me say that I don't like this any more than you do. Contrary to what many people believe, soldiers are not mindless vandals. Some of us have an active interest in such things as archaeology and believe me I do appreciate the importance of what you have been doing here. I've had an interest in the subject ever since I was posted out to the Middle East, but I have my orders and, even if it goes against the grain, an order must be obeyed. Do you understand?'

'I understand,' John said. 'But I would like you to understand the importance of some of the discoveries we have recently made on this dig. As a direct result of what we have found, most of the history books will have to be rewritten. I can tell you that we originally thought that this was the site of an Iron Age village. We now know it to be Stone Age, but millennia ahead of its rightful time. That's just how important this dig is to all concerned.'

'Really?' Colonel Fraser looked genuinely interested. 'Go on.'

John felt encouraged by this. Despite his initial anger, he was beginning to like the colonel for his apparent honesty and directness of approach. 'Among the things we've found are a clock-like mechanism, a dagger that is made of some sort of corrosion resistant steel and a statuette that would rival the work of Praxiteles in the fineness and delicacy of its execution; all of these dating from the Mesolithic period. That thing in the cabin that you are fencing off is another of those discoveries.'

The colonel looked puzzled. 'Just what is in that cabin?'

'You really don't know, do you?' John decided to tell him, despite Fox's threat of prosecution if he divulged anything of the cylinder's existence. 'I shouldn't be telling you this, but I will. Some time ago, we unearthed something that remains a puzzle to us. Put simply, it is a smooth cylinder that appears to be made of some strange ceramic material and is like nothing on earth.'

'So what's dangerous about it?'

'It seems to possess the property of being able to read people's minds and implant thoughts of its own. Three members of the team, including myself, have been affected by this. Now I don't believe in little green men, but I am now fully prepared to believe that it may be extraterrestrial in origin. It employs a technology that we don't understand and is far in advance of anything that exists on this planet, even today. We had it examined by an aerospace engineer and he said that it appears to be made from some kind of super ceramic material unknown on earth. He also said that the technology to make such a substance doesn't yet exist, and yet it was known to these Stone Age people.'

'Hmm.' The colonel thought for a moment. 'I'd like to see this cylinder of yours.'

'I'm afraid you can't. The cabin is locked and Detective Inspector Fox has taken the keys. In any case, I wouldn't advise you to go anywhere near it. When we first found it, it was inert and it could be safely handled, although it was extremely heavy for its size. Shortly after that, it began to psychologically affect anyone who approached it. Since then, its power has been steadily increasing so that now it's unsafe even to enter the cabin. Look, I have no objection to your securing the cabin, but does it have to be over such a wide area? Its range doesn't extend that far or anywhere near it.'

'What do you mean by its range?'

'I mean the range at which it can affect people's minds. For that to happen, you must be within about three metres or so of it. Further away, its effect is too weak to cause any damage.'

'I'm sorry,' the colonel said, 'I know I may sound a bit thick, but just how does this thing affect people's minds?'

John decided to tell him the full story, including the nightmares and James's lapsing into a coma following his second prolonged exposure to it. Colonel Fraser listened attentively as he spoke while finding much of what he said hard to believe. Had he not been listening to a serious minded down-to-earth academic, he would have dismissed him as a crank if not a lunatic or else a downright liar. But he found John's account of these events convincing enough to believe, albeit with some difficulty.

'Can I meet the other members of your team?' he said when John had finished.

'Sure,' he said, 'but they'll tell you the same story.'

'Still, I'd be interested to meet them.'

John led him over to the Land Rover where the others stood, watching them. Here he introduced him to the other members of the team. Bernard was particularly suspicious of him at first, having already experienced Fox's charade of friendship. Still, like John, he found the colonel intelligent and sympathetic to their plight. Despite his initial misgivings, he decided that he liked the man after all and wished that they could be on the same side. His liking of the colonel increased further when he confessed to an interest in ancient civilisations and a fascination with their project. He even believed him when he said that he was genuinely sorry to be interfering with their work.

Finally, the colonel left them with the assurance that his men would endeavour to keep the damage down to the barest minimum, adding: 'If you want to carry on working here, then I have no objection. Our job is just to erect the fence. If Inspector Fox has a problem with that, then that's his worry, not mine. I wish you good luck, but I must ask you to stay away from the area where we are working. It's just a matter of health and safety, you understand. By the way, just for the record, I have heard nothing about the cylinder. OK?'

'Well,' Bernard said after he had gone. 'It could have been worse, I suppose.'

'It's bad enough,' John said. 'Come on, we might as well take the rest of the day off. There's no point in hanging around here.'

'Do you know what?' Bernard said. 'I actually found myself liking that bloke.'

John had to agree.

'Do you think he's really on our side?'

'I don't know. He's sympathetic, but that doesn't mean he's on our side. I told him about the cylinder. He knew nothing about it. No one had told him. He thought it was a bomb or something of the sort that was too unstable to defuse.'

Bernard stared at him. 'You told him about the cylinder?'

John shrugged. 'I didn't see why not.'

'You will if Fox finds out.'

John started to walk back towards the Land Rover. 'Bollocks to Fox.'

78

Sergeant Gallagher was sitting up reading when a young woman doctor entered the isolation ward. He looked up and put his book down on the bed.

The doctor flashed him an encouraging smile. 'You'll be very pleased to hear that there's nothing wrong with you. We've checked and tested you for everything we can think of and found nothing untoward, so you're free to go.'

He thought about the dreams and his planned request to see a psychiatrist, but decided to let it go. A psychiatrist would not be able to sort out what was currently on his mind. Only one thing could do that. He had to get back to the cylinder in order to finish what he had inadvertently started.

'I'll contact your superior and tell him that you're OK, shall I?' the doctor said.

'No, that's all right, I'll do it myself. Thanks.'

The doctor left and the swing doors swished shut behind her. Gallagher got out of bed and found his clothes. He dressed and walked out into the corridor, feeling free. Outside in the car park, he switched on his mobile phone to call Fox, paused and then switched it off again. He would not call him immediately. As far as Fox was concerned, he was still being held in isolation until the doctors thought him fit to be discharged. That time was not now. He had more important business on his agenda.

He decided to go for a walk.

Leaving the hospital behind him, he headed out into the country, trusting his memory to find the location of the cylinder. He wandered the narrow country roads hoping to spot something that might look familiar. This was not easy, since he had only been up to the site in the car and now that he was a pedestrian, the roads took on a different aspect. He had a rough idea of the direction in which he should be heading, but it was no better than that. He wished that he had taken more notice of the minor landmarks that all roads possess; such things as a peculiarly shaped tree or a rock that protrudes from the bank – little things that mark the way for the experienced traveller, but to his untrained eye there was little to distinguish one road from another. He remembered one important detail, though. The site was on high ground, so as long as he went uphill he should be heading in the right general direction. That made sense.

For two hours he wandered the network of minor roads, seeing few people apart from the occasional farm tractor, a Post Office van and a couple of touring cyclists and still he seemed to be no nearer to the site than he had been two hours ago. He was just beginning to think he was hopelessly lost when he spotted something that did look familiar. It was a stunted hawthorn tree with a sloping trunk, its crown flat-topped by the winds that occasionally raged across the exposed landscape. He had seen that tree before, or one like it growing by the roadside, and he decided to follow this particular road, confident that it would soon lead him to the site and the cylinder.

His pulse quickened as he spotted something else that looked familiar. It was a large, solitary grey boulder about fifty yards from the road and it looked out of place, as if it had been placed there or casually dropped by some passing giant. He knew now that the cabin must be close and he slowed down, not wishing to blunder upon the site while everyone was working there. That would immediately arouse suspicion. He continued along the road, listening for the sound of voices or approaching vehicles and scanning the landscape for any sign of the cabin. There was none. Then he saw a small slate roof and guessed that he had found it at last. He slowed his pace down to a cautious walk and left the road, crossing the hard standing that had been put there as a parking place and following the path to the site. He knew that this was the right place by the presence of fresh tyre prints on the narrow dirt track road which he now followed, wherever possible keeping under cover of the gorse bushes and anything else that might screen him from the diggings. As the site came into view, he crouched and then lay flat on his stomach.

Something was wrong. Instead of the archaeologists' Land Rovers, a large army lorry was parked near the site and soldiers were swarming all over the place, erecting what looked like high fence posts around the cabin. He wondered how he could have failed to notice the heavy vehicle's tyre tracks on the path. He was supposed to be observant. He looked again at the site and knew straight away what had happened. Fox must have called the Army in to isolate the cylinder. He had told him that he might do this and it was obvious that now he had. This presented a problem.

He looked at his watch. It was after five o'clock and he guessed that the soldiers would soon finish work for the day. He would wait. He gazed at the cabin and remembered with a silent curse that the door was locked and that Fox had taken charge of the keys. If he was to get to the cylinder again he would have to break and enter. Well, if that was what it took to conclude the business, he would do it. The only thing that mattered was to see the cylinder again. Fox could do what he liked. That didn't matter. The cylinder was the only thing that mattered now.

He left the vicinity of the dirt road and hid in a shallow dip on the far side of a gorse thicket. The departing soldiers in their lorry would never spot him there, even if they were looking for him, which of course they were not. He wondered if sentries would be posted overnight to guard the cabin. They might, he reasoned, but it was unlikely. No one was likely to visit such a godforsaken place after nightfall. He would approach the cabin at dusk and then the cylinder would be within his reach. All he had to do then was prize the padlocks off the door to gain access to it.

He plucked a blade of grass and toyed with it, turning it between his finger and thumb and noticing the longitudinal ribs and veins that formed its structure, together with the tiny hairs that covered its outer surface. He had never really looked that closely at a blade of grass before. More than that, he fancied he saw the complex arrangement of cells that constituted its outer layer and beneath them, other layers of cells that went through to its core, each cell having its own specific purpose. It was beautiful and, at the same time, awesome. He had never looked at a blade of grass like this before. In fact, he had never really looked at a blade of grass or a leaf or, for that matter, any natural object. He had always taken these things for granted as just being there. In that sense, they were little different from the bricks and paving slabs that constituted his urban world. To him, all trees and wild flowers were the same. Now he was seeing a blade of grass as if for the first time. To all intents and purposes, it was for the first time. He began to realise that he had missed so much in life because he had never really looked before. He was observant, he had been trained to be, but he had never used his eyes as he was using them now. It was as if he was seeing everything for the first time. He watched the squadrons of insects that buzzed among the yellow flowers of the gorse, each with its own mission – the bees and hoverflies, wasps, beetles and other flying insects that he could not identify. They were all part of a grand and impeccable design, with each one performing a valuable function, even if that function was at times obscure. Everything had a purpose, even the flies. He could see that now.

These thoughts were entirely new to him and he wondered if this was yet another aspect of the odd effect that the cylinder was having upon his mind.

He looked again in the direction of the site. The soldiers were still at work erecting the large fence posts around the cabin. At the rate they were working, they would be finished by tomorrow so if he was going to act, it would have to be tonight. He might not get another chance. He wondered if they were going to work through the night, but he could see no floodlights or anything to indicate this to be the case. What he had at first sight taken to be a generator turned out to be a posthole borer, so it looked unlikely that they would be working for much longer. Once the light began to fade they would pack up for the night, or so he hoped.

Eventually, he heard shouted orders and the sound of tools being thrown into the back of the truck and he deduced that they were packing up for the night. He watched as they hooked the posthole borer to the back of the truck and then climbed on board. It would not be long now. Finally, the three remaining men climbed up into the cab and the truck drove off in low gear. It drove around the cabin in a wide circle, avoiding the diggings before turning up the track along which he had walked. It passed close to where he lay but, as he had expected, no one spotted him.

He waited until the sound of the lorry died away before he stood and got a better look at the cabin. As he had hoped, no sentries had been posted so this would be easy. All he had to do was gain access to the cabin and he set to work thinking of a way to do this. He needed a crowbar or something that would serve as one, but that was a problem for later. Had he thought about what he was doing, he would never have entertained the idea, but he was driven by an urge that overrode all common sense and morality. He could not see or understand that the cylinder had become an obsession that was now affecting all that he did.

As he crossed the perimeter ring of fence posts and approached the cabin, his heart was pounding. It was close now. He remembered the metal spike that had been driven into the ground and over which he had tripped when he and Fox had first investigated the cabin. It was still there. He pulled at it but it would not come. It had been driven into the ground almost up to its head and it was firmly embedded. He kicked it with the heel of his shoe, first one way and then another. It moved a bit, but it remained stubborn, so he looked around for a rock that would act as an improvised hammer. Sure enough he found one and began to hit the head of the stake sideways, first one way and then another, backwards and forwards, left and right until it worked loose. Now he was able to draw it from the ground. It came out with a dragging reluctance.

Placing it in the hasp of the first lock, he levered until the metal plate of the hasp came away from the woodwork. The second padlock was dealt with in the same way. If anything, this one was easier than the first. He propped the stake against the wall of the cabin and pushed at the door. It swung open with ease and there before him, glowing in the half light of the cabin's interior, was the cylinder.

It invited him to enter.

79

James and Angel were back in the great hall. Just how long they had been in the little private anteroom he had no idea, but in that time he had learned a lot about himself and many other things, many of which he was still unaware. During this time, he had made love to Angel on a number of occasions and each time he had found her a willing and able partner, since there did not seem to be much about the many aspects of sex that she did not already know. This did not fit easily with her apparent youth and innocence, for although she had the body of an adolescent, she had the sexual appetite of a mature woman, together with the same emotional understanding. This was not surprising for, although apparently young, she had not been born in the accepted sense of the word; therefore she had no age. What was surprising was that she was so completely human as to be perfectly formed in both body and nervous system so that she possessed the emotional and sensual responses of any normal woman. Here, however, the similarity ended, for the intimate contact of their lovemaking further assisted the subliminal transfer of thought between them – something of which he was largely unaware, so that the sex act became an unwitting two-way transfer of ideas. The changes in his psyche caused by this were so gradual as to be unnoticeable, but nevertheless they were taking place, unseen and inexorable. By virtue of this, he did not need to consciously readjust himself to his newly emerging mind. He simply got used to his new mindset. Now he had to get used to something else; the twisted perspective of the great hall that had so confused him before.

After their last intense coupling during which more thoughts were subconsciously transferred, followed by the almost ritual body wash, she had taken his hand and led him to that part of the wall where they had entered the chamber. As if on command, a slit in the wall had opened and allowed them through the barrier into the great hall where the other people sat or stood still as if in a trance.

Here once more he felt unsteady on his feet and she had to support him. He staggered drunkenly as the sense of vertigo returned. He tried to apply his mind to the distorted perspective of the place, but it was difficult. It was as if light itself was bent and everything was both large and small at the same time. This meant that he could not even guess the size or the distance of anything around him. He knew that Angel and the other people were of average size, but this still gave him little idea of scale. The topless pillars were at once both slight and massive; the squares beneath his feet were of an indeterminate size, even when he tried to measure them against his own foot it somehow did not work. It was as if he was walking on the air above them. He could not feel the ground.

'Hold me, please,' he said to Angel, who was already supporting him.

She drew him close and held him firmly. 'You won't fall,' she said.

He knew that she was conducting him towards the cylinder. What was to happen when he reached it he could not guess, but he knew that it was to play a key part in whatever happened when he got there and held it. He knew that he had to hold it. This thought both excited and disturbed him, for he felt that he was about to enter a new phase and possibly yet another dimension. He was not sure that he was ready for this, even if Angel thought he was. He wanted to ask her if he was ready, but dismissed it as a pointless question. The answer was already there before him and a decided matter as far as she was concerned.

He looked behind and saw that the others were following at a discrete distance. It was obvious that they were to witness whatever was about to take place and he called to mind the ancient scene of initiation of the prehistoric people that had first encountered the cylinder on earth. Now, millennia later, this scene was about to be re-enacted. He would have to be brave. The silence of the others was unnerving. In all his time he had never heard any of them utter a word. It was as if they were superbly made androids whose inventor had forgotten to fit with a voice box. Perhaps that was what they were, yet Angel was one of them and she had proved beyond all doubt that she was not an android. It did not make sense.

They seemed to be walking for a long time and yet the cylinder did not appear to be getting any nearer. He could still not judge its size any more than he could estimate the size of anything else around him. The sense of confusion that this caused was almost nauseating, rather like motion sickness and he wanted to lie down and close his eyes. Angel's grip on him grew firmer as she put her arm around his waist and drew him close. It was as if she sensed his distress and disorientation, which in all probability she did, for her empathy towards his feelings was at times uncanny. She touched his forehead. It was hot as if the fever was returning and she slowed down. The others drew close and gathered around them. A dark skinned, powerfully built man stepped forward and helped to support him. His strength was reassuring.

'It won't be long now,' Angel whispered to him.

The dark skinned man smiled but said nothing. Other eyes smiled into his and he wondered if these were smiles of encouragement or sympathy.

One by one, the others touched him as they slowly proceeded towards the waiting cylinder. The contact of the others both reassured him and renewed his strength. He sensed something like love in their touch.

'Why don't you speak?' he asked one of the women.

'They may not speak yet,' Angel said. 'Their time is later.'

'Later?' He deduced that 'later' meant after he had finished with the cylinder, or it had finished with him as the case may be.

Angel gave his waist a gentle squeeze. 'You may kneel,' she whispered.

He realised that they were standing in front of the cylinder. He was not aware that they were so close. Obediently and with some difficulty, he knelt in front of it, assisted by Angel and the dark skinned man. He knew what to do. He reached out and touched the cylinder. Instantly, he was aware of the now familiar sight of the complex circular pattern, but this time it was superimposed upon the cartouche. Overlying that was a third, delicate design that resembled a trefoil. The three patterns combined and interacted to form another, incredibly complicated pattern of geometrical shapes, curves, circles and parabolas, all intertwining into a three dimensional shape that inverted itself into a branching tube into which he was falling headlong into blackness, but not for long. Ahead of him was a light; a mere pinpoint at first, but getting larger and brighter as he approached

332

it. He was aware that he had seen something like this before in one of his visions, but there was no time to think about that now. This was real. He was approaching the star or whatever it was at a terrifying speed and was afraid that he would crash into its surface, not that that mattered. He would be incinerated long before he ever got there. Yet he was not incinerated. The blue-white brilliance of the object moderated to a cool opal glow without the searing stellar heat and radiation that should already have burnt him to a crisp and still he was heading towards the light, but it did not come any closer. It was the core of something much larger – something like a switching station. He barely sensed the change of direction as he left the light behind him and was hurtling along the same branched tube towards another bright object. This one was less bright than the first, but still white hot in its intensity. It grew in size until it filled his field of view and once more he was afraid that he would be incinerated by its heat and radiation before being crushed to a microdot by its gravitational pull. No such thing happened. Its light grew no stronger but, like the first, it moderated to a pearly glow and he was drifting down towards its surface. It was so close now that he could no longer determine its shape or size, nor could he see any sign of a solid surface beneath him. It was like descending into an ever thickening mist.

Eventually, he stopped. There was no sense of having landed in the conventional sense of the word. He just stopped moving and lay upon a surface so soft it might have been air. He could not feel it beneath him and yet he knew it was there. If he put his hand down it stopped against something firm, yet yielding. He looked around. Everything was white. He could see no horizon. Like the place where he had come from, the landscape went on forever, but this one was empty. There were no biomorphic shapes and no sound. In fact there was no visible sign of life. He felt lost and utterly alone in a featureless landscape without even a blade of grass to indicate that he was not the only living thing there. He felt as if he had been the victim of a cruel trick in which he had been marooned and left to die in this vast wilderness. This thought made him angry. He fought to control this anger, reasoning that Angel would be incapable of such a low trick; at least he hoped that the trust he had in her had not been misplaced and that he had not been carelessly catapulted off to what looked like the last place in the universe without a thought for his plight and for no reason that he could see. He wished that she was with him. Perhaps then he might have some idea of what he was doing here. As it was, he was alone and confused with nothing to guide him in a world so strange that it resembled nothing at all. It was Limbo.

'Where am I?' he asked aloud to no one.

Not surprisingly, there was no answer.

'Angel?' He thought that calling her name might open up the telepathic link that had existed between them. It did not.

He bit the back of his hand, wondering what he had done to be sent to this empty place. He felt as if he had been banished for some unknown misdemeanour and that there was no way back. The cylinder had sent him out, but there was no cylinder here so he was marooned. If this place was indeed a star, then he felt that it would have been better if he had been vaporised by its fiery energy before he had had time to realise what was happening, but he had not been vaporised. Whatever it was that had brought him here had taken care to protect him from its destructive forces, but what was that thing and why was it not here to meet him?

He stood up. As in the other place, his body felt light and he had some difficulty balancing. This time, however, the reason for his vertigo was different. Whereas he had formerly had difficulty with false perspective, here there was no perspective at all. He was in a virtual white-out with nothing visible above or below him, or anywhere around him. He cast no shadow in the cool, diffused light. He might have been a phantom drifting through a vast, limitless white void. He sat down again, feeling dejected. There was no point wandering around in a place where everything was the same and where nothing seemed to be the general rule. This was the end.

He cradled his head in his hands and moaned, wondering again what he had done to warrant being sent to this godforsaken wilderness where nothing happened nor could ever happen.

Then something did happen. It was not a dramatic event; there was no voice and nothing touched him, but he became aware that he was not alone. He felt a sudden inner warmth that grew in intensity as if a small fire had been lit deep inside his chest. This fire then spread downwards and outwards, radiating from its core to his entrails and out to his limbs where it burned like a new life force within him. If he closed his eyes he could see it; a bright yellow ball of fire with arms that branched, reaching all parts of his body, lapping at his heart and coursing through his arteries, bringing to him a feeling of ecstasy that was orgasmic in its intensity. The fire was in his head now, burning and sparking with dazzling brilliance as thoughts raced randomly

334

through his mind. This experience should have been terrifying, but it was not. He was aware of his voice crying aloud for joy as the inner flames reached his toes and his fingertips. If those flames had consumed him then and there, he would have been glad to have died in such a state of bliss. His life was unimportant, but he was not to die. He knew that he was to live, but that his life would never be the same again. His old self was dead already. It had died a long time ago. This new self would not die – ever.

He lay back with his eyes closed. Never had he known such peace. He knew now that this place was not the wilderness that he had first supposed. On the contrary, here was a life form so powerful that he could not begin to understand it. This life form had touched his soul and implanted something that he could not define yet. Perhaps he might never be able to define it, but it would stay with him for all time, he was sure of that. The bright fireball that burned within his core would never go out.

With a sigh he fell asleep as a lover might sleep after making love.

When he opened his eyes he was back in the great hall, still kneeling before the cylinder and surrounded by the people who were singing a low, droning chant as the ancient people had done so long ago. He looked around and saw Angel who was standing behind him. She put her hands beneath his arms and helped him to his feet.

'Don't tell me what you saw,' she said. 'I know that it was good.'

He nodded, unable to speak for a moment.

A blonde haired woman came up to him and touched his cheek. 'You are one of us now,' she said.

The powerful dark skinned man who had helped him towards the cylinder approached him and looked into his eyes. 'See!' he said. 'The fire still burns.'

The people were all talking now. One by one, they all approached him and gazed into his eyes. All agreed that the fire still burned, whatever that might mean, he did not know.

He walked with them towards the section of the wall through which he and Angel had entered the hall. This time he needed no assistance, having at last overcome his former feeling of vertigo. He now understood and accepted the perspective tricks that the great hall played on his eyes. His recent experience must have had something to do with this.

The blonde haired woman took his hands and kissed them. 'We shall see you again, but not now.'

The others followed suit and he felt that this was the last time that he would see them, even if they said that they would see him again. He turned to Angel.

'Come,' she said and the slit in the wall opened before them.

They passed through it into the small anteroom where once more they were alone. The slit closed silently behind them.

'This feels like goodbye,' he said at last.

'You must soon return to your own world,' she said. 'You have learned more than you know yet and have been to places that none of your kind has ever known, even the ancient ones.'

He felt reluctant to leave this place, alien as it might have been once. Now it was home. Mostly, he would miss Angel. In the brief time that he had known her, she had come to be the mainstay of his life; his spiritual guide and lover – his *raison d'être*. He knew that he would never meet her like on Earth. He had had many relationships, but never one like this and yet he knew that he did not belong here. As close as these perfect beings were to him, they were still forgeries created for his benefit. After he had gone they would revert to their former amoeboid forms and become once more a part of the massive super organism that had shaped everything around him.

He tried to smile, but it was hard for him in his current state of mind. 'If it must be so, then so be it. I shall miss you.'

'You needn't. I shall always be with you as you shall always be with me. A part of you will always be here.' She indicated her belly.

He pondered this and then the full implication of what she had said hit him. 'Are you pregnant?'

'No. We cannot cross breed, but from your seed I carry your life pattern.'

'So you can clone me?'

'We do not need to clone you. You are here and a part of you will always be here. In any event, we shall meet again. Remember, I am here for you. I shall always be here for you.'

'You mean I shall return?'

'The others returned. They are still here. They died long ago in your world, or their bodies did. Though their earthly bodies perished they exist yet.'

'Why have I not met them?'

'You have. They were around you when you held the cylinder.'

'They were...' He saw it now. This left him with nothing to say.

'When you return, it will be as if you had never been away.'

He put his arms around her and kissed her. Never had he felt such love as this for anyone before. It saddened him to think that they would soon be parted, if only for a time and time here was without meaning. Still, he would leave her with some more of his life pattern, as she had called it. For one more time they made love with a renewed vigour.

80

That evening, John sat with Bernard in the bar of the White Hart. Chris and Lynda had gone out for the evening while Barbara was staying at the university for the night and was not due back until some time the following day. Their mood was sombre.

John toyed with his drink but showed little interest in it. It was currently hard for him to summon up much interest in anything. He had been in charge of the most important project of his career and it hurt him to have it taken away like this.

Bernard nudged his arm. 'Guess who's just come in.'

John turned to look, a thunderous scowl on his face, half expecting to see Fox coming through the door. It was Colonel Fraser, dressed in civvies and clearly off duty. With his faded blue jeans and navy blue Guernsey sweater, he might have been entering a yacht club. He ordered a pint of bitter and came over to where they sat.

'Mind if I join you?'

John indicated a vacant chair. 'Sit down.'

He drew the chair over and joined them at the table. 'Well,' he began, 'you'll be pleased to hear that we expect to be finished in a couple of days or so, after which we'll leave you in peace to get on with your work.'

'Thanks,' John said, but his heart was not in it. This was reflected in the flat tone of his voice.

The colonel detected the listless mood of the two men and thought for a moment, trying to think of something to say that might break the air of gloom that hung over the table like a thundercloud. He leaned forward and lowered his voice. 'I would like to know more about that cylinder of yours. While I was up there, I took the liberty of peeping through the window of that cabin. I couldn't see much. Has there been a fire in there recently?' He paused for a moment. 'This conversation is strictly off the record, by the way.'

'Yes,' John said. 'We actually had that cylinder under control when those bloody detectives came nosing around and buggered it all up with their clumsiness.'

'Under control, you say?'

'One member of our team had the idea that it could be shielded with an improvised Faraday cage,' Bernard said. 'We knocked one up out of chicken wire and it worked, then Fox or his sidekick broke the earth lead to the screen and the whole bloody issue got burned away. Do you know how much power it takes to burn up a roll of chicken wire?'

'A lot,' the colonel said.

'Well, that's how much power that thing has now and that's why we daren't pull a stunt like that again. That thing has enough power to blow us all into the next world.'

'It might be destroyed with a controlled explosion.'

Bernard grunted. 'I very much doubt it. There's no telling what might happen if you tried that. At the very least, nothing would happen and if it did I wouldn't want to be standing within twenty miles of it if it blew. Don't even think of it.'

'Besides,' John added. 'I'm not prepared to see a unique object like that wantonly destroyed. Even if we can't handle it, it remains a priceless piece of our history.'

The colonel raised a placating hand. 'I have no intention of doing any such thing. Look, I didn't become a colonel in the Royal Engineers by being a complete idiot. I just want to know more about what we're supposed to be dealing with, that's all. If I could, I would prefer to work with you on this. Unfortunately, Fate has put us on opposite sides of the issue and I'm no more happy about it than you are.'

John nodded. He had no reason to doubt the colonel's word, despite the still fresh memory of Fox's false offer of friendship. He liked to think that he could read faces and he fancied he detected a degree of earnestness in the colonel's visage. 'I think we have helped you in every way we can,' he said. 'I'm only surprised that you weren't told about it beforehand.'

The colonel pulled a wry face. 'That's a soldier's lot, I'm afraid. We're not accustomed to reasons why. We're just told to get on with it and don't ask questions.'

'I still think a radius of three metres around the cabin would have been more than sufficient,' Bernard said.

'I agree, but we were told thirty, so thirty it has to be.'

'That'll be bloody Fox again,' John growled. 'The man's a fucking idiot.'

The colonel was silent here, unwilling to discuss any possible contact he might have had with Fox, much less express an opinion. If he agreed with John's assessment of the inspector, he was not going to say so. 'About this colleague of yours – the one in hospital – did he spend a lot of time with the cylinder?'

'More than anyone else here,' John said.

'And you still don't know what's wrong with him, do you?'

'No one does. They've tested him for everything they can think of and nothing seems to be physically wrong with him. The fact remains he's still in a coma and that cylinder has something to do with it, of that I'm certain.'

'Would it be possible to see him?'

'I don't know what good it would do. Sure, you can see him, but he won't be able to tell you anything. He's unconscious.'

'I suppose you're right. I'm just curious to know more about whatever that thing is. It fascinates me.'

'It fascinated James Masters too,' Bernard said. 'That's why he's unconscious.'

'Well,' the colonel stood up. 'I've spent enough time here and I have to get back. I'll see you in the morning if you're coming up to the site.'

'Don't count on it,' John said.

Bernard looked at John. Here was proof, if proof were needed, that his heart had gone out of the project. The presence of the Army had finished it for him.

Colonel Fraser sensed it too. He sat down again. 'Professor, I understand how you must feel about all this, but you really should continue with the project. I shall see that my men don't interfere with your work in any way. I may be a soldier, but I have been interested in archaeology ever since I was posted out to the Middle East and I discovered an old Arab coin while clearing some rather dodgy ordnance that had been left lying around. We get all the best jobs, you know.'

For the first time that evening, John smiled. Despite himself, he liked this officer.

'We might as well go up and see how things are going,' Bernard said.

'Very well,' John said.

'Good.' The Colonel stood up and headed for the door. 'I'll see you there.' With that he left them.

'Well,' Bernard said, 'we might as well have a look at the damage.'

'Hmmm…' John stroked his chin. 'I'm not sure I want to see it. Let's face it, mate; we've lost, haven't we?'

'I'm not giving up yet.'

'No?'

'No.'

They fell silent again. After a while, John said, 'I wonder what damage Barbara has inflicted on Fox's news blackout on the cylinder.'

'Eh?'

'I think she might have spilled the beans to Bill in the museum – a couple of weeks ago, of course.'

Bernard grinned. 'Nice one. I'd like to see Fox's face when he finds out that half the academic world already knows about it. He'll go loopy.'

'Well he might, but if everyone keeps it quiet it'll be too late for him to do anything about it. So far, she has told Lars Ericsson in Uppsala who already knew about it anyway, David Emmett of Princeton University and now, closer to home, Bill Reynar. All of them will talk to others, but quietly, so by the time it becomes general knowledge, her tracks will be well covered and it'll be impossible to make any charge against her stick. After all, it's already old news. Fox just doesn't know it yet.'

'Serve the bugger right,' Bernard chuckled.

81

Colonel Fraser and his working party arrived early at the site. They parked their lorry and the men piled out amid shouted orders and the clatter of spades. Rolls of heavy wire netting and razor wire were thrown from the back of the truck where they were carried over to the posts that already marked the perimeter of the no-go area around the cabin. Further, smaller concrete posts appeared. These were to provide an inner fence around the cabin. Colonel Fraser had omitted to tell John about that.

It was Sergeant Blakemore who first noticed the open door of the cabin. He cautiously approached and looked inside. There, in the dim light of the cabin's interior, he saw a man sitting on the earthen floor with his hands on a glowing cylindrical object, seemingly oblivious to all that was going on around him. For a moment he hesitated, uncertain that what he was seeing was real. At first he could not believe the evidence of his eyes and then he acted.

'Hey, you, get out of there – now!' he roared.

The man took no notice of him.

Colonel Fraser came running over. 'What is it, Sergeant?'

'Someone in the cabin, Sir.'

'What?' Fraser looked at the open cabin door and swore under his breath. Without thinking, he strode into the cabin and almost immediately reeled against the wall as a loud bell-like note rang inside his head. He groped his way to the door and staggered out into the open, unable to speak for a moment.

'You all right, Sir?' Sergeant Blakemore caught his arm.

He shook his head as if to clear it. 'I think so. Stay away from there, Sergeant. I don't know what that thing is, but it's not safe to approach it. Bugger, that thing really whacked me. How are we going to get that man out of there?'

'I shouted at him, Sir, but he didn't seem to hear me.'

'Didn't he? We'll see about that.' The colonel approached the door again. 'You, man. Get out of there – now!'

'My words exactly,' the sergeant muttered, 'with the same result.'

Fraser withdrew from the doorway, unsure what to do. He had no wish to go back in there and he was certainly not going to risk sending any of his men in. He had just been zapped by something emitted from that glowing object. He was not going to risk the same thing happening to anyone else on his detail.

'I'll rush in and drag him out,' the sergeant said, starting towards the doorway.

'No!' Fraser barked. 'No one's going in there. It's too dangerous.'

'Then what are we supposed to do, Sir?'

Fraser made a decision. 'We can do nothing for him. Leave him there until the professor and his team arrive. They might have some idea how to deal with this, but I'm not going to risk any of my men by sending them in there.'

'What is that thing?'

'Damned if I know. No one told me we'd be dealing with something like this. Just keep the men away from there, Sergeant. That's an order.'

'Sir!' The sergeant walked back towards the truck. 'I'll fix you a brew, Sir.'

'Thanks, Sergeant.'

It was mid morning before John and the team arrived at the site. John's despondent mood had not lifted and he had taken some persuading to turn out at all, but Bernard's persistence had finally paid off and so they drove out to the site. When they got there, Bernard parked the Land Rover behind the army lorry and the team got out. John was pleased to note that Colonel Fraser had been as good as his word and the damage to the site had been kept to a minimum.

They had only just got out of the Land Rover when the Colonel came running over, shouting something that they failed at first to comprehend.

'What is it?' Bernard asked.

'We've had a break-in,' Fraser said. There's someone in there with that thing.' He pointed towards the cabin.

'What!' John ran towards the cabin, followed by Colonel Fraser and the team. It was easy to see even from a distance that the door had been forced again. The padlocks hung uselessly from the torn-off hasps and the iron fencing stake was propped against the wall of the cabin.

When he reached the open door he stopped, open mouthed. There in front of him, squatting before the cylinder, sat the serene figure of Sergeant Gallagher.

'Gallagher!' he roared. 'What the bloody hell do you think you're doing?' He backed away from the door, knowing too well that his question had been essentially a rhetorical one. It was quite obvious what Gallagher was doing.

'We shouted at him,' Fraser said, 'but he doesn't seem to hear us.'

'He won't,' John said. 'This is exactly what happened to James Masters.'

'Can't you get him out?' Fraser asked.

'No. We'll just have to wait until he's ready to come out by himself. If anyone goes in there, that thing will have them as well.'

'I know,' Fraser said. 'It hit me with something.'

'You went in there?'

'I forgot. I saw the open door and him in there and I rushed in without thinking. That's when it hit me. It nearly knocked me flying. What is that thing in there?'

'We don't know, but we do know what it does. How do you feel now?'

'I feel fine. Sergeant Blakemore fixed me up with a brew and I'm OK.'

'Good, but I'd better warn you that you may well have been psychologically affected by your contact with that thing. You may get some strange dreams and the like. We've all had them.'

'You told me.'

'I didn't tell you what they are like though, did I? I might as well tell you now that some of them are pretty nasty. If necessary, see your MO about it. You may have to.'

'We'll see.' He looked back towards the cabin. 'Who is that man?'

'Detective Sergeant Gallagher, Special Branch. He blundered in there a couple of days ago and got a full dose off that thing. This is the follow-up.'

'That's one in the eye for Inspector Fox,' Bernard muttered to Chris who grinned in agreement. Even John had to suppress a smile despite the tastelessness of his remark.

'How long will he stay in there?' Fraser asked.

'As long as it takes; whatever *it* may be,' John said. 'All we can do is wait.'

'It could take hours,' Bernard said. 'We don't know how long he's been in there.' He thought for a moment. 'Do you suppose he's conscious?'

John had not thought of this. The fact that James had remained conscious for some time after his second contact with the cylinder did not necessarily mean that Gallagher would follow the same pattern. If Gallagher was unconscious, then someone would have to go in there and get him out. There would be no volunteers.

He looked at this watch. 'We'll give him half an hour. If he's not out by then, I'll go in and drag him out.'

'Don't be a bloody fool,' Bernard said. 'You know better than anyone else what another exposure to that thing might do to you. Do you want to end up like James?'

'I'll take that chance. Colonel, do you have a rope?'

'Yes,' Fraser said.

'Then tie it around me. If I look like I'm about to linger for too long, drag me out of there, ready or not.'

Bernard shook his head. 'See you in hospital.'

'I'll detail a couple of men for the job. We have rope in the truck.' The colonel called Sergeant Blakemore over and ordered him to get a rope from the truck.

The sergeant ran to the lorry and returned with a skein of rope. John looked at it. 'That'll do.' He turned back to Colonel Fraser. 'Now remember, if I look as if I'm enjoying it, haul me out of there, double quick.'

'Enjoying it?' Fraser echoed. 'You mean you actually like being hit on the head by that thing?'

'It only hits you like that once,' John said. 'After that it works on a more subtle level. There's no more flash-bang-wallop; just a gentle feeling of... I don't know what, but it's subversive. That's how it seems to catch people.'

'A tender trap,' Bernard said.

'Something of the sort,' John agreed.

Bernard looked at him. 'You do know what you're doing, I suppose...'

'I know exactly what I'm doing and I know the risk, but what else are we to do? We can't exactly leave him there now, can we?'

'Why not?'

John ignored Bernard's flippancy and tied a bowline in the end of the rope with a loop large enough to slip over his shoulders and fit around his chest with comfort. 'This is purely a last resort,' he said, letting the rope's end drop. He had no intention of using it immediately. He looked back inside the cabin. Gallagher still sat there, stock still and oblivious to all that was going on around him. There was no obvious sign that he was alive. Not even a muscle twitched to indicate the presence of life. It occurred to him that he might be dead or at least in a catatonic state. After all, no one knew how long he had been in there or, if he had been there all night, what such a prolonged exposure might do to him.

He turned back to Colonel Fraser. 'Do you or any of your men have a mobile phone that works up here?'

The colonel produced his mobile. 'Yes, but it's in a blind spot.'

'Wonderful! Ours don't work up here either. Look, we shall probably have to get him to the hospital ASAP. Never mind. One of us will drive him there.'

'He must have only just been discharged,' Bernard observed.

'Well, he's going straight back in again. He's going to end up like James, assuming he's still alive, that is.' He turned back towards the cabin. 'Sergeant Gallagher, can you hear me?'

Still there was no response from Gallagher.

'Right,' he said, picking up the rope and putting the loop around his chest. 'I'm not waiting any longer. 'Get two or three of your men and remember what I said; if you think I might be lingering in there for too long, haul me out. I'll try to drag him out with me.' He licked his lips with a dry tongue. His heart was pounding and his palms were wet. He did not know exactly what would happen when he entered the cabin. The cylinder's power was many times more now than it had been when he had first encountered it and he guessed that mere proximity in the same room would be sufficient to receive a full blast of whatever it had to offer.

Colonel Fraser called three men over and ordered them to take the free end of the rope and to pull like hell on his command. The soldiers took up their positions, ready for the order, should it come.

'OK,' John said, 'I'm going in.'

As soon as he entered the cabin he could feel the cylinder's energy crackling in the air around him, as if it was charged to a high potential, but this felt different from any normal electrical field. Instead of the uncomfortable prickling sensation and ozone smell usually associated with high voltages, he felt light-headed and drawn towards the cylinder rather than repelled as would be normal, so that he had to resist the urge to walk straight up to it and join Gallagher in his communion. Images flashed through his mind, few of them with any meaning or significance and somewhere he heard a brittle five note tune repeated over and over again, varying slightly as it progressed and grew in intensity. He tried to ignore this by telling himself that the sound was in his head and that only he could hear it, but it was difficult to ignore the insistent rhythm of the sound that seemed to grow louder as he cautiously approached the stationary figure of Gallagher, pausing from time to time in an effort to clear his head and to look at the cylinder which was glowing brightly now, even in the light from the open door. He was aware of a voice somewhere calling his name, but he ignored it. It was not important. The cylinder was important. It was beautiful. He had never really seen it like this before and he realised that all along he had misjudged it by regarding it as an evil force. It was not evil. It could never be evil and still the images came, too rapid for his brain to process them: images from its past and what appeared to be images of things to come in some place that he could not possibly identify. It was like nothing on earth. He tried to clear his head of these pictures and concentrate upon Gallagher, but it was becoming increasingly difficult to concentrate on anything but the sounds and the images.

'Grab him, man!' It sounded like Bernard's voice.

Obediently, he caught Gallagher under the arms and began to pull. The semiconscious detective offered little resistance and he was able to pull him away from the cylinder without too much difficulty. Gallagher turned and stared weakly into the eyes of his captor as if imploring him to leave him there as he was pulled clear of the glowing object and towards the door. He was aware of a shouted order as the rope around his chest tightened and drew him towards the light and then he was out in the open air, feeling muzzy and still clinging to the slumped body of Gallagher. He released his grip on the detective and let him sit at his feet, then he stepped back two paces and staggered drunkenly so that Colonel Fraser had to support him. Two soldiers tried to attend to Gallagher who was sitting where he had left him, looking dazed and confused, as if something important had been interrupted without any valid reason.

Bernard came over and helped the colonel with John. 'How are you feeling?'

John straightened himself up and shook his head. 'I'm OK, I think. That thing's too strong to go anywhere near it now. God knows what it's done to him.'

Bernard looked at the slumped figure of Gallagher. 'He looks rough, but then I suppose he should, the daft sod.'

'He was driven to it. He had no choice as James had no choice.'

Colonel Fraser looked puzzled. 'You told me it had the power to alter people's minds, but I never would have believed this if I hadn't seen it for myself. That thing in there is more dangerous than I thought.'

'It's not...' John checked himself. He had been about to protest that it was not dangerous. Now he knew that he had been affected by it. He was beginning to think it was beneficent.

Both Bernard and Fraser looked at him. 'You were about to say that it's not dangerous, weren't you?' Bernard said. 'Can you explain the logic underlying that statement?'

John sought hard to find an answer. 'Forget it,' he said. 'My thoughts are mixed up at the moment but I'll be all right. Concentrate on Gallagher. He's the one who needs help, not me.'

Bernard went over to where Gallagher still sat, attended by the soldiers. 'He's barely conscious,' he said. 'We'd better get him to hospital.'

'You'd better drive,' John said. 'I don't think I'm safe yet.'

Colonel Fraser studied him closely. 'Are you sure you're all right?'

'I'm Ok. Can you secure that door again?'

Fraser nodded. 'I'll have a couple of men do it immediately.'

'Be careful not to let them any closer to the cylinder than that.'

'You don't have to tell me. I'm perfectly aware of the danger.'

John was tempted once more to state that there was no danger, but he held it back. He went over to where Bernard squatted beside
348

Gallagher and helped him to carry the semiconscious man to the Land Rover. 'I'll ride in the back with him,' he said. 'Chris, you'd better sit the other side. Help me to support him.'

'Sure,' Chris said.

No one spoke as they drove to the hospital. They were preoccupied with their own thoughts while John tried hard to imagine what on earth he would say when he brought in another of the cylinder's victims, this time a Special Branch officer. That would look good, particularly so since he could not mention anything about the cylinder even if he wanted to.

82

It was early afternoon when Barbara arrived back in town. She parked the Land Rover in the White Hart's car park, collected her room key and took her case and laptop up to her room. She put the cases on the floor and sat on the bed, wondering if John and the team were still on the site or if they had been prohibited from going there by Fox as he had threatened.

She opened her mobile phone and called John's number. To her surprise he answered. 'Hello John, I've just got back and I'm in the White Hart. Where are you?'

'We've just left the hospital,' John's voice came back.

'Have you seen James?'

'No, but we've got another customer for them.'

'What?'

'I'll tell you when we get back. There's been a lot going on. We'll see you shortly.'

'OK.' She closed her phone and sat there for a minute, wondering what on earth had happened while she had been away. She looked at her watch and hoped they would not be long. Then she decided it was time for lunch and went downstairs to the bar. Although hungry, she decided that a bar meal and a drink would suffice.

She sat in the bar eating her lunch when John and the team entered. Bernard ordered the drinks while John sat down beside her.

'Right,' she said. 'I think you'd better tell me what's been going on.'

John stared ahead, looking at nothing in particular. He seemed to be lost in thought. 'A lot has happened while you were away.'

'Well, tell me about it then. What were you doing at the hospital?'

'It's Gallagher,' he said. 'He's done the same thing as James did.'

'He's what?'

'He was discharged from hospital and he went straight up to the site, broke into the cabin and grabbed hold of the cylinder. The Army found him this morning.'

'Army? What's all this about the Army? Look, you'd better tell me what's been happening while I was away. What's the Army doing up there...' She broke off as the realisation dawned on her. 'This is Fox's doing, isn't it?'

'It's all Fox's doing – him and his MI5 cronies in Whitehall or whoever they are. They've buggered up the whole project.'

'Here you are.' Bernard put a pint of bitter on the table in front of him. 'You look as if you need it.'

Chris and Lynda joined them at the table.

'Right,' Barbara said, 'enough of the small talk. I want to know exactly what's happening here.'

Between them, John and Bernard told her all that had happened since the Army had moved in, ending with the discovery of Sergeant Gallagher in the cabin that morning and John's successful if ill advised effort to get him out of there.

She stared at John. 'You went in there? How do you feel now?'

'I don't know,' he said. 'It's too early to say. I think I'm all right, but...'

'I think we'd better keep an eye on you for a while,' she said, 'just to make sure.'

'He's all right compared to Gallagher,' Bernard said. 'We left him at the hospital not knowing what day of the week it is. Fox'll go bloody ballistic when he finds out what's happened to his opposite number.'

'Let him,' John said. 'I did warn him that this might happen. Well, now it has and serves him right. He should listen.'

'Be all the same if he did,' Barbara said. 'It would've happened anyway.'

'The cylinder exerts a will of its own,' John agreed. 'You know, when I was in there I could feel it. It was all I could do to concentrate on getting him out of there and not succumbing to it.' The others stared at him and he went on. 'It was as if it was calling me – inviting me to touch it and I wanted to – I really wanted to. I wanted to join Gallagher in front of it and enter into whatever it was that he had entered into. I know it sounds daft now, but that was how I felt at the time. It was as much as I could do to resist it. By the way,' he turned to Barbara, 'it has also hit Colonel Fraser, the Commanding Officer of the squad up there. I advised him to see the Medical Orderly if the dreams start as they may well do. I warned him about that.'

'You did what?' Barbara was taken aback.

Bernard hid his face. 'Too much information, I fear,' he muttered.

'It was only fair to warn him,' John insisted. 'After all, he knows about it already now, so there's no point in hiding this information away from him. Damn it, if the dreams do come, and they probably will, his reaction to the cylinder and to us will be more hostile than if we had not warned him. It stands to reason. There's nothing we can do to prevent him from finding out the truth about the thing now, is there?'

No one spoke.

'Look,' he went on, 'the Army was called in to fence off the area around the hut. Colonel Fraser wasn't given any precise reason for it. I couldn't hide the truth from him, especially after Gallagher broke in last night and everyone saw what was in there. What else could I do but tell him the truth? The cat was already out of the bag anyway.'

Barbara's initial anger subsided. 'I suppose you had no choice but to tell him. But he's a soldier and he will think like a soldier. If he perceives it as a serious threat, he will stop at nothing to render the thing harmless by whatever means are at his disposal, and if that means blowing the hut, site and all off the map, then he will do it.'

'No he won't.'

'What makes you so sure?'

'I'm not sure. I only trust he will realise the potential danger of such an action. I told him that at best it might not work and at worst it could produce the biggest bang in recorded history. I think he listened.'

'I think the cylinder's made you soft in the head. You have disclosed its existence to the Army – the very thing you didn't want to happen and you've also put yourself in breach of the Official Secrets Act. If Fox finds out you will go to prison. Do you understand?'

He began to feel hot, a sure sign that he was losing his temper. 'Listen, you understand. I had no choice in the matter, especially after Gallagher blew the gaff on the whole shooting match by breaking in like that. Fuck it, what was I supposed to tell him: that it was all the product of his overactive imagination? I wasn't dealing with a five year old.'

'Calm down, the pair of you,' Bernard said, intervening. He had seen the look in John's face and knew that he was about to blow. 'John's right. He had no choice in the matter. Once Fraser and his squad had seen Gallagher in the hut with the cylinder the truth was out and there was no point trying to lie our way out of it. Colonel Fraser is an intelligent man and he would have seen through any attempt to fool him. You can't hide a thing like that, especially when it's staring you in the face.'

They both calmed down. John's impending spate subsided and Barbara relaxed. 'I'm sorry,' she said. 'I was unreasonable, I suppose. The secret's out anyway. Soon half the academic world will know about it. I took the liberty of informing Bill Reynar of its existence. That was my chief reason for going back to the university. I told him in strict confidence of course, but word will leak out, it's bound to.'

'Another black eye for Fox,' Bernard observed dryly. 'What with Gallagher and all, he will go nuts when he finds out that his secret isn't a secret at all. It'll come out slowly, of course, so the truth will dawn only slowly.'

'What of Gallagher?' Barbara asked.

'It's a carbon copy of what happened to James,' Bernard said. 'He must have broken in during the night, God knows when, but they found him there in the morning. Now he's in hospital like James. He'd only just been discharged that very day. They commented on that when we took him in.'

'What did you tell them when you brought him in?'

'We told them we found him like that,' John said. 'They recognised me immediately as one of those who took James in. Bringing in two dazed men begins to look like carelessness. I felt a bit awkward.'

'They must be getting suspicious,' Bernard added.

'They're bound to,' she said. 'It'll only be a matter of minutes before Fox finds out. They're bound to tell him.'

'Then he'll be gunning for us,' John said. 'If he comes round here and he probably will, we tell him the truth. After all, we didn't force Gallagher to break in and anyway, it was the Army that found him there, not us. We just drove him to the hospital, that's all. We've got nothing to hide.'

'Try convincing Fox of that,' she said.

'Colonel Fraser will testify on our behalf. He was there.'

'You really believe he is on your side, don't you?'

'We all do,' John said.

'Then I hope for all our sakes he really is. You believed Fox once, remember?'

As if on cue, Inspector Fox entered the bar and spotted the group immediately. He came straight over to them. 'I want to talk,' he said.

Bernard looked up. 'OK, go ahead.'

'Not here; at the station.'

Bernard opened his mouth, no doubt to utter some caustic retort, but John cut him short. 'This'll be about Gallagher, won't it?'

'Sergeant Gallagher is in hospital.'

'I know,' Bernard said. 'We took him there. He was found this morning with that cylinder that by the way doesn't exist. Therefore, he must be swinging the lead.'

Fox scowled at him. 'That's enough of your lip. I've had more than enough from you already. Now don't push me. Gallagher has lapsed into a coma and they don't know what's wrong with him.'

'Sorry,' John said, 'but I don't know how we can help you.'

'You found him. Where was he?'

'First, we didn't find him; the Army did, and second, he was found in the cabin cuddling that thing in there. All we did was take him to the hospital once we had got him out. Other than that, we know no more about what happened up there than you do. He was discharged from hospital yesterday, by the way. He must have made a beeline for the place as soon as they let him go. I warned you that this might happen.'

Fox quietened down. His aggressive mood faded and his shoulders slumped. He looked beaten. For a moment, John almost felt sorry for him. He softened his tone. 'Look mate, if there was a way to help you with this, I would do what I could, but there's not much that I or anyone else can do now. If it's any comfort to you, that thing hit me again while I was getting him out of there, so don't think I'm being obstructive. I just can't help you.'

'You got him out of there?'

'Yes.'

Fox considered this. His manner became almost mild. 'I think I owe you an apology. I didn't know.'

'Talk to Colonel Fraser. He'll tell you the same as I.'

'Thanks.' This was a different Fox from the one who only moments before had been so bombastic. 'I'll do that.'

He left the bar and walked out into the street.

'That's right,' Bernard said. 'Piss off.'

'He's a worried man,' Barbara said.

'He has a right to be worried,' John said. 'He's losing control of the situation and I know what that feels like.'

83

John lay in bed beside Barbara who was fast asleep, but for him sleep would not come. They had made love on going to bed after which she had slept almost immediately, being tired after the morning's long journey back from the university. He had tried to sleep, but his recently renewed experience with the cylinder had awakened a new interest in the enigmatic object. He was convinced that it had communicated something important to him. The trouble was he could not bring it to mind. He remembered the rapid sequence of images that had passed through his mind while he had been in the cabin, but they made little sense. They had been snatched; a sample and no more than that. He wondered what had gone through Gallagher's mind in the time that he had been with it and what it might have done to him in that time. Would he be like James Masters? If so, would he emerge from his apparent coma in a transformed state as he assumed James would, or would the experience overload his brain and either kill him or put him into a persistent vegetative state?

He fell into a half sleep. Images came and went unbidden and these too conspired to keep sleep at bay. Sometimes these were images from the ancient past, now familiar, but there were others too, such as the tantalising vision of a bizarre, dreamlike landscape that seemed to be inhabited by formless things for which he had no name and that defied description. They moved, or rather drifted in a seemingly random way that at the same time had a certain order and as they moved they changed shape. As alien as this landscape was, he had a feeling that he had been there before, perhaps in an earlier dream.

He was now convinced that the scenes from the past were genuine. The detail was now sharp enough to observe the weave of the clothing of the people that inhabited his vision, as well as the brooches and other adornments that they wore. It was all so vivid that he felt as if he was actually there among them, if not one of their number. He could even smell them. He recalled the previous visions that he had had of this ancient world. This was every bit as real but he was not dreaming now. He was wide awake and still the images came; some of them everyday scenes of life in the city, while others were scarifying images of human sacrifice and ritual murder in the name of some angry god that the priests had assumed inhabited the cylinder. It was obvious to him now that they had misinterpreted its purpose despite its efforts to teach them otherwise. He knew that it had attempted to correct this aberration, but without success. The priesthood had been too strong or else too stubborn to listen or understand. They had followed the old ways and were not going to change them on what might have been, after all, a mere whim. Also, they had belonged to a privileged and often corrupt caste. Consequently, they had resisted change on the grounds that this might diminish their exalted and feared status in what had become a predatory and feared society. It therefore followed that the ultimate downfall of this society was as predictable as it was inevitable. He now understood what James had meant when he had told them that they had not given it time. They had not given it time to tell the full story and issue the gruesome history of these people as a warning to others. Consequently, everything so far had been taken out of its proper context. The nightmares had been a necessary part of this process.

This thought made him sit up in bed. He had to write this down. He switched on the bedside light, got out of bed and pulled on his dressing gown. Then he went over to the dressing table, found a pen and paper and began to write. It was all so obvious and clear that he wondered how he had not seen it before. He had misjudged the cylinder's purpose all along – they all had, from the original People of the Cylinder to those who had rediscovered it. How could he have been so stupid? Bit by bit, the pieces were falling into place. The loathing that he had felt for the object had been wrong in every way. It was not evil – it never had been. It was just a tool placed there to transfer the guidance of its makers to whatever life forms it might encounter. It was not there to dictate its will, merely to act as a guide and teacher. Whether or not this might work was of little consequence to whoever put it there. It was a seed. If it germinated and grew to enhance whatever intelligent life forms it might encounter, then it was a success. If not, then it did not matter. It was up to humanity to absorb its guidance or disregard it. It made no difference to the cylinder or to whatever it was that had placed it there.

It occurred to him that there might be other cylinders in other parts of the world, as yet undiscovered. Some might be lying at the bottom of the sea, forever inert in the cold black depths. These would never be found, but others could be scattered almost anywhere over the seven continents. Maybe a few of these others had also been found in ancient times and these might have helped to propagate some of the more precocious early civilisations. This was pure speculation and he discounted the idea on that premise, but it remained a possibility.

Barbara stirred and muttered something unintelligible but did not wake. She was dreaming. He broke off writing for a while and studied her sleeping form. He wished he was an artist so that he could draw her as she lay, partly uncovered by the bedclothes, her head to one side and her breasts rising and falling in time with her slow breathing. One arm lay across her midriff while the other lay along her side. Her lips mouthed something and were still once more. He would have liked to have made love to her again, but he did not want to wake her just to satisfy his sexual appetite. He turned his attention back to his writing, but he had written all that he could think of for the time being and he put the pen down. Although tired, sleep still eluded him. He could not get the cylinder out of his mind and he had to resist an insane urge to take one of the Land Rovers, drive up to the site and fulfil his communion with it. He needed more information and only the cylinder could supply that information. The rest was supposition.

His mind began to move towards the possibility of gaining access to it, but this was as irrational as it was dangerous. It was right for the authorities to deny general access to such an object and yet he felt that it was unfair to deny it so comprehensively, even to controlled scientific research which he felt was necessary if the thing was ever to be understood. Without that access, the full story would never be known and that would be a bitter blow for the scientific world. Whichever way he looked at it, it seemed that everyone involved in this matter was doomed to lose the battle, be it to destroy the cylinder or to save it. Fox had lost his battle to keep it under wraps, even if he did not know it yet, the Army's attempt to fence it off was little more than a half-hearted attempt to deny access to it, James was still unconscious and now one of the most important archaeological projects of all time had to all intents and purposes foundered. He might be able to continue with it at as soon as the Army had finished

358

their work, but he and the team had lost their motivation to continue with the same degree of enthusiasm. He could sense this from being and working with them. It was over. Fox and the Army had seen to that.

He yawned. His body was tired but his mind was still awake. It was going to be a long night if he did not get some sleep. He went to the mini bar, selected a miniature bottle of Scotch whisky, emptied it into a glass and gulped it down, enjoying the burning sensation of the neat spirit and hoping that its resultant alcoholic stupor might help him to sleep. He read his notes and returned to bed, letting his dressing gown fall to the floor. He would pick it up in the morning.

Barbara stirred again as he switched off the light. He did not want to wake her but it was too late. Her hand brushed his face. 'Are you still awake?'

'I can't switch off.'

'It's that cylinder again, isn't it?'

'I keep thinking about it. I can't get it out of my mind.' He wanted to tell her about his revised opinion of it, but he decided that at this time of night and with her being so tired, he would say nothing about it for now. He would keep it until the morning or maybe later when a better opportunity might present itself.

She propped herself up on one arm. 'Why did you go in there? You knew very well what would happen if you did.'

'Someone had to get the daft bugger out. I decided that since I had already been exposed to it, it couldn't do much more to me than it has already done. Therefore it might as well be me who took the risk. I reckoned without its increased power, though. It must be up to full strength now.'

She sighed. 'It was a silly thing to do – brave but silly. Don't be surprised if the nightmares come again.'

'I don't think they will come again. I think I understand it now.'

'Understand what?'

'I think I understand the cylinder and what it does. I'll explain it later.'

'You're not making sense,' she began and then something did make sense. 'You really have been affected by it, haven't you? Damn it, John, it's got you.'

He did not answer this. Maybe the cylinder had got him. Maybe it had to get him in order that he should better understand its

359

purpose. After all, half knowledge was worse than no knowledge at all. He needed to know more about it and still the images drifted before his eyes. A girl who bore more than a passing resemblance to the figure represented by the statuette appeared briefly before she faded into the darkness of the room and was replaced by an intense white light that seemed to grow in size and intensity until it cooled to a pearly glow. A scintillating trefoil pattern intensified and then evolved into a triangle before settling onto the surface of a glowing disc where it burned with a renewed brilliance. He smiled. It was beautiful.

'John, are you still there?' There was a note of concern in her voice.

'Yes.'

'Don't let go. I don't want you lapsing into a coma like the others.'

He kissed her. 'I don't think I will. There's too much to do.'

'You're not giving up on the dig, then?'

'No.' The truth was he was not thinking about the dig.

'Good,' she said. 'You shouldn't give up. Despite everything, we still have faith in you and the project.'

'Don't you think some of the enthusiasm has gone out of it? I mean I can feel it. I've felt it ever since Fox started sticking his nose into our business. Chris and Lynda are just paying it lip service now and Bernard gets into a foul temper every time he sees Fox. I've never known him dislike anyone the way he dislikes that man.'

'He sees Fox as a threat to your project and that makes him his enemy as well as yours. That's not lack of enthusiasm. That's loyalty. Now, think of that and try and get some sleep. You'll be fit for nothing in the morning.'

'I'll try.' He tried to concentrate on her words and put the cylinder and its images to the back of his mind but they would not stay there. Her words had been meant to comfort him. To some extent they worked, but he still felt that the initial enthusiasm for the project had gone, especially since the Army had moved in and taken such a disproportionately large area, albeit on the periphery of the site. Even if Colonel Fraser was as sensitive as he claimed to be regarding their requirements, he had been given no option but to construct a high fence around the cabin with a radius of thirty metres. This was excessive and quite unnecessary in the opinion of everyone concerned, but he had been given no choice. Fox had filed his report and the

Army had been ordered to act on it, regardless of the importance of the dig. He wondered how Colonel Fraser felt about the project now that he had seen the cylinder, felt its effect and witnessed Gallagher's entrancement after it had captured his mind. That would be bound to influence his attitude towards it and justify his action in fencing the thing off in the interest of public safety.

Barbara's breathing became slow and even. She was asleep again. Still sleep would not come for him as he stared at the darkened ceiling. Again he saw the trefoil pattern and the triangle – the recurring factor of three. Barbara had already noticed that three was a constant factor in everything to do with the cylinder, even to its proportions, a measured ratio of exactly three to one. A trefoil pattern was on its hull; one of three patterns and the last one to be noticed just before the cylinder had begun to become active. He recalled that it had not been noticed before and that Barbara had insisted that it had not been there the previous day when she had examined it thoroughly. It had just appeared, small and faint. Now it had significance. He was not sure what that significance was yet, but he would find out.

He pulled himself up sharply. Barbara was right. It had got him. He had despised the thing from the moment it had first begun to affect him and his two key workers and he was not going to be coerced into loving it now, and yet deep inside he did love it. It had insinuated its way into his psyche and become an important part of him. Once more he felt the urge to be with it again, if only to understand it better and he fought hard to resist that urge. He wondered if it would ever leave him.

He closed his eyes and tried to sleep, forcing himself to think of anything but the cylinder. Eventually sleep overtook him; a profound sleep with just one dream. It was dominated by the cylinder.

84

In the ward where James lay, the monitor screen indicated an extraordinary level of brain activity before it settled down to something approaching normality. In the dim light of the night time ward, two eyes opened and looked around.

James Masters was awake.

85

Colonel Fraser had a restless night in which he dreamed of things that he as a soldier was better equipped to deal with than the members of the archaeological team, but even he was unprepared for some of the scarifying images that came to him that night. He had once witnessed the aftermath of a car bomb in Basra where the mutilated bodies of the dead and injured littered the road amid scattered body parts and pools of blood, so he at first connected the vision of slaughter that came to him with the trauma of that incident. What he could not connect was the overall scenario of what he saw in his dream. This was not Basra; it was some place that he had never seen before and the people were not Iraqis, they were wild and primitive, armed with what looked like Stone Age weapons and iron swords that were wielded with devastating effect on anyone who got in the way.

For some time he lay awake, pondering this hellish dream. He remembered John's warning that disturbing dreams might come following his exposure to the cylinder and he thought that he had mentally prepared himself for this eventuality, but he had not prepared himself for what came to him that night. John had advised him to see the Medical Orderly should these dreams persist. Perhaps he might, but for now he would tackle this on his own. He had witnessed post-traumatic stress disorder following the car bomb incident that had led to one of his men being discharged from the Army on medical grounds. He was not about to cash in his military career on the strength of one dream. Still, it had disturbed him. He would talk to John about it in the morning. After all, he had more experience of these dreams and perhaps was better able to advise him on how they might be controlled, if they could be controlled. Failing that, it would be a private talk with the MO.

He went back to sleep again. Another dream came, less violent than the first, in which he saw a group of people gathered around the cylinder and apparently worshiping it. They uttered a long, monotonous drone of a chant that was accompanied by a brittle, repeated five note phrase that came from somewhere, possibly from the cylinder itself.

He awoke from this, now convinced that the cylinder had implanted these dreams and visions into his mind.

No further dreams came to him that night.

86

James sat on the side of the bed. He had detached the leads from his head, leaving the ones that had been attached to his chest in place, knowing that to detach them would trigger an alarm and bring someone running. Before detaching these, he reached up and switched the monitor off. Now he could be free of them and he peeled off the last of the sticky patches that held the electrodes in place. Then he carefully withdrew the tube by which he had been artificially fed.

He knew what he had to do, but first he had to find his clothes. He searched his bedside locker in vain. His clothes were not there. Having been unconscious at the time, he was oblivious of the fact that he had been naked when admitted to the hospital. After an unsuccessful search of the small private ward in which he had lain, he gave up. Searching the general ward, he found a tee shirt and tracksuit bottoms that more or less fitted in the locker of a sleeping patient and he dressed as quickly and quietly as he could manage. In another locker he found a jacket and put that on. It was a size too big and hung slackly on his slim frame, but it would do. He searched the ward for shoes that fitted and eventually found a pair of rather scruffy trainers, together with a pair of socks. Then, dressed in his stolen clothes, he left the ward. All this time, no one woke up and no one saw him.

Somehow he knew that he was not alone. Another of his kind was nearby. He had to find that person.

He passed the ward sister's desk. She appeared not to see him. A nurse spotted him in the corridor and was about to speak but, after making eye contact with him, she carried on as if he was not there. No one saw him as he walked the hospital corridors. Some time would elapse before he was missed; he had seen to that. A newly awakened instinct told him where Sergeant George Gallagher lay and within minutes he found him, lying as he had lain, wired to a similar monitor and apparently unconscious. He knew as he approached that the man had not been fully prepared for the coming journey, if that was the right word for it. He would put that right. He had no way of knowing that the unconscious man was a Special Branch officer.

The duty nurse looked up from the desk as he approached and was about to challenge him before resuming her paperwork as if he was not there. It was as if she had not seen him. In a sense, she had not.

He passed the desk and, on approaching Gallagher, he reached out and touched his forehead. A quick mind scan told him that the detective's communion with the cylinder had been interrupted quite close to the end of the transfer. This would be a simple matter to correct. After that he could leave him to his own devices and let the remainder of the process take its course.

On the desk a telephone trilled and the nurse answered it. She looked across to where James stood over Gallagher and continued her muted conversation, finally replacing the receiver and returning to her paperwork. She still had not seen him.

James remained with Gallagher for about half an hour before he was satisfied that the process was complete. Then he straightened up and, with a last look at the prone detective, he left the ward. He had done what he could. The rest was now up to Gallagher. He wondered if he might be taken in charge by Angel or if one of the others would care for him in his new world. Only he would know.

He left the ward and walked along the network of corridors to the main entrance. There was more work to do. He left the hospital behind and headed towards the town. It was a long walk and days of lying in bed had taken their toll on his body. His legs felt weak and he had to stop periodically to rest and recover his strength. He did not know how long he had been away. It might have been hours or months. It did not matter. Time had lost all meaning. The weakness in his limbs was a minor matter. He would soon recover his strength with normal exercise. What he needed was somewhere to rest for whatever remained of the night. He had no watch but he guessed that the time was about three fifteen from the time he had left the hospital. There would be nowhere to rest at this hour of the morning. He thought of going up to the cabin and spending the night there with the cylinder, but it was too far. Anyway, he did not need the cylinder any more. As far as he was concerned, it had done its job. It could do no more for him now.

He was not physically tired, but he needed to rest in order to recover from the walk into town with his weakened muscles and to adjust to his new mental powers. He was not willing to test them for their own sake. He had already demonstrated his ability to condition people's minds so that they failed to see or recognise him, even if he was standing directly in front of them. If they did see him, they would instantly forget it. It had been necessary to employ that power in the hospital if he was to communicate with Gallagher and slip out unnoticed, but it was not to be misused. To do so would diminish his power. Angel, or whatever it was that had spoken through her in that other world, had seen to that. That had been one of the lessons learned from the past to ensure that the misuse of heightened intellect that had ended in tragedy so long ago could never happen again. He determined that, outwardly at least, he would be an ordinary man with extraordinary powers, but these powers were to be kept hidden and never misused. History would not be repeated this time.

The road was dark, lit only by a fitful crescent moon that at times lit his way but mostly did not. Consequently, his progress was slow, even after his eyes had adjusted to the almost complete absence of light. He was in constant danger of turning his ankle on one of the potholes that pocked the roadside, but he persisted, treading cautiously, almost feeling his way. He remembered the vertigo that had afflicted him in the great hall and how he had eventually overcome that. This was similar and could be overcome in like manner. He concentrated on this and the going became easier. As long as the road was clear he kept to the middle, pulling over to the edge only when a car approached, but there were few cars at this time of night and mostly he had the road to himself. A police car approached and he backed into the hedge, fixing the car with a stare until it passed. The driver did not see him.

Streetlights informed him that he was at last approaching the town. He wandered down the high street to the White Hart, passing through the courtyard to the car park. His car had not been towed away as he had feared and was where he had left it. He tried the door, but it was locked and, of course, he had no keys. He stared hard at the door and concentrated on the lock mechanism, unsure if he could manipulate its electronics. To his mild surprise, he heard a satisfying clunk as the doors unlocked and he got in, adjusting the seat to the fully reclining position. With a sigh he lay back in the seat and stared up at the darkened windows of the hotel. He was tired now. The walk from the hospital with weakened muscles together with the mental exertion of making himself appear invisible and then psychokinetically unlocking the car door had taken their toll on his mind and body. He thought of Barbara. She was the one who had reached out for him while he was away; he remembered that now and he thought of extending his thoughts to her so that she would know that he was safe but he decided against the idea. It was better to let her rest undisturbed and anyway he was too tired to exercise his mental powers further. He would see her later. He wondered how the others would react to his sudden reappearance after so long an absence from their world. He would have to be careful. His disappearance from the hospital would soon be noticed, if it had not been already, and as likely as not a search would be made for him involving the police. This was not necessarily a problem. He was equipped to deal with that. He had already demonstrated his ability to evade the eyes of people whom he did not wish to see him. He had only to extend a thought to render himself effectively invisible, so evading the police would be an easy matter. In any case, he did not need to evade them. He had committed no crime.

He thought again of Angel. Already she seemed like something remembered from another time and yet in that time she had become a vital part of him – a part that he had thought would be missed when she was gone. She was gone now and yet something of her remained within him; something indefinable. If he closed his eyes he could see her. If he listened he could hear her voice inside his head, not reiterating words that she had already said, but giving him new guidance. Somewhere inside him she was still alive and still Angel. Although distant beyond imagination something of her remained close. He would never leave her. He could not. By the same token, she would not leave him and here was another way of controlling his new power, for if he in any way abused it the most vital part of her would leave him and he would be lost. This was another device to ensure that history did not repeat itself. The super intelligence that had encompassed him had taken great care not to repeat its earlier mistakes. He was therefore aware that any abuse of its power would result in a severe penalty; the loss of that power. He could not afford to let that happen.

He closed his eyes and slept. In the morning he would renew his acquaintance with the team. They would not recognise him immediately. It was better that way. Soon enough they would become aware that he was no longer in hospital and then he would be forced to make himself known to them. Until then he would be a stranger.

87

In the morning John and Barbara arrived late in the breakfast room. John had had a bad night with his mixed thoughts regarding the cylinder, so consequently he slept later than he had intended. This seemed to be becoming a habit with him.

They joined the others at the breakfast table. Bernard gave them a curt good morning and asked them if they were going to visit James in the hospital.

Barbara went over to the sideboard where she poured herself a grapefruit juice. 'We might as well,' she said as she rejoined them at the table.

'Any point in going up to the dig?' Bernard asked John.

'Yes,' he said after a pause for thought. 'We'll take a look and see what the Army has done to the place. I'd also like to know what the cylinder has done to Colonel Fraser after he got zonked by it yesterday.'

'You caught a packet off it too. How do you feel this morning?'

'Tired,' he said noncommittally. This was not the time to talk about the thoughts that had invaded his mind and prevented him from sleeping for most of the night.

'You should be taking it easy,' Barbara said. 'You had an awful night last night. You woke me up with your restlessness.'

'I'm sorry,' he said. 'I don't think we'll be doing much work today anyway – not with things the way they are.'

'I wonder how Gallagher is,' Bernard said.

John looked at him. 'Do you care?'

'Not a lot,' he said, 'but I wonder if he has been affected in the same way that James was.'

'Fox said he had slipped into a coma so it looks as if he has. We'll have a look at him if you like.'

Barbara looked up at this. 'You seem very concerned.'
'I am,' he said.

After breakfast, John and Barbara drove to the hospital. On their way out, neither of them looked at James's car in the hotel's car park. Had they looked at it, they might have noticed someone sleeping in the nearly horizontal driver's seat. Instead, they got into the Land Rover and headed for the hospital.

On arriving there, they went to the ward where James was supposed to be. Here they were met by the ward sister who inquired if they had seen him. Both looked blank.

'He absconded last night,' she said. 'It looks as if he just got up and walked out. No one saw him. He was reported missing early this morning.'

John and Barbara exchanged glances. In that moment all thought of seeing Gallagher vanished. There was little they could do for him anyway.

'Someone must have seen him,' John said. 'He's not the invisible man.'

The sister shook her head. 'No one saw him,' she insisted. 'He was here last night and then he wasn't. It's as if he simply vanished.'

'OK,' John said. 'I think I know where we'll find him.' He turned to Barbara. 'I'll bet a pound to a pinch he's up at the site again.'

James was not at the site. They drove there where they were met by Colonel Fraser who was anxious to talk to them about his dreams that night, but their minds were on James. John went over to the cabin. The door was closed, but the locks had not yet been repaired. He opened it. The cylinder floated just above the floor where it had been the previous day. The smell of charred furniture still permeated the interior. James was not there.

He shut the door and looked around as if James might be standing somewhere nearby. He was confident that he would find him with the cylinder. Now he was at a loss to know where he might be. He rejoined the others.

'Well?' Barbara said.

'He's not there.'

Barbara looked worried. 'In that case we have no option but to inform the police of his absence,' she said. 'I mean, we don't know what condition he's in, do we? He could be wandering around, brain damaged and unable to look after himself. He could be dead for all we know.'

'I doubt it,' John said, 'but you're right. We should tell the police.'

'You mean Fox,' Bernard said.

'I mean anyone who might be able to find him. We can't do it.'

Colonel Fraser spoke up. 'I could have my men out this evening looking for him.'

'Thanks,' John said, 'but you only have a limited number of men at your disposal. Besides, they won't thank you for having them out combing the countryside for a missing person after they've finished a day's work. It's better we call the police.'

'Well, I'll ask my men to keep an eye out for him if it helps.'

'They don't know what he looks like,' John pointed out.

'Do you have a photograph?'

'No.'

Barbara gave him a brief description of James, adding that as likely as not he would be unshaven and generally unkempt. She had no idea how he might have dressed himself since she remembered that he had been naked when admitted to the hospital, and she had taken charge of his clothes and personal effects and had sent his crumpled suit to the cleaner's. This left her with only the vaguest of descriptions, but it was the best she could do.

Fraser thanked her and assured her that he would pass her description on to his men. He put off telling John about the disturbing dreams of that night. That would do for later. This was neither the time nor the place to burden him with his troubles.

They got into the Land Rovers and drove back to town. There was nothing more to do.

88

James awoke feeling refreshed. His first task was to contact Barbara and let her know that he was well. He looked at the car clock. Half past ten. He had slept longer than he had meant to. After an indeterminate time in a place where time in the conventional sense did not exist, he had to readjust to a world where time once more held sway.

He thought of Barbara. At first he could not locate her so he extended the field of his search. Still he could not find her. He did not yet know the physical range of his thought power, but from this he deduced that it must have a limit. He concentrated harder. Still no contact was made. For a moment he wondered if he still possessed the mental powers that had been implanted into him and he began to fear that he might have contravened the code of conduct that had been given to him with these powers. This could not be. So far, he had only exercised these powers to evade the eyes of the hospital staff and patients, and to avoid being spotted by a passing police patrol car. This did not amount to abuse. It was self preservation, as had been the purloining of other people's clothes in order to effect his escape from the hospital, if that was the right word for it.

He looked around. Apart from a small number of cars, the car park was empty. The Land Rovers were not there. From this he deduced that the team must have gone up to the site.

One of the hotel staff came out from the back of the hotel and spotted him. He caught her eye and she carried on as if she had seen nothing. Here was evidence that his powers had not diminished. That was a relief. He concentrated again on Barbara but still he failed to find her. He would try again later. Meanwhile, he had to eat. He had no idea when he had last eaten, having been drip fed while in hospital, but he was hungry. He needed breakfast.

He got out of the car and decided to have a look around the town. There was bound to be a café or somewhere where he could eat, but he would have to be careful. Word that he had absconded from the hospital was bound to be out by now and it was almost certain that the police would be looking for him. He could deal with that, but there remained the ever present possibility of his being observed without his knowledge and here he was vulnerable. Unless he could transmit his power of suggestion to the observer, he would be seen. He would have to take that chance. Food was a priority.

It did not take him long to find the small café so frequently visited by John and Barbara. He found a vacant table and sat down.

A waitress came over and he ordered a light breakfast of scrambled eggs and coffee. Then he sat back and looked out of the window. Life outside appeared to be normal. There were no signs of a major manhunt and no extra police on the street. From this evidence it was possible that his absence had not yet been reported. He relaxed and waited for his breakfast. He realised that he had no money, but he would deal with that minor problem when the time came.

'Scrambled eggs and coffee?' The waitress put the tray on the table and he thanked her.

He sipped his coffee and started in on his breakfast, pausing for a moment to concentrate again on contacting Barbara. First there was nothing and then there was; faint at first, but getting stronger. Then it was clear. She was approaching.

Sitting beside John in the Land Rover, Barbara suddenly stiffened.

John looked at her. 'What is it?'

'I… I don't know. James, can you hear me?' There was a pause. 'Where are you?'

John slowed the Land Rover down to a crawl. 'Barbara, what's the matter?'

She put her hands to her head. 'It's James. He's talking to me, I know he is. James, where are you?'

John could only hear Barbara's side of the conversation. It was like listening to someone talking on the telephone.

She continued her conversation if that was what it was in silence, only mouthing the occasional word, interspersed with long pauses. Finally, she turned to John. 'Forget about the police. We're going to the café. James is there.'

There was a toot from Bernard's Land rover and John stopped. Bernard pulled up behind them and got out. 'What's up?'

374

'I don't know,' John said. 'It's Barbara. Something's happened.'

Barbara leaned across and spoke to Bernard through the open window. 'We're not going to the police. I know where James is.'

'What?' Bernard stepped back.

'Don't ask. I'll explain it later. Just don't go to the police, OK?'

Bernard shrugged. 'OK. See you back in town.' He turned and walked back to his Land Rover. With another toot, he drove past them and disappeared around a bend in the road.

'Right,' John said when he had gone. 'Now perhaps you'll tell me just what's going on.'

'I think James just contacted me,' she said. 'I can't explain it. I heard his voice inside my head. Let's go to the café, I think we'll find him there.'

He opened his mouth to say something but thought better of it and drove off again. She had claimed to have had these telepathic links before. As yet they were unproven. Now it was time to put them to the test.

Back in town, they parked the Land Rover next to Bernard's in the hotel's car park and went to the café where they normally went. This was where James had told her he would be. There were just seven people in there. Two women sat at one table and a man whom they did not recognise sat at a table near the window drinking coffee. An empty plate was in front of him. Presumably he had just finished his breakfast. A middle-aged couple sat in the corner and a younger couple sat further away, sharing some secret over a pot of coffee.

John looked at them all in turn. James was not there. Barbara sat down near the window, feeling despondent. She was sure he would be there. John sat down opposite her. He had no wish to say anything regarding her supposed telepathic message, but it looked as if she had been wrong. Words were unnecessary. Her face told him what he needed to know.

He touched her hand. 'He may have decided not to wait.'

'I was sure we'd see him here,' she said despondently.

He looked around again. It was obvious that James was not there. There was no need to tell her.

The stranger at the nearby table got up and came over to where they sat. 'Barbara,' he said softly.

Surprised, she looked up. 'James!' she exclaimed. 'I didn't recognise you. Neither of us did.'

James smiled. 'That was intended. It's good to see you again.'

John realised that he was gaping and closed his mouth. This defied belief. Here was James whom they had both failed to recognise, now clearly recognisable and talking to Barbara as calmly as if he had just returned from a holiday in Bermuda. He could not understand how they had failed to recognise him, especially after having visited him on an almost daily basis while he had been in hospital. He tried to remember the stranger who had sat at the next table but could recall nothing of the man's appearance. He began to understand how he had managed to slip out of the hospital undetected, but it still made little sense.

The waitress came over and they ordered coffee. James declined.

Barbara had by now recovered her composure. She leaned forward and spoke in hushed tones. 'We've been worried to death since we discovered you were missing this morning. The sister at the hospital said you vanished last night, but no one saw you go.'

James smiled but said nothing.

'How did you do that?' she persisted.

'I can't talk about it here,' he said, 'there are too many people.'

'We'll go somewhere quieter. There are a lot of things I want to know besides that. We both want to know.' She indicated John.

'I'll tell you, but not here.'

'How are you feeling?'

'I'm fine,' he said. 'Never felt better.'

She tried to think of something else to say. This was difficult. She wanted to ask him so many questions, but they all involved matters that she could not discuss anywhere where they were likely to be overheard by a listening public. It was known that Fox used this café from time to time, so James was taking a terrible risk by just being there.

The waitress arrived and put two cups of coffee on the table, then returned to her post behind the counter.

John and Barbara drank their coffee, trying to look as casual as possible while James sat with them looking relaxed. This did not make sense to John. He could be detected at any time and yet he seemed to be totally unconcerned by the fact.

John and Barbara finished their coffee and stood up. John went to the counter and paid the bill, including James's meal; then together they accompanied James out into the high street, still anxious that he might be detected, particularly if Fox was around.

'Right,' she said as soon as they were outside, 'let's find somewhere to talk.'

89

They walked out of town and into the country where they stopped by a farm gate and leaned against it. They might have been a little group of holidaymakers admiring the view.

'This'll do,' James said.

'Right,' Barbara said, 'there are a lot of things we'd like to know. Why did you abscond from the hospital? You've already had the police out looking for you. Now they're going to be really concerned.'

'I've done nothing wrong,' he said.

'It's not what you've done,' she said, 'it's the nature of your work. That's why Special Branch is involved. You were reported as a missing person and they are here trying to find out what happened to you. If you'd just been an ordinary Joe they wouldn't have bothered, but given your position in the aerospace industry working on stuff that we know nothing about... well, what do you think?'

James smiled. 'Special Branch, you say? I must be important.'

'They think you are. Isn't that enough?'

'Hmmm...' He thought for a moment. 'I'll deal with that, don't worry.'

'You haven't met Inspector Fox,' John said. 'He's not an easy man to get on with.'

'I'll deal with him.'

Barbara's eyes narrowed. 'You're confident of that, aren't you?'

James nodded. He did not want to boast of his newly acquired powers, but he was confident that he could deal with this Inspector Fox and send him away with nothing significant to report.

John studied him. There was little doubt in his mind that something in his manner had changed. He was quieter, but that was not it. It was nothing he could quite define. He guessed that Barbara must have noticed it too, but if she did she said nothing.

'Why did we not recognise you immediately?' he asked. 'Damn it, we'd seen you on an almost daily basis since you were admitted to hospital and yet we didn't recognise you sitting at the next table. How was that?'

'What did I look like?'

He thought about this. Again, nothing came to mind. 'I don't know,' he admitted.

'That's how it works,' James said. 'If I don't want to be seen, people won't see me. If I don't wish to be recognised, then they won't recognise me. If this Inspector Fox of yours walked past me now he wouldn't see me, or if he did he wouldn't recognise me.'

'That doesn't explain it,' John said.

'It's just a trick I learned while I was away.'

'What do you mean, *while I was away*?' Barbara asked.

'While you thought I was in a coma I was in another place – I don't know where, but there'll be another one there now.'

John thought about this. 'Sergeant Gallagher,' he muttered.

'Sergeant Gallagher?'

'He's one of the Special Branch officers that came here looking for you,' John said.

James laughed. 'Well well, if that don't beat all. It looks as if he found me.'

'I'm glad you think it's funny.' This unexpected levity annoyed John. Although he had no great liking for Gallagher, he did not think it at all funny that the man was now in hospital as a result of having had his brain frazzled by the cylinder.

James became serious. 'John, in spite of what you think, he's in no danger where he is. He will be well cared for and looked after, believe me. I've been there and I know.'

'Where exactly were you?' Barbara asked, remembering her visions of him in a strange landscape and in the great hall with some other people and one attractive girl in particular.

She listened as he told her about the place where he had been; at first in a formless landscape and then in an igloo-like enclosure. He then described the great hall with its distorted perspective and the sickness that had befallen him there; how he was tended by the being whom he had nicknamed Angel and his eventual recovery. She noted with a jolt that his description of Angel fitted exactly the girl she had seen in her vision. So she really had seen him there and he had indeed communicated with her. It had not been a dream.

He described as best he could the mental changes that had been induced into him, the full extent of which he had yet to discover. Their failure to recognise him had been an illustration of his newly acquired power. As if to further demonstrate this power he suddenly vanished and then reappeared, smiling at their startled faces.

'I didn't disappear,' he said. 'I just exerted my will so that you would simply fail to see me. I was here all the time. It's a psychological trick, that's all.'

'A bloody dangerous one,' John commented.

'Only if it's misused,' he said. 'I cannot misuse it; they thought of that.'

'Who did?'

'I don't know exactly. I never saw the intelligence that made the cylinder and everything else that surrounded me while I was there. I think it spoke to me through Angel. She was my guide and she taught me how to use my powers creatively. She also taught me how not to use them. They learned from their earlier mistakes, you see, so what happened back in the Stone Age can never happen again. To misuse the power as they did would be to lose it. That's the safety factor that has now been built into it and that is the penalty for its misuse, so if you're thinking I could use it to rob a bank of anything like that, you would be wrong. They, or Angel would know and I would lose my power – instantly. I wouldn't want that to happen.' The eagerness with which he spoke gave him the air of a religious zealot; something that both John and Barbara found disturbing. It was like talking to an overenthusiastic convert to a new and eccentric religion.

'They think of everything,' John said dryly.

Barbara too was sceptical. It all sounded too good to be true. There had to be a flaw. 'What exactly is the cylinder's purpose?' she asked.

'I don't know yet,' James said. 'Its original purpose was to advance any civilisation it might come into contact with. That might still be its prime purpose. It also acts as a gate between their world and ours.'

'What makes them think we need their help to advance?' she said. 'We can do that for ourselves without anyone's help.'

James looked at her. 'Are you sure?'

She was not sure, but she resented the arrogance inherent in the assertion that civilisations needed outside help to develop. It was meddlesome as it was highhanded. It was not wanted. She wanted to tell him that she had heard enough, but she refrained from doing so, curious to know what else he might tell her about this magical, mystical Wonderland of his.

'Its purpose is to guide, not to instruct,' he went on. 'I sense your scepticism and I understand it. I think I've said enough for now.'

'What are you going to do now?' Barbara asked him, changing the subject.

'There is a lot to do, but not immediately. I need to get myself sorted out before I can do anything else.'

'We thought you might return to the cylinder.'

'I don't need it any more. It's served its purpose as far as I'm concerned.'

John listened to this with some unease. If James felt he no longer needed the cylinder, then that meant that his power had grown to the point where he now possessed the same, if not even greater properties than the thing itself. If that was so, then he was a walking bomb. He could brainwash anyone he chose to by the process of thought transference; something that he had already demonstrated, albeit harmlessly, on Barbara. Since his own first traumatic encounter with the cylinder he had tried to avoid all contact with it. Now both he and Barbara were talking to nothing less than someone who had become an emissary of the cylinder. It was Mohammed and the mountain. They had not gone to the cylinder – through James it had come to them. Yet he felt none of the stunning effects that had hit him when he had last approached it in order to get Gallagher out of the cabin. Indeed, had he not known that James's mind had been altered, he might have been talking to a normal man. This indicated that although James possessed this power, he could control it; either that or it was working on him in such a subtle way that he was unaware of the fact. He discounted this, reasoning that he would be well aware of any intrusive thoughts that might be trying to work their way in, no matter how subtle they might be. There was nothing that he could detect. Despite this, he felt uneasy in his company.

As if he sensed his thoughts, James turned to him and smiled. 'You needn't worry that I might be trying to brainwash you. If I really wanted to do that I would have already done it. Remember, my purpose is to guide, not to instruct or coerce. I cannot and will not tamper with anyone's mind against their will. That would be an abuse of my power and I would risk losing it.'

This did little to ease John's concern. 'What about those who failed to see or recognise you, including us? Is that not mind-tampering?'

'It's self-preservation,' he said. 'If the wrong people ever came to know the powers that I possess, they would certainly want me out of the way or else they would require me to misuse my power and thus risk losing it. They might even kill me. It's better for now that I avoid those people and if that means I have to tweak their minds so that they don't see me, then so be it. I didn't harm them in any way – I can't do that.'

John was still not convinced. He let the matter drop. There was no point in trying to argue with someone who was convinced that he was right.

'Where are you staying tonight?' Barbara asked.

'I'll see if they've got a room in the White Hart,' he said. 'That's if you don't mind.'

'Why should we?'

He shrugged. 'I get the feeling that you don't trust me. You needn't fear. I'll make myself as scarce as I can and I shan't play any mind games with you, I promise.'

'Listen,' she said, 'it's not that we don't trust you. Christ, James, how long have we known each other? It's not that at all, it's just...'

'Fear of the unknown?' he prompted.

She looked at him. 'If you want the truth, that's exactly what it is.'

'Listen,' he said, 'if it makes you feel better, I shall go to the police and tell them that I'm alive and well. That'll get Fox off your back. What will they charge me with; falling unconscious? They can't lock me up for that.'

'Be careful,' she said.

'I will.'

'I don't doubt it,' John said.

James turned to face him. 'John, I know you don't like me and never have. I wish I could do something to change your opinion of me, but it's obvious that I can't do anything about that. Never mind, I shall just have to live with it. I'll see you back at the hotel.' He walked back down the road towards the town.

382

'Well,' Barbara said as soon as he was out of earshot. 'It's good to see that your rudeness hasn't deserted you.'

He was about to protest this charge, but he changed his mind. He had been rude. Instead, he apologised and, watching James as he walked away from them, said: 'What has it done to him?'

She shook her head. 'I'm not sure I want to know.'

He plucked a grass stem and chewed on it, enjoying the faint sweetness of the sap on his tongue. James was right. He had done nothing wrong and he could hardly be arrested for absconding from a general hospital unless he was there for his own protection and it was unlikely that the police would deem that to be the case. Therefore, they were powerless to prevent him from doing whatever it was that he had come back to do. He had not divulged this purpose to either John or Barbara. In fact it was probable that he did not know it himself yet, so it was all supposition. They could not pin a charge on that. James could walk into the police station and they could do nothing.

'Well,' he said. 'He's got us over a barrel and neither we nor Fox or anyone else can do anything about it. We might as well sit back and enjoy the ride.'

She smiled. 'You'd better hold onto your hat. It could be a wild one.'

90

That evening John, Barbara and Bernard sat in the bar. Chris and Lynda had gone to the local cinema and James was presumably up in his room. John and Barbara were in many ways glad he was not with them. They had not seen him since their conversation earlier in the day, but an unobserved glance at the hotel register had told Barbara that he had indeed booked in early that afternoon. He had slightly altered his name to Jim Masterson and scribbled an illegible signature, but the handwriting was recognisably his. She wondered if the manager might recognise him as the man who had been found unconscious in his room. If he did, she reasoned, he would probably forget it instantly. James would see to that.

She remembered that she still had his clothes, money and credit cards, together with other personal effects. She would return these to him at the first opportunity. As far as she could see, he was destitute.

In the bar, Bernard's eyes narrowed as they told him of James's newly acquired powers briefly demonstrated during their meeting that afternoon. As yet he had not seen him, but what he heard made him think that they were dealing with someone who was potentially one of the most dangerous men alive if his powers were not curbed, and it looked as if it was in no one's power to do that. He could always stay one jump ahead of the rest. The cylinder might be contained, but to have its power and more besides transferred to a living human being meant that it was now in effect uncontrolled and at large. This was a disturbing thought.

It was while he was mulling over this that Colonel Fraser entered the bar, bought himself a drink, looked around and joined them at the table. 'Any luck with your missing person?' he asked.

'Yes,' Barbara said. 'We found him. He's OK.' She hoped that this would bring the topic to a swift conclusion.

'Good,' he said and let the matter drop, at least for now. He had other things on his mind. The previous night's disturbing dreams still dominated his thoughts and he was anxious to discuss them in an effort to seek some sort of guidance from those who claimed to have experienced the same phenomenon.

They listened as he outlined the dreams that he had had that night. 'I could put it down to post-traumatic stress disorder,' he said, 'but it wasn't like that. It was so graphic and it was set in some distant time and place like no place I've ever seen. Anyway, if it was PTSD I would have had it before now. I've never had dreams like these.'

'It's that cylinder,' John said. 'The same thing happened to us soon after we first came into contact with it and I warned you that this might happen. They will decrease after a while.' As he spoke, he wondered what past trauma had prompted Fraser to cite post-traumatic stress disorder as the possible cause of his dreams, but he decided not to pursue the matter.

'How long after?' Fraser looked worried.

'Days – weeks; it varies. We still get them now, but not as frequently as we used to. If they persist, I suggest you see your MO and see if he can sort it out for you. We just had to let it take its course.'

Fraser shook his head. 'I don't want another night like last night.'

'It's only fair to warn you that you might well have another and several more after that, and some of them are really awful. It seems to happen to everyone who gets zapped by the thing. It's as if it's replaying some of its memories through your mind.'

'It is,' Barbara said. 'That's what it does – that and other things.'

'What other things?'

She was silent for a moment while she collected her thoughts. 'Well,' she began slowly. 'Some people feel an urge to return to it. That's what happened to Detective Sergeant Gallagher. He couldn't help doing what he did. He was driven to it.' She paused and looked at him. 'Have you felt an urge to be with it again?'

'No,' he said.

'Good. It seems that only more prolonged exposure to it prompts that urge in people; people like Sergeant Gallagher and James Masters. Both of them had considerably more exposure to it than you did.'

'About James Masters,' he began. 'What's he like now that you've found him?'

She swore silently to herself. She had not intended to revive this topic. 'He seems OK,' she lied.

'Does he still get the dreams?'

She decided to tell him the truth, or at least a part of it. 'No. He never had them. It seems you only get them if you have been briefly exposed to it. A full exposure such as he received has a different, more profound effect.'

She stopped, unsure that she wanted to continue with this conversation. Right now, the fewer people who knew about James the better as far as she and the team were concerned. The thought occurred to her that it was probably within James's power to cure the nightmares. After all, if he knew what caused them he would be in the best position to cure them, but the possible risk was too great to consider. There was no knowing what else he might do while he was messing about with someone else's mind.

No one noticed that James had entered the room and was standing at the bar. He had not used his mind influence to disguise himself; they had simply failed to see him. He bought a drink, putting it on his room number, then came over and sat down at their table looking relaxed, almost casual in his manner. There was no sign of the enthusiasm that had so fired him earlier on. He greeted them with a smile and introduced himself using his real name to Colonel Fraser, extending his hand as he did so.

Fraser shook his hand and introduced himself without his rank. Since he was not in uniform it was possible that James might have taken him to be a colleague of John's from the university.

'Well,' he announced to them, 'you needn't worry about Inspector Fox any more. I've met him and he's OK. I made it clear to him that I've got nothing to hide and he's fine about it. He's worried about Gallagher, though.'

'You've been to the police?' Barbara said.

'I said I would.'

'Yes.' She said slowly. 'You did, didn't you?' She had not thought that he would actually do it and she wondered if he had used his mental powers on Fox to get him off the case, but then when she thought about it, he had done nothing wrong. There was no case to answer.

Colonel Fraser saw a chance here to ask him about his experience with the cylinder. John's words had done nothing to ease his mind concerning the dreams that, if he was right, threatened to continue and even get worse, if that was possible. He reflected that circumstances had been different for John and his colleagues. They had all been affected at much the same time and therefore they had been able to support each other through the worst of it. He was alone and in command of a troop of soldiers. This put him in a very different position. They had not taken this into account.

He looked at James. 'You've had some experience of that cylinder thing up there, haven't you?'

James nodded. 'Yes, a little.'

John held his breath, noting his understatement and wondering what was coming next. Both he and Barbara had tried to keep Fraser off the subject of the cylinder wherever possible, particularly in connection with James. Now it was all about to be blown wide open, especially if he was in the same enthusiastic mood as he had been earlier that day. He wanted to stop this conversation before it went any further, but he could do nothing without making matters worse.

'I'm told you didn't get the nightmares that the others got,' Fraser continued.

James stared at him. 'You have seen the cylinder?'

'Yes, and it's affected me in some way. I'm getting these dreams…'

John and Barbara exchanged glances while Bernard took a large swig of his beer. Whatever happened next was beyond their control. If Fraser saw their reaction, he chose to ignore it.

'How long were you with it?'

Fraser shrugged. 'I don't know. Only a few seconds, I guess.'

'Not long enough. That's why you're getting them. Here…' He put a hand on Fraser's forehead.

'What's all this?' Bernard asked.

John and Barbara stared as Fraser's face became calm and expressionless. Both he and James seemed to be oblivious of their presence. They appeared to be in some kind of silent communion. Minutes ticked by and neither man moved.

'How long is this going on for?' Bernard said, looking uncomfortable.

'I don't know but I'm going to stop it,' John said.

'No,' Barbara said. 'Leave them. It could be dangerous to do anything right now. Look at them.'

Small beads of sweat showed on Fraser's brow and he was shaking with some invisible exertion as James stared fixedly into his eyes.

'Stop this!' Bernard ordered, but neither man seemed to hear him.

Barbara leaned across to him. 'Leave them and don't draw attention. People are starting to look.'

She was right. The barman had stopped what he was doing and was staring in their direction. Two customers were also looking. John got up and went over to the bar on the pretext of ordering a drink.

'It's about chakras or something like that.' He said as casually as he could manage. 'The fellow suffers from migraines and the other bloke thinks he can fix it with some ancient Indian cure. I don't know much about it. It's all mumbo-jumbo to me.'

The barman made a wry face and pulled a pint for him. He paid him and returned to the table where James still sat, holding Fraser's forehead.

'What did you say?' Barbara asked him as he sat down.

'I put him off with some story about chakras and migraines,' he said.

'It seems to have worked,' she observed.

James finally let go and sat back. 'That should've sorted the problem out,' he said as casually as if he had just finished a routine repair job. 'You'll be all right in a minute.'

Fraser sat back and wiped his forehead.

'What have you done to him?' Barbara asked.

'I've cured his nightmare problem,' he said. 'They shouldn't trouble him again.'

'What else have you done to him?' John demanded.

'Nothing, I assure you. He should be all right in a minute.'

'We'll see.' John was unconvinced.

'He only had a partial exposure, the same as you,' he said. 'That's what produces the nightmares. They're snapshots of its history taken out of context. I've corrected that now.' He looked at Fraser. 'You shouldn't have any more trouble.'

Fraser blinked. 'Thanks,' he said slowly. 'I think I see it now.' It was clear from his changed manner that James's mind technique had had some effect upon him. 'I didn't know it had witnessed such dreadful things. No wonder it gave me the horrors.'

'You know its history?' John asked.

'I think so. I don't know yet.'

James turned to John and Barbara. 'I could do the same for you.'

'Not here, you won't!' John snorted.

'Later, perhaps,' Barbara said and John looked at her, wondering if she was serious.

Fraser got up and went to the bar to refill his glass. John followed him.

'OK,' He said once he was sure that no one was listening. 'I want to know exactly what happened back there.'

Fraser thought for a moment. 'I don't know exactly. I heard this voice inside my head and there were these images like the ones I had in my dreams, but these were in context and somehow I understood what happened and why it happened. Somehow, all the terror left me at that point – I can't explain it, but it seems to have worked. I don't think I'll be so afraid to sleep tonight, anyway.'

'Did you get any other thoughts – any desire to see the cylinder again?'

'No, but I think I understand it better now.'

John thought about this. He wanted to know if James had induced more than just the cylinder's history into him. 'Do you think you're doing the right thing, fencing it off like that?' he asked, anxious to know if Fraser's attitude towards the cylinder had changed at all.

'If you want an honest answer, no, I don't.'

This perhaps was proof enough.

91

John slept fitfully that night. He awoke from a dream of indiscriminate slaughter such as he had had before, but it was not this that disturbed him. By virtue of an uncomfortable familiarity due to their still too frequent appearances, these dreams were becoming less frightening than when they had started, not that this made them any less unpleasant. What overshadowed his thoughts now was the question of James and the effect that the cylinder had had on him after his period of apparent unconsciousness. He wondered if the story of his time in that other world was true or if had been one long hallucination. There was no easy answer for this. His natural inclination was to assume the latter to be the case. If this was so then it was the longest hallucination in history. Also, there was enough continuity in his story to give it a coherent narrative and thus lend it a degree of credibility that made it hard to dismiss out of hand. Added to this, his undoubted ability to influence people's minds was proof that something in him had changed. He could not doubt this. Both he and Barbara had witnessed it. The disappearing trick that he had shown them was something that could have been performed by any good stage illusionist, but it was harder to explain the effect that he had had upon Colonel Fraser who had clearly been disturbed by the onset of the cylinder-induced dreams with which they were only too familiar. A visible change had come over the officer and this was much harder to explain away as a simple conjuring trick. James had offered to do the same for him and Barbara and he had brusquely declined the offer. Now he was not so sure.

He thought of the dream that had awoken him. It had been another scene of human sacrifice and, although he was becoming inured to these scenes of wanton bloodletting, these dreams were no less disturbing for that. He pondered James's offer again. Although he was beginning to understand more clearly the history of the cylinder's influence on the people it had first contacted and now saw these glimpses of its bloody past more in context than before, he still found the intrusion of these images disturbing and he knew that Barbara continued to be similarly affected by them.

Something else was on his mind. A lot of what James had told them coincided with some of his more recent thoughts. What if the intelligence that had put the cylinder there really had learned from its earlier mistakes and taken measures to ensure that the unfortunate events of the past could not happen again? Would the cylinder's influence be more benign as a result and was its purpose really to guide and not instruct? There were too many questions without answers; something that he always found annoying.

It was then that he made a decision. He would find out.

92

The next morning he, Barbara and Bernard went up to the site. As usual, he wanted to inspect its condition, but he was also anxious to see Colonel Fraser to find out if James's mental trick had worked.

They found the colonel looking refreshed and alert. On seeing them he came over and greeted each in turn. Together, they walked away from the area where the men were still erecting the fence.

'Where's James?' Fraser asked.

John shrugged. 'Probably sleeping late; we haven't seen him this morning.'

Barbara noticed that his uncaring attitude towards James had not changed. She also noticed that as he spoke his eyes kept drifting towards the cabin. This was evidence in her eyes that his mind was becoming increasingly fixed upon the cylinder and she wondered if he might be looking for a chance to gain access to it. Given the uncertain state of mind that he had been in lately, this was a possibility. He would need watching.

'How did you sleep last night?' John asked.

'Fine,' Fraser said. 'Whatever he did to me seems to have worked. There were no bad dreams and I woke up this morning feeling great. No problems.'

'Glad to hear it.'

'We should be finished today and then I suppose you can get on with your work undisturbed.' Fraser indicated the half completed fence. Something in the flat way he said this hinted a loss of enthusiasm for the job. This was new.

John looked at the cabin again. He was now convinced that what they were doing here was wrong. Not long ago he had hated the cylinder with a passion. He had even considered the vague possibility of destroying it. Now he was beginning to see it in a different light. This was not due to any possible influence that James might have had over him. He liked to think that he was too independently minded to be influenced by anyone and in any case, he had already begun to waver in his formerly entrenched view before James had spoken to him and before his last exposure to the cylinder, although he could not deny that this incident might have contributed something to his change of heart. Be that as it may, he had reasoned for himself that it had been intended to be of benefit to humanity. It had gone wrong, but that had largely been the fault of the people at that particular time who had misinterpreted its purpose. Now it was to be lost forever to a world that stood to reap the benefits that such an object might bestow upon it. It would be held under lock and key until some means could be found to either disable or destroy it. Even Colonel Fraser had admitted that he believed that what he was doing was wrong. They had all been wrong. He recalled Barbara's words after he had forcibly removed her from the cylinder while it held James in its power: '*We always destroy that which we cannot understand.*' He had assumed that it had been the cylinder talking through her. Perhaps it had been, but she had been right. They were now in the process of putting it beyond the reach of everyone because they had failed to understand it. They had failed to understand it all along.

He looked at Barbara as he recalled these words. She had understood its purpose once. Since then her attitude had changed and she had become increasingly opposed to it and everything associated with it. The nightmares would have had a lot to do with this, but it was odd that as she became more sceptical about the cylinder, he was becoming closer to it by degrees. It was as if their respective attitudes towards it were swinging in opposition to each other.

'John.' Barbara's voice stirred him from his reverie. 'Colonel Fraser's talking to you.'

'Sorry,' he said, 'I was miles away. Another restless night, I'm afraid.'

Fraser looked at him. 'Do you still get the nightmares?'

'I had one last night.'

'You didn't say,' Barbara said.

'I think I'm getting used to them now and anyway, it was only the one.' He tried to look nonchalant but it did not work. He decided to reveal his feelings on the matter of the cylinder. 'I was also thinking that what we're doing here is wrong. We're denying the world of science something that I'm convinced would be of incalculable value to it. Can this be right?'

They all looked blank. Bernard broke the silence. 'John, I don't believe I'm hearing this from you. You know as well as anyone else what that thing does.'

'Do I? Do we? We know nothing about it and I'll tell you why. We let it frighten us off. We hid from it when all the time it was reaching out to contact us. Look at James. We're afraid of him now because he has acquired certain powers. Something, I don't know what, gave him those powers and we're still running away from it. That thing in there could change the world and we're incarcerating it behind acres of fencing. How can that be right?'

'I think you've taken leave of your senses,' Bernard said.

'I think I've just found them,' he corrected him.

Barbara stared at him. 'I do believe you're thinking of going in there with that thing. Are you?'

He did not answer.

'He's gone mad,' Bernard said to himself.

'I don't think so,' Barbara said. 'What if he is right and that thing in there really is of benefit to us all? Would it be right to hide it away for all time?'

'You too?' Bernard looked at her, open mouthed.

Fraser intervened. 'I'm not in a position to judge this matter, you understand, but I've learned a few things about that cylinder. I don't know how, but I do know that the mistakes of the past can never be repeated, so the various nasty things that happened back then are unlikely to happen again. I've already told you I believe that what we're doing here is wrong. I still believe that. There's nothing I can do about it, because to stop work on the fence would be to disobey a direct order and that would be tantamount to mutiny. In any case it would change nothing, since someone else would come along and finish it off and the end result would be the same.'

John turned away. There was nothing more to do. Barbara caught his arm.

'Where are you going?'

'It's over,' he said. 'There's nothing more to do here so we might as well complete our notes on our findings and go back to the university. The cylinder doesn't exist. It never did exist.'

'Don't be ridiculous,' she said. 'We've only just begun and the cylinder *does* exist. Fox tried to hush it up, but that'll never work.' She lowered her voice. 'The news is out, remember? Despite Fox's efforts, it won't go away.'

He listened to her words but absorbed few of them. Not for the first time since the discovery of the cylinder, he was overtaken by a particular kind of melancholia – the sort that comes with a loss of control over a given situation. Yet it was not over yet. There remained the question of James and Sergeant Gallagher. James was at large and Gallagher soon would be, assuming he would recover as James did, emerging as a new kind of human being. The irony of this did not escape him. He had begun by investigating the past and had discovered the future.

It was then that the thought hit him. They were fencing off something that was no longer needed. Its power had been transferred to James and he was waiting.

'OK,' he said to Barbara. 'You're right. We shall carry on tomorrow. It'll be business as usual and bugger the cylinder.'

She took his arm and led him to one side. 'John, are you sure you're feeling all right? Only you've not been acting rationally of late. We've all noticed it. One minute you want to abandon the project and the next you're ready to carry on with it. What's the matter?'

'I wish I knew. Nothing makes sense any more.'

She took his hands and looked into his eyes. 'One thing does, doesn't it? One thing makes sense to you. John, don't you realise the danger you might be facing?'

'There isn't any danger, I see that now. There never was any danger.'

'How do you know?'

'When I was in there, getting Gallagher out, I had a series of images and messages, most of which were confusing and untranslatable. One thing did present itself, however, and that was an overall feeling that no harm would come to me. For that moment I felt safe.'

'That's the oldest trick in the book,' she said. 'I felt something similar when I was with it, remember? I even believed it for a while until it wore off. I think it's brainwashed you.'

He shook his head. 'I've worked a lot of this out for myself. Both James and the cylinder have served to corroborate what I have already come to believe.'

'John, you're starting to frighten me now.'

'There's no need to be frightened.'

'I wish I could believe you.'

'Talk to James. He'll tell you more than I can.'

'You can't stand the man. Why has he suddenly become your guru in this?'

'He hasn't. It's just that what he has to say more or less confirms what I've already worked out for myself.'

'Anyway,' she said, 'it'll soon be locked away for good. Then no one will be able to go near it.'

He smiled. 'Are you sure?'

She was not sure. His smile worried her. Something in it indicated the presence of some secret knowledge embedded deep in his psyche of which perhaps even he was unaware.

She took his hand. 'Come on,' she said. 'There's work to do tomorrow.'

93

That evening they were joined in the bar by Colonel Fraser who bought himself a drink and sat down with them. 'I've come to say goodbye,' he said. 'We've finished work up there and we're leaving in the morning, so you'll be free once more to work unhindered by me and my squaddies.'

'Right,' John said without much enthusiasm.

'We've taken every care not to disturb your diggings,' the colonel continued. 'You shouldn't notice too much damage.'

'Thanks,' Barbara said. 'So we can carry on up there tomorrow.'

'As far as I'm concerned you can. I'm only sorry for the disruption I've caused you all. I just wish I could be there with you. From what I've heard, you've made some amazing discoveries up there.'

'You wouldn't believe it,' Bernard said.

James wandered into the bar and joined them at the table.

'Here,' Barbara said, handing him his wallet. 'I've been looking after your stuff while you were away.'

'Thanks,' he said, pocketing the wallet without checking its contents. This suggested to her a degree of trust that up to here had not been reciprocated by either her or the team. He went to the bar and bought himself a drink, then returned to the table. He looked casual and relaxed and to see him it was hard to believe that his mind might have been altered in any way. He had shaved and his hair was once more tidy. He had swapped his borrowed assortment of clothing for something better fitting, probably bought from a local charity shop. Barbara wondered where he had got the money to make the purchase. She had only just returned his wallet to him and she hoped that he had not stolen them from the shop in question. With his newly acquired powers this was possible, but he had stated more than once that these powers could not be abused on pain of losing them.

As if in answer to her unasked question, he patted the wallet and said: 'I can settle one or two minor debts now. I persuaded the lady in the shop to let me have these on account.' He indicated his new clothes. 'I promised her that I would repay her tomorrow; now I can.' He smiled. This was more like the James that she used to know. Still she wondered just how he might have 'persuaded' the woman in the shop to part with the goods and trust a total stranger to repay her the following day.

'What else have you been up to?' she asked him in as conversational a tone as she could manage. 'We haven't seen you all day.'

'Oh, this and that; you know,' he said vaguely.

She did not know. However, she decided to let the matter drop.

'All we need now is Inspector Fox and we've got a full house,' Bernard muttered.

The colonel ignored his comment and turned to James. 'Thanks for sorting out my little problem. I don't know what you did exactly, but it worked.'

'Good.' James smiled. 'The dreams won't trouble you again. Neither should that unpleasantness in Iraq. I took the liberty of sorting that out as well.'

Fraser stared at him. 'What do you know about that?'

'Enough.'

John listened to this. To the best of his knowledge, Fraser had never been specific about any particular trauma in his life, whatever that might have been. The only possible explanation for this was that James must have probed Fraser's mind. There was no other way he could have gained such hidden knowledge. He would have to speak to him on this matter, but not now while the others were listening. He did not want to risk any further conflict with the team by displaying what they already considered to be an unhealthy interest in the cylinder's effects. It had caused enough trouble already.

It was while he was pondering this that Inspector Fox entered the bar and looked around.

'Bingo!' Bernard called, but not so loud that he might hear.

'Oh, fuck,' John muttered. 'I wonder what he wants.'

Fox ordered a drink and joined them at the table. 'Well,' he said, 'it looks like this is goodbye. I'm off back to London tomorrow and you'll be left in peace to get on with your work.'

'What about Sergeant Gallagher?' Barbara asked.

'I've left a contact number at the hospital. If there are any developments, they'll let me know. Meanwhile, I'd like to thank you for your cooperation regarding this matter.'

John wondered if this comment was meant to be ironic or if it was just a routine form of police courtesy spoken out of a sense of duty but signifying nothing. No one as best as he could recall had been particularly cooperative. He wondered if James might have tampered with his mind as well. This was something else he would have to talk to him about.

'He's not in any danger,' James said.

Fox looked at him. 'You seem very sure of that.'

James said nothing.

'He's a good officer,' Fox said. 'I must remind you that you are still bound by the Official Secrets Act regarding this matter. Not a word of it may be passed to anyone for any reason. Is that clear?'

They all agreed that it was clear. The fact that the word was already out was something that he could find out for himself.

'I'm afraid the same must go for you, Colonel. You know what I'm talking about, don't you?'

Fraser nodded. 'Your secret's safe with me, Inspector.'

'Right.' Fox finished his drink and stood up. 'I'll be off then.'

'See you.' Bernard waved his hand in a mock friendly gesture.

He turned and left the bar.

'Missing you already!' Bernard called after him.

'Bernard, that's enough,' Barbara said.

He made a naughty schoolboy's face. 'Sorry,' he said, but it was obvious that he did not mean it.

Colonel Fraser stood up and got ready to go. 'I must be off as well,' he said. 'I hope we meet again some time. When I finally retire from the Army I'll seek you out. Some of my skills may be of use to you, you never know.'

They bid him farewell and he left.

'He was a decent bloke,' Bernard said.

John had to agree. While he could not understand Bernard's continuing antipathy towards Fox, he shared his liking for Fraser.

Bernard got up to refill his glass. 'Well,' he said, 'it looks like business as usual tomorrow. That'll be nice.'

John wondered if it really would be business as usual or could ever be again. The cylinder would still be there, safe behind fencing and razor wire, but still there. He became aware of James's voice inside his head. At first he could not understand the words, but bit by bit, more came through.

...have to listen... there is much... understand... nothing to fear... failure to understand led to downfall... will love you because that is... fear of love? ...not understand... never did...

He looked at Barbara and wondered if she could hear the same as he. Her face was calm and she seemed to be watching Bernard at the bar. He could not guess. The voice continued, fading in and out.

...aware of you... not hurt or damage... cannot... understand ...t...?

'Understand what?' He said this louder than he had meant to and he coughed in an effort to disguise the immediate feeling of embarrassment that followed this outburst.

Barbara looked at him and the voice ceased abruptly. 'Sorry, what was that?'

'Nothing,' he lied. 'I was thinking aloud.' He looked at James who was toying with a beer mat and he wondered if he really had been trying to communicate with him or if he had just imagined it. The voice, if fractured, had been loud and clear, but it made little sense. It had been too disjointed for that. It was clear that she had not heard it, hence her puzzlement. He leaned towards her. 'Barbara, can we talk somewhere?'

'Sure.' She looked at James. 'Excuse us, will you?'

They went out into the hotel lobby. 'What is it?' she asked.

'I think James was trying to communicate with me just now.' He paused, thinking how improbable this sounded. 'It's as if he was trying to insinuate something into me – his thoughts, perhaps... I don't know.'

'Are you sure?'

'As sure as I can be. I distinctly heard his voice inside my head just then. Didn't you hear it too?'

'No, but I believe you. Look, lately you've been thinking a lot about the cylinder, haven't you? Supposing he picked up on that and tuned in? We're going to have to watch him. He's getting sneaky.'

'Thanks,' he said, relieved that she was taking him seriously.

400

'What exactly did you hear?'

'I don't know. It was all in bits so it made little sense.'

She pondered this new turn of events. Not long ago he was showing all the signs of a growing obsession with the cylinder. Now he was expressing concern because James might have tried out his telepathic powers on him; something that the cylinder had been trying to do since shortly after its discovery. It was evident that he was becoming increasingly confused. Given his unique circumstances, this was not surprising. She decided that she would have something to say to James about this, but later. This was not the time.

'Let's go back to the bar,' she said. 'If it happens again, don't say anything, just give me a gentle nudge. We don't want to draw any attention to what's going on.'

They returned to the bar where Bernard and James were still at the table.

'What was that about?' Bernard asked as they sat down.

'Just a private chat,' Barbara said. 'Nothing special.'

Bernard rubbed his hands together. 'Well, now that we've got the police and the Army out of our hair, we can get on with our work undisturbed.'

'I could help you with that,' James said.

Bernard looked at him. 'How could you help us?' He laughed. 'Forgive me, but you're an engineer, not an archaeologist.'

'With all due respect, I think I know more about the people you are investigating than you do. I know their history; how they lived and what they did. Can you think of anyone better able to help you?'

Bernard gaped and was about to say something, but John cut him short. 'OK,' he said. 'We'll give it a go. Your knowledge would be useful if you could help us locate more evidence of their culture. I'll give you a briefing later.'

James smiled and Bernard shut up. He was not keen on the idea of the team being joined by someone who was, after all, still an outsider and he wondered at John's sudden acceptance of him. Barbara too wondered at this sudden change of heart in one who had previously not attempted to hide his dislike for the young man. Although James was an old friend of hers, she had since his apparent recovery come to regard him with suspicion. It was plain to her that he had become little more than an agent for what looked increasingly like an alien intelligence and the possibility that he could be using his newly acquired powers to recruit John to its side was too obvious to ignore. The thought that he might have been attempting to recruit John angered her more than she could adequately express at this particular time. It would keep for later. In the light of John's recent revision of his thoughts surrounding the cylinder, he would be ripe for such subversion. On the other hand, reason dictated that John was right to include James on the project. Given his professed intimate knowledge of the culture in question, it was hard to think of anyone better qualified to guide them to the places where their most important artefacts might be hidden. For this reason alone, she was prepared to accept him as a useful member of the team, but she remained suspicious of his motives. Also, no one had any clue as to whether or not his supposed knowledge of this culture was in any way accurate. It had been implanted by the cylinder. By this very token it was not reliable evidence as far as she was concerned. The time was right to have a serious talk with both him and John in an effort to find out what he was planning. She resolved to address this matter as soon as possible. John was going to have a talk with him anyway and she decided that she would be present at this meeting whether he liked it or not.

Bernard excused himself to go to the lavatory and she picked this moment to make her move. 'I'd like to join you at this meeting,' she said. 'I suggest we meet in our room where we can talk in private. I don't want people eavesdropping, you understand.'

Both James and John agreed to this.

'Good,' she said. Things were coming to a head.

94

They sat in John and Barbara's room. John and Barbara sat together on the edge of the bed while James sat on a chair near the dressing table. For a while, no one spoke until Barbara, who had become increasingly incensed at the thought of James's underhand attempt to probe John's mind, broke the silence.

'Right,' she began, 'I want to know just what game you are trying to play with us. First, why did you try to communicate telepathically with John?'

James shifted in his seat and looked at her. 'You know, do you?'

'He told me.'

John felt his face flush. He would rather have asked this question himself. After all, he was the one whose mind had been probed, if only with partial success. 'You did, didn't you?' he said. 'Don't try to deny it.'

James sighed. 'I tried, but it was difficult. I'm sorry. I shouldn't have tried it at all without your permission.'

'Shouldn't have tried it at all?' Barbara repeated, her voice rising. 'How could you even contemplate the idea? Don't you think our minds have been screwed up enough already without you fiddling about with them? Damn your insolence!'

James looked ashamed. 'I'm sorry.'

'Sorry?'

'I'm sorry, I really am. I took an unforgivable liberty and I apologise. I shouldn't have done it, but I thought the time might be right. Now I know I was wrong. I'm sorry.'

'It's not enough to be sorry,' she said. 'How do you think we can ever use you on the dig if we can't trust you?'

John controlled his sense of outrage and tried to maintain a calmer, more reasonable tone. 'I really ought to hit you for that. Why did you do it?'

'It was a test – an experiment if you like. I sensed you might be undergoing a change of heart regarding the cylinder and were beginning to see things differently. I wanted to explain some of these things to you so that you might understand it better.'

John forgot his anger and leaned forward. 'Just how much do you know about it?'

'More than enough to know its purpose – what it did and what it may yet do if only you would let it.'

'We'll never know now that it's been put beyond use.'

James laughed. 'Did they think that would stop it?'

They both stared at him with a growing sense of unease. They had already guessed that its power might have been transferred to him, now it looked as if they were about to find out. They exchanged glances as they realised that he had them at his mercy should he feel inclined to exercise his powers over them. Too late the realisation dawned on them that they had walked into a trap of their own making.

Barbara's anger dissolved and was supplanted by a growing sense of panic. James had them just where he wanted them. She had an urge to run out of the room, but she kept her seat and maintained her composure as best as she could manage. In the same instant she fancied she saw a warm light radiating from his eyes and she knew in that moment that she was panicking for no reason at all. He was not going to hurt them. He could hurt no one. Their fears had been founded on imperfect knowledge and were therefore groundless. She looked at John. His rage appeared to have evaporated and his face was calmer than she had seen it for a long time. It looked as though he too had seen the warm, radiant light that seemed to burn behind James's eyes. A sense of peace settled over them like a soft, comforting blanket and they were ready, even glad to receive it. All that time spent resisting the cylinder had been wasted. Now it was time to rethink everything that they had done since it had first come to light. She smiled as she realised that they had all made the same fundamental error.

They had never understood the cylinder because they had not given it time. Now that was about to change. They would give it time.

www.ingramcontent.com/pod-product-compliance
Lightning Source LLC
Chambersburg PA
CBHW020834030726
47496CB00001B/230